I0526163

THE PRODIGAL JUDGE

VAUGHAN KESTER

1st WORLD
LIBRARY
Literary Society

The Prodigal Judge

Vaughan Kester

© 1st World Library – Literary Society, 2005
PO Box 2211
Fairfield, IA 52556
www.1stworldlibrary.org
First Edition

LCCN: 2006902783

Softcover ISBN: 1-4218-1913-9
Hardcover ISBN: 1-4218-1813-2
eBook ISBN: 1-4218-2013-7

Purchase *"The Prodigal Judge"*
as a traditional bound book at:
www.1stWorldLibrary.org/purchase.asp?ISBN=1-4218-1913-9

1st World Library Literary Society is a nonprofit
organization dedicated to promoting literacy by:

- Creating a free internet library accessible from any computer worldwide.
- Hosting writing competitions and offering book publishing scholarships.

Readers interested in supporting literacy
through sponsorship, donations or
membership please contact:
literacy@1stworldlibrary.org
Check us out at: www.1stworldlibrary.ORG
and start downloading free ebooks today.

The Prodigal Judge
contributed by Tim, Ed & Rodney
in support of
1st World Library Literary Society

CHAPTER I

THE BOY AT THE BARONY

The Quintards had not prospered on the barren lands of the pine woods whither they had emigrated to escape the malaria of the low coast, but this no longer mattered, for the last of his name and race, old General Quintard, was dead in the great house his father had built almost a century before and the thin acres of the Barony, where he had made his last stand against age and poverty, were to claim him, now that he had given up the struggle in their midst. The two or three old slaves about the place, stricken with a sense of the futility of the fight their master had made, mourned for him and for themselves, but of his own blood and class none was present.

Shy dwellers from the pine woods, lanky jeans-clad men and sunbonneted women, who were gathering for the burial of the famous man of their neighborhood, grouped themselves about the lawn which had long since sunk to the uses of a pasture lot. Singly or by twos and threes they stole up the steps and across the wide porch to the open door. On the right of the long hall another door stood open, and who wished could enter the drawing-room, with its splendid green and gold paper, and the wonderful fireplace with the Dutch tiles that graphically depicted the story of Jonah and the whale.

Here the general lay in state. The slaves had dressed their old master in the uniform he had worn as a colonel of the continental line, but the thin shoulders of the wasted figure no longer filled the buff and blue coat. The high-bred face, once proud and masterful no doubt, as became the face of a Quintard, spoke of more than age and poverty - it was infinitely sorrowful. Yet there was something harsh and unforgiving in the lines death had fixed there, which might have been taken as the visible impress of that mystery, the bitterness of which had misshaped the dead man's nature; but the resolute lips had closed for ever on their secret, and the broken spirit had gone perhaps to learn how poor a thing its pride had been.

Though he had lived continuously at the Barony for almost a quarter of a century, there was none among his neighbors who could say he had looked on that thin, aquiline face in all that time. Yet they had known much of him, for the gossip of the slaves, who had been his only friends in those years he had chosen to deny himself to other friends, had gone far and wide over the county.

That notable man of business, Jonathan Crenshaw - and this superiority was especially evident when the business chanced to be his own - was closeted in the library with a stranger to whom rumor fixed the name of Bladen, supposing him to be the legal representative of certain remote connections of the old general's.

Crenshaw sat before the flat-topped mahogany desk in the center of the room with several well-thumbed account-books open before him. Bladen, in riding dress, stood by the window.

"I suppose you will buy in the property when it comes up for sale?" the latter was saying.

Mr. Crenshaw had already made it plain that General Quintard's creditors would have lean pickings at the Barony, intimating that he himself was the chiefest of these and the one to suffer most grievously in pocket. Further than this, Mr. Bladen saw that the old house was a ruin, scarcely habitable, and that the thin acres, though they were many and a royal grant, were of the slightest value. Crenshaw nodded his acquiescence to the lawyer's conjecture touching the ultimate fate of the Barony.

"I reckon, sir, I'll want to protect myself, but if there are any of his own kin who have a fancy to the place I'll put no obstacle in their way."

"Who are the other creditors?" asked Bladen.

"There ain't none, sir; they just got tired waiting on him, and when they began to sue and get judgment the old general would send me word to settle with them, and their claims passed into my hands. I was in too deep to draw out. But for the last ten years his dealings were all with me; I furnished the supplies for the place here. It didn't amount to much, as there was only him and the darkies, and the account ran on from year to year."

"He lived entirely alone, saw no one, I understand," said Bladen.

"Alone with his two or three old slaves - yes, sir. He wouldn't even see me; Joe, his old nigger, would fetch orders for this or that. Once or twice I rode out to see him, but I wa'n't even allowed inside that door; the message I got was that he couldn't be disturbed, and the last time I come he sent me word that if I annoyed him again he would be forced to terminate our business relations. That was pretty strong talk, wa'n't it, when you consider that I could have sold the roof from over his head and the land from under his feet? Oh, well, I just put it down to childishness." There was a brief pause, then Crenshaw spoke again. "I reckon, sir, if you know anything about the old general's private affairs you don't feel no call to speak on that point?" he observed, and with evident regret. He had hoped that Bladen would clear up the mystery, for certainly it must have been some sinister tragedy that had cost the general his grip on life and for twenty years and more had made of him a recluse, so that the faces of his friends had become as the faces of strangers.

"My dear sir, I know nothing of General Quintard's private, history. I am even unacquainted with my clients, who are distant cousins, but his nearest kin - they live in South Carolina. I was merely instructed to represent them in the event of his death and to look after their interests."

"That's business," said Crenshaw, nodding.

"All I know is this: General Quintard was a conspicuous man in these parts fifty years ago; that was before my time, Mr. Crenshaw, and I take it, too, it was before yours; he married a Beaufort."

"So he did," said Crenshaw, "and there was one child, a daughter; she married a South Carolinian by the name of Turberville. I remember that, fo' they were married under the gallery in the hall. Great folks, those Turbervilles, rolling rich. My father was manager then fo' the general - that was nearly forty years ago. There was life here then, sir; the place was alive with niggers and the house full of guests from one month's end to another." He drummed on the desktop. "Who'd a thought it wa'n't to last for ever!"

"And what became of the daughter who married Turberville ?"

"Died years ago," said Crenshaw. "She was here the last time about thirty years back. It wa'n't so easy to get about in those days, no roads to speak of and no stages, and besides, the old general wa'n't much here nohow; her going away had sort of broken up his home, I reckon. Then the place stood empty fo' a few years, most of the slaves were sold off, and the fields began to grow up. No one rightly knew, but the general was supposed to be traveling up yonder in the No'th, sir. As I say, things ran along this way quite a while, and then one morning when I went to my store my clerk says, 'There's an old white-headed nigger been waiting round here fo' a word with you, Mr. Crenshaw.' It was Joe, the general's body servant, and when I'd shook hands with him I said, 'When's the master expected back?' You see, I thought Joe had been sent on ahead to open the house, but he says, 'General Quintard's at the Barony now,' and then he says, 'The general's compliments, sir, and will you see that this order is filled?' Well, Mr. Bladen, I and my father had factored the Barony fo' fifteen years and upward, but that was the first time the supplies fo' the general's table had ever been toted here in a meal sack!

"I rode out that very afternoon, but Joe, who was one of your mannerly niggers, met me at the door and says, 'Mr. Crenshaw, the general appreciates this courtesy, but regrets that he is unable to see you, sir.' After that it wa'n't long in getting about that the general was a changed man. Other folks came here to welcome him back and he refused to see them, but the reason of it we never learned. Joe, who probably knew, was one of your close niggers; there was, no getting anything out of him; you could talk with that darky by the hour, sir, and he left you feeling emptier than if he'd kept his mouth shut."

They were interrupted by a knock at the door.

"Come in," said Crenshaw, a trifle impatiently, and in response to his bidding the door opened and a small boy entered the room dragging after him a long rifle. Suddenly overcome by a speechless shyness, he paused on the threshold to stare with round, wondering eyes at the two men. "Well, sonny, what do you want?" asked Mr. Crenshaw indulgently.

The boy opened his mouth, but his courage failed him, and with his courage went the words he would have spoken.

"Who is this?" asked Bladen.

"I'll tell, you presently," said Crenshaw. "Come, speak up, sonny, what do you want?"

"Please, sir, I want this here old spo'tin' rifle," said: the child. "Please, sir, I want to keep it," he added.

"Well, you run along on out of here with your old spo'tin' rifle!" said Crenshaw good-naturedly.

"Please, sir, am I to keep it?"

"Yes, I reckon you may keep it - least I've no objection." Crenshaw glanced at Bladen.

"Oh, by all means," said the latter. Spasms of delight shook the small figure, and with a murmur that was meant for thanks he backed from the room, closing the door. Bladen glanced inquiringly at Crenshaw.

"You want to know about him, sir? Well, that's Hannibal Wayne Hazard."

"Hannibal Wayne Hazard?" repeated Bladen.

"Yes, sir; the general was the authority on that point, but who Hannibal Wayne Hazard is and how he happens to be at the Barony is another mystery - just wait a minute, sir -" and quitting his chair Mr. Crenshaw hurried from the room to return almost immediately with a tall countryman. "Mr. Bladen, this is Bob Yancy. Bob, the gentleman, wants to hear about the woman and the child; that's your story."

"Howdy, sir," said Mr. Yancy. He appeared to meditate on the mental effort that was required of him, then he took a long breath. "It was this a-ways -" he began with a soft drawl, and then paused. "You give me the dates, Mr. John, fo' I disremember."

"It was four year ago come next Christmas," said Crenshaw.

"Old Christmas," corrected Mr. Yancy. "Our folks always kept the old Christmas like it was befo' they done mussed up the calendar. I'm agin all changes," added Mr. Yancy.

"He means the fo'teenth of December," explained Mr. Crenshaw.

"Not wishin' to dispute your word, Mr. John, I mean Christmas," objected Yancy.

"Oh, very well, he means Christmas then!" said Crenshaw.

"The evening befo', it was, and I'd gone to Fayetteville to get my Christmas fixin's; there was right much rain and some snow falling." Mr. Yancy's guiding light was clearly accuracy. "Just at sundown I hooked up that blind mule of mine to the cart and started fo' home. As I got shut of the town the stage come in and I seen one passenger, a woman. Now that mule is slow, Mr. John; I'm free to say there are faster mules, but a set of harness never went acrost the back of a slower critter than that one of mine." Yancy, who thus far had addressed himself to Mr. Crenshaw, now turned to Bladen. "That mule, sir, sees good with his right eye, but it's got a gait like it was looking fo' the left-hand side of the road and wondering what in thunderation had got into it that it was acrost the way; mules are gifted with some sense, but mighty little judgment."

"Never mind the mule, Bob," said Crenshaw.

"If I can't make the gentleman believe in the everlasting slowness of that mule of mine, my story ain't worth a hill of beans," said Yancy.

"The extraordinary slowness of the mule is accepted without question, Mr. Yancy," said Bladen.

"I'm obliged to you," rejoined Yancy, and for a brief moment he appeared to commune with himself, then he continued. "A mile out of town I heard some one sloshing through the rain after me; it was dark by that time and I couldn't see who it was, so I pulled up and waited, and then I made out it was a woman. She spoke when she was alongside the cart and says, 'Can you drive me on to the Barony?' and it came to me it was the same woman I'd seen leave the stage. When I got down to help her into the cart I saw she was toting a child in her arms."

"What did the woman look like, Bob?" said Crenshaw.

"She wa'n't exactly old and she wa'n't young by no manner of means; I remember saying to myself, that child ain't yo's, whose ever it is. Well, sir, I was willing enough to talk, but she wa'n't, she hardly spoke until we came to the red gate, when she says, 'Stop, if you please, I'll walk the rest of the way.' Mind you, she'd known without a word from me we were at the Barony. She give me a dollar, and the last I seen of her she was hurrying through the rain toting the child in her arms."

Mr. Crenshaw took up the narrative.

"The niggers say the old general almost had a fit when he saw her. Aunt Alsidia let her into the house; I reckon if Joe had been alive she wouldn't have got inside that door, spite of the night!"

"Well?" said Bladen.

"When morning come she was gone, but the child done stayed behind; we always reckoned the lady walked back to Fayetteville sometime befo' day and took the stage. I've heard Aunt Alsidia tell as how the old general said that morning, pale and shaking like, 'You'll find a boy asleep in the red room; he's to be fed and cared fo', but keep him out of my sight. His name is Hannibal Wayne Hazard.' That is all the general ever said on the matter. He never would see the boy, never asked after him even, and the boy lived in the back of the house, with the niggers to look after him. Now, sir, you know as much as we know, which is just next door to nothing."

The old general was borne across what had once been the west lawn to his resting-place in the neglected acre where the dead and gone of his race lay, and the record of the family was complete, as far as any man knew. Crenshaw watched the grave take shape with a melancholy for which he found no words, yet if words could have come from the mist of ideas in which his mind groped vaguely he would have said that for themselves the deeds of the Quintards had been given the touch of finality, and that whether for good or for evil, the consequences, like the ripple which rises from the surface of placid waters when a stone is dropped, still survived somewhere in the world.

The curious and the idle drifted back to the great house; then the memory of their own affairs, not urgent, generally speaking, but still of some casual interest, took them down the disused carriage-way to the red gate and so off into the heat of the summer day. Crenshaw's wagon, driven by Crenshaw's man, vanished in a cloud of gray dust with the two old slaves, Aunt Alsidia and Uncle Ben, who were being taken to the Crenshaw place to be cared for pending the settlement of the Quintard estate. Bladen parted from Crenshaw with expressions of pleasure at having had the opportunity of making his acquaintance, and further delivered himself of the civil wish that they might soon meet again. Then Crenshaw, assisted by Bob Yancy, proceeded to secure the great house against intrusion.

"I make it a p'int to always stay and see the plumb finish of a thing," explained Yancy. "Otherwise you're frequently put out by hearing of what happened after you left; I can stand anything but disapp'intment of that kind."

They passed from room to room securing doors and windows, and at last stepped out upon the back porch.

"Hullo!" said Yancy, pointing.

There on a bench by the kitchen door was a small figure. It was Hannibal Wayne Hazard asleep, with his old spo'tin' rifle across his knees. His very existence had been forgotten.

"Well, I declare to goodness!" said Crenshaw.

"What are you going to do with him, Mr. John?"

This question nettled Crenshaw.

"I don't know as that is any particular affair of mine," he said. Now, Mr. Crenshaw, though an excellent man of business, with an unblinking eye on number one, was kindly, on the whole, but there was a Mrs. Crenshaw, to whom he rendered a strict account of all his deeds, and that sacred institution, the home, was only a tolerable haven when these deeds were nicely calculated to fit with the lady's exactions. Especially was he aware that Mrs. Crenshaw was averse to children as being inimical to cleanliness and order, oppressive virtues that drove Crenshaw himself in his hours of leisure to the woodshed, where he might spit freely.

"I reckon you'd rather drop a word with yo' missus before you toted him home?" suggested Yancy, who knew something of the nature of his friend's domestic thraldom.

"A woman ought to be boss in her own house," said Crenshaw.

"Feelin' the truth of that, I've never married, Mr. John; I do as I please and don't have to listen to a passel of opinion. But I was going to say, what's to hinder me from toting that boy to my home? There are no calico petticoats hanging up in my closets."

"And no closets to hang 'em in, I'll be bound!" rejoined Crenshaw. "But if you'll take the boy, Bob, you shan't lose by it."

Yancy rested a big knotted hand on the boy's shoulder.

"Come, wake up, sonny! Yo' Uncle Bob is ready fo' to strike out home," he said. The child roused with a start and stared into the strange bearded face that was bent toward him. "It's yo' Uncle Bob," continued Yancy in a wheedling tone. "Are you the little nevvy what will help him to hook up that old blind mule of hisn ? Here, give us the spo'tin' rifle to tote!"

"Please, sir, where is Aunt Alsidia?" asked the child.

Yancy balanced the rifle on his great palm and his eyes assumed a speculative cast.

"I wonder what's to hinder us from loading this old gun, and firing this old gun, and hearing this old gun go-bang! Eh?"

The child's blue eyes grew wide.

"Like the guns off in the woods?" he asked, in a breathless whisper.

"Like the guns a body hears off in the woods, only louder - heaps louder," said Yancy. "You fetch out his plunder, Mr. John," he added in a lower tone.

"Do it now, please," the child cried, slipping off the bench.

"I was expectin' fo' to hear you name me Uncle Bob, sonny; my little nevvies get almost anything they want out of me when they call me that-a-ways."

"Please, Uncle Bob, make it go bang!"

"You come along, then," and Mr. Yancy moved off in the direction of his mule, the child following. "Powder's what we want fo' to make this old spo'tiu' rifle talk up, and I reckon we'll find some in a horn flask in the bottom of my cart." His expectations in this particular were realized, and he loaded the rifle with a small blank charge. 'Now," he said, shaking the powder into the pan by a succession of smart taps on the breech, "sometimes these old pieces go off and sometimes they don't; it depends on the flint, but you stand back of your Uncle Bob, sonny, and keep yo' fingers out of yo' ears, and when you say - bang! - off she goes."

There was a moment of delightful expectancy, and then -

"Bang!" cried the child, and on the instant the rifle cracked. "Do it againQ Please, Uncle Bob!" he cried, wild with delight.

"Now if you was to help yo' Uncle Bob hook up that old mule of hisn and ride home with him, fo' he's going pretty shortly, you and Uncle Bob could do right much shootin' with this old rifle." Mr. Crenshaw had appeared with a bundle, which he tossed into the cart. Yancy turned to him. "If you meet any inquiring friends, Mr. John, I reckon you may say that my nevvy's gone fo' to pay me a visit. Most of his time will be agreeably spent shootin' with this rifle at a mark, and me holdin' him so he won't get kicked clean off his feet."

Thereafter beguiling speech flowed steadily from Mr. Yancy's bearded lips, in the midst of which relations were established between the mule and cart, and the boy quitted the Barony for a new world.

"Do you reckon if Uncle Bob was to let you, you could drive, sonny?"

"Can she gallop?" asked the boy.

Mr. Yancy gave him a hurt glance.

"She's too much of a lady to do that," he said. "No, I 'low this ain't 'so fast as running or walking, but it's a heap quicker than standing stock-still." The afternoon sun waned as they went deeper and deeper into the pine woods, but at last they came to their journey's end, a widely scattered settlement on a hill above a branch.

"This," said Mr. Yancy, "are Scratch Hill, sonny. Why Scratch Hill? Some say it's the fleas; others agin hold it's the eternal bother of making a living here, but whether fleas or living you scratch fo' both."

Vaughan Kester

CHAPTER II

YANCY TELLS A MORAL TALE

In the deep peace that rested like a benediction on the pine-clad slopes of Scratch Hill the boy Hannibal followed at Yancy's heels as that gentleman pursued the not arduous rounds of temperate industry which made up his daily life, for if Yancy were not completely idle he was responsible for a counterfeit presentment of idleness having most of the merits of the real article. He toiled casually in a small cornfield and a yet smaller truck patch, but his work always began late, when it began at all, and he was easily dissuaded from continuing it; indeed, his attitude toward it seemed to challenge interference.

In the winter, when the weather conditions were perfectly adjusted to meet certain occult exactions he had come to require, Yancy could be induced to go into the woods and there labor with his ax. But as he pointed out to Hannibal, a poor man's capital was his health, and he being a poor man it behooved him to have a jealous care of himself. He made use of the dull days of mingled mist and drizzle for hunting, work being clearly out of the question; one could get about over the brown floor of the forest in silence then, and there was no sun to glint the brass mountings of his rifle. The fine days he professed to regard with keen suspicion as weather breeders, when it was imprudent to go far from home, especially in the direction of the Crenshaw timber lands, which for years had been the scene of all his gainful industry, and where he seemed to think nature ready to assume her most sinister aspect. Again in the early spring, when the young oak leaves were the size of squirrel's ears and the whippoorwills began calling as the long shadows struck through the pine woods, the needs of his corn ground battled with his desire to fish. In all such crises of the soul Mr. Yancy was fairly vanquished before the struggle began; but to the boy his activities were perfectly ordered to yield the largest return in contentment.

The Barony had been offered for sale and bought in by Crenshaw for eleven thousand dollars, this being the amount of his claim. Some six months later he sold the plantation for fifteen thousand dollars to Nathaniel Ferris, of Currituck County.

"There's money in the old place, Bob, at that figure," Crenshaw told Yancy.

"There are so," agreed Yancy, who was thinking Crenshaw had lost no time in getting it out.

They were seated on the counter in Crenshaw's store at Balaam's Cross Roads, where the heavy odor of black molasses battled with the sprightly smell of salt fish. The merchant held the Scratch Hiller in no small esteem. Their intimacy was of long standing, for the Yancys going down and the Crenshaws coming up had for a brief space flourished on the same social level. Mr. Crenshaw's rise in life, however, had been uninterrupted, while Mr. Yancy, wrapped in a philosophic calm and deeply averse to industry, had permitted the momentum imparted by a remote ancestor to carry him where it would, which was steadily away from that tempered prosperity his family had once boasted as members of the land-owning and slaveholding class.

"I mean there's money in the place fo' Ferris," Crenshaw explained.

"I reckon yo're right, Mr. John; the old general used to spend a heap on the Barony and we all know he never got a cent back, so I reckon the money's there yet.

"Bladen's got an answer from them South Carolina Quintards, and they don't know nothing about the boy," said Crenshaw, changing the subject. "So you can rest easy, Bob; they ain't going to want him."

"Well, sir, that surely is a passel of comfort to me. I find I got all the instincts of a father without having had none of the instincts of a husband."

A richer, deeper realization of his joy came to Yancy when he had turned his back on Balaam's Cross Roads and set out for home through the fragrant silence of the pine woods. His probable part in the young life chance had placed in his keeping was a glorious thing to the man. He had not cared to speculate on the future; he had believed that friends or kindred must sooner or later claim Hannibal, but now he felt wonderfully secure in Crenshaw's opinion that this was not to be.

Just beyond the Barony, which was midway between Balaam's and the Hill, down the long stretch of sandy road he saw two mounted figures, then as they drew nearer he caught the flutter of skirts and recognized one of the horsewomen. It was Mrs. Ferris, wife of the Barony's new owner. She reined in her horse abreast of his cart.

"Aren't you Mr. Yancy?" she asked.

"Yes, ma'am, that's me - Bob Yancy." He regarded her with large gray eyes that were frankly approving in their expression, for she was more than commonly agreeable to look upon.

"I am Mrs. Ferris, and I am very pleased to make your acquaintance."

"The same here," murmured Yancy with winning civility.

Mrs. Ferris' companion leaned forward, her face averted, and stroked her horse's neck with gloved hand.

"This is my friend, Miss Betty Malroy."

"Glad to know you, ma'am," said Yancy.

Miss Malroy faced him, smiling. She, too, was very good to look upon, indeed she was quite radiant with youth and beauty.

"We are just returning from Scratch Hill - I think that is what you call it?" said Mrs. Ferris.

"So we do," agreed Yancy.

"And the dear little boy we met is your nephew, is he not, Mr. Yancy?" It was Betty Malroy who spoke.

"In a manner he is and in a manner he ain't," explained Yancy, somewhat enigmatically.

"There are quite a number of children at Scratch Hill?" suggested Mrs. Ferris.

"Yes, ma'am, so there are; a body would naturally notice that."

"And no school - not a church even!" continued Mrs. Ferris in a grieved tone.

"Never has been," rejoined Yancy cheerfully. He seemed to champion the absence of churches and schools on the score of long usage.

"But what do the people do when they want to go to church?" questioned Mrs. Ferris.

"Never having heard that any of 'em wanted to go I can't say just offhand, but don't you fret none about that, ma'am; there are churches; one's up at the Forks, and there's another at

Balaam's Cross Roads."

"But that's ten miles from Scratch Hill, isn't it?"

"It's all of that," said Yancy. He sensed it that the lady before him, was a person of much force and energy, capable even of reckless innovation. Mr. Yancy himself was innately conservative; his religious inspiration had been drawn from the Forks and Balaam's Cross Roads. It had seemed to answer very well. Mrs. Ferris fixed his wavering glance.

"Don't you think it is too bad, Mr. Yancy, the way those children have been neglected? There is nothing for them but to run wild."

"Well, I seen some right good children fetched up that-a-ways - smart, too. You see, ma'am, there's a heap a child can just naturally pick up of himself."

"Oh!" and the monosyllable was uttered rather weakly. Mr. Yancy's name had been given her as that of a resident of weight and influence in the classic region of Scratch Hill. Miss Malroy came to her friend's rescue.

"Mrs. Ferris thinks the children should have a chance to learn at home. Poor little tots! - they can't walk ten or fifteen miles to Sunday-school, now can they, Mr. Yancy ?"

"Bless yo' heart, they won't try to!" said Yancy reassuringly. "Sunday's a day of rest at Scratch Hill. So are most of the other days of the week, but we all aspire to take just a little mo' rest on Sunday than any other day. Sometimes we ain't able to, but that's our aim."

"Do you know the old deserted cabin by the big pine? - the Blount place?" asked Mrs. Ferris.

"Yes, ma'am, I know it."

"I am going to have Sunday-school there for those children; they shan't be neglected any longer if I can help it - I should feel guilty, quite guilty! Now won't you let your little nephew come? Perhaps they'll not find it so very terrible, after all." From which Mr. Yancy concluded that when she invaded it, skepticism had rested as a mantle on Scratch Hill.

"Every one said we would better talk with you, Mr. Yancy, and we were hoping to meet you as we came along," supplemented Miss Malroy, and her words of flattery were wafted to him with so sweet a smile that Yancy instantly capitulated.

"I reckon you-all can count on my nevvy," he said.

When he reached Scratch Hill, in the waning light of day, Hannibal, in a state of high excitement, met him at the log shed, which served as a barn.

"I hear you-all have been entertaining visitors while Uncle Bob was away," observed Yancy, and remembering what Crenshaw had told him, he rested his big hand on the boy's head with a special tenderness.

"There's going to be a school in the cabin in the old field!" said the boy. "May I go? - Oh, Uncle Bob, will you please take me?"

"When's this here school going to begin, anyhow?"

"To-morrow at four o'clock, she said, Uncle Bob."

"She's a quick lady, ain't she? Well, I expected you'd be hopping around on one leg when you named it to me. You wait until Sunday and see what I do fo' my nevvy," said Yancy.

He was as good as his implied promise, but the day began discouragingly with an extra and, as it seemed to Hannibal, an unnecessary amount of soap and water.

"You owe it to yo'self to show a clean skin in the house of worship. Just suppose one of them nice ladies was to cast her eye back of yo' ears! She'd surely be put out to name it offhand whether you was black or white. I reckon I'll have to barber you some, too, with the shears."

"What's school like, Uncle Bob?" asked Hannibal, twisting and squirming under the big resolute hands of the man.

"I can't just say what it's like."

"Why, didn't you ever go to school, Uncle Bob?"

"Didn't I ever go to school! Where do you reckon I got my education, anyhow? I went to school several times in my young days."

"On a Sunday, like this?"

"No, the school I tackled was on a week-day."

"Was it hard?" asked Hannibal, who was beginning to cherish secret misgivings; for surely all this soap and water must have some sinister portent

"Well, some learn easier than others. I learned middling easy - it didn't take me long - and when I felt I knowed enough I just naturally quit and went on about my business."

"But what did you learn?" insisted the boy.

"You-all wouldn't know if I told you, because you-all ain't ever been to school yo'self. When you've had yo' education we'll talk over what I learned - it mostly come out of a book." He hoped his general statement would satisfy Hannibal, but it failed to do so.

"What's a book. Uncle Bob?" he demanded.

"Well, whatever a body don't know naturally he gets out of a book. I reckon the way you twist, Nevvy, mebby you'd admire fo' to lose an ear!" and Mr. Yancy refused further to discuss the knowledge he had garnered in his youth.

Hannibal and Yancy were the first to arrive at the deserted cabin in the old field that afternoon. They found the place had been recently cleaned and swept, while about the wall was ranged a row of benches; there was also a table and two chairs. Yancy inspected the premises with the eye of mature experience.

"Yes, it surely is a school; any one with an education would know that. Just look! - ain't you glad yo' Uncle Bob slicked you up some, now you see what them ladies has done fo' to make this place tidy?"

Shy children from the pine woods, big brothers with little sisters and big sisters with little brothers, drifted out of the encircling forest. Coincident with the arrival of the last of these stragglers Mrs. Ferris and Miss Malroy appeared, attended by a colored groom.

"It was so good of you to come, Mr. Yancy! The children won't feel so shy with you here," said Mrs. Ferris warmly, as Yancy assisted her to dismount, an act of courtesy that called for his finest courage.

Mrs. Ferris' missionary spirit manifested itself agreeably enough on the whole. When she had ranged her flock in a solemn-faced row on the benches, she began by explaining why Sunday was set apart for a day of rest, touching but lightly on its deeper significance as a day of worship as well; then she read certain chapters from the Bible, finishing with the story of David, a narrative that made a deep impression upon Yancy, comfortably seated in the doorway.

"Can't you tell the children a story, Mr. Yancy? Something about their own neighborhood I think would be nice, something with a moral," the pleasant earnest voice of Mrs. Ferris roused the Scratch Hiller from his meditations.

"Yes, ma'am, I reckon I can tell 'em a story." He stood up, filling the doorway with his bulk. "I can tell you-all a story about this here house," he said, addressing himself to the children. He smiled happily. "You-all don't need to look so solemn, a body ain't going to snap at you! This house are the old Blount cabin, but the Blounts done moved away from it years and years ago. They're down Fayetteville way now. There was a passel of 'em and they was about as common a lot of white folks as you'd find anywhere; I know, because I come to a dance here once and Dave Blount called me a liar right in this very room." He paused, that this impressive fact might disseminate itself. Hannibal slid forward in his seat, his earnest little face bent on Yancy.

"Why did he call you a liar, Uncle Bob?" he demanded.

"Well, I scarcely know, Nevvy, but that's what he done, and he stuck some words in front of it that ain't fitten I should repeat."

Miss Malroy's cheeks had become very red, and Mrs. Ferris refused to meet her eye, while the children were in a flutter of pleased expectancy. They felt the wholly contemporary interest of Yancy's story; he was dealing with forms of speech which prevailed and were usually provocative of consequences more or less serious. He gave them a wide, sunny smile.

"When Dave Blount called me that, I struck out fo' home." At this surprising turn in the narrative the children looked their disgust, and Mrs. Ferris shot Betty a triumphant glance. "Yes, ma'am, I struck out across the fields fo' home, I didn't wish to hear no mo' of that loose kind of talk. When I got home I found my old daddy setting up afo' the fire, and he says, 'You come away early, son.' I told him what Dave Blount had called me and he says, 'You acted like a gentleman, Bob, with all them womenfolks about.'"

"You had a very good and sensible father, Mr. Yancy. How much better than if -" began Mrs. Ferris, who feared that the moral might elude him.

"Yes, ma'am, but along about day he come into the loft where I was sleeping and says to me, 'Sun-up, Bob - time fo' you to haul on yo' pants and go back yonder and fetch that Dave Blount a smack in the jaw.'" Mrs. Ferris moved uneasily in her chair: "I dressed and come here, but when I asked fo' Dave he wouldn't step outside, so I just lost patience with his foolishness and took a crack at him standing where I'm standing now, but he ducked and you can still see, ma'am" - turning to the embarrassed Mrs. Ferris - "where my knuckles made a dint in the door-jamb. I got him the next lick, though!"

Mr. Yancy's moral tale had reached its conclusion; it was not for him to boast unduly of his prowess.

"Uncle Bob, you lift me up and show me them dints!" and Hannibal slipped from his seat.

"Oh, no!" said Betty Malroy laughing. She captured the boy and drew him down beside her on a corner of her chair. "I am sure you don't want to see the dents - Mr. Yancy's story, children, is to teach us how important it is to guard our words - and not give way to hasty speech -"

"Betty!" cried Mrs. Ferris indignantly.

"Judith, the moral is as obvious as it is necessary."

Mrs. Ferris gave her a reproachful look and turned to the children.

"You will all be here next Sunday, won't you? - and at the same hour?" she said, rising.

There was a sudden clatter of hoofs beyond the door. A man,

Vaughan Kester

well dressed and well mounted had ridden into the yard. As Mrs. Ferris came from the cabin he flung himself out of the saddle and, hat in hand, approached her.

"I am hunting a place called the Barony; can you tell me if I am on the right road?" he asked. He was a man in the early thirties, graceful and powerful of build, with a handsome face.

"It is my husband you wish to see? I am Mrs. Ferris."

"Then General Quintard is dead?" His tone was one of surprise.

"His death occurred over a year ago, and my husband now owns the Barony; were you a friend of the general's ?"

"No, Madam; he was my father's friend, but I had hoped to meet him." His manner was adroit and plausible.

Mrs. Ferris hesitated. The stranger's dress and bearing was that of a gentleman, and he could boast of his father's friendship with General Quintard. Any doubts she may have had she put aside.

"Will you ride on with us to the Barony and meet my husband, Mr. - ?" she paused.

"Murrell - Captain Murrell. Thank you; I should like to see the old place. I should highly value the privilege," then his eyes rested on Miss Malroy.

"Betty, let me present Captain Murrell."

The captain bowed, giving her a glance of bold admiration.

By this time the children had straggled off into the pine woods as silently as they had assembled; only Yancy and Hannibal remained. Mrs. Ferris turned to the former.

"If you will close the cabin door, Mr. Yancy, everything will be ready for next Sunday," she said, and moved toward the horses, followed by Murrell. Betty Malroy lingered for a moment at Hannibal's side.

"Good-by, little boy; you must ask your Uncle Bob to bring you up to the big house to see me," and stooping she kissed him. "Good-by, Mr. Yancy, I liked your story."

Hannibal and Yancy watched them mount and ride away, then the boy said:

"Uncle Bob, now them ladies have gone, won't you please show me them dints you made in the doorjamb?"

CHAPTER III

TROUBLE AT SCRATCH HILL

Captain Murrell had established himself at Balaam's Cross Roads. He was supposed to be interested in the purchase of a plantation, and in company with Crenshaw visited the numerous tracts of land which the merchant owned; but though he professed delight with the country, he was plainly in no haste to become committed to any one of the several propositions Crenshaw was eager to submit. Later, and still in the guise of a prospective purchaser, he met Bladen, who also dealt extensively in land, and apparently if anything could have pleased him more than the region about the Cross Roads it was the country adjacent to Fayetteville.

From the first he had assiduously cultivated his acquaintance with the new owners of the Barony. He was now on the best of terms with Nat Ferris, and it was at the Barony that he lounged away his evenings, gossiping and smoking with the planter on the wide veranda.

"The Barony would have suited me," he told Bladen one day. They had just returned from an excursion into the country and were seated in the lawyer's office.

"You say your father was a friend of the old general's?" said Bladen.

"Years ago, in the north - yes," answered Murrell.

"Odd, isn't it, the way he chose to spend the last years of his life, shut off like that and seeing no one?"

Murrell regarded the lawyer in silence for a moment out of his deeply sunk eyes.

"Too bad about the boy," he said at length slowly.

"How do you mean, Captain?" asked Bladen.

"I mean it's a pity he has no one except Yancy to look after him," said Murrell, but Bladen showed no interest and Murrell went on. "Don't you reckon he must have touched General Quintard's life mighty close at some point?"

"Well, if so, it eluded me," said Bladen. "I went through General Quintard's papers and they contained no clue to the boy's identity that I could discover. Fact is, the general didn't leave much beyond an old account-book or two; I imagine that before his death he destroyed the bulk of his private papers; it looked as if he'd wished to break with the past. His mind must have been affected."

"Has Yancy any legal claim on the boy?" inquired Murrell.

"No, certainly not; the boy was merely left with Yancy because Crenshaw didn't know what else to do with him."

"Get possession of him, and if I don't buy land here I'll take him West with me," said Murrell quietly. Bladen gave him a swift, shrewd glance, but Murrell, smiling and easy, met it frankly. "Come," he said, "it's a pity he should grow up wild in the pine woods - get him away from Yancy - I am' willing to spend five hundred dollars on this if necessary."

"As a matter of sentiment?"

"As a matter of sentiment."

Bladen considered. He was not averse to making five hundred dollars, but he was decidedly averse to letting slip any chance to secure a larger sum. It flashed in upon him that Murrell had uncovered the real purpose of his visit to North Carolina; his interest in land had been merely a subterfuge.

"Well?" said Murrell.

"I'll have to think your proposition over," said Bladen.

The immediate result of this conversation was that within twenty-four hours a man driving two horses hitched to a light buggy arrived at Scratch Hill in quest of Bob Yancy, whom he found at dinner and to whom he delivered a letter. Mr. Yancy was profoundly impressed by the attention, for holding the letter at arm's length, he said

"Well, sir, I've lived nigh on to forty years, but I never got a piece of writing befo' - never, sir. People, if they was close by, spoke to me, if at a distance they hollered, but none of 'em ever wrote." After gazing at the written characters with satisfaction Mr. Yancy made a taper of the letter and lit his pipe, which he puffed meditatively. "Sonny, when you grow up you must learn so you can send writings to yo' Uncle Bob fo' him to light his pipe with."

"What was in the paper, Uncle Bob?" asked Hannibal.

"Writin'," said Mr. Yancy, and smoked.

"What did the writin' say, Uncle Bob?" insisted the boy.

"It was private," said Mr. Yancy, "very private."

"What's your answer?" demanded the stranger.

"That's private, too," said Mr. Yancy. "You tell him I'll be monstrous glad to talk it over with him any time he fancies to come out here."

"He said something about some one I was to carry back with me," objected the man.

"Who said that?" asked Mr. Yancy.

"Bladen did."

"How's a body to know who yore talking about unless you name him?" said Yancy severely.

"Well, what am I to tell him?"

"It's a free country and I got no call to dictate. You-all can tell him whatever you like." Further than this Mr. Yancy would not commit himself, and the man went as he came.

The next day Yancy had occasion to visit Balaam's Cross Roads. Ordinarily Hannibal would have gone with him, but he was engaged in digging out a groundhog's hole with Oglethorpe Bellamy, grandson of Uncle Sammy Bellamy, the patriarch of Scratch Hill. Mr. Yancy forbore to interrupt this enterprise which he considered of some educational value, since the ground-hog's hole was an old one and he was reasonably certain that a family of skunks had taken possession of it. When Yancy reached the Cross Roads, Crenshaw gave him a disquieting opinion as to the probable contents of his letter, for he himself had heard from Bladen that he had decided to assume the care of the boy.

"So you reckon it was that -" said Yancy, with a deep breath.

"It's a blame outrage, Bob, fo' him to act like this!" said the merchant with heat.

"When do you reckon he's going to send fo' him?" asked Yancy.

"Whenever the notion strikes him."

"What about my having notions too?" inquired Yancy, flecked into passion, and bringing his fist down on the counter with a crash.

"You surely ain't going to oppose him, Bob?"

"Does he say when he's going to send fo' my nevvy ?"

"He says it will be soon."

"You take care of my mule, Mr. John," said Yancy, and turned his back on his friend.

"I reckon Bladen will have the law on his side, Bob!"

"The law be damned - I got what's fair on mine, I don't wish fo' better than that," exclaimed Yancy, over his shoulder. He strode from the store and started down the sandy road at a brisk run. Miserable forebodings of an impending tragedy leaped up within him, and the miles were many that lay between him and the Hill.

"He'll just naturally bust the face off the fellow Bladen sends!" thought Crenshaw, staring after his friend.

That run of Bob Yancy's was destined to become a classic in the annals of the neighborhood. Ordinarily a man walking briskly might cover the distance between the Cross Roads and the Hill in two hours. He accomplished it in less than an hour, and before he reached the branch that flowed a full quarter of a mile from his cabin he was shouting Hannibal's name as he ran. Then as he breasted the slope he came within sight of a little group in his own dooryard. Saving only Uncle Sammy Bellamy, the group resolved itself into the women and children of the Hill, but there was one small figure he missed, and the color faded from his cheeks while his heart stood still. The patriarch hurried toward him, leaning on his cane, while his grandson clung to the skirts of his coat, weeping bitterly.

"They've took your nevvy, Bob!" he cried, in a high, thin voice.

"Who's took him?" asked Yancy hoarsely. He paused and glanced from one to another of the little group.

"Hit were Dave Blount. Get your gun, Bob, and go after him - kill the miserable sneaking cuss!" cried Uncle Sammy, who believed in settling all difficulties by bloodshed as befitted a veteran of the first war with England, he having risen to the respectable rank of sergeant in a company of Morgan's riflemen; while at sixty-odd in '12, when there was recruiting at the Cross Roads, his son had only been able to prevent his tendering his services to his country by hiding his trousers. "Fetch his rifle, some of you fool women!" cried Uncle Sammy. "By the Fayetteville Road, Bob, not ten minutes ago - you can cut him off at Ox Road forks!"

Yancy breathed a sigh of relief. The situation was not entirely desperate, for, as Uncle Sammy said, he could reach the Ox Road forks before Blount possibly could, by going as the crow flies through the pine woods.

"Hit wouldn't have happened if there'd been a man on the Hill, but there was nothing but a passel of women about the place. I heard the boys crying when Dave Blount lifted your nevvy into the buggy," said Uncle Sammy; "all I could do was to cuss him across two fields. I hope you blow his hide full of holes!" for a rifle had been placed in Yancy's hands.

"Thank you-all kindly," said Yancy, and turning away he struck off through the pine woods. A brisk walk of twenty minutes brought him to the Ox Road forks, as it was called, where he could plainly distinguish the wheel and hoof marks left by the buggy and team as it went to Scratch Hill, but there was only the single track.

This important point being settled, sense of sweet peace stole in upon Yancy's spirit. He stood his rifle against a tree, lit his pipe with flint and steel, and rested comfortably by the wayside. He had not long to wait, for presently the buggy hove in sight; whereupon he coolly knocked the ashes from his pipe, pocketed it, and prepared for action. As the buggy came nearer he recognized his ancient enemy in the person of the man who sat at Hannibal's side, and stepping nimbly into the road seized the horses by their bits. At sight of him Hannibal shrieked his name in an ecstasy of delight.

"Uncle Bob - Uncle Bob -" he, cried.

"Yes, it's Uncle Bob. You can light down, Nevvy. I reckon you've rid far enough," said Yancy pleasantly.

"Leggo them horses!" said Mr. Blount, recovering somewhat from the effect of Yancy's sudden appearance.

"Light down, Nevvy," said Yancy, still pleasantly. Blount turned to the boy as if to interfere. "Don't you put the weight of yo' finger on the boy, Blount!" warned Yancy. "Light down, Hannibal!"

Hannibal instantly availed himself of the invitation. At the same moment Blount struck at Yancy with his whip and his horses reared wildly, thinking the blow meant for them. Seeing that the boy had reached the ground in safety, Yancy relaxed his hold on the team, which instantly plunged forward. Then as the buggy swept past him he made a dexterous grab at Blount and dragged him out over the wheels into the road, where, for the second time in his life, he proceeded to fetch Mr. Blount a smack in the jaw. This he followed up with other smacks variously distributed about his countenance.

"You'll sweat for this, Bob Yancy!" cried Blount, as he vainly sought to fend off the blows.

"I'm sweating now - scandalous," said Mr. Yancy, taking his unhurried satisfaction of the other. Then with a final skilful kick he sent Mr. Blount sprawling. "Don't let me catch you around these diggings again, Dave Blount, or I swear to God I'll be the death of you!"

Hannibal rode home through the pine woods in triumph on his Uncle Bob's mighty shoulders.

"Did you get yo' ground-hog, Nevvy?" inquired Mr. Yancy presently when they had temporarily exhausted the excitement of Hannibal's capture and recovery.

"It weren't a ground-hog, Uncle Bob - it were a skunk!"

"Think of that!" murmured Mr. Yancy.

CHAPTER IV

LAW AT BALAAM'S CROSS-ROADS

But Mr. Yancy was only at the beginning of his trouble. Three days later there appeared on the borders of Scratch Hill a lank gentleman armed with a rifle, while the butts of two pistols protruded from the depths of his capacious coat pockets. He made his presence known by whooping from the edge of the branch, and his whoops shaped themselves into the name of Yancy. It was Charley Balaam, old Squire Balaam's nephew. The squire lived at the crossroads to which his family had given its name, and dispensed the little law that found its way into that part of the county. The whoops finally brought Yancy to his cabin door.

"Can I see you friendly, Bob Yancy?" Balaam demanded with the lungs of a stentor, sheltering himself behind the thick bole of a sweetgum, for he observed that Yancy held his rifle in the crook of his arm and had no wish to offer his person as a target to the deadly aim of the Scratch Hiller who was famous for his skill.

"I reckon you can, Charley Balaam, if you are friendly," said Yancy.

"I'm a family man, Bob, and I ask you candid, do you feel peevish?"

"Not in particular," and Yancy put aside his rifle.

"I'm a-going to trust you, Bob," said Balaam. And forsaking the shelter of the sweetgum he shuffled up the slope.

"How are you, Charley?" asked Yancy, as they shook hands.

"Only just tolerable, Bob. You've been warranted - Dave Blount swore hit on to you." He displayed a sheet of paper covered with much writing and decorated with a large seal. Yancy viewed this formidable document with respect, but did not offer to take it.

"Read it," he said mildly. Balaam scratched his head.

"I don't know that hit's my duty to do that, Bob. Hit's my duty to serve it on to you. But I can tell you what's into hit, leavin' out the law - which don't matter nohow."

At this juncture Uncle Sammy's bent form emerged from the path that led off through the woods in the direction of the Bellamy cabin. With the patriarch was a stranger. Now the presence of a stranger on Scratch Hill was an occurrence of such extraordinary rarity that the warrant instantly became a matter of secondary importance.

"Howdy, Charley. Here, Bob Yancy, you shake hands with Bruce Carrington," commanded Uncle Sammy. At the name both Yancy and Balaam manifested a quickened interest. They saw a man in the early twenties, clean-limbed and broad-shouldered, with a handsome face and shapely head. "Yes, sir, hit's a grandson of Tom Carrington that used to own the grist-mill down at the Forks. Yo're some sort of wild-hog kin to him, Bob - yo' mother was a cousin to old Tom. Her family was powerful upset at her marrying a Yancy. They say Tom cussed himself into a 'pleptic fit when the news was fetched him."

"Where you located at, Mr. Carrington?" asked Yancy. But Carrington was not given a chance to reply. Uncle Sammy saved him the trouble.

"Back in Kentucky. He tells me he's been follerin' the water. What's the name of that place where Andy Jackson fit the British?"

"New Orleans," prompted Carrington good naturedly.

"That's hit - he takes rafts down the river to New Orleans, then he comes back on ships to Baltimore, or else he hoofs it no'th overland." Uncle Sammy had acquired a general knowledge of the stranger's habits and pursuits in an incredibly brief space of time. "He wants to visit the Forks," he added.

"I'm shortly goin' that way myself, Mr. Carrington, and I'll be pleased of your company - but first I got to get through with Bob Yancy," said Balaam, and again he produced the warrant. "If agreeable to you, Bob, I'll ask Uncle Sammy, as a third party friendly to both, to read this here warrant," he said.

"Who's been a-warrantin' Bob Yancy?" cried Uncle Sammy, with shrill interest.

"Dave Blount has."

"I knowed hit - I knowed he'd try to get even!" And Uncle Sammy struck his walking-stick sharply on the packed earth of Yancy's dooryard. "What's the charge agin you, Bob?"

"Read hit," said Balaam. "Why, sho' - can't you read plain writin', Uncle Sammy?" for the patriarch was showing signs of embarrassment.

"If you gentlemen will let me -" said Carrington pleasantly. Instantly there came a relieved chorus from the three in one breath.

"Why, sure!"

"Would my spectacles help you any, Mr. Carrington ?" asked Uncle Sammy officiously.

"No, I guess not."

"They air powerful seein' glasses, and I'm aweer some folks read a heap easier with spectacles than without 'em." After a moment's scrutiny of the paper that Balaam had thrust in his hand, Carrington began:

"To the Sheriff of the County of Cumberland: Greetings."

"He means me," explained Balaam. "He always makes 'em out to the sheriff, but they are returned to me and I serve 'em." Carrington resumed his reading

"Whereas, It is alleged that a murderous assault has been committed on one David Blount, of Fayetteville, by Robert Yancy, of Scratch Hill, said Blount sustaining numerous bruises and contusions, to his great injury of body and mind; and, whereas, it is further alleged that said murderous assault was wholly unprovoked and without cause, you will forthwith take into custody the person of said Yancy, of Scratch Hill, charged with having inflicted the bruises and contusions herein set forth in the complaint of said Blount, and instantly bring him into our presence to answer to these various and several crimes and misdemeanors. You are empowered to seize said Yancy wherever he may be at; whether on the hillside or in the valley, eating or sleeping, or at rest.

"De Lancy Balaam, Magistrate.

"Fourth District, County of Cumberland, State of North Carolina. Done this twenty-fourth day of May, 1835.

"P.S. Dear Bob: Dave Blount says he ain't able to chew his meat. I thought you'd be glad to know."

Smilingly Carrington folded the warrant and handed it to Yancy.

"Well, what are you goin' to do about hit, Bob?" inquired Balaam.

"Maybe I'd ought to go. I'd like to oblige the squire," said Yancy.

"When does this here co't set?" demanded Uncle Sammy.

"Hit don't do much else since he's took with the lumbago," answered Balaam somewhat obscurely.

"How are the squire, Charley?" asked Yancy with grave concern.

"Only just tolerable, Bob."

"What did he tell you to do?" and Yancy knit his brows.

"Seems like he wanted me to find out what you'd do. He recommended I shouldn't use no violence."

"I wouldn't recommend you did, either," assented Yancy, but without heat.

"I'd get shut of this here law business, Bob," advised Uncle Sammy.

"Suppose I come to the Cross Roads this evening?"

"That's agreeable," said the deputy, who presently departed in company with Carrington.

Some hours later the male population of Scratch Hill, with a gravity befitting the occasion, prepared itself to descend on the Cross Roads and give its support to Mr. Yancy in his hour of need. To this end those respectable householders armed themselves, with the idea that it might perhaps be necessary to correct some miscarriage of justice. They were shy enough and timid enough, these remote dwellers in the pine woods, but, like all wild things, when they felt they were cornered they were prone to fight; and in this instance it was clearly iniquitous that Bob Yancy's right to smack Dave Blount should be questioned. That denied what was left of human liberty. But beyond this was a matter of even greater importance: they felt that Yancy's possession of the boy was somehow involved.

Yancy had declared himself simply but specifically on this point. Law or no law, he would kill whoever attempted to take the boy from him, and Scratch Hill believing to a man that in so doing he would be well within his rights, was prepared to join in the fray. Even Uncle Sammy, who had not been off the Hill in years, announced that no consideration of fatigue would keep him away from the scene of action and possible danger, and Yancy loaned him his mule and cart for the occasion. When the patriarch was helped to his seat in the ancient vehicle he called loudly for his rifle.

"Why, pap, what do you want with a weapon?" asked his son indulgently. "If there air shootin' I may take a hand in it. Now you-all give me a fair hour's start with this mule critter of Bob's, and if nothin' busts I'll be at the squire's as soon as the best of you."

Uncle Sammy was given the time allowance he asked and then Scratch Hill wended its way down the path to the branch and the highroad. Yancy led the straggling procession, with the boy trotting by his side, his little sunburned fist clasped in the man's great hand. He, too, was armed. He carried the old spo'tin' rifle he had brought from the Barony, and suspended from his shoulder by a leather thong was the big horn flask with its hickory stopper his Uncle Bob had fashioned for him, while a deerskin pouch held his bullets and an extra flint or two. He understood that beyond those smacks he had seen his Uncle Bob fetch Mr. Blount, he himself was the real cause of this excitement, that somebody, it was not plain to his mind just who, was seeking to get him away from Scratch Hill, and that a mysterious power called the Law would sooner or later be invoked to this dread end. But he knew this much clearly, nothing would induce him to leave his Uncle Bob! And his thin little fingers nestled warmly against the man's hardened palm. Yancy looked down and gave him a sunny, reassuring smile.

"It'll be all right, Nevvy," he said gently.

"You wouldn't let 'em take me, would you, Uncle Bob?" asked the child in a fearful whisper.

"Such an idea ain't entered my head. And this here warranting is just some of Dave Blount's cussedness."

"Uncle Bob, what'll they do to you?"

"Well, I reckon the squire'll feel obliged to do one of two things. He'll either fine me or else he won't."

"What'll you do if he fines you?"

"Why, pay the fine, Nevvy - and then lick Dave Blount again for stirring up trouble. That's the way we most in general do. I mean to say give him a good licking, and that'll make him stop his foolishness."

"Wasn't that a good licking you gave him on the Ox Road, Uncle Bob?" asked Hannibal.

"It was pretty fair fo' a starter, but I'm capable of doing a better job," responded Yancy.

They overtook Uncle Sammy as he turned in at the squire's.

"I thought I'd come and see what kind of law a body gets at this here co't of yours," the patriarch explained to Mr. Balaam, who, forgetting his lumbago, had hurried forth to greet him.

"But why did you fetch your gun, Uncle Sammy?" asked the

magistrate, laughing.

"Hit were to be on the safe side, Squire. Where air them Blounts?"

"Them Blounts don't need to bother you none. There air only Dave, and he can't more than half see out of one eye to-day."

The squire's court held its infrequent sittings in the best room of the Balaam homestead, a double cabin of hewn logs. Here Scratch Hill was gratified with a view of Mr. Blount's battered visage, and it was conceded that his condition reflected creditably on Yancy's physical prowess and was of a character fully to sustain that gentleman's reputation; for while he was notoriously slow to begin a fight, he was reputed to be even more reluctant to leave off once he had become involved in one.

"What's all this here fuss between you and Bob Yancy?" demanded the squire when he had administered the oath to Blount. Mr. Blount's statement was brief and very much to the point. He had been hired by Mr. Bladen, of Fayetteville, to go to Scratch Hill and get the boy who had been temporarily placed in Yancy's custody at the time of General Quintard's death.

"Stop just there!" cried the magistrate, leveling a pudgy finger at Blount. "This here co't is already cognizant of certain facts bearing on that p'int. The boy was left with Bob Yancy mainly because nobody else would take him. Them's the facts. Now go on!" he finished sternly.

"I only know what Bladen told me," said Blount sullenly.

"Well, I reckon Mr. Bladen ought to feel obliged to tell the truth," said the squire.

"He done give me the order from the judge of the co't - I was to show it to Bob Yancy -"

"Got that order?" demanded the squire sharply. With a smile, damaged, but clearly a smile, Blount produced the order. Hmm - app'inted guardeen of the boy -" the squire was presently heard to murmur. The crowded room was very still now, and more than one pair of eyes were turned pityingly in Yancy's direction. When the long arm of the law reached out from Fayetteville, where there was a real judge and a real sheriff, it clothed itself with very special terrors. The boy looked up into Yancy's face. That tense silence had struck a chill through his heart.

"It's all right," whispered Yancy reassuringly, smiling down upon him. And Hannibal, comforted, smiled back, and nestled his head against his Uncle Bob's side.

"Well, Mr. Blount, what did you do with this here order?" asked the squire.

"I went with it to Scratch Hill," said Blount.

"And showed it to Bob Yancy ?" asked the squire.

"No, he wa'n't there. But the boy was, and I took him in my buggy and drove off. I'd got as far as the Ox Road forks when I met Yancy -"

"What happened then? - but a body don't need to ask! Looks like the law was all you had on your side!" and the squire glanced waggishly about the room.

"I showed Yancy the order -"

"You lie, Dave Blount; you didn't!" said Yancy. "But I can't say as it would have made no difference, Squire. He'd have taken his licking just the same and I'd have had my nevvy out of that buggy!"

"Didn't he say nothing about this here order from the colt, Bob?"

"There wa'n't much conversation, Squire. I invited my nevvy to light down, and then I snaked Dave Blount out over the wheel."

"Who struck the first blow?"

"He did. He struck at me with his buggy whip."

"What you got to say to this, Mr. Blount?" asked the squire.

"I say I showed him the order like I said," answered Blount doggedly. Squire Balaam removed his spectacles and leaned back in his chair.

"It's the opinion of this here co't that the whole question of assault rests on whether Bob Yancy saw the order. Bob Yancy swears he didn't see it, while Dave Blount swears he showed it to him. If Bob Yancy didn't know of the existence of the order he was clearly actin' on the idea that Blount was stealin' his nevvy, and he done what any one would have done under the circumstances. If, on the other hand, he knowed of this order from the co't, he was not only guilty of assault, but he was guilty of resistin' an officer of the co't." The squire paused impressively. His audience drew a long breath. The impression prevailed that the case was going against Yancy, and more than one face was turned scowlingly on the fat little justice.

"Can a body drap a word here?" It was Uncle Sammy's thin voice that cut into the silence.

"Certainly, Uncle Sammy. This here co't will always admire to listen to you."

"Well, I'd like to say that I consider that Fayetteville co't mighty officious with its orders. This part of the county won't take nothin' off Fayetteville! We don't interfere with Fayetteville, and blamed if we'll let Fayetteville interfere with us!" There was a murmur of approval. Scratch Hill remembered the rifles in its hands and took comfort.

"The Fayetteville co't air a higher co't than this, Uncle Sammy," explained the squire indulgently.

"I'm aweer of that," snapped the patriarch. "I've seen hit's steeple."

"Air you finished, Uncle Sammy?" asked the squire deferentially.

"I 'low I am. But I 'low that if this here case is goin' agin Bob Yancy I'd recommend him to go home and not listen to no mo' foolishness."

"Mr. Yancy will oblige this co't by setting still while I finish this case," said the squire with dignity. "As I've already p'inted out, the question of veracity presents itself strongly to the mind of this here colt. Mr. Yancy has sworn to one thing, Mr. Blount to another. Now the Yancys air an old family in these parts; Mr. Blount's folks air strangers, but we don't know nothing agin them -"

"And we don't know nothing in their favor," Uncle Sammy interjected.

"Dave's grandfather came here from Virginia about fifty years back and settled near Scratch Hill -"

"We never knowed why he left Virginia or why he came here," said Uncle Sammy, and knowing what local feeling was, was sure he had shot a telling bolt.

"Then, about twenty-five years ago Dave's father pulled up and went to Fayetteville. Nobody ever knowed why - and I don't remember that he ever offered any explanation -" continued the squire.

"He didn't - he just left," said Uncle Sammy.

"Consequently," pursued the squire, somewhat vindictively,

"we ain't had any time in which to form an opinion of the Blounts; but for myself, I'm suspicious of folks that keep movin' about and who don't seem able to get located permanent nowheres, who air here to-day and away tomorrow. But you can't say that of the Yancys. They air an old family in the country, and naturally this co't feels obliged to accept a Yancy's word before the word of a stranger. And in view of the fact that the defendant did not seek litigation, but was perfectly satisfied to let matters rest where they was, it is right and just that all costs should fall on the plaintiff."

CHAPTER V

THE ENCOUNTER

Betty Malroy had ridden into the squire's yard during the progress of the trial and when Yancy and Hannibal came from the house she beckoned the Scratch Hiller to her. She was aware that Mr. Yancy, moving along the line of least industrial resistance, might be counted of little worth in any broad scheme of life. Nat Ferris had strongly insisted on this point, as had Judith, who shared her husband's convictions; consequently, the rumors of his present difficulty had merely excited them to adverse criticism. They had been sure the best thing that could happen the boy would be his removal from Yancy's guardianship, but this was not at all her conclusion. She considered Mr. Bladen heartless and his course without justification, and she regarded Yancy's affection for the boy as in itself constituting a benefit that quite outweighed his unprogressive example.

"You are not going to lose your nephew, are you, Mr. Yancy?" she asked eagerly, when Yancy stood at her side.

"No, ma'am." But his sense of elation was plainly tempered by the knowledge that for him the future held more than one knotty problem.

"I am very glad! I know Hannibal will be much happier with you than with any one else," and she smiled brightly at the boy, whose small sunburned face was upturned to hers.

"I think that-a-ways myself, Miss Betty, but this trial was only for my smacking Dave Blount, who was trying to steal my nevvy," explained Yancy.

"I hope you smacked him well and hard!" said the girl, whose mood was warlike.

"I ain't got no cause to complain, thank you," returned Mr. Yancy pleasantly.

"I rode out to the Hill to say good-by to Hannibal and to you, but they said you were here and that the trial was today."

Captain Murrell, with Crenshaw and the squire, came from the house, and Murrell's swarthy face lit up at sight of the girl. Yancy, sensible of the gulf that yawned between himself and what was known as "the quality," would have yielded his place, but Betty detained him.

"Are you going away, ma'am?" he asked with concern.

"Yes - to my home in west Tennessee," and a cloud crossed her smooth brow.

"That surely is a right big distance for you to travel, ma'am," said Yancy, his mind opening to this fresh impression. "I reckon it's rising a hundred miles or mo'," he concluded, at a venture.

"It's almost a thousand."

"Think of that! And you are that ca'm!" cried Yancy admiringly, as a picture of simply stupendous effort offered itself to his mind's eye. He added: "I am mighty sorry you are going. We-all here shall miss you - specially Hannibal. He just regularly pines for Sunday as it is."

"I hope he will miss me a little - I'm afraid I want him to!" She glanced down at the boy as she spoke, and into her eyes, very clear and very blue and shaded by long dark lashes, stole a look of wistful tenderness. She noted how his little hand was clasped in Yancy's, she realized the perfect trust of his whole attitude toward this big bearded man, and she was conscious of a sudden feeling of profound respect for the Scratch Hiller.

"But ain't you ever coming back, Miss Betty?" asked Hannibal rather fearfully, smitten with the awesome sense of impermanence which dogs our footsteps.

"Oh, I hope so, dear - I wish to think so. But you see my home is not here." She turned to Yancy, "So it is settled that he is to remain with you?"

"Not exactly, Miss Betty. You see, there's an order from the Fayetteville co't fo' me to give him up to this man Bladen."

"But Uncle Bob says -" began Hannibal, who considered his Uncle Bob's remarks on this point worth quoting.

"Never mind what yo' Uncle Bob said," interrupted Yancy hastily.

"Oh, Mr. Yancy, you are not going to surrender him - no matter what the court says!" cried Betty. The expression on Yancy's face was so grim and determined on the instant with the latent fire that was in him flashing from his eyes that she added quickly, "You know the law is for you as well as for Mr. Bladen!"

"I reckon I won't bother the law none," responded Yancy briefly. "Me and my nevvy will go back to Scratch Hill and there won't be no trouble so long as they leave us be. But them Fayetteville folks want to keep away -" The fierce light slowly died out of his eyes. "It'll be all right, ma'am, and it's mighty good and kind of you fo' to feel the way you do. I'm obliged to you."

But Betty was by no means sure of the outcome Yancy seemed

to predict with such confidence. Unless Bladen abandoned his purpose, which he was not likely to do, a tragedy was clearly pending for Scratch Hill. She saw the boy left friendless, she saw Yancy the victim of his own primitive conception of justice. Therefore she said:

"I wonder you don't leave the Hill, Mr. Yancy. You could so easily go where Mr. Bladen would never find you. Haven't you thought of this?"

"That are a p'int," agreed Yancy slowly. "Might I ask what parts you'd specially recommend?" lifting his grave eyes to hers.

"It would really be the sensible thing to do!" said Betty. "I am sure you would like West Tennessee - they say you are a great hunter." Yancy smiled almost guiltily.

"I like a little spo't now and then yes, ma'am, I do hunt some," he admitted.

"Miss Betty, Uncle Bob's the best shot we got! You had ought to see him shoot!" said Hannibal.

"Mr. Yancy, if you should cross the mountains, remember I live near Memphis. Belle Plain is the name of the plantation - it's not hard to find; just don't forget - Belle Plain."

"I won't forget, and mebby you will see us there one of these days. Sho', I've seen mighty little of the world - about as far as a dog can trot it a couple of hours!"

"Just think what it will mean to Hannibal if you become involved further with Mr. Bladen." Betty spoke earnestly, bending toward him, and Yancy understood the meaning that lay back of her words.

"I've thought of that, too," the Scratch Hiller answered seriously. Betty glanced toward the squire and Mr. Crenshaw.

They were standing near the bars that gave entrance to the lane. Murrell had left them and was walking briskly down the road toward Crenshaw's store where his horse was tied. She bent down and gave Yancy her slim white hand.

"Good-by, Mr. Yancy - lift Hannibal so that I can kiss him!" Yancy swung the child aloft. "I think you are such a nice little boy, Hannibal - you mustn't forget me!" And touching her horse lightly with the whip she rode away at a gallop.

"She sho'ly is a lady!" said Yancy, staring after her. "And we mustn't forget Memphis or Belle Plain, Nevvy."

Crenshaw and the squire approached.

"Bob," said the merchant, "Bladen's going to have the boy - but he made a mistake in putting this business in the hands of a fool like Dave Blount. I reckon he knows that now."

"I reckon his next move will be to send a posse of gun-toters up from Fayetteville," said the squire.

"That's just what he'll do," agreed Crenshaw, and looked disturbed.

"They certainly air an unpeaceable lot - them Fayetteville folks! It's always seemed to me they had a positive spite agin this end of the county," said the squire, and he pocketed his spectacles and refreshed himself with a chew of tobacco. "Bladen ain't actin' right, Bob. It's a year and upwards since the old general 'died. He let you go on thinking the boy was to stay with you and now he takes a notion to have him!"

"No, sir, it ain't right nor reasonable. And what's more, he shan't have him!" said Yancy, and his tone was final.

"I don't know what kind of a mess you're getting yourself into, Bob, I declare I don't!" cried Crenshaw, who felt that he was largely responsible for the whole situation.

"Looks like your neighbors would stand by you," suggested the squire.

"I don't want them to stand by me. It'll only get them into trouble, and I ain't going to do that," rejoined Yancy, and lapsed into momentary silence. Then he resumed meditatively, "There was old Baldy Ebersole who shot the sheriff when they tried to arrest him for getting drunk down in Fayetteville and licking the tavern-keeper -"

"Sho', there wa'n't no harm in Baldy!" said the squire, with heat. "When that sheriff come along here looking for him, I told him p'inted that Baldy said he wouldn't be arrested. A more truthful man I never knowed, and if the damn fool had taken my word he'd be living yet!"

"But you-all know what trouble killing that sheriff made fo' Baldy!" said Yancy. "He told me often he regretted it mo' than anything he'd ever done. He said it was most aggravatin' having to always lug a gun wherever he went. And what with being suspicious of strangers when he wa'n't suspicious by nature, he reckoned in time it would just naturally wear him out."

"He stood it until he was risin' eighty," said Crenshaw.

"His, father lived to be ninety, John, and as spry an old gentleman as a body'd wish to see. I don't uphold no man for committing murder, but I do consider the sheriff should have waited on Baldy to get mo' reasonable, like he'd done in time if they'd just let him alone - but no, sir, he reckoned the law wa'n't no respecter of persons. He was a fine-appearin' man, that sheriff, and just elected to office. I remember we had to leave off the tail-gate to my cart to accommodate him. Yes, sir, they pretty near pestered Baldy into his grave - and seein' that pore old fellow pottering around year after year always toting a gun was the patheticest sight I most ever seen, and I made up my mind then if it ever seemed necessary for me to kill a man, I'd leave the county or maybe the state," concluded the squire.

Vaughan Kester

"Don't you reckon it would be some better to leave the state afo' you. done the killing?" suggested Yancy.

"Well, a man might. I don't know but what he'd be justified in getting shut of his troubles like that."

When Betty Malroy rode away from Squire Balaam's Murrell galloped after her. Presently she heard the beat of his horse's hoofs as he came pounding along the sandy road and glanced back over her shoulder. With an exclamation of displeasure she reined in her horse. She had not wished to ride to the Barony with him, yet she had no desire to treat him with discourtesy, especially as the Ferrises were disposed to like him. Murrell quickly gained a place at her side.

"I suppose Ferris is at the Barony?" he said, drawing his horse down to a walk.

"I believe he is," said Betty with a curt little air.

"May I ride with you?" he gave her a swift glance. She nodded indifferently and would have urged her horse into a gallop again, but he made a gesture of protest. "Don't - or I shall think you are still running away from me," he said with a short laugh.

"Were you at the trial?" she asked. "I am glad they didn't get Hannibal away from Yancy."

"Oh, Yancy will have his hands full with that later - so will Bladen," he added significantly. He studied her out of those deeply sunken eyes of his in which no shadow of youth lingered, for men such as he reached their prime early, and it was a swiftly passing splendor. "Ferris tells me you are going to West Tennessee?" he said at length.

"Yes."

"I know your half-brother, Tom Ware - I know him   very

well." There was another brief silence.

"So you know Tom?" she presently observed, and frowned slightly. Tom was her guardian, and her memories of him were not satisfactory. A burly, unshaven man with a queer streak of meanness through his character. She had not seen him since she had been sent north to Philadelphia, and their intercourse had been limited to infrequent letters. His always smelled of strong, stale tobacco, and the well-remembered whine in the man's voice ran through his written sentences.

"You've spent much of your time up North?" suggested Murrell.

"Four years. I've been at school, you know. That's where I met Judith."

"I hope you'll like West Tennessee. It's still a bit raw compared with what you've been accustomed to in the North. You haven't been back in all those four years?" Betty shook her head. "Nor seen Tom - nor any one from out yonder?" For some reason a little tinge of color had crept into Betty's cheeks. "Will you let me renew our acquaintance at Belle Plain? I shall be in West Tennessee before the summer is over; probably I shall leave here within a week," he said, bending toward her. His glance dwelt on her face and the pliant lines of her figure, and his sense swam. Since their first meeting the girl's beauty had haunted and allured him; with his passionate sense of life he was disposed to these violent fancies, and he had a masterful way with women just as he had a masterful way with men. Now, however, he was aware that he was viewed with entire indifference. His vanity, which was his whole inner self, was hurt, and from the black depths of his nature his towering egotism flashed out lawless and perverted impulses. "I must tell you that I am not of your sort, Miss Malroy -" he continued hurriedly. "My people were plain folk out of the mountains. For what I am I have no one to thank but myself. You must be aware of the prejudices of the planter class, for it is your class. Perhaps I haven't been quite frank at the Barony - I felt it was asking too much when you were there. That was a door I didn't want closed to me!"

"I imagine you will be welcome at Belle Plain. You are Tom's friend." Murrell bit his lip, and then laughed as his mind conjured up a picture of the cherished Tom. Suddenly he reached out and rested his hand on hers. He lived in the shadow of chance not always kind, his pleasures were intoxicating drafts snatched in the midst of dangers, and here was youth, sweet and perfect, that only needed awakening.

"Betty - if I might think -" he began, but his tongue stumbled. His love-making was usually of a savage sort, but some quality in the girl held him in check. The words he had spoken many times before forsook him. Betty drew away from him, an angry color on her cheeks and an angry light in her eyes. "Forgive me, Betty!" muttered Murrell, but his heart beat against his ribs, and passion sent its surges through him. "Don't you know what I'm trying to tell you?" he whispered. Betty gathered up her reins. "Not yet -" he cried, and again he rested a heavy hand on hers. "Don't you know what's kept me here? It was to be near you - only that - I've been waiting for this chance to speak. It was long in coming, but it's here now - and it's mine!" he exulted. His eyes burned with a luminous fire, he urged his horse nearer and they came to a halt. "Look here - I'll follow you North - I swear I love you - say I may!"

"Let me go - let me go!" cried Betty indignantly.

"No - not yet!" he urged his horse still nearer and gathered her close. "You've got to hear me. I've loved you since the first moment I rested my eyes on you - and, by God, you shall love me in return!" He felt her struggle to free herself from his grasp with a sense of savage triumph. It was the brute force within him that conquered with women just as it conquered with men.

Bruce Carrington, on his way back to Fayetteville from the Forks, came about a turn in the road. Betty saw a tall, handsome fellow in the first flush of manhood; Carrington, an angry girl, very beautiful and very indignant, struggling in a man's grasp.

At sight of the new-comer, Murrell, with an oath, released Betty, who, striking her horse with the whip galloped down the road toward the Barony. As she fled past Carrington she bent low in her saddle.

"Don't let him follow me!" she gasped, and Carrington, striding forward, caught Murrell's horse by the bit.

"Not so fast, you!" he said coolly. The two men glared at each other for a brief instant.

"Take your hand off my horse!" exclaimed Murrell hoarsely, his mouth hot and dry with a sense of defeat.

"Can't you see she'd rather be alone?" said Carrington.

"Let go!" roared Murrell, and a murderous light shot from his eyes.

"I don't know but I should pull you out of that saddle and twist your neck!" said Carrington hotly. Murrell's face underwent a swift change.

"You're a bold fellow to force your way into a lover's quarrel," he said quietly. Carrington's arm dropped at his side. Perhaps, after all, it was that. Murrell thrust his hand into his pocket. "I always give something to the boy who holds my horse," he said, and tossed a coin in Carrington's direction. "There - take that for your pains!" he added. He pulled his horse about and rode back toward the cross-roads at an easy canter.

Carrington, with an angry flush on his sunburnt cheeks, stood staring down at the coin that glinted in the dusty road, but he was seeing the face of the girl, indignant, beautiful - then he glanced after Murrell.

"I reckon I ought to have twisted his neck," he said with a deep breath.

CHAPTER VI

BETTY SETS OUT FOR TENNESSEE

Bruce Carrington came of a westward-looking race. From the low coast where they had first settled, those of his name had followed the rivers to their headwaters. The headwaters had sent them forth toward the foot-hills, where they made their, clearings and built their cabins in the shadow of the blue wall that for a time marked the furthest goal of their desires. But only for a time. Crossing the mountains they found the headwaters once more, and following the streams out of the hills saw the roaring torrents become great placid rivers.

Carrington's father had put the mountains at his back thirty years before. The Watauga settlements had furnished him a wife, and some four years later Bruce was born on the banks of the Ohio. The senior Carrington had appeared on horseback as a wooer, but had walked on foot as a married man, each shift of residence he made having represented a descent to a lower social level. On the death of his wife he had embarked in the river trade with all that enthusiasm and hope he had brought to half-a-dozen other occupations, for he was a gentleman of prodigious energy.

Bruce's first memories had to do with long nights when he perched beside his father on the cabin roof of their keel-boat and watched the stars, or the blurred line of the shore where it lay against the sky, or the lights on other barges and rafts drifting as they were drifting, with their wheat and corn and whisky to that common market at the river's mouth.

Sometimes they dragged their boat back up-stream, painfully, laboriously; three or four months of unremitting toil sufficed for this, when the crew sweated at the towing ropes from dawn until dark, that the rich planters in Kentucky and Tennessee might have tea and wine for their tables, and silks and laces for their womenfolk. More often they abandoned their boat and tramped north, armed and watchful, since cutthroats and robbers haunted the roads, and river-men, if they had not drunk away their last dollar in New Orleans, were worth spoiling. Or, if it offered, they took passage on some fast sailing clipper bound for Baltimore or Philadelphia, and crossed the mountains to the Ohio and were within a week or two of home.

Bruce Carrington had seen the day of barge and raft reach its zenith, had heard the first steam packet's shrieking whistle which sounded the death-knell of the ancient order, though the shifting of the trade was a slow matter and the glory of the old did not pass over to the new at once, but lingered still in mighty fleets of rafts and keel-boats and in the Homeric carousals of some ten thousand of the half-horse, half-alligator breed that nightly gathered in New Orleans. Broad-horns and mud-sills they were called in derision. A strange race of aquatic pioneers, jeans and leather clad, the rifle and the setting-pole equally theirs, they came out of every stream down which a scow could be thrust at flood-time; from tiny settlements far back among the hills; from those bustling sinks of iniquity, the river towns. But now, surely, yet almost imperceptibly, their commerce was slipping from them. At all the landings they were being elbowed by the newcomers - men who wore brass buttons and gold braid, and shiny leather shoes instead of moccasins; men with white hands and gold rings on their fingers and diamonds in their shirts - men whose hair and clothing kept the rancid smell of oil and smoke and machinery.

After the reading of the warrant that morning, Charley Balaam had shown Carrington the road to the Forks, assuring him when they separated that with a little care and decent use of his eyes it would be possible to fetch up there and not pass plumb through the settlement without knowing where he was. But Carrington had found the Forks without difficulty. He had seen the old mill his grandfather had built almost a hundred years before, and in the churchyard he had found the graves and read the inscriptions that recorded the virtues of certain dead and gone Carringtons. It had all seemed a very respectable link with the past.

He was on his way to Fayetteville, where he intended to spend the night, and perhaps a day or two in looking around, when the meeting with Betty and Murrell occurred. As Murrell disappeared in the direction of Balaam's, Carrington took a spiteful kick at the unoffending coin, and strode off down the Fayetteville pike. But the girl's face remained with him. It was a face he would like to see again. He wondered who she was, and if she lived in the big house on the other road, the house beyond the red gate which Charley Balaam had told him was called the Barony.

He was still thinking of the girl when he ate his supper that night at Cleggett's Tavern. Later, in the bar, he engaged his host in idle gossip. Mr. Cleggett knew all about the Barony and its owner, Nat Ferris. Ferris was a youngish man, just married. Carrington experienced a quick sinking of the heart. A fleeting sense of humor succeeded - had he interfered between man and wife? But surely if this had been the case the girl would not have spoken as she had.

He wound Mr. Cleggett up with sundry pegs of strong New England rum. He had met a gentleman and lady on the road that day; he wondered, as he toyed with his glass, if it could have been the Ferrises? Mounted? Yes, mounted. Then it was Ferris and his wife - or it might have been Captain Murrell and Miss Malroy the captain was a strapping, black-haired chap who rode a big bay horse. Miss Malroy did not live in that part of the country; she was a friend of Mrs. Ferris', belonged in

Kentucky or Tennessee, or somewhere out yonder - at any rate she was bringing her visit to an end, for Ferris had instructed him to reserve a place for her in the north-bound stage on the morrow.

Carrington suddenly remembered that he had some thought of starting north in the morning himself, but he was still undecided. How about it if he deferred his decision until the stage was leaving? Mr. Cleggett consulted his bookings and was of the opinion that his chances would not be good; and Carrington hastily paid down his money. Later in the privacy of his own room he remarked meditatively, viewing his reflection in the mirror that hung above the chimneypiece, "I reckon you're plain crazy!" and seemed to free himself from all further responsibility for his own acts whatever they might be.

The stage left at six, and as Carrington climbed to his seat the next morning Mr. Cleggett was advising the driver to look sharp when he came to the Barony road, as he was to pick up a party there. It was Carrington who looked sharp, and almost at the spot where he had seen Betty Malroy the day before he saw her again, with Ferris and Judith and a pile of luggage best-owed by the wayside. Betty did not observe him as the coach stopped, for she was intent on her farewells with her friends. There were hasty words of advice from Ferris, prolonged good-byes to Judith, tears - kisses - while a place was being made for her many boxes and trunks. Carrington viewed the luggage with awe, and listened without shame. He gathered that she was going north to Washington; that her final destination was some point either on the Ohio or Mississippi, and that her name was Betty. Then the door slammed and the stage was in motion again.

Carrington felt sensibly enriched by the meager facts now in his possession. He was especially interested in her name. Be liked the sound of it. It suited her. He even tried it under his breath softly. Betty - Betty Malroy - next he fell to wondering if those few hurried words she had addressed to him could possibly be construed as forming a basis for a further acquaintance. Or wasn't it far more likely she would prefer to forget the episode of the previous day, which had clearly been anything but agreeable?

All through the morning they swung forward in the heat and dust and glare, with now and then a brief pause when they changed horses, and at midday rattled into the shaded main street of a sleepy village and drew up before the tavern where dinner was waiting them - a fact that was announced by a bare-legged colored boy armed with a club, who beat upon a suspended wagon tire.

Betty saw Carrington when she took her seat, and gave a scarcely perceptible start of surprise. Then her face was flooded with a rich color. This was the man who saw her with Captain Murrell yesterday I What must he think of her! There was a brief moment of irresolution and then she bowed coldly.

"You just barely managed it. I reckon nobody could misun-derstand that. By no means cordial - but of course not!" Carrington reflected. His own handsome face had been expressionless when he returned her bow, and Betty could not have guessed how consoled and comforted he was by it. With great fortitude and self-denial he forbore to look in her direction again, but he lingered at the table until the last moment that he might watch her when she returned to the coach. Mr. Carrington entertained ideals where women were concerned, and even though he had been the one to profit by it he would not have had Betty depart in the minutest particular from those stringent rules he laid down for her sex. Consequently that distant air she bore toward him filled him with satisfaction. It was quite enough for the present - for the present - that three times each day his perseverance and determination were rewarded by that curt little acknowledgment of her indebtedness to him.

It was four days to Richmond. Four days of hot, dusty travel, four nights of uncomfortable cross-road stations, where Betty suffered sleepless nights and the unaccustomed pangs of early rising. She occasionally found herself wondering who Carrington was. She approved of the manner in which he conducted himself. She liked a man who could be unobtrusive. Traveling like that day after day it would have been so easy for him to be officious. But he never addressed her and refused to see any opportunity to assist her in entering or quitting the stage, leaving that to some one else. Presently she was sorry she had bowed to him that first day - so self-contained and unpresuming a person as he would evidently have been quite satisfied to overlook the omission. Then she began to be haunted by doubts. Perhaps, after all, he had not recognized her as the girl he had met in the road! This gave her a very queer feeling indeed - for what must he think of her? And the next time she bowed to this perfect stranger she threw a chilling austerity into the salutation quite at variance with her appearance, for the windy drive had tangled her hair and blown it in curling wisps about her face. This served to trouble Carrington excessively, and furnished him with food for reflection through all his waking moments for the succeeding eight and forty hours.

The next morning he found himself seated opposite her at breakfast. He received another curt little nod, cool and distant, as he took his seat, but he felt strongly that a mere bowing acquaintance would no longer suffice; so he passed her a number of things she didn't want, and presently ventured the opinion that she must find traveling as they were, day after day, very fatiguing. Surprised at the sound of his voice, before she knew what she was doing, Betty said, "Not at all," closed her red lips, and was immediately dumb.

Carrington at once relapsed into silence and ventured no further opinion on any topic. Betty was left wondering whether she had been rude, and when they met again asked if the stage would reach Washington at the advertised hour. She had been consulting the copy of Badger's and Porter's Register which Ferris had thrust into her satchel the morning she left the Barony, and which, among a multiplicity of detail as to hotels and taverns, gave the runnings of all the regular stage lines, packets, canal-boats and steamers, by which one could travel over the length and breadth of the land. "You stop in Washington?" said Carrington.

Betty shook her head. "No, I am going on to Wheeling."

"You're fortunate in being so nearly home," he observed. "I am going on to Memphis." He felt it was time she knew this, or else she might think his movements were dictated by her own.

Betty exclaimed: "Why, I am going to Memphis, too!"

"Are you? By canal to Cumberland, and then by stage over the National Road to Wheeling?"

Betty nodded. "It makes one wish they'd finish their railroads, doesn't it? Do you suppose they'll ever get as far west as Memphis?" she said.

"They say it's going to be bad for the river trade when they're built on something besides paper," answered Carrington. "And I happen to be a flatboat-man, Miss Malroy."

Betty gave him a glance of surprise.

"Why, how did you learn my name?" she asked.

"Oh, I heard your friends speak it," he answered glibly. But Betty's smooth brow was puckered thoughtfully. She wondered if he had - and if he hadn't. It was very odd certainly that he should know it.

"So the railroads are going to hurt the steamboats?" she presently said.

"No, I didn't say that. I was thinking of the flatboats that have already been hurt by the steamers," he replied. Now to the western mind the river-men typified all that was reckless and wild. It was their carousals that gave an evil repute to such towns as Natchez. But this particular river-man looked harmless. "Carrington is my name, Miss Malroy," he added.

No more was said just then, for Betty became reserved and he did not attempt to resume the conversation. A day later they rumbled into Washington, and as Betty descended from the coach, Carrington stepped to her side.

"I suppose you'll stop here, Miss Malroy?" he said, indicating the tavern before which the stage had come to a stand. "Yes," said Betty briefly.

"If I can be of any service to you -" he began, with just a touch of awkwardness in his manner.

"No, I thank you, Mr. Carrington," said Betty quickly.

"Good night . . . good-by," he turned away, and Betty saw his tall form disappear in the twilight.

CHAPTER VII

THE FIGHT AT SLOSSON'S TAVERN

Murrell had ridden out of the hills some hours back. He now faced the flashing splendors of a June sunset, but along the eastern horizon the mountains rose against a somber sky. Night was creeping into their fastnesses. Already there was twilight in those cool valleys lying within the shadow of mighty hills. A month and more had elapsed since Bob Yancy's trial. Just two days later man and boy disappeared from Scratch Hill. This had served to rouse Murrell to the need of immediate action, but he found, where Yancy was concerned, Scratch Hill could keep a secret, while Crenshaw's mouth was closed on any word that might throw light on the plans of his friend.

"It's plain to my mind, Captain, that Bladen will never get the boy. I reckon Bob's gone into hiding with him," said the merchant, with spacious candor.

The fugitives had not gone into hiding, however; they had traversed the state from east to west, and Murrell was soon on their trail and pressing forward in pursuit. Reaching the mountains, he heard of them first as ten days ahead of him and bound for west Tennessee, the ten days dwindled to a week, the week became five days, the five days three; and now as he emerged from the last range of hills he caught sight of them. They were half a mile distant perhaps, but he was certain that the man and boy he saw pass about a turn in the road were the man and boy he had been following for a month.

He was not mistaken. The man was Bob Yancy and the boy was Hannibal. Yancy had acted with extraordinary decision. He had sold his few acres at Scratch Hill for a lump sum to Crenshaw - it was to the latter's credit that the transaction was one in which he could feel no real pride as a man of business - and just a day later Yancy and the boy had quitted Scratch Hill in the gray dawn, and turned their faces westward. Tennessee had become their objective point, since here was a region to which they could fix a name, while the rest of the world was strange to them. As they passed the turn in the road where Murrell had caught his first sight of them, Yancy glanced back at the blue wall of the mountains where it lay along the horizon.

"Well, Nevvy," he said, "we've put a heap of distance between us and old Scratch Hill; all I can say is, if there's as much the other side of the Hill as there is this side, the world's a monstrous big place fo' to ramble about in." He carried his rifle and a heavy pack. Hannibal had a much smaller pack and his old sporting rifle, burdens of which his Uncle Bob relieved him at brief intervals.

For the past ten days their journey had been conducted in a leisurely fashion. As Yancy said, they were seeing the world, and it was well to take a good look at it while they had a chance. He was no longer fearful of pursuit and his temperament asserted itself - the minimum of activity sufficed. Usually they camped just where the night overtook them; now and then they varied this by lodging at some tavern, for since there was money in his pocket, Yancy was disposed to spend it. He could not conceive that it had any other possible use.

Suddenly out of the silence carne the regular beat of hoofs. These grew nearer and nearer, and at last when they were quite close, Yancy faced about. He instantly recognized Murrell and dropped his rifle into the crook of his arm. The act was instinctive, since there was no reason to believe that the captain had the least interest in the boy. Smilingly Murrell reined in his horse.

"Why - Bob Yancy!" he cried, in apparent astonishment.

"Yes, sir - Bob Yancy. Does it happen you are looking fo' him, Captain?" inquired Yancy.

"No - no, Bob. I'm on my way West. Shake hands." His manner was frank and winning, and Yancy met it with an equal frankness.

"Well, sir, me and my nevvy are glad to meet some one we've knowed afore. The world are a lonesome place once you get shut of yo'r own dooryard," he said. Murrell slipped from his saddle and fell into step at Yancy's side as they moved forward.

"They were mightily stirred up at the Cross Roads when I left, wondering what had come of you," he observed.

"When did you quit there?" asked Yancy.

"About a fortnight ago," said Murrell. "Every one approves of your action in this matter, Yancy," he went on.

"That's kind of them," responded Yancy, a little dryly. There was no reason for it, but he was becoming distrustful of Murrell, and uneasy.

"Bladen's hurt himself by the stand he's taken it this matter," Murrell added.

They went forward in silence, Yancy brooding and suspicious. For the last mile or so their way had led through an unbroken forest, but a sudden turn in the road brought them to the edge of an extensive clearing. Close to the road were several buildings, but not a tree had been spared to shelter them and they stood forth starkly, the completing touch to a civilization that was still in its youth, unkempt, rather savage, and ruthlessly utilitarian. A sign, the work of inexpert hands, announced the somewhat dingy structure of hewn logs that stood nearest the roadside a tavern. There was a horse rack in front of it and a trampled space. It was flanked by its several sheds and barns on one hand and a woodpile on the other. Beyond the woodpile a rail fence inclosed a corn-field, and beyond the barns and sheds a similar fence defined the bounds of a stumpy pasture-lot.

From the door of the tavern the figure of a man emerged. Pausing by the horse rack he surveyed the two men and boy, if not with indifference, at least with apathy. Just above his head swung the sign with its legend, Slosson - Entertainment;" but if he were Slosson, one could take the last half of the sign either as a poetic rhapsody on the part of the painter, or the yielding to some meaningless convention, for in his person, Mr. Slosson suggested none of those qualities of brain or heart that trenched upon the lighter amenities of life. He was black-haired and bull-necked, and there was about him a certain shagginess which a recent toilet performed at the horse trough had not served to mitigate.

"Howdy?" he drawled.

"Howdy?" responded Mr. Yancy.

"Shall you stop here?" asked Murrell, sinking his voice. Yancy nodded. "Can you put us up?" inquired Murrell, turning to the tavern-keeper.

"I reckon that's what I'm here for," said Slosson. Murrell glanced about the empty yard. "Slack," observed Slosson languidly. "Yes, sir, slack's the only name for it." It was understood he referred to the state of trade. He looked from one to the other of the two men. As his eyes rested on Murrell, that gentleman raised the first three fingers of his right hand. The gesture was ever so little, yet it seemed to have a tonic effect on Mr. Slosson. What might have developed into a smile had he not immediately suppressed it, twisted his bearded lips as he made an answering movement. "Eph, come here, you!" Slosson raised his voice. This call brought a half-grown black boy from about a corner of the tavern, to whom Murrell relinquished his horse.

"Let's liquor," said the captain over his shoulder, moving off in the direction of the bar.

"Come on, Nevvy!" said Yancy following, and they all entered the tavern.

"Well, here's to the best of good luck!" said Murrell, as he raised his glass to his lips.

"Same here," responded Yancy. Murrell pulled out a roll of bills, one of which he tossed on the bar. Then after a moment's hesitation he detached a second bill from the roll and turned to Hannibal.

"Here, youngster - a present for you;" he said good-naturedly. Hannibal, embarrassed by the unexpected gift, edged to his Uncle Bob's side.

"Ain't you-all got nothing to say to the gentleman?" asked Yancy.

"Thank you, sir," said the boy.

"That sounds a heap better. Let's see - why, if it ain't ten dollars - think of that!" said Yancy, in surprise.

"Let's have another drink," suggested Murrell.

Presently Hannibal stole out into the yard. He still held the bill in his hand, for he did not quite know how to dispose of his great wealth. After debating this matter for a moment he knotted it carefully in one corner of his handkerchief. But this did not quite suit him, for he untied the knot and looked at the bill again, turning it over and over in his hand. Then he folded it carefully into the smallest possible compass and once more tied a corner of his handkerchief about it, this time with two knots instead of one; these he afterward tested with his teeth.

"I 'low she won't come undone now!" he said, with satisfaction. He stowed the handkerchief away in his trousers pocket, ramming it very tight with his fist. He was much relieved when this was done, for wearing a care-free air he sauntered across the yard and established himself on the top rail of the corn-field fence.

The colored boy, armed with an ax, appeared at the woodpile and began to chop in the desultory fashion of his race, pausing every few seconds to stare in the direction of his white compatriot, who met his glance with reserve. Whereupon Mr. Slosson's male domestic indulged in certain strange antics that were not rightly any part of woodchopping. This yet further repelled Hannibal.

"The disgustin' chattel!" he muttered under his breath, quoting his Uncle Bob, with whom, in theory at least, race feeling was strong. Yancy appeared at the door of the bar and called to him, and as the boy slid from the fence and ran toward him across the yard, the Scratch Hiller sauntered forth to meet him.

"I reckon it's all right, Nevvy," he said, "but we don't know nothing about this here Captain Murrell - as he calls himself - though he seems a right clever sort of gentleman; but we won't mention Belle Plain." With this caution he led the way into the tavern and back through the bar to a low-ceilinged room where Murrell and Slosson were already at table. It was intolerably hot, and there lingered in the heavy atmosphere of the place stale and unappetizing odors. Only Murrell attempted conversation and he was not encouraged; and presently silence fell on the room except for the rattle of dishes and the buzzing of flies. When they had finished, the stale odors and the heat drove them quickly into the bar again, where for a little time Hannibal sat on Yancy's knee, by the door. Presently he slipped down and stole out into the yard.

The June night was pulsing with life. Above him bats darted in short circling flights. In the corn-field and pasture-lot the fireflies lifted from their day-long sleep, showing pale points of light in the half darkness, while from some distant pond or stagnant watercourse came the booming of frogs, presently to swell into a resonant chorus. These were the summer night sounds he had known as far back as his memory went.

In the tavern the three men were drinking - Murrell with the idea that the more Yancy came under the influence of Slosson's corn whisky the easier his speculation would be managed. Mr. Yancy on his part believed that if Murrell went to bed reasonably drunk he would sleep late and give him the opportunity he coveted, to quit the tavern unobserved at break of day. Gradually the ice of silence which had held them mute at supper, thawed. At first it was the broken lazy speech of men who were disposed to quiet, then the talk became brisk - a steady stream of rather dreary gossip of horses and lands and negroes, of speculations past and gone in these great staples.

Hannibal crossed to the corn-field. There, in the friendly gloom, he examined his handkerchief and felt of the rolled-up bill. Then he made count of certain silver and copper coins which he had in his other pocket. Satisfied that he had sustained no loss, he again climbed to the top rail of the fence where he seated himself with an elbow resting on one knee and his chin in the palm of his hand.

"I got ten dollars and seventy cents - yes, sir - and the clostest shooting rifle I ever tossed to my shoulder." He seemed but small to have accomplished such a feat. He meditated for a little space. "I reckon when we strike the settlements again I should like to buy my Uncle Bob a present." With knitted brows he considered what this should be, canvassing Yancy's needs. He had about decided on a ring such as Captain Murrell was wearing, when he heard the shuffling of bare feet over the ground and a voice spoke out of the darkness.

"When yo' get to feelin' like sleep, young boss, Mas'r Slosson he says I show yo' to yo' chamber." It was Slosson's boy Eph.

"Did you-all happen to notice what they're doing in the tavern now?" asked Hannibal.

"I low they're makin' a regular hog-killin' of it," said Eph smartly. Hannibal descended from the fence.

"Yes, you can show me my chamber," he said, and his tone was severe. What a white man did was not a matter for a black man to criticize. They went toward the open door of the tavern. Mr. Slosson's corn whisky had already wrought a marked transformation in the case of Slosson himself. His usually terse speech was becoming diffuse and irrelevant, while vacant laughter issued from his lips. Yancy was apparently unaffected by the good cheer of which he had partaken, but Murrell's dark face was flushed. The Scratch Hiller's ability to carry his liquor exceeded anything he had anticipated.

"You-all run along to bed, Nevvy," said Yancy, as Hannibal entered the room. "I'll mighty soon follow you."

Eph secured a tin candle-stick with a half-burnt candle in it and led the way into the passage back of the bar.

"Mas'r Slosson's jus' mo' than layin' back!" he said, as he closed the door after them.

"I reckon you-all will lay back, too, when you get growed up," retorted Hannibal.

"No, sir, I won't. White folks won't let a nigger lay back. Onliest time a nigger sees co'n whisky's when he's totin' it fo' some one else."

"I reckon a nigger's fool enough without corn whisky," said

Hannibal. They mounted a flight of stairs and passed down a narrow hall. This brought them to the back of the building, and Eph pushed open the door on his right.

"This heah's yo' chamber," he said, and preceding his companion into the room, placed the candle on a chair.

"Well - I low I clean forgot something!" cried Hannibal.

"If it's yo' bundle and yo' gun, I done fotched 'em up heah and laid 'em on yo' bed," said Eph, preparing' to withdraw.

"I certainly am obliged to you," said Hannibal, and with a good night, Eph retired, closing the door after him, and the boy heard the patter of his bare feet as he scuttled down the hall.

The moon was rising and Hannibal went to the open window and glanced out. His room overlooked the back yard of the inn and a neglected truck patch. Starting from a point beyond the truck patch and leading straight away to the woodland beyond was a fenced lane, with the corn-field and the pasture-lot on either hand. Immediately below his window was the steeply slanting roof of a shed. For a moment he considered the night, not unaffected by its beauty, then, turning from the window, he moved his bundle and rifle to the foot of the bed, where they would be out of his way, kicked off his trousers, blew out the candle and lay down. The gossip of the men in the bar ran like a whisper through the house, and with it came frequent bursts of noisy laughter. Listening for these sounds the boy dozed off.

Yancy had become more and more convinced as the evening passed that Murrell was bent on getting him drunk, and suspicion mounted darkly to his brain. He felt certain that he was Bladen's agent. Now, Mr. Yancy took an innocent pride in his ability to "cool off liquor." Perhaps it was some heritage from a well living ancestry that had hardened its head with Port and Madeira in the days when the Yancys owned their acres and their slaves. Be that as it may, he was equal to the task he had set himself. He saw with satisfaction the flush mount to Murrell's swarthy cheeks, and felt that the limit of his capacity was being reached. Mr. Slosson had become a sort of Greek chorus. He anticipated all the possible phases of drunkenness that awaited his companions. He went from silence to noisy mirth, when his unmeaning laughter rang through the house; he told long witless stories as he leaned against the bar; he became melancholy and described the loss of his wife five years before. From melancholy he passed to sullenness and seemed ready to fasten a quarrel on Yancy, but the latter deftly evaded any such issue.

"What you-all want is another drink," he said affably. "With all you been through you need a tonic, so shove along that extract of cornshucks and molasses!"

"I'm a rip-staver," said Slosson thickly. "But I've knowed enough sorrow to kill a horse."

"You have that look. Captain, will you join us?" asked Yancy. Murrell shook his head, but he made a significant gesture to Slosson as Yancy drained his glass.

"Have a drink with me!" cried Slosson, giving way to drunken laughter.

"Don't you reckon you'll spite yo' appetite fo' breakfast, neighbor?" suggested Yancy.

"Do you mean you won't drink with me?" roared Slosson.

"The captain's dropped out and I 'low it's about time fo' these here festivities to come to an end. I'm thinking some of going to bed myself," said Yancy. He kept his eyes fixed on Murrell. He realized that if the latter could prevent it he was not to leave the bar. Murrell stood between him and the door; more than this, he stood between him and his rifle, which leaned against the wall in the far corner of the room. Slosson roared out a protest to his words. "That's all right, neighbor," retorted Yancy over his shoulder, "but I'm going to bed." He never shifted his glance from Murrell's face. Seowling now, the captain's eyes blazed back their challenge as he thrust his right hand under his coat. "Fair play - I don't know who you are, but I know what you want!" said Yancy, the light in his frank gray eyes deepening. Murrell laughed and took a forward step. At the same moment Slosson snatched up a heavy club from back of the bar and dealt Yancy a murderous blow. A single startled cry escaped the Scratch Hitler; he struck out wildly as he lurched toward Murrell, who drew his knife and drove it into his shoulder.

Groping wildly, Yancy reached his rifle and faced about. His scalp lay open where Slosson's treacherous blow had fallen and his face was covered with blood; even as his fingers stiffened they found the hammer, but Murrell, springing forward, kicked the gun out of his hands. Dashing the blood from his eyes, Yancy threw himself on Murrell. Then, as they staggered to and fro, Yancy dully bent on strangling his enemy, Slosson - whom the sight of blood had wonderfully sobered - rushed out from the bar and let loose a perfect torrent of blows with his club. Murrell felt the fingers that gripped him grow weak, and Yancy dropped heavily to the floor.

How long the boy slept he never knew, but he awoke with a start and a confused sense of things. He seemed to have heard a cry for help. But the tavern was very silent now. The distant murmur of voices and the shouts of laughter had ceased. He lifted himself up on his elbow and glanced from the window. The heavens were pale and gray. It was evidently very late, probably long after midnight but where was his Uncle Bob?

He sank back on his pillow intent and listening. What he had heard, what he still expected to hear, he could not have told, but he was sure he had been roused by a cry of some sort. A chilling terror that gripped him fast and would not let him go, mounted to his brain. Once he thought he heard cautious steps beyond his door. He could not be certain, yet he imagined the

Vaughan Kester

bull-necked landlord standing with his ear to some crack seeking to determine whether or not he slept. His thin little body grew rigid and a cold sweat started from him. He momentarily expected the latch to be lifted, then in the heavy silence he caught the sound of some stealthy movement beyond the lath and plaster partition, and an instant later an audible footfall. He heard the boards creak and give, as the person who had been standing before his door passed down the hall, down the stairs, and to the floor below.

Limp and shivering, he drew his scanty covering tight about him. In the silence that succeeded, he once more became aware of the tireless chorus of the frogs, the hooting of the owls, and the melancholy and oft-repeated call of the whippoorwill. But where was his Uncle Bob? Why didn't he come to bed? And whose was that cry for help he had heard? Memories of idle tales of men foully dealt with in these lonely taverns, of murderous landlords, and mysterious guests who were in league with them, flashed through his mind.

Murrell had followed them for this - and had killed his Uncle Bob, and he would be sent back to Bladen! The law had said that Bladen could have him and that his Uncle Bob must give him up. The law put men in prison - it hanged them sometimes - his Uncle Bob had told him all about it - by the neck with ropes until they were dead! Maybe they wouldn't send him back; maybe they would do with him what they had already done with his Uncle Bob; he wanted the open air, the earth under his feet, and the sky over his head. The four walls stifled him. He was not afraid of the night, be could run and hide in it - there were the woods and fields where he would be safe.

He slid from the bed, and for a long moment stood cold and shaking, his every sense on the alert. With infinite caution he got into his trousers and again paused to listen, since he feared his least movement might betray him. Reassured, he picked up his battered hat from the floor and inch by inch crept across the squeaking boards to the window. When the window was reached he paused once more to listen, but the quiet that was everywhere throughout the house gave him confidence. He straddled the low sill, and putting out his hand gripped the stock of his rifle and drew that ancient weapon toward him. Next he secured his pack, and was ready for flight.

Encumbered by his belongings, but with no mind to sacrifice them, he stepped out upon the shed and made his way down the slant of the roof to the eaves. He tossed his bundle to the ground and going down on his knees lowered his rifle, letting the muzzle fall lightly against the side of the shed as it left his hand, then he lay flat on his stomach and, feet first, wriggled out into space. When he could no longer preserve his balance, he gave himself a shove away from the eaves and dropped clear of the building.

As he recovered himself he was sure he heard a door open and close, and threw himself prone on the ground, where the black shadow cast by the tavern hid him. At the same moment two dark figures came from about a corner of the building. He could just distinguish that they carried some heavy burden between them and that they staggered as they moved. He heard Slosson curse drunkenly, and a whispered word from Murrell. The two men slowly crossed the truck patch, and the boy's glance followed them, his eyes starting from his head. Just at the mouth of the lane they paused and put down their burden; a few words spoken in a whisper passed between them and they began to drag some dark thing down the lane, their backs bent, their heads bowed and the thing they dragged bumping over the uneven ground.

They passed out of sight, and breathless and palsied, Hannibal crept about a corner of the tavern. He must be sure! The door of the bar stood open; the lamps were still burning, and the upturned chairs and a broken table told of the struggle that had taken place there. The boy rested his hand on the top step as he stared fearfully into the room. His palm came away with a great crimson splotch. But he was not satisfied yet. He must be sure - sure! He passed around the building as the men had

　　　　Vaughan Kester

done and crossed the truck patch to the mouth of the lane. Here he slid through the fence into the corn-field, and, well sheltered, worked his way down the rows. Presently he heard a distant sound - a splash - surely it was a splash - .

A little later the men came up the lane, to disappear in the direction of the tavern. Hannibal peered after them. His very terrors, while they wrenched and tortured him, gave him a desperate kind of courage. As the gloom hid the two men, he started forward again; he must know the meaning of that sound - that splash, if it was a splash. He reached the end of the cornfield, climbed the fence, and entered a deadening of slashed and mutilated timber. In the long wet grass he found where the men had dragged their burden. He reached down and swept his hand to and fro - once - twice - the third time his little palm came away red and discolored.

There was the first pale premonition of dawn in the sky, and as he hurried on the light grew, and the black trunks of trees detached themselves from the white mist that filled the woods and which the dawn made visible. There was light enough for him to see that he was following the trail left by the men; he could distinguish where the dew had been brushed from the long grass. Advancing still farther, he heard the clear splash of running water, an audible ripple that mounted into a silver cadence. Day was breaking now. The lifeless gray along the eastern horizon had changed to orange. Still following the trail, he emerged upon the bank of the Elk River, white like the woods with its ghostly night sweat.

The dull beat of the child's heart quickened as he gazed out on the swift current that was hurrying on with its dreadful secret. Then the full comprehension of his loss seemed to overwhelm him and he was utterly desolate. Sobs shook him, and he dropped on his knees, holding fast to the stock of his rifle.

"Uncle Bob - Uncle Bob, come back! Can't you come back!" he wailed miserably. Presently he staggered to his feet. Convulsive sobs still wrenched his little body. What was he to do? Those men - his Uncle Bob's murderers - would go to his room; they would find his empty bed and their search for him would begin! Not for anything would he have gone back through the corn-field or the lane to the road. He had the courage to go forward, but not to retrace his steps; and the river, deep and swift, barred his path. As he glanced about, he saw almost at his feet a dug-out, made from a single poplar log. It was secured to an overhanging branch by a length of wild grape-vine. With one last fearful look off across the deadening in the direction of the tavern, he crept down to the water's edge and entered the canoe. In a moment, he had it free from its lashing and the rude craft was bumping along the bank in spite of his best efforts with the paddle. Then a favoring current caught it and swept it out toward the center of the stream.

It was much too big and clumsy for him to control without the stream's help, though he labored doggedly with his paddle. Now he was broadside to the current, now he was being spun round and round, but always he was carried farther and farther from the spot where he had embarked. He passed about a bend; and a hundred yards beyond, about a second bend; then the stream opened up straight before him a half-mile of smooth running water. Far down it, at the point where the trees met in the unbroken line of the forest and the water seemed to vanish mysteriously, he could distinguish a black moving object; some ark or raft, doubtless.

In the smoother water of the long reach, Hannibal began to make head against the flood. The farther shore became the nearer, and finally he drove the bow of his canoe up on a bit of shelving bank, and seizing his pack and rifle, sprang ashore. Panting and exhausted, he paused just long enough to push the canoe out into the stream again, and then, with his rifle and pack in his hands, turned his small tear-stained face toward the wooded slope beyond. As he toiled up it in the wide silence of the dawn, a mournful wind burst out of the north, filling the air about him with withered leaves and the dead branches of trees.

CHAPTER VIII

ON THE RIVER

Betty stood under a dripping umbrella in the midst of a drenching downpour, her boxes and trunks forming a neat pyramid of respectable size beside her. She was somewhat perturbed in spirit, since they contained much elaborate finery all in the very latest eastern fashion, spoils that were the fruit of a heated correspondence with Tom, who hadn't seemed at all alive to the fact that Betty was nearly eighteen and in her own right a young woman of property. A tarpaulin had been thrown over the heap, and with one eye on it and the other on the stretch of yellow canal up which they were bringing the fast packet Pioneer, she was waiting impatiently to see her belongings transferred to a place of safety.

Just arrived by the four-horse coach that plyed regularly between Washington and Georgetown, she had found the long board platform beside the canal crowded with her fellow passengers, their number augmented by those who delight to share vicariously in travel and to whom the departure of a stage or boat was a matter of urgent interest requiring their presence, rain or shine. Suddenly she became aware of a tall, familiar figure moving through the crowd. It was Bruce Carrington. At the same moment he saw her, and with a casual air that quite deceived her, approached; and Betty, who had been feeling very lonely and very homesick, was somehow instantly comforted at sight of him. She welcomed him almost as a friend.

"You're leaving to-night?" he asked.

"Yes - isn't it miserable the way it rains? And why are they so slow - why don't they hurry with that boat?"

"It's in the last lock now," explained Carrington.

"My clothes will all be ruined," said Betty. He regarded the dress she wore with instant concern. "No - I mean the things in my trunks; this doesn't matter," and Betty nodded toward the pile under the steaming tarpaulin. Carrington's dark eyes opened with an expression of mild wonder. And so those trunks were full of clothes - Oh, Lord! - he looked down at the flushed, impatient face beside him with amusement.

"I'll see that they are taken care of," he said, for the boat was alongside the platform now; and gathering up Betty's hand luggage, he helped her aboard.

By the time they had reached Wheeling, Betty had quite parted with whatever superficial prejudice she might have had concerning river-men. This particular one was evidently a very nice river-man, an exception to his kind. She permitted him to assume the burden of her plans, and no longer scanned the pages of her Badger's and Porter's with a puckered brow. It reposed at the bottom of her satchel. He made choice of the steamer on which she should continue her journey, and thoughtfully chose The Naiad - a slow boat, with no reputation for speed to sustain. It meant two or three days longer on the river, but what of that? There would be no temptation in the engine-room to attach a casual wrench or so to the safety-valve as an offset to the builder's lack of confidence in his own boilers. He saw to it that her state-room was well aft - steamers had a trick of blowing up forward.

Ne had now reached a state of the utmost satisfaction with himself and the situation. Betty was friendly and charming. He walked with her, and he talked with her by the hour; and always he was being entangled deeper and deeper in the web of her attraction. "When alone he would pace the deck recalling every word she had spoken. There was that little air of high breeding which was Betty's that fascinated him. He had known something of the other sort, those who had arrived at prosperity with manners and speech that still reflected the meaner condition from which they had risen.

"I haven't a thing to offer her - this is plain madness of mine!" he kept telling himself, and then the expression of his face would become grim and determined. No more of the river for him - he'd get hold of some land and go to raising cotton; that was the way money was made.

Slow as The Naiad was, the days passed much too swiftly for him. When Memphis was reached their friendly intercourse would come to an end. There would be her brother, of whom she had occasionally spoken - he would be pretty certain to have the ideas of his class.

As for Betty, she liked this tall fellow who helped her through the fatigue of those long days, when there was only the unbroken sweep of the forest on either hand, with here and there a clearing where some outrageous soul was making a home for himself. The shores became duller, wilder, more uninteresting as they advanced, and then at last they entered the Mississippi, and she was almost home.

Betty was not unexcited by the prospect. She would be the mistress of the most splendid place in West Tennessee. She secretly aspired to be a brilliant hostess. She could remember when the doors of Belle Plain were open to whoever had the least claim to distinction - statesmen and speculators in land; men who were promoting those great schemes of improvement, canals and railroads; hard-featured heroes of the two wars with England - a diminishing group; the men of the modern army, the pathfinders, and Indian fighters, and sometimes a titled foreigner. She wondered if Tom had maintained the traditions of the place. She found that Carrington had heard of Belle Plain. He spoke of it with respect, but with a noticeable lack of enthusiasm, for how could he feel enthusiasm when he must begin his chase after fortune with bare hands? - he suffered acutely whenever it was mentioned. The days, like any other days, dwindled. The end of it all was close at hand. Another twenty-four hours and Carrington reflected there would only be good-by to say.

"We will reach New Madrid to-night," he told her. They were watching the river, under a flood of yellow moonlight.

"And then just another day - Oh, I can hardly wait!" cried Betty delightedly. "Soon I shall hope to see you at Belle Plain, Mr. Carrington," she added graciously.

"Thank you, your - your family -" he hesitated.

"There's only just Tom - he's my half-brother. My mother was left a widow when I was a baby. Later, some years after, she married Tom's father."

"Oh - then he's not even your half-brother?"

"He's no relation at all - and much older. When Tom's father died my mother made Tom, manager, and still later he was appointed my guardian."

"Then you own Belle Plain?" and Carrington sighed.

"Yes. You have never seen it? - it's right on the river, you know?" then Betty's face grew sober: "Tom's dreadfully queer - I expect he'll require a lot of managing!"

"I reckon you'll be equal to that!" said-Carrington, convinced of Betty's all-compelling charm.

"No, I'm not at all certain about Tom - I can see where we shall have serious differences; but then, I shan't have to struggle single-handed with him long; a cousin of my mother's is coming to Belle Plain to make her home with me - she'll make' him behave," and Betty laughed maliciously. "It's a great nuisance being a girl!"

Then Betty fell to watching for the lights at New Madrid, her elbows resting on the rail against which she was leaning, and the soft curve of her chin sunk in the palms of her hands. She wondered absently what Judith would have said of this riverman. She smiled a little dubiously. Judith had certainly vindicated the sincerity of her convictions regarding the importance of family, inasmuch as in marrying Ferris she had married her own second cousin. She nestled her chin a little closer in her palms. She remembered that they had differed seriously over Mr. Yancy's defiance, of the law as it was supposed to be lodged in the sacred person of Mr. Bladen's agent, the unfortunate Blount. Carrington, with his back against a stanchion, watched her discontentedly.

"You'll be mighty glad to have this over with, Miss Malroy -" he said at length, with a comprehensive sweep toward the river.

"Yes - shan't you?" and she opened her eyes questioningly.

"No," said Carrington with a short laugh, drawing a chair near hers and sitting down.

Betty, in surprise, gave him a quick look, and then as quickly glanced away from what she encountered in his eyes. Men were accustomed to talk sentiment to her, but she had hoped - well, she really had thought that he was, superior to this weakness. She had enjoyed the feeling that here was some one, big and strong and thoroughly masculine, with whom she could be friendly without - she took another look at him from under the fringe of her long lashes. He was so nice and considerate - and good looking - he was undeniably this last. It would be a pity! And she had already determined that Tom should invite him to Belle Plain. She didn't mind if he was a river-man - they could be friends, for clearly he was such an exception. Tom should be cordial to him. Betty stared before her, intently watching the river. As she looked, suddenly pale points of light appeared on a distant headland.

"Is that New Madrid? - Oh, is it, Mr. Carrington?"' she cried eagerly.

"I reckon so," but he did not alter his position.

"But you're not looking!"

"Yes, I am - I'm looking at you. I reckon you'll think me crazy, Miss Malroy-presumptuous and all that but I wish Memphis could be wiped off the map and that we could go on like this for ever! - no, not like this but together - you and I" he took a deep breath. Betty drew a little farther away, and looked at him reproachfully; and then she turned to the dancing lights far down the river. Finally she said slowly:

"I thought you were - different."

"I'm not," and Carrington's hand covered hers.

"Oh - you mustn't kiss my hand like that -"

"Dear - I'm just a man - and you didn't expect, did you, that I could see you this way day after day and not come to love you?" He rested his arm across the back of her chair and leaned toward her.

"No - no -" and Betty moved still farther away.

"Give me a chance to win your love, Betty!"

"You mustn't talk so - I am nothing to you -"

"Yes, you are. You're everything to me," said Carrington doggedly.

"I'm not - I won't be!" and Betty stamped her foot.

"You can't help it. I love you and that's all there is about it. I know I'm a fool to tell you now, Betty, but years wouldn't make any difference in my feeling; and I can't have you go, and perhaps never see you again, if I can help it. Betty - give me a chance - you don't hate me -"

"But I do - yes, I do - indeed -"

"I know you don't. Let me see you again and do what I can to make you care for me!" he implored. But he had a very indignant little aristocrat to deal with. She was angry with him, and angry with herself that in spite of herself his words moved her. She wouldn't have it so! Why, he wasn't even of her class - her kind! "Betty, you don't mean -" he faltered.

"I mean - I am extremely annoyed. I mean just what I say." Betty regarded him with wrathful blue eyes. It proved too much for Carrington. His arm, dropped about her shoulders.

"You shall love me -" She was powerless in his embrace. She felt his breath on her cheek, then he kissed her. Breathless and crimson, she struggled and pushed him from her. Suddenly his arms fell at hisside; his face was white. "I was a brute to do that! - Betty, forgive me! I am sorry - no, I can't be sorry!"'

"How do you dare! I hope I may never see you again - I hate you -" said Betty furiously, tears in her eyes and her pulses still throbbing from his fierce caress.

"Do you mean that?" he asked slowly, rising.

"Yes - yes - a million times, yes!"

"I don't believe you - I can't - I won't!" They were alongside the New Madrid wharf now, and a certain young man who had been impatiently watching The Naiad's lights ever since they became visible crossed the gang-plank with a bound.

"Betty - why in the name of goodness did you ever, choose this tub? - everything on the river has passed it!" said the newcomer. Betty started up with a little cry of surprise and pleasure.

"Charley!"

Carrington stepped back. This must be the brother who had come up the river from Memphis to meet her - but her brother's name was Tom! He looked this stranger - this Charley - over with a hostile eye, offended by his good looks, his confident manner, in which he thought he detected an air of ownership, as if - certainly he was holding her hands longer than was necessary! Of course, other men were in love with her, such a radiant personality held its potent attraction for men, but for all that, she was going to belong to him - Carrington! She did like him; she had shown it in a hundred little ways during the last week, and he would give her up to no man - give her up? - there wasn't the least tie between them - except that kiss - and she was furious because of it. There was nothing for him to do but efface himself. He would go now, before the boat started - and an instant later, when Betty, remembering, turned to speak to him, his place by the rail was deserted.

CHAPTER IX

JUDGE SLOCUM PRICE

Athat day Hannibal was haunted by the memory of what he had heard and seen at Slosson's tavern. More than this, there was his terrible sense of loss, and the grief he could not master, when his thin, little body was shaken by sobs. Marking the course of the road westward, he clung to the woods, where his movements were as stealthy as the very shadows themselves. He shunned the scattered farms and the infrequent settlements, for the fear was strong with him that he might be followed either by Murrell or Slosson. But as the dusk of evening crept across the land, the great woods, now peopled by strange shadows, sent him forth into the highroad. He was beginning to be very tired, and hunger smote him with fierce pangs, but back of it all was his sense of bitter loss, his desolation, and his loneliness.

"I couldn't forget Uncle Bob if I tried -" he told himself, with quivering lips, as he limped wearily along the dusty road, and the tears welled up and streaked his pinched face. Now before him he saw the scattered lights of a settlement. All his terrors, the terrors that grouped themselves about the idea of pursuit and capture, rushed back upon him, and in a panic he plunged into the black woods again.

But the distant lights intensified his loneliness. He had lived a whole day without food, a whole day without speech. He began to skirt the settlement, keeping well within the thick gloom of the woods, and presently, as he stumbled forward, he came to a small clearing in the center of which stood a log dwelling. The place seemed deserted. There was no sign of life, no light shone from the window, no smoke issued from the stick-and-mud chimney.

Tilted back in a chair by the door of this house a man was sleeping. The hoot of an owl from a near-by oak roused him. He yawned and stretched himself, thrusting out his fat legs and extending his great arms. Then becoming aware of the small figure which had stolen up the path as he slept and now stood before him in the uncertain light, he fell to rubbing his eyes with the knuckles of his plump hands. The pale night mist out of the silent depths of the forest had assumed shapes as strange.

"Who are you?" he demanded, and his voice rumbled thickly forth from his capacious chest. The very sound was sleek and unctuous.

"I'm Hannibal," said the small figure. He was meditating flight; he glanced over his shoulder toward the woods.

"No, you ain't. He's been dead a thousand years, more or less. Try again," recommended the man.

"I'm Hannibal Wayne Hazard," said the boy. The man quitted his chair.

"Well - I am glad to know you, Hannibal Wayne Hazard. I am Slocum Price - Judge Slocum Price, sometime major-general of militia and ex-member of congress, to mention a few of those honors my fellow countrymen have thrust upon me." He made a sweeping gesture with his two hands outspread and bowed ponderously.

The boy saw a man of sixty, whose gross and battered visage told its own story. There was a sparse white frost about his ears; and his eyes, pale blue and prominent, looked out from under beetling brows. He wore a shabby plum-colored coat and tight, drab breeches. About his fat neck was a black stock, with just a suggestion of soiled linen showing above it. His figure was corpulent and unwieldy.

The man saw a boy of perhaps ten, barefoot, and clothed in homespun shirt and trousers. On his head was a ruinous hat much too large for him, but which in some mysterious manner he contrived to keep from quite engulfing his small features, which were swollen and tear-stained. In his right hand he carried a bundle, while his left clutched the brown barrel of a long rifle.

"You don't belong in these parts, do you?" asked the judge, when he had completed his scrutiny.

"No, sir," answered the boy. He glanced off down the road, where lights were visible among the trees. "What town is that?" he added.

"Pleasantville - which is a lie - but I am neither sufficiently drunk nor sufficiently sober to cope with the possibilities your question offers. It is a task one should approach only after extraordinary preparation," and the sometime major-general of militia grinned benevolently.

"It's a town, ain't it?" asked Hannibal doubtfully. He scarcely understood this large, smiling gentleman who was so civilly given to speech with him, yet strangely enough he was not afraid of him, and his whole soul craved human companionship.

"It's got a name - but you'll excuse me, I'd much prefer not to tell you how I regard it - you're too young to hear. But stop a bit - have you so much as fifty cents about you?" and the judge's eyes narrowed to a slit above their folds of puffy flesh. Hannibal, keeping his glance fixed on the man's face, fell back a step. "I can't let you go if you are penniless - I can't do that!" cried the judge, with sudden vehemence. "You shall be my guest for the night. They're a pack of thieves at the tavern," he lowered his voice. "I know 'em, for they've plucked me!" To make sure of his prey, he rested a fat hand on the boy's shoulder and drew him gently but firmly into the shanty. As they crossed the threshold he kicked the door shut, then with flint and steel he made a light, and presently a candle was sputtering in his hands. He fitted it into the neck of a tall bottle, and as the light flared up the boy glanced about him.

The interior was mean enough, with its rough walls, dirt floor and black, cavernous fireplace. A rude clapboard table did duty as a desk, a fact made plain by a horn ink-well, a notary's seal, and a rack with a half-dozen quill pens. Above the desk was a shelf of books in worn calf bindings, and before it a rickety chair. A shakedown bed in one corner of the room was tastefully screened from the public gaze by a tattered quilt.

"Boy, don't be afraid. Look on me as a friend," urged the judge, who towered above him in the dim candle-light. "Here's comfort without ostentation. Don't tell me you prefer the tavern, with its corrupt associations!" Hannibal was silent, and the judge, after a brief moment of irresolution, threw open the door. Then he bent toward the small stranger, bringing his face close to the child's, while his thick lips wreathed themselves in a smile ingratiatingly genial. "You can't look me squarely in the eye and say you prefer the tavern to these scholarly surroundings?" he said banteringly.

"I reckon I'll be glad to stop," answered Hannibal. The judge clapped him playfully on the back.

"Such confidence is inspiring! Make yourself perfectly at home. Are you hungry?"

"Yes, sir. I ain't had much to eat to-day," replied Hannibal cautiously.

"I can offer you food then. What do you say to cold fish?" the judge smacked his lips to impart a relish to the idea. "I dare swear I can find you some corn bread into the bargain. Tea I haven't got. On the advice of my physician, I don't use it. What do you say - shall we light a fire and warm the fish?"

"I 'low I could eat it cold."

"No trouble in the world to start a fire. All we got to do is to go out, and pull a few palings off the fence," urged the judge.

"It will do all right just like it is," said Hannibal.

"Very good, then! " cried the judge gaily, and he began to assemble the dainties he had enumerated. "Here you are!" he cleared his throat impressively, while benignity shone from every feature of his face. "A moment since you allowed me to think that you were solvent to the extent of fifty cents -" Hannibal looked puzzled. The judge dealt him a friendly blow on the back, then stood off and regarded him with a glance of great jocularity, his plump knuckles on his hips and his arms akimbo. "I wonder" - and his eyes assumed a speculative squint "I wonder if you could be induced to make a temporary loan of that fifty cents? The sum involved is really such a ridiculous trifle I don't need to point out to you the absolute moral certainty of my returning it at an early date - say to-morrow morning; say to-morrow afternoon at the latest; say even the day after at the very outside. Meantime, you shall be my guest. The landlady's son has found my notarial seal an admirable plaything - she has had to lick the little devil twice for hooking it - my pens and stationery are at your disposal, should you desire to communicate to absent friends; you can have the run of my library!" the judge fairly trembled in his eagerness. It was not the loss of his money that Hannibal most feared, and the coin passed from his possession into his host's custody. As it dropped into the latter's great palm he was visibly moved. His moist, blue eyes became yet more watery, while his battered old face assumed an expression indicating deep inward satisfaction. "Thank you, my boy! This is one of those intrinsically trifling benefits which, conferred at the moment of acute need, touch the heart and tap the unfailing springs of human gratitude - I must step down to the tavern - when I return, please God, we shall know more of each other." While he was still speaking he had produced a jug from behind the quilt that screened his bed, and now, bareheaded, and with every indication of haste, took himself off into the night.

Left alone, Hannibal gravely seated himself at the table. What the judge's larder lacked in variety it more than made up for in quantity, and the boy was grateful for this fact. He was half famished, and the coarse, abundant food was of the sort to which he was accustomed. Presently he heard the judge's heavy, shuffling step as he came up the path from the road, and a moment later his gross bulk of body filled the doorway. Breathing hard and perspiring, the judge entered the shanty, but his eagerness, together with his shortness of breath, kept him silent until he had established himself in his chair beside the table, with the jug and a cracked glass at his elbow. Then, bland and smiling, he turned toward his guest.

"Will you join me?" he asked.

"No, sir. Please, I'd rather not," said Hannibal.

"Do you mean that you don't like good liquor?" demanded the judge. "Not even with sugar and a dash of water? - say, now, don't you like it that way, my boy?"

"I ain't learned to like it no ways," said Hannibal.

"You amaze me - well - well - the greater the joy to which you may reasonably aspire. The splendid possibilities of youth are yours. My tenderest regards, Hannibal!" and he nodded over the rim of the cracked glass his shaking hand had carried to his lips. Twice the glass was filled and emptied, and then again, his roving, watery eyes rested meditatively on the child, who sat very erect in his chair, with his brown hands crossed in his lap. "Personally, I can drink or not," explained the judge. "But I hope I am too much a man of the world to indulge in any intemperate display of principle." He proved the first clause of his proposition by again filling and emptying his glass. "Have you a father?" he asked suddenly. Hannibal shook his head. "A mother?" demanded the judge.

"They both of them done died years and years ago," answered the boy. "I can't tell you how long back it was, but I reckon I don't know much about it. I must have been a small child."

"Ho - a small child!" cried the judge, laughing. He cocked his head on one side and surveyed Hannibal Wayne Hazard with a glance of comic seriousness. "A small child and in God's name what do you call yourself now? To hear you talk one would think you had dabbled your feet in the Flood!"

"I'm most ten," said Hannibal, with dignity.

"I can well believe it," responded the judge. "And with this weight of years, where did you come from and how did you get here?"

"From across the mountains."

"Alone?"

"No, sir. Mr. Yancy fetched me - part way." The boy's voice broke when he spoke his Uncle Bob's name, and his eyes swam with tears, but the judge did not notice this.

"And where are you going?"

"To West Tennessee."

"Have you any friends there?"

"Yes, sir."

"You've money enough to see you through?" and what the judge intended for a smile of fatherly affection became a leer of infinite cunning.

"I got ten dollars."

"Ten dollars -" the judge smacked his lips once. "Ten dollars" he repeated, and smacked his lips twice. There was a brief silence, in which he seemed to give way to pleasant reveries.

From beyond the open door of the shanty came a multitude of night sounds. The moon had risen, and what had been a dusty country road was now a streak of silver in the hot light. The purple flush on the judge's face, where the dignity that belonged to age had gone down in wreck, deepened. The sparse, white frost above his ears was damp with sweat. He removed his stock, opened his shirt at the neck, and cast aside his coat; then he lighted a blackened pipe, filled his glass, and sank back in his chair. The long hours of darkness were all before him, and his senses clothed themselves in rich content. Once more his glance rested on the boy. Here, indeed, was a guest of whom one might make much and not err - he felt all the benevolence of his nature flow toward him. Ten dollars!

"Certainly the tavern would have been no place for you! Well, thank God, it wasn't necessary for you to go there. You are more than welcome here. I tell you, when you know this place as I know it, you'll regard every living soul here with suspicion. Keep 'em at arm's length!" he sank his voice to an impressive whisper. "In particular, I warn you against a certain Solomon Mahaffy. You'll see much of him; I haven't known how to rebuff the fellow without being rude - he sticks to me like my shadow. He's profited by my charity and he admires my conversation and affects my society, but don't tell him you have so much as a rusty copper, for he will neither rest nor eat nor sleep until he's plucked you - tell him nothing - leave him to me. I keep him - there -" the judge extended his fat hands, "at arm's length. I say to him metaphorically speaking - 'so close, but no closer. I'll visit you when sick, I'll pray with you when dying, I'll chat with you, I'll eat with you, I'll smoke with you, and if need be, I'll drink with you - but be your intimate? Never! Why? Because be's a damned Yankee! These are the inextinguishable feelings of a gentleman. I am aware they are out of place in this age, but what's bred in the bone will show in the flesh. Who says it won't, is no gentleman himself and a liar as well! My place in the world was determined two or three hundred years ago, and my ancestors spat on such cattle as Mahaffy and they were flattered by the attention!" The judge, powerfully excited by his denunciation of the unfortunate Mahaffy, quitted his chair and, lurching somewhat as he did so, began to pace the floor.

"Take me for your example, boy! You may be poor, you may possibly be hungry you'll often be thirsty, but through it all you will remain that splendid thing - a gentleman! Lands, niggers, riches, luxury, I've had 'em all; I've sucked the good of 'em; they've colored my blood, they've gone into the fiber of my brain and body. Perhaps you'll contend that the old order is overthrown, that family has gone to the devil? You are right, and there's the pity of it! Where are the great names? A race of upstarts has taken their place - sons of nobody - nephews of nobody - cousins of nobody - I observe only deterioration in the trend of modern life. The social fabric is tottering - I can see it totter -" and he tottered himself as he said this.

The boy had watched him out of wide eyes, as ponderous and unwieldy he shuffled back and forth in the dim candlelight; now shaking his head and muttering, the judge dropped into his chair.

"Well, I'm an old man-the spectacle won't long offend me. I'll die presently. The Bench and Bar will review my services to the country, the militia will fire a few volleys at my graveside, here and there a flag will be at half-mast, and that will be the end -" He was so profoundly moved by the thought that he could not go on. His voice broke, and he buried his face in his arms. A sympathetic moisture had gathered in the child's eyes. He understood only a small part of what his host was saying, but realized that it had to do with death, and he had his own terrible acquaintance with death. He slipped from his chair and stole to the judge's side, and that gentleman felt a cool hand rest lightly on his arm.

"What?" he said, glancing up.

"I'm mighty sorry you're going to die," said the boy softly.

"Bless you, Hannibal!" cried the judge, looking wonderfully cheerful, despite his recent bitterness of spirit. "I'm not experiencing any of the pangs of mortality now. My dissolution ain't a matter of to-night or to-morrow - there's some life in Slocum Price yet, for all the rough usage, eh? I've had my fun - I could tell you a thing or two about that, if you had hair on your chin!" and the selfish lines of his face twisted themselves into an exceedingly knowing grin.

"You talked like you thought you were going to die right off," said Hannibal gravely, as he resumed his chair. The judge was touched. It had been more years than he cared to remember since he had launched a decent emotion in the breast of any human being. For a moment he was silent, struck with a sense of shame; then he said:

"You are sure you are not running away, Hannibal? I hope you know that boys should always tell the truth - that hell has its own especial terrors for the boy who lies? Now, if I thought the worst of you, I might esteem it my duty to investigate your story." The judge laid a fat forefinger against the side of his nose, and regarded him with drunken gravity. Hannibal shook with terror. This was what he had feared. "That's one aspect of the case. Now, on the other hand, I might draw up a legal instrument which could not fail to be of use to you on your travois, and would stop all questions. As for my fee, it would be trifling, when compared with the benefits I can see accruing to you."

"No, I ain't running away. I ain't got no one to run away from," said the boy chokingly. He was showing signs of fatigue. His head drooped and he met the judge's glance with tired, sleepy eyes. The latter looked at him and then said suddenly:

"I think you'd better go to bed."

"I reckon I had," agreed Hannibal, slipping from his chair.

"Well, take my bed back of the quilt. You'll find a hoe there.
You can dig up the dirt under the shuck tick with it - which
helps astonishingly. What would the world say if it could
know that judge Slocum Price makes his bed with a hoe!
There's Spartan hardihood!" but the boy, not knowing what
was meant by Spartan hardihood, remained silent. "Nearing
threescore years and ten, the allotted span as set down by the
Psalmist - once man of fashion, soldier, statesman and lawgiver
- and makes his bed with a hoe! What a history!" muttered the
judge with weary melancholy, as one groping hand found the
jug while the other found the glass. There was a pause, while
he profited by this fortunate chance. "Well, take the bed," he
resumed hospitably.

"I can sleep most anywhere. I ain't no ways particular," said
Hannibal.

"I say, take the bed!" commanded the judge sternly. And
Hannibal quickly retired behind the quilt. "Do you find it
comfortable?" the judge asked, when the rustling of the shuck
tick informed him that the child had lain down.

"Yes, sir," said the boy.

"Have you said your prayers?" inquired the judge:.

"No, sir. I ain't said 'em yet."

"Well, say them now. Religion is as becoming in the young as
it is respectable in the aged. I'll not disturb you to-night, for it
is God's will that I should stay up and get very drunk."

CHAPTER X

BOON COMPANIONS

Some time later the judge was aware of a step on the path beyond his door, and glancing up, saw the tall figure of a man pause on his threshold. A whispered curse slipped from between his lips. Aloud he said:

"Is that you, Mr. Mahaffy?" He got no reply, but the tall figure, propelled by very long legs, stalked into the shanty and a pair of keen, restless eyes deeply set under a high, bald head were bent curiously upon him.

"I take it I'm intruding," the new-comer said sourly.

"Why should you think that, Solomon Mahaffy? When has my door been closed on you?" the judge asked, but there was a guilty deepening of the flush on his face. Mr. Mahaffy glanced at the jug, at the half-emptied glass within convenient reach of the judge's hand, lastly at the judge himself, on whose flame-colored visage his eyes rested longest.

"I've heard said there was honor among thieves," he remarked.

"I know of no one better fitted to offer an opinion on so delicate a point than just yourself, Mahaffy," said the judge, with a thick little ripple of laughter.

But Solomon Mahaffy's long face did not relax in its set expression.

"I saw your light," he explained, "but you seem to be raising first-rate hell all by yourself."

"Oh, be reasonable, Solomon. You'd gone down to the steamboat landing," said the judge plaintively. By way of answer, Mahaffy shot him a contemptuous glance. "Take a chair - do, Solomon!" entreated the judge.

"I don't force my society on any man, Mr. Price," said Mahaffy, with austere hostility of tone. The judge winced at the "Mr." That registered the extreme of Mahaffy's disfavor.

"You feel bitter about this, Solomon?" he said.

"I do," said Mahaffy, in a tone of utter finality.

"You'll feel better with three fingers of this trickling through your system," observed the judge, pushing a glass toward him.

"When did I ever sneak a jug into my shanty?" asked Mahaffy sternly, evidently conscious of entire rectitude in this matter.

"I deplore your choice of words, Solomon," said the judge. "You know damn well that if you'd been here I couldn't have got past your place with that jug! But let's deal with conditions. Here's the jug, with some liquor left in it - here's a glass. Now what more do you want?"

"Have I ever been caught like this?" demanded Mahaffy.

"No, you've invariably manifested the honorable disabilities of a gentleman. But don't set it all down to virtue. Maybe you haven't had the opportunity, maybe the temptation never came and found you weak and thirsty. Put away your sinful pride, Solomon - a sot like you has no business with the little niceties of selfrespect."

"Do I drink alone?" insisted Mahaffy doggedly.

"I never give you the chance," retorted his friend. Mr. Mahaffy drew near the table. "Sit down," urged the judge.

"I hope you feel mean?" said Mahaffy.

"If it's any satisfaction to you, I do," admitted the judge.

"You ought to." Mahaffy drew forward a chair. The judge filled his glass. But Mr. Mahaffy's lean face, with its long jaws and high cheek-bones, over which the sallow skin was tightly drawn, did not relax in its forbidding expression, even when he had tossed off his first glass.

"I love to see you in a perfectly natural attitude like that, Solomon, with your arm crooked. What's the news from the landing?"

Mahaffy brought his fist down on the table.

"I heard the boat churning away round back of the bend, then I saw the lights, and she tied up and they tossed off the freight. Then she churned away again and her lights got back of the trees on the bank. There was the lap of waves on the shore, and I was left with the half-dozen miserable loafers who'd crawled out to see the boat come in. That's the news six days a week!"

By the river had come the judge, tentatively hopeful, but at heart expecting nothing, therefore immune to disappointment and equipped for failure. By the river had come Mr. Mahaffy, as unfit as the judge himself, and for the same reason, but sour and bitter with the world, believing always in the possibility of some miracle of regeneration.

Pleasantville's weekly paper, The Genius of Liberty, had dwelt at length upon those distinguished services judge Slocum Price had rendered the nation in war and peace, the judge having graciously furnished an array of facts otherwise difficult of access. That he was drunk at the time had but added to the splendor of the narrative. He had placed his ripe wisdom, the talents he had so assiduously cultivated, at the services of his fellow citizens. He was prepared to represent them in any or all the courts. But he had remained undisturbed in his condition of preparedness; that erudite brain was unconcerned with any problem beyond financing his thirst at the tavern, where presently ingenuity, though it expressed itself with a silver tongue, failed him, and he realized that the river's spent floods had left him stranded with those other odds and ends of worthless drift that cumbered its sun-scorched mud banks.

Something of all this passed through his mind as he sat there sodden and dreamy, with the one fierce need of his nature quieted for the moment. He had been stranded before, many times, in those long years during which he had moved steadily toward a diminishing heritage; indeed, nothing that was evil could contain the shock of a new experience. He had fought and lost all his battles - bitter struggles to think of even now, after the lapse of years, and the little he had to tell of himself was an intricate mingling of truth and falsehood, grotesque exaggeration, purposeless mendacity.

He and Mahaffy had met exactly one month before, on the deck of the steamer from which they had been put ashore at the river landing two miles from Pleasantville. Mahaffy's historic era had begun just there. Apparently he had no past of which he could be brought to speak. He admitted having been born in Boston some sixty years before, and was a printer by trade; further than this, he had not revealed himself, drunk or sober.

At the judge's elbow Mr. Mahaffy changed his position with nervous suddenness. Then he folded his long arms.

"You asked if there was any news, Price; while we were waiting for the boat a raft tied up to the bank; the fellow aboard of it had a man he'd fished up out of the river, a man who'd been pretty well cut to pieces."

"Who was he?" asked the judge.

"Nobody knew, and he wasn't conscious. I shouldn't be surprised if he never opens his lips again. When the doctor had looked to his cuts, the fellow on the raft cast off and went on down the Elk."

It occurred to the judge that he himself had news to impart. He must account for the boy's presence.

"While you've been taking your whiff of life down at the steamboat landing, Mahaffy, I've been experiencing a most extraordinary coincidence." The judge paused. By a sullen glare in his deep-sunk eyes Mr. Mahaffy seemed to bid him go on. "Back east -" the judge jerked his thumb with an indefinite gesture "back east at my ancestral home -" Mahaffy snorted harshly. "You don't believe I had an ancestral home? - well, I had! It was of brick, sir, with eight Corinthian columns across the front, having a spacious paneled hall sixty feet long. I had the distinguished honor to entertain General Andrew Jackson there."

"Did you get those dimensions out of the jug?" inquiry Mahaffy, with a frightful bark that was intended for a sarcastic laugh.

"Sir, it is not in your province to judge me by my present degraded associates. Near the house I have described - my father's and his father's before him, and mine now - but for the unparalleled misfortunes which have pursued me - lived a family by the name of Hazard. And when I went to the war of 'i2 -"

"What were you in that bloody time, a sutler?" inquired Mahaffy insultingly.

"No, sir - a colonel of infantry! - I say, when I went to the war, one of these Hazards accompanied me as my orderly. His grandson is back of that curtain now - asleep - in my bed!"

Mahaffy put down his glass.

"You were like this once before," he said darkly. But at that instant the shuck tick rattled noisily at some movement of the sleeping boy. Mahaffy quitted his chair, and crossing the room, drew the quilt aside. A glance sufficed to assure him that in part, at least, the judge spoke the truth. He let the curtain fall into place and resumed his chair.

"He's an orphan, Solomon; a poor, friendless orphan. Another might have turned him away from his door - I didn't; I hadn't the heart to. I bespeak your sympathy for him."

"Who is he?" asked Mahaffy.

"Haven't I just told you?" said the judge reproachfully. Mahaffy laughed.

"You've told me something. Who is he?"

"His name is Hannibal Wayne Hazard. Wait until he wakes up and see if it isn't."

"Sure he isn't kin to you?" said Mahaffy.

"Not a drop of my blood flows in the veins of any living creature," declared the judge with melancholy impressiveness. He continued with deepening feeling, "All I shall leave to posterity is my fame."

"Speaking of posterity, which isn't present, Mr. Price, I'll say it is embarrassed by the attention," observed Mahaffy.

There was a long silence between them. Mr. Mahaffy drank, and when he did not drink he bit his under lip and studied the judge. This was always distressing to the latter gentleman. Mahaffy's silence he could never penetrate. What was back of it - judgment, criticism, disbelief - what? Or was it the silence of emptiness?

Was Mahaffy dumb merely because he could think of nothing to say, or did his silence cloak his feelings-and what were his feelings? Did his meditations outrun his habitually insulting speech as he bit his under lip and glared at him? The judge always felt impelled to talk at such times, while Mahaffy, by that silence of his, seemed to weigh and condemn whatever he said.

The moon had slipped below the horizon. Pleasantville had long since gone to bed; it was only the judge's window that gave its light to the blackness of the night. There was a hoofbeat on the road. It came nearer and nearer, and presently sounded just beyond the door. Then it ceased, and a voice said:

"Hullo, there!" The judge scrambled to his feet, and taking up the candle, stepped, or rather staggered, into the yard. Mahaffv followed him.

"What's wanted?" asked the judge, as he lurched up to horse and rider, holding his candle aloft. The light showed a tail fellow mounted on a handsome bay horse. It was Murrell.

"Is there an inn hereabouts?" he asked.

"You'll find one down the road a ways," said Mahaffy. The judge said nothing. He was staring up at Murrell with drunken gravity.

"Have either of you gentlemen seen a boy go through here to-day? A boy about ten years old?" Murrell glanced from one to the other. Mr. Mahaffy's thin lips twisted themselves into a sarcastic smile. He turned to the judge, who spoke up quickly.

"Did he carry a bundle and rifle?" he asked. Murrell gave eager assent.

"Well," said the judge, "he stopped here along about four o'clock and asked his way to the nearest river landing." Murrell gathered up his reins, and then that fixed stare of the judge's seemed to arrest his attention.

"You'll know me again," he observed.

"Anywhere," said the judge.

"I hope that's a satisfaction to you," said Murrell.

"It ain't - none whatever," answered the judge promptly. "For I don't value you - I don't value you that much!" and he snapped his fingers to illustrate his meaning.

CHAPTER XI

THE ORATOR Or THE DAY

"Hanibal" the judge's voice and manner were rather stern. "Hannibal, a man rode by here last night on a big bay horse. He said he was looking for a boy about ten years old - a boy with a bundle and rifle." There was an awful pause. Hannibal's heart stood still for a brief instant, then it began to beat with terrific thumps against his ribs. "Who was that man, Hannibal?"

"I - please I don't know -" gasped the child.

"Hannibal, who was that man?" repeated the judge.

"It were Captain Murrell." The judge regarded him with a look of great steadiness. He saw his small face go white, he saw the look of abject terror in his eyes. The judge raised his fist and brought it down with a great crash on the table, so that the breakfast dishes leaped and rattled. "We don't know any boy ten years old with a rifle and bundle!" he said.

"Please - you won't let him take me away, judge I want to stop with you!" cried Hannibal. He slipped from his chair, and passing about the table, siezed the judge by the hand. The judge was visibly affected.

"No!" he roared, with a great oath. "He shan't have you - I'll see him in the farthest corner of hell first! Is he kin to you?"

"No," said Hannibal.

"Took you to raise, did he - and abused you - infernal hypocrite!" cried the judge with righteous wrath.

"He tried to get me away from my Uncle Bob. He's been following us since we crossed the mountains."

"Where is your Uncle Bob?"

"He's dead." And the child began to weep bitterly. Much puzzled, the judge regarded him in silence for a moment, then bent and lifted him into his lap.

"There, my son -" he said soothingly. "Now you tell me when he died, and all about it."

"He were killed. It were only yesterday, and I can't forget him! I don't want to - but it hurts - it hurts terrible!" Hannibal buried his head in the judge's shoulder and sobbed aloud. Presently his small hands stole about the judge's neck, and that gentleman experienced a strange thrill of pleasure.

"Tell me how he died, Hannibal," he urged gently. In a voice broken by sobs the child began the story of their flight, a confused narrative, which the judge followed with many a puzzled shake of the head. But as he reached his climax - that cry he had heard at the tavern, the men in the lane with their burden - he became more and more coherent and his ideas clothed themselves in words of dreadful simplicity and directness. The judge shuddered. "Can such things be?" he murmured at last.

"You won't let him take me?"

"I never unsay my words," said the judge grandly. "With God's help I'll be the instrument for their destruction." He frowned with a preternatural severity. Eh - if he could turn a trick like that, it would pull him up! There would be no more jeers and laughter.

What credit and standing it would give him! His thoughts slipped along this fresh channel. What a prosecution he would conduct - what a whirlwind of eloquence he would loose! He began to breathe hard. His name should go from end to end of the state! No man could be great without opportunity - for years he had known this - but here was opportunity at last! Then he remembered what Mahaffy had told him of the man on the raft. This Slosson's tavern was probably on the upper waters of the Elk. Yancy had been thrown in the river and had been picked up in a dying condition. "Hannibal," be said, "Solomon Mahaffy, who was here last night, told me he saw down at the river landing, a man who had been fished up out of the Elk - a man who had been roughly handled."

"Were it my Uncle Bob?" cried Hannibal, lifting a swollen face to his.

"Dear lad, I don't know," said the judge sympathetically. "Some people on a raft had picked him up out of the river. He was unconscious and no one knew him. He was apparently a stranger in these parts."

"It were Uncle Bob! It were Uncle Bob - I know it were my Uncle Bob! I must go find him!" and Hannibal slipped from the judge's lap and ran for his rifle and bundle.

"Stop a bit!" cried the judge. "He was taken on past here, and he was badly injured. Now, if it was your Uncle Bob, he'll come back the moment he is able to travel. Meantime, you must remain under my protection while we investigate this man Slosson."

But alas - that thoroughfare which is supposed to be paved exclusively with good resolutions, had benefited greatly by Slocum Price's labors in the past, and he was destined to toil still in its up-keep. He borrowed the child's money and spent it, and if any sense of shame smote his torpid conscience, he hid it manfully. Not so Mr. Mahaffy; for while he profited by his friend's act, he told that gentleman just what he thought of him with insulting candor. On the eighth day there was sobriety for the pair. Deep gloom visited Mr. Mahaffy, and the judge was a prey to melancholy.

It was Saturday, and in Pleasantville a jail-raising was in progress. During all the years of its corporate dignity the village had never boasted any building where the evil-doer could be placed under restraint; hence had arisen its peculiar habit of dealing with crime; but a leading citizen had donated half an acre of ground lying midway between the town and the river landing as a site for the proposed structure, and the scattered population of the region had assembled for the raising. Nor was Pleasantville unprepared to make immediate use of the jail, since the sheriff had in custody a free negro who had knifed another free negro and was awaiting trial at the next term of court.

"We don't want to get there too early," explained the judge, as they quitted the cabin. "We want to miss the work, but be on hand for the celebration."

"I suppose we may confidently look to you to favor us with a few eloquent words?" said Mr. Mahaffy.

"And why not, Solomon?" asked the judge.

"Why not, indeed!" echoed Mr. Mahaffy.

The opportunity he craved was not denied him. The crowd was like most southwestern crowds of the period, and no sooner did the judge appear than there were clamorous demands for a speech. He cast a glance of triumph at Mahaffy, and nimbly mounted a convenient stump. He extolled the climate of middle Tennessee, the unsurpassed fertility of the soil; he touched on the future that awaited Pleasantville; he apostrophized the jail; this simple structure of logs in the shadow of the primeval woods was significant of their love of justice and order; it was a suitable place for the detention of a citizen of a great republic; it was no mediaeval dungeon, but a forest-embowered retreat where, barring mosquitoes and malaria, the party under restraint would be put to no needless hardship; he would have the occasional companionship of the gentlemanly sheriff; his friends, with such wise and proper restrictions as the law saw fit to impose, could come and impart the news of the day to him through the chinks of the logs.

"I understand you have dealt in a hasty fashion with one or two horse-thieves," he continued. "Also with a gambler who was put ashore here from a river packet and subsequently became involved in a dispute with a late citizen of this place touching the number of aces in a pack of cards. It is not for me to criticize! What I may term the spontaneous love of justice is the brightest heritage of a free people. It is this same commendable ability to acquit ourselves of our obligations that is making us the wonder of the world! But don't let us forget the law - of which it is an axiom, that it is not the severity of punishment, but the certainty of it, that holds the wrong-doer in check! With this safe and commodious asylum the plow line can remain the exclusive aid to agriculture. If a man murders, curb your natural impulse! Give him a fair trial, with eminent counsel!" The judge tried not to look self-conscious when he said this. "If he is found guilty, I still say, don't lynch him! Why? Because by your hasty act you deny the public the elevating and improving spectacle of a legal execution!" When the applause had died out, a lank countryman craning his neck for a sight of the sheriff, bawled out over the heads of the crowd:

"Where's your nigger? We want to put him in here!"

"I reckon he's gone fishin'. I never seen the beat of that nigger to go fishin'," said the sheriff.

"Whoop! Ain't you goin' to put him in here?" yelled the countryman.

"It's a mighty lonely spot for a nigger," said the sheriff doubtingly.

"Lonely? Well, suppose he ups and lopes out of this?"

"You don't know that nigger," rejoined the sheriff warmly. "He ain't missed a meal since I had him in custody. Just as regular as the clock strikes he's at the back door. Good habits - why, that darky is a lesson to most white folks!"

"I don't care a cuss about that nigger, but what's the use of building a jail if a body ain't goin' to use it?"

"Well, there's some sense in that," agreed the sheriff.

"There's a whole heap of sense in it!"

"I suggest" - the speaker was a young lawyer from the next county - "I suggest that a committee be appointed to wait on the nigger at the steamboat landing and acquaint him with the fact that with his assistance we wish completely to furnish the jail."

"I protest -" cried the judge. "I protest -" he repeated vigorously. "Pride of race forbids that I should be a party to the degradation of the best of civilization! Is your jail to be christened to its high office by a nigger? Is this to be the law's apotheosis? No, sir! No nigger is worthy the honor of being the first prisoner here!" This was a new and striking idea. The crowd regarded the judge admiringly. Certainly here was a man of refined feeling.

"That's just the way I feel about it," said the sheriff. "If I'd athought there was any call for him I wouldn't have let him go fishing, I'd have kept him about."

"Oh, let the nigger fish - he has powerful luck. What's he usin', Sheriff; worms or minnies?"

"Worms," said the sheriff shortly.

Presently the crowd drifted away in the direction of the tavern. Hannibal meantime had gone down to the river. He haunted its banks as though he expected to see his Uncle Bob appear any moment. The judge and Mahaffy had mingled with the others in the hope of free drinks, but in this hope there lurked the germ of a bitter disappointment. There was plenty of drinking, but they were not invited to join in this pleasing rite, and after a period of great mental anguish Mahaffy parted with the last stray coin in the pocket of his respectable black trousers, and while his flask was being filled the judge indulged in certain winsome gallantries with the fat landlady.

"La, Judge Price, how you do run on!" she said with a coquettish toss of her curls.

"That's the charm of you, ma'am," said the judge. He leaned across the bar and, sinking his voice to a husky whisper, asked, "Would it be perfectly convenient for you to extend me a limited credit?"

"Now, Judge Price, you know a heap better than to ask me that!" she answered, shaking her head.

"No offense, ma'am," said the judge, hiding his disappointment, and with Mahaffy he quitted the bar.

"Why don't you marry the old girl? You could drink yourself to death in six months," said Mahaffy. "That would be a speculation worth while - and while you live you could fondle those curls!"

"Maybe I'll be forced to it yet," responded the judge with gloomy pessimism.

With the filling of Mahaffy's flask the important event of the day was past, and both knew it was likely to retain its preeminence for a terrible and indefinite period; a thought that

Vaughan Kester

enriched their thirst as it increased their gravity while they were traversing the stretch of dusty road that lay between the cavern and the judge's shanty. When they had settled themselves in their chairs before the door, Mahaffy, who was notably jealous of his privileges, drew the cork from the flask and took the first pull at its contents. The judge counted the swallows as registered by that useful portion of Mahaffy's anatomy known as his Adam's apple. After a breathless interval, Mahaffy detached himself from the flask and civilly passing the cuff of his coat about its neck, handed it over to the judge. In the unbroken silence that succeeded the flask passed swiftly from hand to hand, at length Mahaffy held it up to the light. It was two-thirds empty, and a sigh stole from between his thin lips. The judge reached out a tremulous hand. He was only too familiar with his friend's distressing peculiarities.

"Not yet!" he begged thickly.

"Why not?" demanded Mahaffy fiercely. "Is it your liquor or mine?" He quitted his chair end stalked to the well where he filled the flask with water. Infinitely disgusted, the judge watched the sacrilege. Mahaffy resumed his chair and again the flask went its rounds.

"It ain't so bad," said the judge after a time, but with a noticeable lack of enthusiasm.

"Were you in shape to put anything better than water into it, Mr. Price?" The judge winced. He always winced at that "Mr."

"Well, I wouldn't serve myself such a trick as that," he said with decision. "When I take liquor, it's one thing; and when I want water, it's another."

"It is, indeed," agreed Mahaffy.

"I drink as much clear water as is good for a man of my constitution," said the judge combatively. "My talents are wasted here," he resumed, after a little pause. "I've brought them the blessings of the law, but what does it signify!"

"Why did you ever come here?" Mahaffy spoke sharply.

"I might ask the same question of you, and in the same offensive tone," said the judge.

"May I ask, not wishing to take a liberty, were you always the same old pauper you've been since I've known you?" inquired Mahaffy. The judge maintained a stony silence.

The heat deepened in the heart of the afternoon. The sun, a ball of fire, slipped back of the tree-tops. Thick shadows stole across the stretch of dusty road. Off in the distance there was the sound of cowbell. Slowly these came nearer and nearer - as the golden light slanted, sifting deeper and deeper into the woods.

They could see the crowd that came and went about the tavern, they caught the distant echo of its mirth.

"Common - quite common," said the judge with somber melancholy.

"I didn't see anything common," said Mahaffy sourly. "The drinks weren't common by a long sight."

"I referred to the gathering in its social aspect, Solomon," explained the judge; "the illiberal spirit that prevailed, which, I observe, did not escape you."

"Skunks!" said Mahaffy.

"Not a man present had the public spirit to set 'em up," lamented the judge. "They drank in pairs, and I'd blistered my throat at their damn jail-raising! What sort of a fizzle would it have been if I hadn't been on hand to impart distinction to the occasion ?"

"I don't begrudge 'em their liquor," said Mahaffy with acid dignity.

"I do," interrupted the judge. "I hope it's poison to 'em.

"It will be in the long run, if it's any comfort to you to know it."

"It's no comfort, it's not near quick enough," said the judge relentlessly. The sudden noisy clamor of many voices, highpitched and excited, floated out to them under the hot sky. "I wonder -" began the judge, and paused as he saw the crowd stream into the road before the tavern. Then a cloud of dust enveloped it, a cloud of dust that came from the trampling of many pairs of feet, and that swept toward them, thick and impenetrable, and no higher than a tall man's head in the lifeless air. "I wonder if we missed anything" continued the judge, finishing what he had started to say.

The score or more of men were quite near, and the judge and Mahaffy made out the tall figure of the sheriff in the lead. And then the crowd, very excited, very dusty, very noisy and very hot, flowed into the judge's front yard. For a brief moment that gentleman fancied Pleasantville had awakened to a fitting sense of its obligation to him and that it was about to make amends for its churlish lack of hospitality. He rose from his chair, and with a splendid florid gesture, swept off his hat.

"It's the pussy fellow!" cried a voice.

"Oh, shut up - don't you think I know him?" retorted the sheriff tartly.

"Gentlemen -" began the judge blandly.

"Get the well-rope!"

The judge was rather at loss properly to interpret these varied remarks. He was not long left in doubt. The sheriff stepped to his side and dropped a heavy hand on his shoulder.

"Mr. Slocum Price, or whatever your name is, your little game is up!"

"Get the well-rope! Oh, hell - won't some one get the well-rope?" The voice rose into a wail of entreaty.

The judge's eyes, rather startled, slid around in their sockets. Clearly something was wrong - but what - what?

"Ain't he bold?" it was a woman's voice this time, and the fat landlady, her curls awry and her plump breast heaving tumultuously, gained a place in the forefront of the crowd.

"Dear madam, this is an unexpected pleasure!" said the judge, with his hand upon his heart.

"Don't you make your wicked old sheep's eyes at me, you brazen thing!" cried the lady.

"You're wanted," said the sheriff grimly, still keeping his hand on the judge's shoulder.

"For what?" demanded the judge thickly. The sheriff had no time in which to answer.

"I want my money!" shrieked the landlady.

"Your money - Mrs. Walker, you amaze me!" The judge drew himself up haughtily, in genuine astonishment.

"I want my money!" repeated Mrs. Walker in even more piercing tones.

"I am not aware that I owe you anything, madam. Thank God, I hold your receipted bill of recent date," answered the judge with chilling dignity.

"Good money - not this worthless trash!" she shook a bill under his nose. The judge recognized it as the one of which he had despoiled Hannibal.

"You have been catched passing counterfeit," said the sheriff. A light broke on the judge, a light that dazzled and stunned. An officious and impatient gentleman tossed a looped end of the well-rope about his neck and the crowd yelled excitedly. This was something like - it had a taste for the man-hunt! The sheriff snatched away the rope and dealt the officious gentleman a savage blow on the chin that sent him staggering backward into the arms of his friends.

"Now, see here, now - I'm going to arrest this old faller! I am going to put him in jail, and I ain't going to have no nonsense - do you hear me?" he expostulated.

"I can explain -" cried the judge.

"Make him give me my money!" wailed Mrs Walker.

"Jezebel!" roared the judge, in a passion of rage.

"Ca'm's the word, or you'll get 'em started!" whispered the sheriff. The judge looked fearfully around. At his side stood Mahaffy, a yellow pallor splotching his thin cheeks. He seemed to be holding himself there by an effort.

"Speak to them, Solomon - speak to them - you know how I came by the money! Speak to them - you know I am innocent!" cried the judge, clutching his friend by the arm. Mahaffy opened his thin lips, but the crowd drowned his voice in a roar.

"He's his "partner -"

"There's no evidence against him," said the sheriff.

A tall fellow, in a fringed hunting-shirt, shook a long finger under Mahaffy's aquiline nose.

"You scoot - that's what - you make tracks! And if we ever see your ugly face about here again, we'll -"

"You'll what?" inquired Mahaffy.

"We'll fix you out with feathers that won't molt, that's what!"

Mr. Mahaffy seemed to hesitate. His lean hands opened and closed, and he met the eyes of the crowd with a bitter, venomous stare. Some one gave him a shove and he staggered forward a step, snapping out a curse. Before he could recover himself the shove was repeated.

"Lope on out of here!" yelled the tall fellow, who had first challenged his right to remain in Pleasantville or its environs. As the crowd fell apart to make way for him, willing hands were extended to give him the needed impetus, and without special volition of his own,

Mahaffy was hurried toward the road. His hat was knocked flat on his head - he turned with an angry snarl, the very embodiment of hate - but again he was thrust forward. And then, somehow, his walk became a run and the crowd started after him with delighted whoopings. Once more, and for the last time, he faced about, giving the judge a hopeless, despairing glance. His tormentors were snatching up sods and stones and he had no choice. He turned, his long strides taking him swiftly over the ground, with the air full of missiles at his back.

Before he had gone a hundred yards he abandoned the road and, turning off across an unfenced field, ran toward the woods and swampy bottom. Twenty men were in chase behind him. The judge was the sheriff's prisoner - that official had settled that point - but Mr. Mahaffy was common property, it was his cruel privilege to furnish excitement; his keen rage was almost equal to the fear that urged him on. Then the woods closed about him. His long legs, working tirelessly, carried him over fallen logs and through tai. tangeled thickets, the voices behind him growing more and more distant as he ran.

CHAPTER XII

THE FAMILY ON THE RAFT

That would unquestionably have been the end of Bob Yancy when he was shot out into the muddy waters of the Elk River, had not Mr. Richard Keppel Cavendish, variously known as Long-Legged Dick, and Chills-and-Fever Cavendish, of Lincoln County, in the state of Tennessee, some months previously and after unprecedented mental effort on his part, decided that Lincoln County was no place for him. When he had established this idea firmly in his own mind and in the mind of Polly, his wife, he set about solving the problem of transportation.

Mr. Cavendish's paternal grandparent had drifted down the Holston and Tennessee; and Mr. Cavendish's father, in his son's youth, had poled up the Elk. Mr. Cavendish now determined to float down the Elk to its juncture with the Tennessee, down the Tennessee to the Ohio, and if need be, down the Ohio to the Mississippi, and keep drifting until he found some spot exactly suited to his taste. Temperamentally, he was well adapted to drifting. No conception of vicarious activity could have been more congenial.

With this end in view he had toiled through late winter and early spring, building himself a raft on which to transport his few belongings and his numerous family; there were six little Cavendishes, and they ranged in years from four to eleven; there was in addition the baby, who was always enumerated separately. This particular infant Mr. Cavendish said he wouldn't take a million dollars for. He usually added feelingly that he wouldn't give a piece of chalk for another one.

June found him aboard his raft with all his earthly possessions bestowed about him, awaiting the rains and freshets that were to waft him effortless into a newer country where he should have a white man's chance. At last the rains came, and he cast off from the bank at that unsalubrious spot where his father had elected to build his cabin on a strip of level bottom subject to periodic inundation. Wishing fully to profit by the floods and reach the big water without delay, Cavendish ran the raft twenty-four hours at a stretch, sleeping by day while Polly managed the great sweep, only calling him when some dangerous bit of the river was to be navigated. Thus it happened that as Murrell and Slosson were dragging Yancy down the lane, Cavendish was just rounding a bend in the Elk, a quarter of a mile distant. Leaning loosely against the long handle of his sweep, he was watching the lane of bright water that ran between the black shadows cast by the trees on either bank. He was in shirt and trousers, barefoot and bareheaded, and his face, mild and contemplative, wore an expression of dreamy contentment.

Suddenly its expression changed. He became alert and watchful. He had heard a dull splash. Thinking that some tree had been swept into the flood, he sought to pierce the darkness that lay along the shore. Five or six minutes passed as the raft glided along without sound. He was about to relapse into his former attitude of listless ease when he caught sight of some object in the eddy that swept alongside. Mr. Cavendish promptly detached himself from the handle of the sweep and ran to the edge of the raft.

"Good Lord - what's that!" he gasped, but he already knew it was a face, livid and blood-streaked. Dropping on his knees he reached out a pair of long arms and made a dexterous grab, and his fingers closed on the collar of Yancy's shirt. "Neighbor, I certainly have got you!" said Cavendish, between his teeth.

He drew Yancy close alongside the raft, and, slipping a hand under each arm, pulled him clear of the water. The swift current swept the raft on down the stream. It rode fairly in the center of the lane of light, but no eye had observed its passing. Mr. Cavendish stood erect and stared down at the blood-stained face, then he dropped on his knees again and began a hurried examination of the still figure. "There's a little life here - not much, but some - you was well worth fishing up!" be said approvingly, after a brief interval. "Polly!" he called, raising his voice.

This brought Mrs. Cavendish from one of the two cabins that occupied the center of the raft. She was a young woman, still very comely, though of a matronly plumpness. She was in her nightgown, and when she caught sight of Yancy she uttered a shriek and fled back into the shanty.

"I declare, Dick, you might ha' told a body you wa'n't alone!" she said reproachfully.

Her cry had aroused the other denizens of the raft. The tow heads of the six little Cavendishes rose promptly from a long bolster in the smaller of the two shanties, and as promptly six little Cavendishes, each draped in a single non-committal garment, apparently cut by one pattern and not at all according to the wearer's years or length of limb, tumbled forth from their shelter.

"Sho', Polly, he's senseless! But you dress and come here quick. Now, you young folks, don't you tetch him!" for the six small Cavendishes, excited beyond measure, were crowding and shoving for a nearer sight of Yancy. They began to pelt their father with questions. Who was it? Sho', in the river? Sho', all cut up like that - who'd cut him? Had he hurt himself? Was he throwed in? When did pop fish him out? Was he dead? Why did he lay like that and not move or speak - sho'! This and much more was flung at Mr. Cavendish all in one breath, and each eager questioner seized him by the hand, the dangling sleeve of his shirt, or his trousers - they clutched him from all sides. "I never seen such a family!" said Mr. Cavendish helplessly. "Now, you-all shut up, or I 'low I'll lay into you!"

Mrs. Cavendish's appearance created a diversion in his favor. The six rushed on her tumultously. They seized her hands or struggled for a fragment of her skirt to hold while they poured out their tale. Pop had fished up a man - he'd been throwed in the river! Pop didn't know if he was dead or not - he was all cut and bloody

"I declare, I've a mind to skin you if you don't keep still! Miss Constance," Polly addressed her eldest child, "I'm surprised at you! You might be a heathen savage for all you got on your back - get into some duds this instant!" Cavendish was on his knees again beside Yancy, and Polly, by a determined effort, rid herself of the children. "Why, he's a grand-looking man, ain't he?" she cried. "La, what a pity!"

"You can feel his heart beat, and he's bleeding some," said Cavendish.

"Let me see - just barely flutters, don't it? Henry, go mind the sweep and see we don't get aground! Keppel, you start a fire and warm some water! Connie, you tear up my other petticoat for bandagesnow, stir around, all of you!" And then began a period of breathless activity. They first lifted Yancy into the circle of illumination cast by the fire Keppel had started on the hearth of flat stones before the shanties. Then, with Constance to hold a pan of warm water, Mrs. Cavendish deftly bathed the gaping wound in Yancy's shoulder where Murrell had driven his knife. This she bandaged with strips torn from her petticoat. Next she began on the ragged cut left by Slosson's club.

"He's got a right to be dead!" said Cavendish.

"Get the shears, Dick - I must snip away some of his hair."

All this while the four half-naked youngest Cavendishes, very still now, stood about the stone hearth in the chill dawn and watched their mother's surgery with a breathless interest. Only the outcast Henry at the sweep ever and anon lifted his voice between sobs of mingled rage and disappointment, and demanded what was doing.

"Think he is going to die, Polly?" whispered Cavendish at length. Their heads, hers very black and glossy, his very blond, were close together as they bent above the injured man.

"I never say a body's going to die until he's dead," said Polly. "He's still breathing, and a Christian has got to do what they can. Don't you think you ought to tie up?"

"The freshet's leaving us. I'll run until we hit the big water down by Pleasantville, and then tie up," said Cavendish.

"I reckon we'd better lift him on to one of the beds - get his wet clothes off and wrap him up warm," said Polly.

"Oh, put him in our bed!" cried all the little Cavendishes.

And Yancy was borne into the smaller of the two shanties, where presently his bandaged head rested on the long communal pillow. Then his wet clothes were hung up to dry along with a portion of the family wash which fluttered on a rope stretched between the two shanties.

The raft had all the appearance of a cabin dooryard. There was, in addition to the two shelters of bark built over a light framework of poles, a pen which housed a highly domestic family of pigs, while half a dozen chickens enjoyed a restricted liberty. With Yancy disposed of, the regular family life was resumed. It was sun-up now. The little Cavendishes, reluctant but overpersuaded, had their faces washed alongside and were dressed by Connie, while Mrs. Cavendish performed the same offices for the baby. Then there was breakfast, from which Mr. Cavendish rose yawning to go to bed, where, before dropping off to sleep, he played with the baby. This left Mrs. Cavendish in full command of her floating dooryard. She smoked a reflective pipe, watching the river between puffs, and occasionally lending a hand at the sweeps. Later the family wash engaged her. It had neither beginning nor end, but serialized itself from day to day. Connie was already proficient at the tubs. It was a knack she was in no danger of losing.

Keppel and Henry took turns at the sweeps, while the three smaller children began to manifest a love for the water they had not seemed to possess earlier in the day. They played along the edge of the raft, always in imminent danger of falling in, always being called back, or seized, just in time to prevent a catastrophe. This ceaseless activity on their part earned them much in the way of cuffings, chastisements which Mrs. Cavendish administered with no great spirit.

"Drat you, why don't you go look at the pore gentleman instead of posterin' a body 'most to death!" she demanded at length, and they stole off on tiptoe to stare at Yancy. Presently Richard ran to his mother's side.

"Come quick - he's mutterin' and mumblin' and moving his head!" he cried. It wfs as the child said. Yancy had roused from his heavy stupor. Words almost inaudible and quite inarticulate were issuing from his lips and there was a restless movement of his head on the pillow.

"He 'pears powerful distressed about something," said Mrs. Cavendish. "I reckon I'd better give him a little stimulant now."

While she was gone for the whisky, Connie, who had squatted down beside the bed, touched Yancy's hand which lay open. Instantly his fingers closed about hers and he was silent; the movement of his head ceased abruptly; but when she sought to withdraw her hand he began to murmur again.

"I declare, what he wants is some one to sit beside him!" said Mrs. Cavendish, who had returned with the whisky, a few drops of which she managed to force between Yancy's lips. All the rest of that day some one of the children sat beside the wounded man, who was quiet and satisfied just as long as there was a small hand for him to hold.

"He must be a family man," observed Mr. Cavendish when Polly told him of this. "We'll tie up at Pleasantville landing and learn who he is."

"He had ought to have a doctor to look at them cuts of his," said Mrs. Cavendish.

It was late afternoon when the landing was reached. Half a score of men were loafing about the woodyard on shore. Mr. Cavendish made fast to a blasted tree, then he climbed the bank; the men regarding him incuriously as he approached.

"Howdy," said Cavendish genially.

"Howdy," they answered.

"Where might I find the nearest doctor?" inquired Cavendish.

"Within about six foot of you," said one of the group.

"Meaning yourself?"

"Meaning myself."

Briefly Cavendish told the story of Yancy's rescue.

"Now, Doc, I want you should cast an eye over the way we've dressed his cuts, and I want the rest of you to come and take a look at him and tell who he is and where he belongs," he said in conclusion.

"I'll know him if he belongs within forty miles of here in any direction," said the doctor. But he shook his head when his eye rested on Yancy. "Never saw him," he said briefly.

"How about them bandages, Doc?" demanded Cavendish.

"Oh, I reckon they'll do," replied the doctor indifferently.

"Will he live?"

"I can't say. You'll know all about that inside the next forty-eight hours. Better let the rest have a look."

"Just feel of them bandages - sho', I got money in my pants!" Mr. Cavendish was rapidly losing his temper, yet he controlled himself until each man had taken a look at Yancy; but always with the same result - a shake of the head. "I reckon I can leave him here?" Cavendish asked, when the last man had looked and turned away.

"Leave him here - why?" demanded the doctor slowly.

"Because I'm going on, that's why. I'm headed for down-stream, and he ain't in any sort of shape to say whether he wants to go or stop," explained Cavendish.

"You picked him up, didn't you?" asked one of the men.

"I certainly did," said Cavendish.

"Well, I reckon if you're so anxious for him to stay hereabout, you'd better stop, yourself," said the owner of the woodyard. "There ain't a house within two miles of here but mine, and he don't go there!"

"You're a healthy lot, you are!" said Cavendish. "I wonder your largeness of heart ain't ruptured your wishbones long ago!" So saying, he retired to the stern of his raft and leaned against the sweep-handle, apparently lost in thought. His visitors climbed the bank and reestablished themselves on the wood-ranks.

Presently Mr. Cavendish lifted his voice and addressed Polly and the six little Cavendishes at the other end of the raft. He asserted that he was the only well-born man within a radius of perhaps a hundred miles - he excepted no one. He knew who his father and mother were, and they had been legally married - he seemed to infer that this was not always the case. Mr. Cavendish glanced toward the shore, then he lifted his voice again, giving it as his opinion that he was the only Christian seen in those parts in the last fifty years. He offered to fight any gentleman who felt disposed to challenge this assertion. He sprang suddenly aloft, knocked his bare heels together and uttered an ear-piercing whoop. He subsided and gazed off into the red eye of the sun which was slipping back of the trees. Presently he spoke again. He offered to lick any gentleman who felt aggrieved by his previous remarks, for fifty cents, for a drink of whisky, for a chew of tobacco, for nothing - with one hand tied behind him! He sprang aloft, cracked his heels together as before and crowed insultingly; then he subsided into silence. An instant later he appeared stung by the acutest pangs of remorse. In a cringing tone he begged Polly to forgive him for bringing her to such a place. He bewailed that they had risked pollution by allowing any inhabitant of that region to set foot on the raft - he feared for the innocent minds of their children, and he implored her pardon. Perhaps it was better that they should cast off at once - unless one of the gentlemen on shore felt himself insulted, in which event he would remain to fight.

Then as he slowly worked the raft out toward the middle of the stream, he repeated all his former remarks, punctuating them with frequent whoops. He recapitulated the terms on which he could be induced to fight-fifty cents, a drink of liquor, a chew of tobacco, nothing! His shouts became fainter and fainter as the raft was swept down-stream, and finally died away in the distance.

CHAPTER XIII

THE JUDGE BREAKS JAIL

The sheriff had brought the judge's supper. He reported that the crowd was dispersing, and that on the whole public sentiment was not particularly hostile; indeed, he went so far as to say there existed a strong undercurrent of satisfaction that the jail should have so speedily justified itself. Moreover, there was a disposition to exalt the judge as having furnished the crowning touch to the day's pleasure.

"I reckon, sir, they'd have felt obliged to string you up if there wa'n't no jail," continued the sheriff lazily from the open door where he had seated himself. "I don't say there ain't them who don't maintain you had ought to be strung up as it is, but people are funny, sir; the majority talk like they might wish to keep you here indefinite. There's no telling when we'll get another prisoner. Tomorrow the blacksmith will fix some iron bars to your window so folks can look in and see you. It will give a heap more air to the place -"

"Unless I do get more air, you will not be troubled long by me!" declared the judge in a tone of melancholy conviction.

The building was intolerably hot, the advantages of ventilation having been a thing the citizens of Pleasantville had over-looked. But the judge was a reasonable soul; he was disposed to accept his immediate personal discomfort with a fine true philosophy; also, hope was stirring in his heart. Hope was second nature with him, for had he not lived all these years with the odds against him?

"You do sweat some, don't you? Oh, well, a man can stand a right smart suffering from heat like this and not die. It's the sun that's dangerous," remarked the sheriff consolingly. "And you had ought to suffer, sir! that's what folks are sent to jail for," he added.

"You will kindly bear in mind, sir, that I have been convicted of no crime!" retorted the judge.

"If you hadn't been so blamed particular you might have had company; politest darky you would meet anywhere. Well, sir, I didn't think the boss orator of the day would be the first prisoner - the joke certainly is on you!"

"I never saw such bloody-minded ruffians! Keep them out and keep me in - all I ask is to vindicate myself in the eyes of the world," said the judge.

"Well," began the sheriff severely, "ain't it enough to make 'em bloody-minded? Any one of 'em might have taken your money and got stuck. Just to think of that is what hets them up." He regarded the judge with a glance of displeasure. "I hate to see a man so durn unreasonable in his p'int of view. And you picked a lady - a widow-lady - say, ain't you ashamed?"

"Well, sir, what's going to happen to me?" demanded the judge angrily.

"I reckon you'll be tried. I reckon the law will deal with you - that is, if the public remains ca'm. Maybe it will come to the conclusion that it'd prefer a lynching - people are funny." He seemed to detach himself from the possible current of events.

"And, waking and sleeping, I have that before me!" cried the judge bitterly.

"You had ought to have thought of that sooner, when you was unloading that money. Why, it ain't even good counterfeit! I wonder a man of your years wa'n't slicker."

"Have you taken steps to find the boy, or Solomon Mahaffy?" inquired the judge.

"For what?"

"How is my innocence going to be established - how am I going to clear myself if my witnesses are hounded out of the county?"

"I love to hear you talk, sir. I told 'em at the raising to-day that I considered you one of the most eloquent minds I had ever listened to - but naturally, sir, you are too smart to be honest. You say you ain't been convicted yet; but you're going to be! There's quite a scramble for places on the jury already. There was pistols drawed up at the tavern by some of our best people, sir, who got het up disputin' who was eligible to serve." The judge groaned. "You should be thankful them pistols wasn't drawed on you, sir," said the sheriff amiably. "You've got a heap to be grateful about; for we've had one lynching, and we've rid one or two parties on a rail after giving 'em a coat of tar and feathers."

The judge shuddered. The sheriff continued placidly:

"I'll take it you'll get all that's coming to you, sir—say about twenty years - that had ought to let you out easy. Sort of round out your earthly career, and leave something due you t'other side of Jordan."

"I suppose there is no use in my pointing out to you that I did not know the money was counterfeit, and that I was quite innocent of any intention to defraud Mrs. Walker?" said the judge, with a weary, exasperated air.

"It don't make no difference where you got the money; you

The Prodigal Judge   135

know that, for you set up to be some sort of a lawyer."

Presently the sheriff went his way into the dusk of the evening, and night came swiftly to fellowship the judge's fears. A single moonbeam found its way into the place, making a thin rift in the darkness. The judge sat down on the three-legged stool, which, with a shake-down bed, furnished the jail. His loneliness was a great wave of misery that engulfed him.

"Well, just so my life ain't cut short!" he whispered.

He had known a varied career, and what he was pleased to call his unparalleled misfortunes had reduced him to all kinds of desperate shifts to live, but never before had the law laid its hands on him. True, there had been times and seasons when he had been grateful for the gloom of the dark ways he trod, for echoes had taken the place of the living voice that had once spoken to his soul; but he could still rest his hand upon his heart and say that the law had always nodded to him to pass on.

Where was Solomon Mahaffy, and where Hannibal? He felt that Mahaffy could fend for himself, but he experienced a moment of genuine concern when he thought of the child. In spite of himself, his thoughts returned to him again and again. But surely some one would shelter and care for him!

"Yes - and work him like a horse, and probably abuse him into the bargain -"

Then there was a scarcely audible rustle on the margin of the woods, a dry branch snapped loudly. A little pause succeeded in which the judge's heart stood still. Next a stealthy step sounded in the clearing. The judge had an agonized vision of regulators and lynchers. The beat of his pulse quickened. He knew something of the boisterous horseplay of the frontier. The sheriff had spoken of tar and feathers - very quietly he stood erect and picked up the stool.

"Heaven helping me, I'll brain a citizen or two before it comes to that!" he told himself.

The cautious steps continued to approach. Some one paused below the closely shuttered window, and a hand struck the boards sharply. A whisper stole into the jail.

"Are you awake, Price?" It was Mahaffy who spoke.

"God bless you, Solomon Mahaffy!" cried the judge unsteadily.

"I've got the boy - he's with me," said Mahaffy.

"God bless you both!" repeated the judge brokenly. "Take care of him, Solomon. I feel better now, knowing he's in good hands."

"Please, Judge -" it was Hannibal

"Yes, dear lad?"

"I'm mighty sorry that ten dollars I loaned you was bad - but you don't need ever to pay it back!"

Mahaffy gave way to mirth.

"Never mind!" said the judge indulgently. "It performed all the essential functions of a perfectly legal currency. Just suppose we had discovered it was counterfeit before I took it to the tavern - that would have been a hardship!"

"It were Captain Murrell gave it to me," explained Hannibal.

"I consecrate myself to his destruction! Judge Slocum Price can not be humiliated with impunity!"

"I should think you would save your wind, Price, until you'd waddled out of danger!" Mahaffy spoke, gruffly.

"How are you going to get me out of this, Solomon - for I suppose you are here to break jail for me," said the judge.

Mahaffy inspected the building. He found that the door was secured by two ponderous hasps to which were fitted heavy padlocks, but the solid wooden shutter which closed the square hole in the gable that served as a window was fastened by a hasp and peg. He withdrew the peg, opened the shutter, and the judge's face, wreathed in smiles, appeared at the aperture.

"The blessed sky and air!" he murmured, breathing deep. "A week of this would have broken my spirit!"

"If you can, Price, you'd better come feet first," suggested Mahaffy.

"Not sufficiently acrobatic, Solomon - it's heads or I lose!" said the judge.

He thrust his shoulders into the opening and wriggled outward. Suddenly his forward movement was arrested.

"I was afraid of that!" he said, with a rather piteous smile. "It's my stomach, Solomon!" Mahaffy seized him by the shoulders with lean muscular hands. "Pull!" cried the judge hoarsely. But Mahaffy's vigorous efforts failed to move him.

"I guess you're stuck, Price!"

"Get your wind, Solomon," urged the judge, "and then, if Hannibal will reach up and work about my middle with his knuckles while you pull, I may get through." But even this expedient failed.

"Do you reckon you can get me back? I should not care to spend the night so!" said the judge. He was purple and panting.

"Let's try you edgewise!" And Mahaffy pushed the judge into

the jail again.

"No," said the judge, after another period of resolute effort on his part and on the part of Mahaffy. "Providence has been kind to me in the past, but it's clear she didn't have me in mind when they cut this hole."

"Well, Price, I guess all we can do is to go back to town and see if I can get into my cabin - I've got an old saw there. If I can find it, I can come again to-morrow night and cut away one of the logs, or the cleats of the door."

"In Heaven's name, do that to-night, Solomon!" implored the judge. "Why procrastinate?"

"Price, there's a pack of dogs in this neighborhood, and we must have a full night to move in, or they'll pull us down before we've gone ten miles!"

The judge groaned.

"You're right, Solomon; I'd forgotten the dogs," and he groaned again.

Mahaffy closed and fastened the shutter, then he and Hannibal stole across the clearing and entered the woods. The judge flung off his clothes and went to bed, determined to sleep away as many hours as possible. He was only aroused by the arrival of his breakfast, which the sheriff brought about eight o'clock.

"Well, if I was in your boots I couldn't sleep like you!" remarked that official admiringly. "But I reckon, sir, this ain't the first time the penitentiary has stared you in the face."

"Then you reckon wrong," said the judge sententiously, as he hauled on his trousers.

"No? - you needn't hurry none. I'll get them dishes when I fetch your dinner," he added, as he took his leave.

A little later the blacksmith appeared and fitted three iron bars to the window.

"I reckon that'll hold you, old feller!" he observed pleasantly.

He was disposed to linger, since he was interested in the mechanical means employed in the making of counterfeit money and thirsted for knowledge at first hand. Also, he had in his possession a one-dollar bill which had come to him in the way of trade and which local experts had declared to be a spurious production. He passed it in between the bars and demanded the judge's opinion of it as though he were the first authority in the land. But he went no wiser than he came.

It was nearing the noon hour when the judge's solitude was again invaded. He first heard the distant murmur of voices on the road and passed an uneasy and restless ten minutes, with his eye to a crack in the door. He was soothed and reassured, however, when at last be caught sight of the sheriff.

"Well, judge, I got company for you," cried the sheriff cheerfully, as he threw open the door. "A hoss-thief!"

He pushed into the building a man, hatless and coatless, with a pair of pale villainous eyes and a tobaccostained chin. The judge viewed the new-comer with disfavor. As for the horse-thief, he gave his companion in misery a coldly critical stare, seated himself on the stool, and with quite a fierce air devoted all his energy to mastication. He neither altered his position nor changed his expression until he and the judge were alone, then, catching the judge's eye, he made what seemed a casual movement with his hand, the three fingers raised; but to the judge this clearly was without significance, and the horse-thief manifested no further interest where he was concerned. He did not even condescend to answer the one or two civil remarks the judge addressed to him.

As the long afternoon wore itself away, the judge lived through the many stages of doubt and uncertainty, for suppose anything had happened to Mahaffy! When the sheriff came with his supper he asked him if he had seen or heard of his friend.

"Judge, I reckon he's lopin' on yet. I never seen a man of his years run as well as he done - it was inspirin' how he got over the ground!" answered the sheriff. Then he attempted conversation with the horse-thief, but was savagely cursed for his pains. "Well, I don't envy you your company none, sir," he remarked as he took leave of the judge.

Standing before the window, the judge watched the last vestige of light fade from the sky and the stars appear. Would Mahaffy come? The suspense was intolerable. It was possibly eight o'clock. He could not reasonably expect Mahaffy until nine or half past; to come earlier would be too great a risk. Suddenly out of the silence sounded a long-drawn whistle. Three times it was repeated. The horse-thief leaped to his feet.

"Neighbor, that means me!" he cried.

The moon was rising now, and by its light the judge saw a number of horsemen appear on the edge of the woods. They entered the clearing, picking their way among the stumps without haste or confusion. When quite close, five of the band dismounted; the rest continued on about the jail or cantered off toward the road. By this time the judge's teeth were chattering and he was dripping cold sweat at every pore. He prayed earnestly that they might hang the horsethief and spare him. The dismounted men took up a stick of timber that had been cut for the jail and not used.

"Look out inside, there!" cried a voice, and the log was dashed against the door; once - twice - it rose and fell on the clapboards, and under those mighty thuds grew up a wide gap through which the moonlight streamed splendidly. The horse-thief stepped between the dangling cleats and vanished. The judge, armed with the stool, stood at bay.

"What next?" a voice asked.

"Get dry brush - these are green logs - we'll burn this jail!"

"Hold on!" the judge recognized the horse-thief as the speaker. "There's an old party in there! No need to singe him!"

"Friend?"

"No, I tried him."

The judge tossed away the stool. He understood now that these men were neither lynchers nor regulators. With a confident, not to say jaunty step, he emerged from the jail.

"Your servant, gentlemen!" he said, lifting his hat.

"Git!" said one of the men briefly, and the judge moved nimbly away toward the woods. He had gained its shelter when the jail began to glow redly.

Now to find Solomon and the boy, and then to put the miles between himself and Pleasantville with all diligence. As he thought this, almost at his elbow Mahaffy and Hannibal rose from behind a fallen log. The Yankee motioned for silence and pointed west.

"Yes," breathed the judge. He noted that Mahaffy had a heavy pack, and the boy his long rifle. For a mile or two they moved forward without speech, the boy in the lead; while at his heels strode Mahaffy, with the judge bringing up the rear.

"How do you feel, Price?" asked Mahaffy at length, over his shoulder.

"Like one come into a fortune! Those horse-thieves gave me a fine scare, but did me a good turn."

Hannibal kept to the woods by a kind of instinct, and the two men yielded themselves to his guidance; but there was no speech between them. Mahaffy trod in the boy's steps, and the judge, puffing like an overworked engine, came close upon his heels. In this way they continued to advance for an hour or more, then the boy paused.

"Go on!" commanded Mahaffy.

"Do you 'low the judge can stand it?" asked Hannibal .

"Bless you, lad!" panted the judge feelingly.

"He's got to stand it - either that, or what do you suppose will happen to us if they start their dogs?" said Mahaffy.

"Solomon's right - you are sure we are not going in a circle, Hannibal?"

"Yes, I'm sure," said Hannibal. "Do you see that star? My Uncle Bob learned me how I was to watch that star when I wanted to keep going straight."

There was another long interval of silence. Bit by bit the sky became overcast. Vague, fleecy rifts of clouds appeared in the heavens. A wind sprang up, murmuring about them, there came a distant roll of thunder, while along the horizon the lightning rushed in broken, jagged lines of fire. In the east there was a pale flush that showed the black, hurrying clouds the winds had summoned out of space.

The booming thunder, first only the sullen menace of the approaching storm, rolled nearer and nearer, and the fierce light came in blinding sheets of flame. A ceaseless, pauseless murmur sprang up out of the distance, and the trees rocked with a mighty crashing of branches, while here and there a big drop of rain fell. Then the murmur swelled into a roar as the low clouds disgorged themselves. Drenched to the skin on the instant, the two men and the boy stumbled forward through the gray wake of the storm.

"What's come of our trail now?" shouted the judge, but the sound of his voice was lost in the rush of the hurrying winds and the roar of the airy cascades that fell about them.

An hour passed. There was light under the trees, faint, impalpable without visible cause, but they caught the first sparkle of the rain drops on leaf and branch; they saw the silvery rivulets coursing down the mossy trunks of old trees; last of all through a narrow rift in the clouds, the sun showed them its golden rim, and day broke in the steaming woods. With the sun, with a final rush of the hurrying wind, a final torrent, the storm spent itself, and there was only the drip from bough and leaf, or pearly opalescent points of moisture on the drenched black trunks of maple and oak; a sapphire sky, high arched, remote overhead; and the June day all about.

"What's come of they trail now?" cried the judge again. "He'll be a good dog that follows it through, these woods!"

They had paused on a thickly wooded hillside.

"We've come eight or ten miles if we have come a rod, Price," said Mahaffy, "and I am in favor of lying by for the day. When it comes dark we can go on again."

The judge readily acquiesced in this, and they presently found a dense thicket which they cautiously entered. Reaching the center of the tangled growth, they beat down the briers and bushes, or cut them away with their knives, until they had a little cleared space where they could build a fire. Then from the pack which Mahaffy carried, the rudiments of a simple but filling meal were produced.

"Your parents took no chances when they named you Solomon!" said the judge approvingly.

CHAPTER XIV

BELLE PLAIN

Now, Tom," said Betty, with a bustling little air of excitement as she rose from the breakfast table that first morning at Belle Plain, "I am ready if you are. I want you to show me everything!"

"I reckon you'll notice some changes," remarked Tom.

He went from the room and down the hall a step or two in advance of her. On the wide porch Betty paused, breathing deep. The house stood on an eminence; directly before it at the bottom of the slight descent was a small bayou, beyond this the forest stretched away in one unbroken mass to the Mississippi. Here and there, gleaming in the brilliant morning light, some great bend of the river was visible through the trees, while the Arkansas coast, blue and distant, piled up against the far horizon.

"What is it you want to see, anyhow, Betty?" Tom demanded, turning on her.

"Everything - the place, Tom - Belle Plain! Oh, isn't it beautiful! I had no idea how lovely it was!" cried Betty, as with her eyes still fixed on the distant panorama of woods and water she went down the steps, Tom at her heels - he bet she'd get sick of it all soon enough, that was one comfort!

"Why, Tom! Why does the lawn look like this?"

"Like what?" inquired Tom.

"Why, this - all weeds and briers, and the paths overgrown?" and as Betty surveyed the unkempt waste that had once been a lawn, a little frown fixed itself on her smooth brow.

Mr. Ware rubbed his chin reflectively with the back of his hand.

"That sort of thing looked all right, Bet," he said, "but it kept five or six of the best hands out of the fields right at the busiest time of the year."

"Haven't I slaves enough?" she asked.

The dull color crept into Ware's cheeks. He hated her for that "I!" So she was going to come that on him, was she? And he'd worked himself like a horse to bring in more land. Why, he'd doubled the acreage in cotton and corn in the last four years! He smothered his sense of hurt and indignation.

"Don't you want to see the crops, Bet? Let me order a team and show you about, you couldn't walk over the place in a week!" he urged.

The girl shook her head and moved swiftly down the path that led from terrace to terrace to the margin of the bayou. At the first terrace she paused. All below was a wilderness of tangled vines and brush. She faced Tom rather piteously. What had been lost was more than he could possibly understand. Her father had planned these grounds which he was allowing a riotous second growth to swallow up.

"It's positively squalid!" cried Betty, with a little stamp of her foot.

Ware glanced about with dull eyes. The air of neglect and

decay which was everywhere visible, and which was such a shock to Betty, had not been reached in a season, he was really convinced that the place looked pretty much as it had always looked.

"I'll tell you, Betty, I'm busy this morning; you poke about and see what you want done and we'll do it," he said, and made a hasty retreat to his office, a little brick building at the other side of the house.

Betty returned to the porch and seating herself on the top step with her elbows on her knees and her chin sunk in the palms of her hands, gazed about her miserably enough. She was still seated there when half an hour later Charley Norton galloped up the drive from the highroad. Catching sight of her on the porch he sprang from the saddle, and, throwing his reins to a black boy, hurried to her side.

"Inspecting your domain, Betty?" he asked, as he took his place near her on the step.

"Why didn't you tell me, Charley - or at least prepare me for this?" she asked, almost tearfully.

"How was I to know, Betty? I haven't been here since you went away, dear - what was there to bring me? Old Tom would make a cow pasture out of the Garden of Eden, wouldn't he - a beautiful, practical, sordid soul he is!"

"What am I going to do, Charley?"

"Keep after him until you get what you want, it's the only way to manage Tom that I know of."

"It's horrid to have to assert one's self!"

"You'll have to with Tom - you must, Betty - he won't understand anything else." Then he added: "Let's look around and see what's needed, a season or two of care will remedy the most of this neglect. Just make Tom put a lot of hands in here with brush-hooks and axes and soon you'll not know the place!"

Norton spent the day at Belle Plain; and though he was there on his good behavior as the result of an agreement they had reached on board The Naiad, he proposed twice.

"My intentions are all right, Betty," he assured her in extenuation. "But I've the worst memory imaginable. Oh, yes, the lower terrace is badly gullied, but it's no great matter, it can be fixed with a little work."

It was soon plain to Betty that Tom's ideals, if he possessed any, had not led him in the direction of what he termed display. His social impulse had suffered atrophy. The house was utterly disorganized; there was a dearth of suitable servants. Those she had known were gone - sold, she learned. Tom explained that there had been no need for them since he had lived pretty much in his office, what had been the use in keeping darkies standing about doing nothing? He had got rid of those show niggers and put their price in husky field hands, who could be made to do a day's work and not feel they were abused.

But Tom was mistaken in his supposition that Betty would soon tire of Belle Plain. She demanded men, and teams, and began on the lawns. This interested and fascinated her. She was out at sun-up to direct her laborers. She had the advantage of Charley Norton's presence and advice for the greater part of each day in the week, and Sundays he came to look over what had been accomplished, and, as Tom firmly believed, to put that little fool up to fresh nonsense. He could have booted him!

As the grounds took shape before her delighted eyes, Betty found leisure to institute a thorough reformation indoors. A number of house servants were rescued from the quarters and she began to instruct them in their new duties.

Tom was sick at heart. The little fool would cripple the place. It gave him acute nausea to see the gangs at work about the lawns; it made him sicker to pass through the house. There were five or six women in the kitchen now - he was damned if he could see what they found to do - there was a butler and a page. Betty had levied on the stables for one of the best teams to draw the family carriage, which had not been in use since her mother's death; there was a coachman for that, and another little monkey to ride on the rumble and hop down and open gates. This came of sending girls away to school - they only learned foolishness.

And those niggers about the house had to be dressed for their new work; the butler, a cracking plow-hand he was, wore better clothes than he - Tom - did. No wonder he was sick; - and waste! Tom knew all about that when the bills began to come in from Memphis. Why, that pink-faced chit, he always referred to her in his own mind now as a pink-faced chit, was evolving a scheme of life that would cost eight or ten thousand dollars a year to maintain, and she was talking of decorators for the house, either from New Orleans or Philadelphia, and new furniture from top to bottom.

Tom felt that he was being robbed. Then he realized with a sense of shock that here was a fortune of over half a million in lands and slaves which he had managed and manipulated all these years, but which was not his. It was true that under the terms of his stepmother's will he would inherit it in the event of Betty's death - well, she looked like dying, a whole lot - she was as strong as a mule, those soft rounded curves covered plenty of vigorous muscle; Tom hated the very sight of her. A pink-faced chit bubbling over with life and useless energy, a perfect curse she was, with all sorts of extravagant tastes and he was powerless to check her, for, although he was still her guardian, there were certain provisions of the will - he consulted the copy he kept locked up in his desk in the office - that permitted her to do pretty much as she pleased with her income. It was a hell of a will! She could spend fifteen or twenty thousand dollars a year if she wanted to and he couldn't prevent it. It was an iniquitous document!

Well, the place could go straight off to the devil, he wouldn't wear out his life economizing for her to waste - he didn't get a thank-you - and he knew that nobody took off the land bigger crops than he did, while bale for bale his cotton outsold all other cotton raised in the county - that was the kind of a manager he was. He wagged his head in self-approval. And what did he get out of it? A lump sum each year with a further lump sum of twenty thousand dollars when she came of age - soon now - or married. Tom's eyes bulged from their sockets - she'd be doing that next, to spite him!

Betty's sphere of influence rapidly extended itself. She soon began to have her doubts concerning the treatment accorded the slaves, and was not long in discovering that Hicks, the overseer, ran things with a heavy hand. Matters reached a crisis one day when, happening to ride through the quarters, she found him disciplining a refractory black. She turned sick at the sight. Here was a slave actually being whipped by another slave while Hicks stood looking on with his hands in his pockets, and with a brutal satisfied air. When he caught sight of the girl, he sang out

"That'll do; he's had enough, I reckon, to learn him!" He added sullenly to Betty, "Sorry you seen this, Miss!"

"How dare you order such a punishment without authority!" cried Betty furiously.

Hicks gave her a black scowl.

"I don't need no authority to whip a shirker," he said insolently, as he turned away.

"Stop!" commanded Betty, her eyes blazing. She strove to keep her voice steady. "You shall not remain at Belle Plain another hour."

Hicks said nothing. He knew it would take more than her saying so to get him off the place. Betty turned her horse and galloped back to the house. She felt that she was in no condition to see Tom just at that moment, and dismounting at the door ran up-stairs to her room.

Meantime the overseer sought out Ware in his office. His manner of stating his grievance was singular. He began by swearing at his employer. He had been insulted before all the quarter - his rage fairly choked him, he could not speak.

Tom seized the opportunity to swear back. He wanted to know if he hadn't troubles enough without the overseer's help? If he'd got himself insulted it was his own affair and he could lump it, generally speaking, and get out of that office! But Tom's fury quickly spent itself. He wanted to know what the matter was.

"Sent you off the place, did she; well, you'll have to eat crow. I'll do all I can. I don't know what girls were ever made for anyhow, damned if I do!" he added plaintively, as a realization of a stupendous mistake on the part of nature overwhelmed him.

Hicks consented to eat crow only after Mr. Ware had cursed and cajoled him into a better and more forgiving frame of mind. Then Tom hurried off to find Betty and put matters right; a more difficult task than he had reckoned on, for Betty was obdurate and her indignation flared up at mention of the incident; all his powers of argument and persuasion were called into requisition before she would consent to Hicks remaining, and then only on that most uncertain tenure, his good behavior.

"Now you come up to the house," said Tom, when he had won his point and gone back to Hicks, "and get done with it. I reckon you talked when you should have kept your blame familiar mouth shut! Come on, and get it over with, and say you're sorry."

Later, after Hicks had made his apology, the two men smoked a friendly pipe and discussed the situation. Tom pointed out that opposition was useless, a losing game, you could get your way by less direct means. She wouldn't stay long at Belle Plain, but while she did remain they must avoid any more crises of the sort through which they had just passed, and presently; she'd be sick of the place. Tom wagged his head. She was sick of it already only she hadn't the sense to know it. It wasn't good enough. Nothing suited-the house - the grounds - nothing!

In the midst of her activities Betty occasionally found time to think of Bruce Carrington. She was sure she did not wish to see him again! But when three weeks had passed she began to feel incensed that he had not appeared. She thought of him with hot cheeks and a quickening beat of the heart. It was anger. Naturally she was very indignant, as she had every right to be! He was the first man who had dared - !

Then one day when she had decided for ever to banish all memory of him from her mind, and never, under any circumstances, to think of him again, he presented himself at Belle Plain.

She was in her room just putting the finishing touches to an especially satisfying toilet when her maid tapped on the door and told her there was a gentleman in the parlor who wished to see her.

"Is it Mr. Norton?" asked Betty.

"No, Miss - he didn't give no name, Miss."

When Betty entered the parlor a moment later she saw her caller standing with his back turned toward her as he gazed from one of the windows, but she instantly recognized those broad shoulders, and the fine poise of the shapely head that surmounted them.

"Oh, Mr. Carrington -" and Betty stopped short, while her face grew rather pale and then crimsoned. Then she advanced quite boldly and held out a frigid hand, which he took carefully. "I didn't know - so you are alive - you disappeared so suddenly that night -"

"Yes, I'm alive," he said, and then with a smile. "But I fear before you get through with me we'll both wish I were not, Betty."

"Don't call me Betty."

"Who was that man who met you at New Madrid? He can't have you, whoever he is!" His eyes dwelt on her tenderly, and the remembered spell of her fresh youthful beauty deepened itself for him.

"Perhaps he doesn't want me -"

"Yes, he does. That was plain as day."

Betty surveyed him from under her lashes. What could she do with this man? Nothing affected him. He seemed to have crossed some intangible barrier and to stand closer to her than any other man had ever stood.

"Do you still hate me, Betty - Miss Malroy - is there anything I can say or do that will make you forgive me?" He looked at her penitently.

But Betty hardened her heart against him and prepared to keep him in place. Remembering that he was still holding her hand, she recovered it.

"Will you sit down?" she indicated a chair. He seated himself and Betty put a safe distance between them. "Are you staying in the neighborhood, Mr. Carrington ?" she asked, rather unkindly.

How did he dare come here when she had forgotten him and her annoyance? And now the sight of him brought back memories of that disagreeable night on that horrid boat - he had deceived her about that boat, too - she would never forgive him for that - she had trusted him and he had clearly shown that he was not to be trusted; and Betty closed her pretty mouth until it was a thin red line and looked away that she might not see his hateful face.

"No, I'm not staying in the neighborhood. When I left you, I made up my mind I'd wait at New Madrid until I could come on down here and say I was sorry."

"And it's taken you all this time?"

Carrington regarded her seriously.

"I reckon I must have come for more time, Betty - Miss Malroy." In spite of herself, Betty glowed under the caressing humor of his tone.

"Really - you must have chosen poorly then when you selected New Madrid. It couldn't have been a good place for your purpose."

"I think if I could have made up my mind to stay there long enough, it would have answered," said Carrington. "But when a down-river boat tied up 'there yesterday it was more than I could stand. You 'see there's danger in a town like New Madrid of getting too sorry. I thought we'd better discuss this point -"

"Mayn't I show you Belle Plain?" asked Betty quickly.

But Carrington shook his head.

"I don't care anything about that," he said. "I didn't come here to see Belle Plain."

"You certainly are candid," said Betty.

"I intend to be honest with you always."

"Dear me - but I don't know that I shall particularly like it. Do you think it was quite fair to select the boat you did, or was your resolution to be always honest formed later?" demanded Betty severely.

He looked at her with great sweetness of expression.

"I didn't advise that boat for speed, only for safety. Betty, doesn't it mean anything to you that I love you? I admit that I wish it had been twice as slow!" he added reflectively, as an afterthought. He looked at her steadily, and Betty's dark lashes drooped as the color mounted to her face.

"I don't," she said quickly. She rose from her chair, and Carrington followed her example with a lithe movement that bespoke muscles in good training. She led the way through the wide hall and out to the porch.

"Now I am going to show you all over the place," she announced resolutely. She stood on the top step, looking off into the flaming west where the sun rode low in the heavens. "Isn't it lovely, Mr. Carringtonisn't it beautiful?"

"Very beautiful!" Carrington's glance was fixed on her face.

"If you don't care to see Belle Plain," began Betty, rather indignantly. "No, I don't, Betty. This is enough for me. I'll come for that some other time if you'll be good enough to let me?"

"Then you expect to remain in the neighborhood?"

"I've given up the river, and I'm going to get hold of some land -"

"Land?" said Betty, with a rising inflection.

"Yes, land."

"I thought you were a river-man?"

"I'm a river-man no longer. I am going to be a planter now. But I'll tell you why, and all about it some other day." Then he held out his hand. "Goodby," he added.

"Are you going - good-by, Mr. Carrington," and Betty's fingers tingled with his masterful clasp long after he had gone.

Carrington sauntered slowly down the path to the highroad.

"She didn't ask me to come back - an oversight," he told himself cheerfully.

Just beyond the gates he met that same young fellow he had seen at New Madrid. Norton nodded good-naturedly as he passed, and Carrington, glancing back, saw that he turned in at Belle Plain. He shrugged his shoulders, and went on his way not rejoicing.

CHAPTER XV

THE SHOOTING-MATCH AT BOGGS'

The judge's faith in the reasonableness of mankind having received a staggering blow, there began a somewhat furtive existence for himself, for Solomon Mahaffy, and for the boy. They kept to little frequented byways, and usually it was the early hours of morning, or the cool of late afternoons when they took the road.

The heat of silent middays found them lounging beside shady pools, where the ripple of fretted waters filled the pauses in their talk. It was then that the judge and Mahaffy exchanged views on literature and politics, on religion and politics, on the public debt and politics, on canals and national roads and more politics. They could and did honestly differ at great length and with unflagging energy on these vital topics, especially politics, for they were as far apart mentally as they were close together morally.

Mahaffy, morose and embittered, regarded the life they were living as an unmixed hardship. The judge entered upon it with infinite zest. He displayed astonishing adaptability, while he brought all the resources of a calm and modest knowledge to bear on the vexed problem of procuring sustenance for himself and for his two companions.

"To an old campaigner like me, nothing could be more delightful than this holiday, coming as it does on the heels of grinding professional activity," he observed to Mahaffy. "This is the way our first parents lived - close to nature, in touch with her gracious beneficence! Sir, this experience is singularly refreshing after twenty years of slaving at the desk. If any man can grasp the possibilities of a likely looking truck-patch at a glance, I am that man, and as for getting around in the dark and keeping the lay of the land - well, I suppose it's my military training. Jackson always placed the highest value on such data as I furnished him. He leaned on me more than any other man, Solomon -"

"I've heard he stood up pretty straight," said Mahaffy affably. The judge's abandoned conduct distressed him not a little, but his remonstrances had been in vain.

"I consider that when society subjected me to the indignity of arrest, I was relieved of all responsibility. Injustice must bear its own fruit," the judge had answered him sternly.

His beginnings had been modest enough: a few ears of corn, a few hills of potatoes, and the like, had satisfied him; then one night he appeared in camp with two streaks of scarlet down the side of his face.

"Are you hurt, Price?" demanded Mahaffy, betraying an anxiety of which he was instantly ashamed.

"Let me relieve your apprehension, Solomon; it's only a trickle of stewed fruit. I folded a couple of pies and put them in the crown of my hat," explained the judge.

"You mean you've been in somebody's springhouse ?"

"It was unlocked, Solomon, This will be a warning to the owner. I consider I have done him a kindness."

Thus launched on a career of plunder, the judge very speedily accumulated a water bucket - useful when one wished to milk cow - an ax from a woodpile, a kettle from a summer kitchen, a tin of soft soap, and an excellent blanket from a wash-line.

"For the boy, Solomon," he said gently, when he caught Mahaffy's steady disapproving glance fixed upon him as he displayed this last trophy.

"What sort of an example are you setting him?"

"The world is full of examples I'd not recommend, Solomon. One must learn to discriminate. A body can no more follow all the examples than he can follow all the roads, and I submit that the ends of morality can as well be served in showing a child what he should not do as in showing him what he should. Indeed, I don't know but it's the finer educational idea!"

Thereafter the judge went through the land with an eye out for wash-lines.

"I'm looking for a change of linen for the boy, Solomon," he said. "Let me bring you a garment or two. Eh - how few men you'll find of my build; those last shirts I got were tight around the armholes and had no more tail than a rabbit!"

Two nights later Mr. Mahaffy accepted a complete change of under linen, but without visible sign of gratitude.

A night later the judge disappeared from camp, and after a prolonged absence returned puffing and panting with three watermelons, which proved to be green, since his activity had been much in advance of the season.

"I don't suppose there is any greater tax on human ingenuity than to carry three watermelons!" he remarked. "The human structure is ideally adapted to the transportation of two - it can be done with comfort; but when a body tackles three he finds that nature herself is opposed to the proceeding! Well, I am going back for a bee-gum I saw in a fence corner. Hannibal will enjoy that - a child is always wanting sweets!"

In this fashion they fared gaily across the state, but as they neared the Mississippi the judge began to consider the future. His bright and illuminating intelligence dealt with this problem in all its many-sidedness.

"I wish you'd enter one of the learned professions, Solomon - have you ever thought of medicine?" he inquired. Mr. Mahaffy laughed. "But why not, Solomon? There is nothing like a degree or a title - that always stamps a man, gives him standing -"

"What do I know about the human system?"

"I should certainly hope you know as much as the average doctor knows. We could locate in one of these new towns where they have the river on one side and the canal on the other, and where everybody has the ague -"

"What do I know about medicine?" inquired Mahaffy.

"As much as Aesculapius, no doubt - even he had to make a beginning. The torch of science wasn't lit in a day - you must be willing to wait; but you've got a good sick-room manner. Have you ever thought of opening an undertaker's shop? If you couldn't cure them you might bury them."

A certain hot afternoon brought them into the shaded main street of a straggling village. Near the door of the principal building, a frame tavern, a man was seated, with his feet on the horse-rack. There was no other sign of human occupancy.

"How do you do, sir?" said the judge, halting before this solitary individual whom he conjectured to be the 'landlord. The man nodded, thrusting his thumbs into the armholes of his vest. "What's the name of this bustling metropolis?" continued the judge, cocking his head on one side.

As he spoke, Bruce Carrington appeared in the tavern door; pausing there, he glanced curiously at the shabby wayfarers.

"This is Raleigh, in Shelby County, Tennessee, one of the states of the Union of which, no doubt, you've heard rumor in your wanderings," said the landlord.

"Are you the voice from the tomb?" inquired the judge, in a tone of playful sarcasm.

Carrington, amused, sauntered toward him.

"That's one for you, Mr. Pegloe!" he said.

"I am charmed to meet a gentleman whose spirit of appreciation shows his familiarity with a literary allusion," said the judge, bowing.

"We ain't so dead as we look," said Pegloe. "Just you keep on to Boggs' race-track, straight down the road, and you'll find that out - everybody's there to the hoss-racing and shooting-match. I reckon you've missed the hoss-racing, but you'll be in time for the shooting. Why ain't you there, Mr. Carrington?"

"I'm going now, Mr. Pegloe," answered Carrington, as he followed the judge, who, with Mahaffy and the boy, had moved off.

"Better stop at Boggs'!" Pegloe called after them.

But the judge had already formed his decision.

Horse-racing and shooting-matches were suggestive of that progressive spirit, the absence of which he had so much lamented at the jail raising at Pleasantville - Memphis was their objective point, but Boggs' became a side issue of importance. They had gained the edge of the village when Carrington overtook them. He stepped to Hannibal's side.

"Here, let me carry that long rifle, son!" he said. Hannibal looked up into his face, and yielded the piece without a word. Carrington balanced it on his big, muscular palm. "I reckon it can shoot - these old guns are hard to beat!" he observed.

"She's the clostest shooting rifle I ever sighted," said Hannibal promptly. "You had ought to see the judge shoot her - my! He never misses!"

Carrington laughed.

"The clostest shooting rifle you ever sighted - eh?" he repeated. "Why, aren't you afraid of it?"

"No," said Hannibal scornfully. "But she kicks you some if you don't hold her right."

There was a rusty name-plate on the stock of the old sporting rifle; this had caught Carrington's eye.

"What's the name here? Oh, Turberville."

The judge, a step or two in advance, wheeled in his tracks with a startling suddenness.

"What?" he faltered, and his face was ashen.

"Nothing, I was reading the name here; it is yours; sir, I suppose?" said Carrington.

The color crept slowly back into the judge's cheeks, but a tremulous hand stole up to his throat.

"No, sir - no; my name is Price - Slocum Price! Turberville - Turberville -" he muttered thickly, staring stupidly at Carrington.

"It's not a common name; you seem to have heard it before?" said the latter.

A spasm of pain passed over the judge's face.

"I - I've heard it. The name is on the rifle, you say?"

"Here on the stock, yes."

The judge took the gun and examined it in silence.

"Where did you get this rifle, Hannibal?" he at length asked brokenly.

"I fetched it away from the Barony, sir; Mr. Crenshaw said I might have it."

The judge gave a great start, and a hoarse inarticulate murmur stole from between his twitching lips.

"The Barony - the Barony - what Barony? The Quintard seat in North Carolina, is that what you mean?"

"Yes," said the boy.

The judge, as though stunned, stared at Hannibal and stared at the rifle, where the rusted name-plate danced before his eyes.

"What do you know of the Barony, Hannibal?" the words came slowly from the judge's lips, and his face had gone gray again.

"I lived at the Barony once, until Uncle Bob took me to Scratch Hill to be with him. It were Mr. Crenshaw said I was to have the old sp'otin' rifle," said Hannibal.

"You - you lived at the Barony?" repeated the judge, and a dull stupid wonder struck through his tone, he passed a shaking hand before his eyes. "How long ago - when?" he continued.

"I don't know how long it were, but until Uncle Bob carried me away after the old general died."

The judge slipped a hand under the child's chin and tilted his face back so that he might look into it. For a long moment he studied closely those small features, then with a shake of the head he handed the rifle to Carrington, and without a word strode forward. Carrington had been regarding Hannibal with a quickened interest.

"Hello!" he said, as the judge moved off. "You're the boy I saw at Scratch Hill!"

Hannibal gave him a frightened glance, and edged to Mr. Mahaffy's side, but did not answer him.

"What's become of Bob Yancy?" Carrington went on. He looked from Mahaffy to the judge; externally neither of these gentlemen was calculated to inspire confidence. Mahaffy, keenly alive to this fact, returned Carrington's glance with a fixed and hostile stare. "Come -" said Carrington good-naturedly, "you surely remember me?"

"Yes, sir; I reckon I do -"

"Can't you tell me about Mr. Yancy?"

"No, sir; I don't know exactly where he is -"

"But how did you get here?" persisted Carrington.

Suddenly Mahaffy turned on him.

"Don't you see he's with us?" he said truculently.

"Well, my dear sir, I certainly intended no offense!" rejoined Carrington rather hotly.

Mahaffy was plainly disturbed, the debased currency of his affection was in circulation where Hannibal was concerned, and he eyed the river-man askance. He was prepared to give him the lie should he set up any claim to the boy.

The judge plodded forward, his shoulders drooped, and his head bowed. For once silence had fixed its seal upon his lips, no inspiring speech fell from them. He had been suddenly swept back into a past he had striven these twenty years and more to forget, and his memories shaped themselves fantastically. Surely if ever a man had quitted the world that knew him, he was that man! He had died and yet he lived - lived horribly, without soul or heart, the empty shell of a man.

A turn in the road brought them within sight of Boggs' racetrack, a wide level meadow. The judge paused irresolutely, and turned his bleared face on his friend.

"We'll stop here, Solomon," he said rather wearily, for the spirit of boast and jest was quite gone out of him. He glanced toward Carrington. "Are you a resident of these parts, sir?" he asked.

"I've been in Raleigh three days altogether," answered Carrington, falling into step at his side, and they continued on across the meadow in silence.

"Do you observe the decorations of those refreshment booths? - the tasteful disposition of our national colors, sir?" the judge presently inquired.

Carrington smiled; he was able to follow his companion's train of thought.

They were elbowing the crowd now. Here were men from the small clearings in homespun and butternut or fringed hunting-shirts, with their women folk trailing after them. Here, too, in lesser numbers, were the lords of the soil, the men who counted their acres by the thousand and their slaves by the score. There was the flutter of skirts among the moving groups, the nodding of gay parasols that shaded fresh young faces, while occasionally a comfortable family carriage with some planter's wife or daughter rolled silently over the turf; for Boggs' race-track was a famous meeting-place where families that saw one another not above once or twice a year, friends who lived a day's hard drive apart even when summer roads were at their best, came as to a common center.

The judge's dull eye kindled, the haggard lines that had streaked his face erased themselves. This was life, opulent and full. These swift rolling carriages with their handsome women, these well-dressed men on foot, and splendidly mounted, all did their part toward lifting him out of his gloom. He settled his hat on his head with a rakish slant and his walk became a strut, he courted observation; he would have been grateful for a word, even a jest at his expense.

A cry from Hannibal drew his attention. Turning, he was in time to see the boy bound away. An instant later, to his astonishment, he saw a young girl who was seated with two men in an open carriage, spring to the ground, and dropping to her knees put her arms about the tattered little figure.

"Why, Hannibal!" cried Betty Malroy.

"Miss Betty! Miss Betty!" and Hannibal buried his head on her shoulder.

"What is it, Hannibal; what is it, dear?"

"Nothing, only I'm so glad to find you!"

"I am glad to see you, too!" said Betty, as she wiped his tears away. "When did you get here, dear?"

"We got here just to-day, Miss Betty," said Hannibal.

Mr. Ware, careless as to dress, with a wiry black beard of a week's growth decorating his chin and giving an unkempt appearance which his expression did not mitigate, it being of the sour and fretful sort; scowled down on the child. He had favored Boggs' with his presence, not because he felt the least interest in horse-racing, but because he had no faith in girls, and especially had he profound mistrust of Betty. She was so much easily portable wealth, a pink-faced chit ready to fall into the arms of the first man who proposed to her. But Charley Norton had not seemed disturbed by the planter's forbidding air. Between those two there existed complete reciprocity of feeling, inasmuch as Tom's presence was as distasteful to Norton as his own presence was distressing to Ware.

"Where is your Uncle Bob, Hannibal?" Betty asked, glancing about, and at her question a shadow crossed the child's face and the tears gathered again in his eyes.

"Ain't you seen him, Miss Betty?" he whispered. He had been sustained by the belief that when he found her he should find his Uncle Bob, too.

"Why, what do you mean, Hannibal - isn't your Uncle Bob with you?" demanded Betty.

"He got hurt in a fight, and I got separated from him way back yonder just after we came out of the mountains." He looked up piteously into Betty's face. "But you think he'll find me, don't you?"

"Why, you poor little thing!" cried Betty compassionately, and again she sank on her knees at Hannibal's side, and slipped her arms about him. The child began to cry softly.

"What ragamuffin's this, Betty?" growled Ware disgustedly.

But Betty did not seem to hear.

"Did you come alone, Hannibal?" she asked.

"No, ma'am; the judge and Mr. Mahaffy, they fetched me."

The judge had drawn nearer as Betty and Hannibal spoke together, but Mahaffy hung back. There were gulfs not to be crossed by him. It was different with the judge; the native magnificence of his mind fitted him for any occasion. He pulled up his stock, and coaxed a half-inch of limp linen down about his wrists, then very splendidly he lifted his napless hat from his shiny bald head and pressing it against his fat chest with much fervor, elegantly inclined himself from the hips.

"Allow me the honor to present myself, ma'am - Price is my name - Judge Slocum Price. May I be permitted to assume that this is the Miss Betty of whom my young protege so often speaks?" The judge beamed benevolently, and rested a ponderous hand on the boy's head.

Tom Ware gave him a glance of undisguised astonishment, while Norton regarded him with an expression of stunned and resolute gravity. Mahaffy seemed to be undergoing a terrible moment of uncertainty. He was divided between two purposes: one was to seize Price by the coat tails and drag him back into the crowd; the other was to kick him, and himself fly that spot. This singular impulse sprang from the fact that he firmly believed his friend's appearance was sufficient to blast the boy's chances in every quarter; nor did he think any better of himself.

Betty looked at the judge rather inquiringly.

"I am glad he has found friends," she said slowly. She wanted to believe that judge Slocum Price was somehow better than he looked, which should have been easy, since it was incredible that he could have been worse.

"He has indeed found friends," said the judge with mellow unction, and swelling visibly. These prosperous appearing people should be of use to him, God willing - he made a sweeping gesture. "I have assumed the responsibility of his future - he is my care."

Now Betty caught sight of Carrington and bowed. Occupied with Hannibal and the judge, she had been unaware of his presence.

Carrington stepped forward.

"Have you met Mr. Norton, and my brother, Mr. Carrington?" she asked.

The two young men shook hands, and Ware improved the opportunity to inspect the new-comer. But as his glance wandered over him, it took in more than Carrington, for it included the fine figure and swarthy face of Captain Murrell, who, with his eyes fixed on Betty, was thrusting his eager way through the crowd.

Murrell had presented himself at Belle Plain the day before. For upward of a year, Ware had enjoyed great peace of mind as a direct result of his absence from west Tennessee, and when he thought of him at all he had invariably put a period to his meditations with, "I hope to hell he catches it wherever he is!" It had really seemed a pernicious thing to him that no one had shown sufficient public spirit to knock the captain on the head, and that this had not been done, utterly destroyed his faith in the good intentions of Providence.

More than this, Betty had spoken of the captain in no uncertain terms. He was not to repeat that visit. Tom must make that point clear to him. Tom might entertain him if he liked at his office, but the doors of Belle Plain were closed against Captain Murrell; he was not to set his foot inside of them.

As Murrell approached, the hot color surged into Betty's face. As for Hannibal, he had gone white to the lips, and his small hand clutched hers desperately; he was remembering all the terror of that hot dawn at Slosson's.

Murrell, with all his hardihood, realized that a too great confidence had placed him in an awkward position, for Betty turned her back on him and began an animated conversation with Carrington and Charley Norton; only Hannibal and the judge continued to regard him; the boy with a frightened, fascinated stare, the judge with a wide sweet smile.

Hicks, the Belle Plain overseer, pushed his way to Murrell's side.

"Here, John Murrell, ain't you going to show us a trick or two?" he inquired.

Murrell turned quickly with a sense of relief.

"If you can spare me your rifle," he said, but his face wore a bleak look. Glancing at Betty, he took up his station with the other contestants, whereupon two or three young planters silently withdrew from the firing-line.

"Don't you think you've seen about enough, Bet?" demanded Tom. "You don't care for the shooting, do you ?"

"That's the very thing I do care for; I think I'd rather see that than the horse-racing," said Betty perversely. This had been her first appearance in public since her home-coming, and she felt that it had been most satisfactory. She had met everybody she had ever known, and scores of new people; her progress had been quite triumphal in spite of Tom, and in spite of Charley Norton, who was plainly not anxious to share her with any one, his devotion being rather of the monopolizing sort.

Betty now seated herself in the carriage, with Hannibal beside her, quietly determined to miss nothing. The judge, feeling that he had come into his own, leaned elegantly against the wheel, and explained the merits of each shot as it was made.

"Our intruding friend, the Captain, ma'am, is certainly a master with his weapon," he observed.

Betty was already aware of this. She turned to Norton.

"Charley, I can't bear to have him win!"

"I am afraid he will, for anything I can do, Betty," said Norton.

"Mr. Carrington, can't you shoot? - do take Hannibal's rifle and beat him," she coaxed.

"Don't be too sure that I can!" said Carrington, laughing.

"But I know you can!" urged Betty.

"I hope you gentlemen are not going to let me walk off with the prize?" said Murrell, approaching the group about the carriage.

"Mr. Norton, I am told you are clever with the rifle."

"I am not shooting to-day," responded Norton haughtily.

Murrell stalked back to the line.

"At forty paces I'd risk it myself, ma'am," said the judge. "But at a hundred, offhand like this, I should most certainly fail - I've burnt too much midnight oil. Eh - what - damn the dog, he's scored another center shot!"

"It would be hard to beat that -" they heard Murrell say.

"At least it would be quite possible to equal it," said Carrington, advancing with Hannibal's rifle in his hands. It was tossed to his shoulder, and poured out its contents in a bright stream of flame. There was a moment of silence.

"Center shot, ma'am!" cried the judge.

"I'll add twenty dollars to the purse!" Norton addressed himself to Carrington. "And I shall hope, sir, to see it go in to your pocket."

"Our sentiments exactly, ma'am, are they not?" said the judge.

"Perhaps you'd like to bet a little of your money?" remarked Murrell.

"I'm ready to do that too, sir," responded Norton quietly.

"Five hundred dollars, then, that this gentleman in whose success you take so great an interest, can neither equal nor better my next shot!" Murrell had produced a roll of bills as he spoke. Norton colored with embarrassment. Carrington took in the situation.

"Wait a minute -" he said, and passed his purse to Norton.

"Cover his money, sir," he added briefly.

"Thank you, my horses have run away with most of my cash," explained Norton.

"Your shot!" said Carrington shortly, to the outlaw.

Murrell taking careful aim, fired, clipping the center.

As soon as the result was known, Carrington raised his rifle; his bullet, truer than his opponent's, drove out the center. Murrell turned on him with an oath.

"You shoot well, but a board stuck against a tree is no test for a man's nerve," he said insolently.

Carrington was charging his piece.

"I only know of one other kind of target," he observed coolly.

"Yes - a living target!" cried Murrell.

The crowd opened from right to left. Betty's face grew white, and uttering a smothered cry she started to descend from the carriage, but the judge rested his hand on her arm.

"No, my dear young, lady, our friend is quite able to care for himself."

Carrington shook the priming into the pan of Hannibal's ancient weapon.

"I am ready for that, too," he said. There was a slow smile on his lips, but his eyes, black and burning, looked the captain through and through.

"Another time -" said Murrell, scowling.

"Any time," answered Carrington indifferently.

CHAPTER XVI

THE PORTAL OF HOPE

"This -" the speaker was judge Price; "this is the place for me: They are a warm-hearted people, sir; a prosperous people, and a patriotic people with an unstinted love of country. A people full of rugged virtues engaged in carving a great state out of the indulgent bosom of Nature. I like the size of their whisky glasses; I like the stuff that goes into them; I despise a section that separates its gallons into too many glasses. Show me a community that does that, and I'll show you a community rapidly tending toward a low scale of living. I'd like to hang out my shingle here and practise law."

The judge and Mr. Mahaffy were camped in the woods between Boggs' and Raleigh. Betty had carried Hannibal off to spend the night at Belle Plain, Carrington had disappeared with Charley Norton; but the judge and Mahaffy had lingered in the meadow until the last refreshment booth struck its colors to the twilight, and they had not lingered in vain. The judge threw himself at full length on the ground, and Mahaffy dropped at his side. About them, in the ruddy glow of their camp-fire, rose the dark wall of the forest.

"I crave opportunity, Solomon - the indorsement of my own class. I feel that I shall have it here," resumed the judge pensively.

But Mahaffy was sad in his joy, sober in his incipient

drunkenness. The same handsome treatment which the judge commended, had been as freely tendered him, yet he saw the end of all such hospitality. This was the worm in the bud. The judge, however, was an eager idealist; he still dreamed of Utopia, he still believed in millenniums. Mahaffy didn't and couldn't. Memory was the scarecrow in the garden of his hopes - you could wear out your welcome anywhere. In the end the world reckoned your cost, and unless you were prepared to make some sort of return for its bounty, the cold shoulder came to be your portion instead of the warm handclasp.

"Hannibal has found friends among people of the first importance. I have made it my business to inquire into their standing, and I find that young lady is heiress to a cool half million. Think of that, Solomon - think of that! I never saw anything more beautiful than her manifestation of regard for my protege -"

"And you made it your business, Mr. Price, to do your very damnedest to ruin his chances," said Mahaffy, with sudden heat.

"I ruin his chances? - I, sir? I consider that I helped his chances immeasurably."

"All right, then, you helped his chances - only you didn't, Price!"

"Am I to understand, Solomon, that you regard my interest in the boy as harmful?" inquired the judge, in a tone of shocked surprise.

"I regard it as a calamity," said Mahaffy, with cruel candor.

"And how about you, Solomon?"

"Equally a calamity. Mr. Price, you don't seem able to grasp just what we look like!"

"The mind's the only measure of the man, Solomon. If anybody can talk to me and be unaware that they are conversing with a gentleman, all I can say is their experience has been as pitiable as their intelligence is meager. But it hurts me when you intimate that I stand in the way of the boy's opportunity."

"Price, what do you; suppose we look like - you and I"

"In a general way, Solomon, I am conscious that our appeal is to the brain rather than the eye," answered the judge, with dignity.

"I reckon even you couldn't do a much lower trick than use the boy as a stepping-stone," pursued Mahaffy.

"I don't see how you have the heart to charge me with such a purpose - I don't indeed, Solomon." The judge spoke with deep feeling; he was really hurt.

"Well, you let the boy have his chance, and don't you stick in your broken oar," cried Mahaffy fiercely.

The judge rolled over on his back, and stared up at the heavens.

"This is a new aspect of your versatile nature, Solomon. Must I regard you as a personally emancipated moral influence, not committed to the straight and narrow path yourself, but still close enough to it to keep my feet from straying?" he at length demanded.

Mahaffy having spoken his mind, preserved a stony silence.

The judge got up and replenished the camp-fire, which had burnt low, then squatting before it, he peered into the flames.

"You'll not deny, Solomon, that Miss Malroy exhibited a real affection for Hannibal?" he began.

"Now don't you try to borrow money of her, Price," said Mahaffy, returning to the attack.

"Solomon - Solomon - how can you?"

"That'll be your next move. Now let her alone; let Hannibal have his luck as it comes to him."

"You seem to forget, sir, that I still bear the name of gentleman!" said the judge.

Mahaffy gave way to acid merriment.

"Well, see that you are not tempted to forget that," he observed.

"If I didn't know your sterling qualities, Solomon, and pay homage to 'em, I might be tempted to take offense," said the judge.

"It's like pouring water on a duck's back to talk to you, Price; nothing strikes in."

"On the contrary, I am at all times ready to listen to reason from any quarter, but I've studied this matter in its many-sided aspect. I won't say we might not do better in Memphis, but we must consider the boy. No; if I can find a vacant house in Raleigh, I wouldn't ask a finer spot in which to spend the afternoon of my life."

"Afternoon?" snapped Mahaffy irritably.

"That's right - carp - ! But you can't relegate me! You can't shove me away from the portal of hope - metaphorically speaking, I'm on the stoop; it may be God's pleasure that I enter; there's a place for gray heads - and there's a respectable slice of life after the meridian is passed."

"Humph!" said Mahaffy.

"I've made my impression; I've been thrown with cultivated minds quick to recognize superiority; I've met with deference and consideration."

"Aren't you forgetting the boy?" inquired Mahaffy. "No, sir! I regard my obligations where he is concerned as a sacred trust to be administered in a lofty and impersonal manner. If his friends - if Miss Malroy, for instance - cares to make me the instrument of her benefactions, I'll not be disposed to stand on my dignity; but his education shall be my care. I'll make such a lawyer of him as America has not seen before! I don't ask you to accept my own opinion of my fitness to do this, but two gentlemen with whom I talked this evening - one of them was the justice of the peace - were pleased to say that they had never heard such illuminating comments on the criminal law. I quoted the Greeks and Romans to 'em, sir; I gave 'em the salient points on mediaeval law; and they were dumfounded and speechless. I reckon they'd never heard such an exposition of fundamental principles; I showed 'em the germ and I showed 'em fruition. Damn it, sir, they were overwhelmed by the array of facts I marshaled for 'em. They said they'd never met with such erudition - no more they had, for I boiled down thirty years of study into ten minutes of talk! I flogged 'em with facts, and then we drank -" The judge smacked his lips. "It is this free-handed hospitality I like; it's this that gives life its gala aspect."

He forgot former experiences; but without this kindly refusal of memory to perform its wonted functions, the world would have been a chill place indeed for Slocum Price. But Mahaffy, keen and anxious, with doubt in every glass he drained, a lurking devil to grin at him above the rim, could see only the end of their brief hour of welcome. This made the present moment as bitter as the last.

"I have a theory, Solomon, that I shall be handsomely supported by my new friends. They'll snatch at the opportunity."

"I see 'em snatching, Mr. Price," said Mahaffy grimly.

"That's right - go on and plant doubt in my heart if you can! You're as hopeless as the grave side!" cried the judge, a spasm of rage shaking him.

"The thing for us to do - you and I, Price - is to clear out of here," said Mahaffy,

"But what of the boy?"

"Leave him with his friends."

"How do you know Miss Malroy would be willing to assume his care? It's scandalous the way you leap at conclusions. No, Solomon, no - I won't shirk a single irksome responsibility," and the judge's voice shook with suppressed emotion. Mahaffy laughed. "There you go again, Solomon, with that indecent mirth of yours! Friendship aside, you grow more offensive every day." The judge paused and then resumed. "I understand there's a federal judgeship vacant here. The president -" Mr. Mahafly gave him a furtive leer. "I tell you General Jackson was my friend - we were brothers, sir - I stood at his side on the glorious blood-wet field of New Orleans! You don't believe me "

"Price, you've made more demands on my stock of credulity than any man I've ever known!"

The judge became somber-faced.

"Unparalleled misfortune overtook me - I stepped aside, but the world never waits; I was a cog discarded from the mechanism of society -" He was so pleased with the metaphor that he repeated it.

"Look here, Price, you talk as though you were a modern job; what's the matter anyhow? - have you got boils?"

The judge froze into stony silence. Well, Mahaffy could sneer - he would show him! This was the last ditch and he proposed to descend into it, it was something to be able to demand the final word of fate - but he instantly recalled that he had been playing at hide-and-seek with inevitable consequences for something like a quarter of a century; it had been a triumph merely to exist. Mahaffy having eased his conscience, rolled over and promptly went to sleep. Flat on his back, the judge stared up at the wide blue arch of the heavens and rehearsed those promises which in the last twenty years he had made and broken times without number. He planned no sweeping reforms, his system of morality being little more than a series of graceful compromises with himself. He must not get hopelessly in debt; he must not get helplessly drunk. Dealing candidly with his own soul in the silence, he presently came to the belief that this might be done without special hardship. Then suddenly the rusted name-plate on Hannibal's old rifle danced again before his burning eyes, and a bitter sense of hurt and loss struck through him. He saw himself as he was, a shabby outcast, a tavern hanger-on, the utter travesty of all he should have been; he dropped his arm across his face.

The first rift of light in the sky found the judge stirring; it found him in his usual cheerful frame of mind. He disposed of his toilet and breakfast with the greatest expedition.

"Will you stroll into town with me, Solomon?" he asked, when they had eaten. Mahaffy shook his head, his air was still plainly hostile. "Then let your prayers follow me, for I'm off!" said the judge.

Ten minutes' walk brought him to the door of the city tavern, where he found Mr. Pegloe directing the activities of a small colored boy who was mopping out his bar. To him the judge made known his needs.

"Goin' to locate, are you?" said Mr. Pegloe.

"My friends urge it, sir, and I have taken the matter under

consideration," answered the judge.

"Sho, do you know any folks hereabouts?" asked Mr. Pegloe.

"Not many," said the judge, with reserve.

"Well, the only empty house in town is right over yonder; it belongs to young Charley Norton out at Thicket Point Plantation."

Ah-h!" said the judge.

The house Mr. Pegloe had pointed out was a small frame building; it stood directly on the street, with a narrow porch across the front, and a shed addition at the back. The judge scuttled over to it. With his hands clasped under the tails of his coat he walked twice about the building, stopping to peer in at all the windows, then he paused and took stock of his surroundings. Over the way was Pegloe's City Tavern; farther up the street was the court-house, a square wooden box with a crib that housed a cracked bell, rising from a gable end. The judge's pulse quickened. What a location, and what a fortunate chance that Mr. Norton was the owner of this most desirable tenement

He must see him at once. As he turned away to recross the street and learn from Mr. Pegloe by what road Thicket Point might be reached, Norton himself galloped into the village. Catching sight of the judge, he reined in. his horse and swung himself from the saddle.

"I was hoping, sir, I might find you," he said, as they met before the tavern.

"A wish I should have echoed had I been aware of it!" responded the judge. "I was about to do myself the honor to wait upon you at your plantation."

"Then I have saved you a long walk," said Norton. He

surveyed the judge rather dubiously, but listened with great civility and kindness as he explained the business that would have taken him to Thicket Point.

"The house is quite at your service, sir," he said, at length.

"The rent -" began the judge. He had great natural delicacy always in mentioning matters of a financial nature.

But Mr. Norton, with a delicacy equal to his own, entreated him not to mention the rent. The house had come to him as boot in a trade. It had been occupied by a doctor and a lawyer; these gentlemen had each decamped between two days, heavily in debt at the stores and taverns, especially the taverns.

"I can't honestly say they owed me, since I never expected to get anything out of them; however, they both left some furniture, all that was necessary for the kind of housekeeping they did, for they were single gentlemen and drew the bulk of their nourishment from Pegloe's bar. I'll turn the establishment over to you with the greatest pleasure in the world, and wish you better luck than your predecessors had - you'll offend me if you refer to the rent again!"

And thus handsomely did Charley Norton acquit himself of the mission he had undertaken at Betty Malroy's request.

That same morning Tom Ware and Captain Murrell were seated in the small detached building at Belle Plain, known as the office, where the former spent most of his time when not in the saddle. Whatever the planter's vices, and he was reputed to possess a fair working knowledge of good and evil, no one had ever charged him with hypocrisy. His emotions lay close to the surface and wrote themselves on his unprepossessing exterior with an impartial touch. He had felt no pleasure when Murrell rode into the yard, and he had welcomed him according to the dictates of his mood, which was one of surly reticence.

"So your sister doesn't like me, Tom - that's on your mind this morning, is it?" Murrell was saying, as he watched his friend out of the corner of his eyes.

"She was mad enough, the way you pushed in on us at Boggs' yesterday. What happened back in North Carolina, Murrell, anyhow?"

"Never you mind what happened."

"Well, it's none of my business, I reckon; she'll have to look out for herself, she's nothing to me but a pest sand a nuisance - I've been more bothered since she came back than I've been in years! I'd give a good deal to be rid of her," said Ware, greatly depressed as he recalled the extraordinary demands Betty had made.

"Make it worth my while and I'll take her off your hands," and Murrell laughed.

Tom favored him with a sullen stare.

"You'd better get rid of that notion - of all fool nonsense, this love business is the worst! I can't see the slightest damn difference between one good looking girl and another. I wish every one was as sensible as I am," he lamented. "I wouldn't miss a meal, or ten minutes' sleep, on account of any woman in creation," and Ware shook his head.

"So your sister doesn't like me?"

"No, she doesn't," said Ware, with simple candor.

"Told you to put a stop to my coming here?"

"Not here - to the house, yes. She doesn't give a damn, so long as she doesn't have to see you."

Murrell, somber-faced and thoughtful, examined a crack in

the flooring.

"I'd like to know what happened back yonder in North Carolina to make her so blazing mad?" continued Ware.

"Well, if you want to know, I told her I loved her."

"That's all right, that's the fool talk girls like to hear," said Ware. He lighted a cigar with an air of wearied patience.

"Open the door, Tom," commanded Murrell.

"It is close in here," agreed the planter.

"It isn't that, but you smoke the meanest cigars I ever smelt, I always think your shoes are on fire. Tom, do you want to get rid of her? Did yot mean that?"

"Oh, shut up," said Tom, dropping his voice to a surly whisper.

There was a brief silence, during which Murrell studied his friend's face. When he spoke, it was to give the conversation a new direction.

"Did she bring the boy here last night? I saw you drive off with him in the carriage."

"Yes, she makes a regular pet of the little ragamuffin - it's perfectly sickening!"

"Who were the two men with him?"

"One of 'em calls himself judge Price; the other kept out of the way, I didn't hear his name."

"Is the boy going to stay at Belle Plain?" inquired Murrell.

"That notion hasn't struck her yet, for I heard her say at

breakfast that she'd take him to Raleigh this afternoon."

"That's the boy I traveled all the way to North Carolina to get for Fentress. I thought I had him once, but the little cuss gave me the slip."

"Eh - you don't say?" cried Ware.

"Tom, what do you know about the Quintard lands; what do you know about Quintard himself?" continued Murrell.

"He was a rich planter, lived in North Carolina. My father met him when he was in congress and got him to invest in land here. They had some colonization scheme on foot this was upward of twenty years ago - but nothing came of it. Ouintard lost interest."

"And the land?"

"Oh, he held on to that."

"Is there much of it?"

"A hundred thousand acres," said Ware.

Murrell whistled softly under his breath.

"What's it worth?"

"A pot of money, two or three dollars an acre anyhow," answered Ware.

"Quintard has been dead two years, Tom, and back yonder in North Carolina they told me he left nothing but the home plantation. The boy lived there up to the time of Quintard's death, but what relation he was to the old man no one knew. What do you suppose Fentress wants with him? He offered me five thousand dollars if I'd bring him West; and he still wants him, only he's lying low now to see what comes of the two old sots - he don't want to move in the dark. Offhand, Tom, I'd say that by getting hold of the boy Fentress expects to get hold of the Quintard land."

"That's likely," said Ware, then struck by a sudden idea, he added, "Are you going to take all the risks and let him pocket the cash? If it's the land he's after, the stake's big enough to divide."

"He can have the whole thing and welcome, I'm playing for a bigger stake." His friend stared at him in astonishment. "I tell you, Tom, I'm bent on getting even with the world! No silver spoon came in the way of my mouth when I was a youngster; my father was too honest - and I think the less of him for it!"

Mr. Ware seemed on the whole edified by the captain's unorthodox point of view.

"My mother was the true grit though; she came of mountain stock, and taught us children to steal by the time we could think! Whatever we stole, she hid, and dared my father to touch us. I remember the first thing of account was when I was ten years old. A Dutch peddler came to our cabin one winter night and begged us to take him in. Of course, he opened his pack before he left, and almost under his nose I got away with a bolt of linen. The old man and woman fought about it, but if the peddler discovered his loss he had the sense not to come back and tell of it! When I was seventeen I left home with three good horses I'd picked up; they brought me more money than I'd ever seen before and I got my first taste of life - that was in Nashville where I made some good friends with whose help I soon had as pretty a trade organized in horseflesh as any one could wish." A somber tone had crept into Murrell's voice, while his glance had become restless and uneasy. He went on: "I'm licking a speculation into shape that will cause me to be remembered while there's a white man alive in the Mississippi Valley!" His wicked black eyes were blazing coals of fire in their deep sockets. "Have you heard what the niggers did at Hayti?"

"My God, John - no, I won't talk to you - and don't you think about it! That's wrong - wrong as hell itself!" cried Ware.

"There's no such thing as right and wrong for me. That'll do for those who have something to lose. I was born with empty hands and I am going to fill them where and how I can. I believe the time has come when the niggers can be of use to me - look what Turner did back in Virginia three years ago! If he'd had any real purpose he could have laid the country waste, but he hadn't brains enough to engineer a general uprising."

Ware was probably as remote from any emotion that even vaguely approximated right feeling as any man could well be, but Murrell's words jarred his dull conscience, or his fear, into giving signs of life.

"Don't you talk of that business, we want nothing of that sort out here. You let the niggers alone!" he said, but he could scarcely bring himself to believe that Murrell had spoken in earnest. Yet even if he jested, this was a forbidden subject.

"White brains will have to think for them, if it's to be more than a flash in the pan," said Murrell unheeding him.

"You let the niggers alone, don't you tamper with them," said Ware. He possessed a profound belief in Murrell's capacity. He knew how the latter had shaped the uneasy population that foregathered on the edge of civilization to his own ends, and that what he had christened the Clan had become an elaborate organization, disciplined and flexible to his ruthless will.

"Look here, what do you think I have been working for - to steal a few niggers?"

"A few - you've been sending 'em south by the boatload! You ought to be a rich man, Murrell. If you're not it's your own fault."

"That furnishes us with money, but you can push the trade too hard and too far, and we've about done that. The planters are uneasy in the sections we've worked over, there's talk of getting together to clean out everybody who can't give a good account of himself. The Clan's got to deal a counter blow or go out of business. It was so with the horse trade; in the end it became mighty unhandy to move the stock we'd collected. We've reached the same point now with the trade in niggers. Between here and the gulf -" he made a wide sweeping gesture with his arm. "I am spotting the country with my men; there are two thousand active workers on the rolls of the Clan, and as many more like you, Tom - and Fentress - on whose friendship I can rely." He leaned toward Ware. "You'd be slow to tell me I couldn't count on you, Tom, and you'd be slow to think I couldn't manage this thing when the time's ripe for it!"

But no trace of this all-sufficient sense of confidence, of which he seemed so certain, showed on Ware's hardened visage. He spat away the stump of his cigar.

"Sure as God, John Murrell, you are overreaching yourself! Your white men are all right, they've got to stick by you; if they don't they know it's only a question of time until they get a knife driven into their ribs - but niggers - there isn't any real fight in a nigger, if there was they wouldn't be here."

"Yet you couldn't have made the whites in Hayti believe that," said Murrell, with a sinister smile.

"Because they were no-account trash themselves!" returned Ware, shaking his head. "We'll all go down in this muss you're fixing for!" he added.

"No, you won't, Tom. I'll look out for my friends. You'll be warned in time."

"A hell of a lot of good a warning will do!" growled Ware.

"The business will be engineered so that you, and those like you, will not be disturbed. Maybe the niggers will have control of the country for a day or two in the thickly settled parts near the towns; longer, of course, where the towns and plantations are scattering. The end will come in the swamps and cane-brakes, and the members of the Clan who don't get rich while the trouble is at its worst, will have to stay poor. As for the niggers, I expect nothing else than that they will be pretty well exterminated. But look what that will do for men like yourself, Tom, who will have been able to hold on to their slaves!"

"I'd like to have some guarantee that I'd be able to; do that! No, sir, the devils will all go whooping off to raise hell." Ware shivered at the picture his mind had conjured up. "Well, thank God, they're not my niggers!" he added.

"You'd better come with me, Tom," said Murrell.

"With you?"

"Yes, I'm going to keep New Orleans for myself; that's a plum I'm going to pick with the help of a few friends, and I'd cheerfully hang for it afterward if I could destroy the city Old Hickory saved - but I expect to quit the country in good time; with a river full of ships I shan't lack for means of escape." His manner was cool and decided. He possessed in an eminent degree the egotism that makes possible great crimes and great criminals, and his degenerate brain dealt with this colossal horror as simply as if it had been a petty theft.

"There's no use in trying to talk you out of this, John, but I just want to ask you one thing: you do all you say you are going to do, and then where in hell's name will you be safe?"

"I'll take my chances. What have I been taking all my life but the biggest sort of chances? - and for little enough!"

Ware, feeling the entire uselessness of argument, uttered a string of imprecations, and then fell silent. His acquaintance with Murrell was of long standing. It dated back to the time when he was growing into the management of Belle Plain. A chance meeting with the outlaw in Memphis had developed into the closest intimacy, and the plantation had become one of the regular stations for the band of horse-thieves of which Murrell had spoken. But time had wrought its changes. Tom was now in full control of Belle Plain and its resources, and he had little heart for such risks as he had once taken.

"Well, how about the girl, Tom?" asked Murrell at length, in a low even tone.

"The girl? Oh, Betty, you mean?" said Ware, and shifted uneasily in his seat. "Haven't you got enough on your hands without worrying about her? She don't like you, haven't I told you that? Think of some one else for a spell, and you'll find it answers," he urged.

"What do you think is going to happen here if I take your advice? She'll marry one of these young bloods!" Ware's lips twitched. "And then, Tom, you'll get your orders to move out, while her husband takes over the management of her affairs. What have you put by anyhow? - enough to stock another place?"

"Nothing, not a damn cent!" said Ware. Murrell laughed incredulously. "It's so! I've turned it all over - more lands, more niggers, bigger crops each year. Another man might have saved his little spec, but I couldn't; I reckon I never believed it would go to her, and I've managed Belle Plain as if I were running it for myself." He seemed to writhe as if undergoing some acute bodily pain.

"And you are in a fair way to turn it all over to her husband when she marries, and step out of here a beggar, unless -"

"It isn't right, John! I haven't had pay for my ability! Why, the place would have gone down to nothing with any management but mine!"

"If she were to die, you'd inherit?"

Ware laughed harshly.

"She looks like dying, doesn't she?"

"Listen to me, Tom. I'll take her away, and Belle Plain is yours
- land, stock and niggers!" said Murrell quietly.

Ware shifted and twisted in his seat.

"It can't be done. I can advise and urge: but I can't command.
She's got her friends, those people back yonder in North
Carolina, and if I made things uncomfortable for her here
she'd go to them and I couldn't stop her. You don't seem to
get it through your head that she's got no earthly use for you!"

Murrell favored him with a contemptuous glance.

"You're like every one else! Certain things you'll do, and
certain other things you won't even try to do - your conscience
or your fear gets in your way."

"Call it what you like."

"I offer to take the girl off your hands; when I quit the country
she shall go with me -"

"And I'd be left here to explain what had become of her!" cried
Ware, in a panic.

"You won't have anything to explain. She'll have disappeared,
that will be all you'll know," said Murrell quietly.

"She'll never marry you."

"Don't you be too sure of that. She may be glad enough to in
the end."

"Oh, you think you are a hell of a fellow with women! Well,
maybe you are with one sort - but what do you know about

her kind?" jeered the planter.

Murrell's brow darkened.

"I'll manage her," he said briefly.

"You were of some account until this took hold of you," complained Ware.

"What do you say? One would hardly think I was offering to make you a present of the best plantation in west Tennessee!" said Murrell.

Ware seemed to suck in hope through his shut teeth.

"I don't want to know anything about this, you are going to swamp yourself yet - you're fixing to get yourself strung up - yes, by thunder, that'll be your finish!"

"Do you want the land and the niggers? I reckon you'll have to take them whether you want them or not, for I'm going to have the girl."

CHAPTER XVII

BOB YANCY FINDS HIMSELF

Mr. Yancy awoke from a long dreamless sleep; heavy-lidded, his eyes slid open. For a moment he struggled with the odds and ends of memory, then he recalled the fight at the tavern, the sudden murderous attack, the fierce blows Slosson had dealt him, the knife thrust which had ended the struggle. Therefore, the bandages that now swathed his head and shoulders; therefore, the need that he should be up and doing - for where was Hannibal?

He sought to lift himself on his elbow, but the effort sent shafts of pain through him; his head seemed of vast size and endowed with a weight he could not support. He sank back groaning, and closed his eyes. After a little interval he opened them again and stared about him. There was the breath of dawn in the air; he heard a rooster crow, and the contented grunting of a pig close at hand. He was resting under a rude shelter of poles and bark. Presently he became aware of a slow gliding movement, and the silvery ripple of water. Clearly he was no longer at the tavern, and clearly some one had taken the trouble to bandage his hurts.

At length his eyes rolling from side to side focused themselves on a low opening near the foot of his shakedown bed. Beyond this opening, and at some little distance, he saw a sunbonneted woman of a plump and comfortable presence. She was leaning against a tub which rested on a rude bench. At her back was another bark shanty similar to the one that sheltered himself, while on either hand a shoreless expanse of water danced and sparkled under the rays of the newly risen sun. As his eyes slowly took in the scene, Yancy's astonishment mounted higher and higher. The lady's sunbonnet quite hid her face, but he saw that she was smoking a cob-pipe.

He was still staring at her, when the lank figure of a man emerged from the other shanty. This man wore a cotton shirt and patched butternut trousers; he way hatless and shoeless, and his hair stood out from his head in a great flaming shock. He, too, was smoking a cob-pipe. Suddenly the man put out a long arm which found its way about the lady's waist, an attention that culminated in a vigorous embrace. Then releasing her, he squared his shoulders, took a long breath, beat his chest with the flat of his hands and uttered a cheerful whoop. The embrace, the deep breath, and the whoop constituted Mr. Cavendish's morning devotions, and were expressive of a spirit of thankfulness to the risen sun, his general satisfaction with the course of Providence, and his homage to the lady of his choice.

Swinging about on his heel, Cavendish passed beyond Yancy's range of vision. Again the latter attempted to lift himself on his elbow, but sky and water changed places before his eyes and he dropped down on his pillow with a stifled sigh. He seemed to be slipping back into the black night from which he had just emerged. Again he was at Scratch Hill, again Dave Blount was seeking to steal his nevvy - incidents of the trial and flight recurred to him - all was confused, feverish, without sequence.

Suddenly a shadow fell obliquely across the foot of his narrow bed, and Cavendish, bending his long body somewhat, thrust his head in at the opening. He found himself looking into a pair of eyes that for the first time in many a long day held the light of consciousness.

"How are you, stranger?" he demanded, in a soft drawl.

"Where am I?" the words were a whisper on Yancy's bearded lips.

"Well, sir, you are in the Tennessee River fo' certain; my wife will make admiration when she hears you speak. Polly! you jest step here."

But Polly had heard Cavendish speak, and the murmur of Yancy's voice in reply. Now her head appeared beside her husband's, and Yancy saw that she was rosy and smiling, and that her claim to good looks was something that could not well be denied.

"La, you are some better, ain't you, sir?" she cried, smiling down on him

"How did I get here, and where's my nevvy ?" questioned Yancy anxiously.

"There now, you ain't in no condition fo' to pester yo'self with worry. You was fished up out of the Elk River by Mr. Cavendish," Polly explained, still smiling and dimpling at him.

"When, ma'am - last night?"

"You got another guess coming to you, stranger!" It was Cavendish who spoke.

"Do you mean, sir, that I been unconscious for a spell?" suggested Yancy rather fearfully, glancing from one to the other.

"It's been right smart of a spell, too; yes, sir, you've laid like you was dead, and not fo' a matter of hours either - but days."

"How long?"

"Well, nigh on to three weeks."

They saw Yancy's eyes widen with a look of dumb horror.

"Three weeks!" he at length repeated, and groaned miserably. He was thinking of Hannibal.

"You was mighty droll to look at when I fished you up out of the river," continued Mr. Cavendish. "You'd been cut and beat up scandalous!"

"And you don't know nothing about my nevvy? - you ain't seen or heard of him, ma'am?" faltered Yancy, and glanced up into Polly's comely face.

Polly shook her head regretfully.

"How come you in the river?" asked Cavendish.

"I reckon I was throwed in. It was a man named Murrell and another man named Slosson. They tried fo' to murder me - they wanted to get my nevvy - I 'low they done it!" and Yancy groaned again.

"You'll get him back," said Polly soothingly.

"Could you-all put me asho'?" inquired Yancy, with sudden eagerness.

"We could, but we won't," said Cavendish, in no uncertain tone.

"Why, la! - you'd perish!" exclaimed Polly.

"Are we far from where you-all picked me up?"

Cavendish nodded. He did not like to tell Yancy the distance they had traversed.

"Where are you-all taking me?" asked Yancy.

"Well, stranger, that's a question I can't answer offhand. The Tennessee are a twister; mebby it will be Kentucky; mebby it will be Illinoy, and mebby it will be down yonder on the Mississippi. My tribe like this way of moving about, and it certainly favors a body's legs."

"How old was your nevvy?" inquired Polly, reading the troubled look in Yancy's gray eyes.

"Ten or thereabouts, ma'am. He were a heap of comfort to me" and the whisper on Yancy's lips was wonderfully tender and wistful.

"Just the age of my Richard," said Polly, her glance full of compassion and pity.

Mr. Cavendish essayed to speak, but was forced to pause and clear his throat. The allusion to Richard in this connection having been almost more than he could endure with equanimity. When he was able to put his thoughts into words, he said:

"I shore am distressed fo' you. I tried to leave you back yonder where I found you, but no one knowed you and you looked so near dead folks wouldn't have it. What parts do you come from?"

"No'th Carolina. Me and my nevvy was a-goin' into west Tennessee to a place called Belle Plain, somewhere near Memphis. We have friends there," explained Yancy.

"That settles it!" cried Cavendish. "It won't be Kentucky, and it won't be Illinoy; I'll put you asho' at Memphis; mebby you'll find yo' nevvy there after all."

"That's the best. You lay still and get yo' strength back as fast as you can, and try not to worry - do now." Polly"s voice was soft and wheedling.

"I reckon I been a heap of bother to you-all," said Yancy.

"La, no," Polly assured him; "you ain't been."

And now the six little Cavendishes appeared on the scene. The pore gentleman had come to - sho! He had got his senses back - sho! he wa'n't goin' to die after all; he could talk. Sho! A body could hear him plain! Excited beyond measure they scurried about in their fluttering rags of nightgowns for a sight and hearing of the pore gentleman. They struggled madly to climb over their parents, and failing this - under them. But the opening that served as a door to the shanty being small, and being as it was completely stoppered by their father and mother who were in no mood to yield an inch, they distributed themselves in quest of convenient holes in the bark edifice through which to peer at the pore gentleman. And since the number of youthful Cavendishes exceeded the number of such holes, the sound of lamentation and recrimination presently filled the morning air.

"I kin see the soles of his feet!" shrieked Keppel with passionate intensity, his small bleached eye glued to a crack.

He was instantly ravished of the sight by Henry.

"You mean hateful thing! - just because you're bigger than Kep!" and Constance fell on the spoiler. As her mother's right-hand man she had cuffed and slapped her way to a place of power among the little brothers.

Mr. Cavendish appeared to allay hostilities.

"I 'low I'll skin you if you don't keep still! Dress! - the whole kit and b'ilin' of you!" he roared, and his manner was quite as ferocious as his words.

But the six little Cavendishes were impressed by neither. They instantly fastened on him like so many leeches. What was the pore gentleman saying? - why couldn't they hear, too? Then they'd keep still, sure they would! Did he say he knowed who throwed him in the river?

"I wonder, Connie, you ain't able to do more with these here children. Seems like you ought to - a great big girl like you," said Mr. Cavendish, reduced to despair.

"It was Henry pickin' on Kep," cried Constance.

"I found a crack and he took it away from me! drug me off by the legs, he did, and filled my stomach full of slivers!" wailed Keppel, suddenly remembering he had a grievance. "You had ought to let me see the pore gentleman!" he added ingratiatingly.

"Well, ain't you been seein' him every day fo' risin' two weeks and upwards? - ain't you sat by him hours at a stretch?" demanded Mr. Cavendish fiercely.

Sho - that didn't count, he only kept a mutterin' - sho! - arollin' his head sideways, sho! And their six tow heads were rolled to illustrate their meaning. And a-pluckin' at a body's hands! - and they plucked at Mr. Cavendish's hands. Sho - did he say why he done that?

"If you-all will quit yo' noise and dress, you-all kin presently set by the pore gentleman. If you don't, I'll have to speak to yo' mother; I 'low she'll trim you! I reckon you-all don't want me to call her? No, by thunderation! - because you-all know she won't stand no nonsense! She'll fan you; she'll take the flat of her hand to you-all and make you skip some; I reckon I'd get into my pants befo' she starts on the warpath. I wouldn't give her no such special opportunity as you're offerin'!" Mr. Cavendish's voice and manner had become entirely confidential and sympathetic, and though fear of their mother could not be said to bulk high on their horizon, yet the small Cavendishes were persuaded by sheer force of his logic to withdraw and dress. Their father hurried back to Yancy.

"I was just thinkin', sir," he said, "that if it would be any comfort to you, we'll tie up to the bank right here and wait until you can travel. I'm powerfully annoyed at having fetched you all this way!"

But Yancy shook his head.

"I'll be glad to go on to Memphis with you. If my nevvy got away from Murrell, that's where I'll find him. I reckon folks will be kind to him and sort of help him along. Why, he ain't much mo' than knee high!"

"Shore they will! there's a lot of good in the world, so don't you fret none about him!" cried Polly.

"I can't do much else, ma'am, than think of him bein' lonesome and hungry, maybe - and terribly frightened. What do you-all suppose he thought when he woke up and found me gone?" But neither Polly nor her husband had any opinion to venture on this point. "If I don't find him in Memphis I'll take the back track to No'th Carolina, stoppin' on the way to see that man Slosson."

"Well, I 'low there's a fit comin' to him when he gets sight of you!" and Cavendish's bleached blue eyes sparkled at the thought.

"There's a heap mo' than a fit. I don't bear malice, but I stay mad a long time," answered Yancy grimly:

"You shouldn't talk no mo'," said Polly. "You must just lay quiet and get yo' strength back. Now, I'm goin' to fix you a good meal of vittles." She motioned Cavendish to follow her, and they both withdrew from the shanty.

Yancy closed his eyes, and presently, lulled by the soft ripple that bore them company, fell into a restful sleep.

"When he told us of his nevvy, Dick, and I got to thinkin' of his bein' just the age of our Richard, I declare it seemed like something got in my throat and I'd choke. Do you reckon he'll ever find him?" said Polly, as she busied herself with preparations for their breakfast.

"I hope so, Polly!" said Cavendish, but her words were a powerful assault on his feelings, which at all times lay close to the surface and were easily stirred.

Under stress of his emotions, he now enjoined silence on his family, fortifying the injunction with dire threats as to the consequences that would descend with lightning - like suddenness on the head of the unlucky sinner who forgot and raised his voice above a whisper. Then he despatched a chicken; sure sign that he and Polly considered their guest had reached the first stage of convalescence.

CHAPTER XVIII

AN ORPHAN MAN OF TITLE

The raft drifted on into the day's heat; and when at last Yancy awoke, it was to find Henry and Keppel seated beside him, each solacing him with a small moist hand, while they regarded him out of the serious unblinking eyes of childhood.

"Howdy!" said he, smiling up at them.

"Howdy!" they answered, a sociable grin puckering their freckled faces.

"Do you find yo'self pretty well, sir?" inquired Keppel.

"I find myself pretty weak," replied Yancy.

"Me and Kep has been watching fo' to keep the flies from stinging you," explained Henry.

"We-all takes turns doin' that," Keppel added.

"Well, and how many of you-all are there?" asked Yancy.

"There's six of we-uns and the baby."

They covertly examined this big bearded man who had lost his nevvy, and almost his life. They had overheard their father and mother discuss his plans and knew when he was recovered from his wounds if he did not speedily meet up with his nevvy at a place called Memphis, he was going back to Lincoln County, which was near where they came from, to have the hide off a gentleman of the name of Slosson. They imagined the gentleman named Slosson would find the operation excessively disagreeable; and that Yancy should be recuperating for so unique an enterprise invested him with a romantic interest. Henry squirmed closer to the recumbent figure on the bed.

"Me and Kep would like mighty well to know how you-all are goin' to strip the hide offen to that gentleman's back," he observed.

Yancy instantly surmised that the reference was to Slosson.

"I reckon I'll feel obliged to just naturally skin him," he explained.

"Sho', will he let you do that?" they demanded.

"He won't be consulted none. And his hide will come off easy once I get hold of him by the scruff of the neck." Yancy's speech was gentle and his lips smiling, but he meant a fair share of what he said.

"Sho', is that the way you do it?" And round-eyed they gazed down on this fascinating stranger.

"I may have to touch him up with a tickler," continued Yancy, who did not wish to prove disappointing. "I reckon you-all know what a tickler is?"

They nodded.

"What if Mr. Slosson totes a tickler, too?" asked Keppel insinuatingly. This opened an inviting field for conjecture.

"That won't make no manner of difference. Why? Because it's

a powerful drawback fo' a man to know he's in the wrong, just as it's a heap in yo' favor to know you're in the right."

"My father's got a tickler; I seen it often," vouchsafed Henry.

"It's a foot long, with a buck horn handle. Gee whiz! - he keeps it keen; but he never uses it on no humans," said Keppel.

"Of course he don't; he's a high-spirited, right-actin' gentleman. But what do you reckon he'd feel obliged to do if a body stole one of you-all?" inquired Yancy.

"Whoop! He'd carve 'em deep!" cried Keppel.

At this moment Mrs. Cavendish appeared, bringing Yancy's breakfast. In her wake came Connie with the baby, and the three little brothers who were to be accorded the cherished privilege of seeing the poor gentleman eat.

"You got a nice little family, ma'am," said Yancy.

"Well, I reckon nobody complains mo' about their children than me, but I reckon nobody gets mo' comfort out of their children either. I hope you-all are a-goin' to be able to eat, you ain't had much nourishment. La, does yo' shoulder pain you like that? Want I should feed you?"

"I am sorry, ma'am, but I reckon you'll have to," Yancy spoke regretfully. "I expect I been a passel of bother to you."

"No, you ain't. Here's Dick to see how you make out with the chicken," Polly added, as Cavendish presented himself at the opening that did duty as a door.

"This looks like bein' alive, stranger," he commented genially. He surveyed the group of which Yancy was the center. "If them children gets too numerous, just throw 'em out."

"You-all ain't told me yo' name yet?" said Yancy.

"It's Cavendish. Richard Keppel Cavendish, to get it all off my mind at a mouthful. And this lady's Mrs. Cavendish."

"My name's Yancy - Bob Yancy."

Mr. Cavendish exchanged glances with Mrs. Cavendish. By a nod of her dimpled chin the lady seemed to urge some more extended confidence on his part. Chills and Fever seated himself at the foot of Yancy's bed.

"Stranger, what I'm a-goin' to tell you, you'll take as bein' said man to man," he began, with the impressive air of one who had a secret of great moment to impart; and Yancy hastened to assure him that whatever passed between them, his lips should be sealed. "It ain't really that, but I don't wish to appear proud afo' no man's, eyes. First, I want to ask you, did you ever hear tell of titles?"

Polly and the children hung breathlessly on Mr. Yancy's reply.

"I certainly have," he rejoined promptly. "Back in No'th Carolina we went by the chimneys."

"Chimneys? What's chimneys got to do with titles, Mr. Yancy?" asked Polly, while her husband appeared profoundly mystified.

"A whole lot, ma'am. If a man had two chimneys to his house we always called him Colonel, if there was four chimneys we called him General."

"La!" cried Polly, smiling and showing a number of new dimples. "Dick don't mean militia titles, Mr. Yancy."

"Them's the only ones I know anything of," confessed Yancy.

"Ever hear tell of lords?" inquired Chills and Fever, tilting his head on one side.

"No." And Yancy was quick to notice the look of disappointment on the faces of his new friends. He felt that for some reason, which was by no means clear to him, he had lost caste.

"Are you ever heard of royalty?" and Cavendish fixed the invalid's wandering glance.

"You mean kings?"

"I shore do."

Yancy regarded him reflectively and made a mighty mental effort.

"There's them Bible kings -" he ventured at length.

Mr. Cavendish shook his head.

"Them's sacred kings. Are you familiar with any of the profane kings, Mr. Yancy?"

"Well, taking them as they come, them Bible kings seemed to average pretty profane." Yancy was disposed to defend this point.

"You must a heard of the kings of England. Sho', wa'n't any of yo' folks in the war agin' him?"

"I'd plumb forgot, why my daddy fit all through that war!" exclaimed Yancy. The Cavendishes were immensely relieved. Polly beamed on the invalid, and the children hunched closer. Six pairs of eager lips were trembling on the verge of speech.

"Now you-all keep still," said Cavendish. "I want Mr. Yancy should get the straight of this here! The various orders of royalty are kings, dukes, earls and lords. Earls is the third from the top of the heap, but lords ain't no slouch; it's a right neat little title, and them that has it can turn round in most any company."

"Dick had ought to know, fo' he's an earl himself," cried Polly exultantly, unable to restrain herself any longer, while a mutter came from the six little Cavendishes who had been wonderfully silent for them.

"Sho', Richard Keppel Cavendish, Earl of Lambeth! 'Sho', that was what he was! Sho'!" and some transient feeling of awe stamped itself upon their small faces as they viewed the long and limber figure of their parent.

"Is that mo' than a Colonel?" Yancy risked the question hesitatingly, but he felt that speech was expected from him.

"Yes," said the possessor of the title.

"Would a General lay it over you any?"

"No, sir, he wouldn't."

Yancy gazed respectfully but uncertainly at Chills and Fever.

"Then all I got to say is that I've traveled considerably, mostly between Scratch Hill and Balaam's Cross Roads, meeting with all kinds of folks; but I never seen an earl afo. I take it they are some scarce."

"They are. I don't reckon there's another one but me in the whole United States."

"Think of that!" gasped Yancy.

"We ain't nothin' fo' style, it bein' my opinion that where a man's a born gentleman he's got a heap of reason fo' to be grateful but none to brag," said Cavendish.

"Dick's kind of titles are like having red hair and squint eyes. Once they get into a family they stick," explained Polly.

"I've noticed that, 'specially about squint eyes." Yancy was glad to plant his feet on familiar ground.

"These here titles go to the eldest son. He begins by bein' a viscount," continued Chills and Fever. He wished Yancy to know the full measure of their splendor.

"And their wives are ladies-ain't they, Dick?"

Cavendish nodded.

"Anybody with half an eye would know you was a lady, ma'am," said Yancy.

"Kep here is an Honorable, same as a senator or a congressman," Cavendish went on.

"At his age, too!" commented Yancy.

"And my daughter's the Lady Constance," said Polly.

"Havin' such a mother she ain't no choice," observed Yancy, with an air of gentle deference.

"Dick's got the family, Mr. Yancy. My folks, the Rhetts, was plain people."

"Some of 'em ain't so noticeably plain, either," said Yancy.

"Sho', you've a heap of good sense, Mr. Yancy!" and Cavendish shook him warmly by the hand. "The first time I ever seen her, I says, I'll marry that lady if it takes an arm! Well, it did most of the time while I was co'tin' her."

"La!" cried Polly, blushing furiously. "You shouldn't tell that, Dick. Mr. Yancy ain't interested."

"Yes, sir, I'd been hearin' about old man Rhett's Polly fo' considerable of a spell," said Cavendish, looking at Polly reflectively. "He lived up at the head waters of the Elk River. Fellows who had been to his place, when girls was mentioned would sort of shake their heads sad-like and say, 'Yes, but you had ought to see old man Rhett's Polly, all the rest is imitations!' Seemed like they couldn't get her off their minds. So I just slung my kit to my back, shouldered my rifle, and hoofed it up-stream. I says, I'll see for myself where this here paragon lays it all over the rest of her sect, but sho - the closter I came to old man Rhett the mo' I heard of Polly!"

"Dick, how you do run on," cried Polly protestingly, but Chills and Fever's knightly soul dwelt in its illusions, and the years had not made stale his romance. Also Polly was beaming on him with a wealth of affection.

"I seen her fo' the first time as I was warmin' the trail within a mile of old man Rhett's. She was carrying a grist of co'n down to the mill in her father's ox cart. When I clapped eyes on her I says, 'I'll marry that lady. I'll make her the Countess of Lambeth - she'll shore do fo' the peerage any day!' That was yo' mommy, sneezic's!" Mr. Cavendish paused to address himself to the baby whom Connie had relinquished to him.

"You bet I made time the rest of the way. I says, 'She's sixteen if she's a day, and all looks!' I broke into old man Rhett's clearin' on a keen run. He was a settin' afo' his do' smokin' his pipe and he glanced me over kind of weary-like and says, 'Howdy!' It wa'n't much of a greetin' the way he said it either; but I figured it was some better than bein' chased off the place. So I stepped indo's, stood my rifle in a corner and hung up my cap. He was watchin' me and presently he drawled out, 'Make yo'self perfectly at home, stranger.'

"I says, 'Squire' - he wa'n't a squire, but they called him that - I says, 'Squire, my name's Cavendish. Let's get acquainted quick. I'm here fo' to co'te yo' Polly. I seen her on the road a spell back and I couldn't be better suited.'

"He says, 'You had ought to be kivered up in salt, young man, else yo'll spile in this climate.'

"I says, 'I'll keep in any climate.'

'He says, 'Polly ain't givin' her thoughts much to marryin', she's busy keepin' house fo' her pore old father.'

"I says, 'I've come here special fo' to arouse them thoughts you mention. If I seem slow '

"He says, 'You don't. If this is yo' idea of bein' slow, I'd wish to avoid you when you was in a hurry.'

"I says, 'Put in yo' spare moments thinkin' up a suitable blessin' fo' us.'

"He says, 'You'll have yo' hands full. There's a number of young fellows hereabouts that you don't lay it over none in p'int of freshness or looks.'

"I says, 'Does she encourage any of 'em?'

"He says, 'Nope, she don't. Ain't I been tellin' you she's givin' her mind to keepin' house fo' her pore old father?'

"I says, 'If she don't encourage 'em none, she shore must disencourage 'em. I 'low she gets my help in that.'

"He says, 'They'll run you so far into the mountings, Mr. Cavendish, you'll never be heard tell of again in these parts.'

"I says, 'I'll bust the heads offen these here galoots if they try that!'

"He asks, grinnin', 'Have you arranged how yo' remains are to be sent back to yo' folks?'

"I says, 'I'm an orphan man of title, a peer of England, and you can leave me lay if it cones to that.'

"'Well,'. he says, 'if them's yo' wishes, the buzzards as good as got you.'" Cavendish lapsed into a momentary silence. It was plain that these were cherished memories.

"That's what I call co'tin!" remarked Mr. Yancy, with conviction.

The Earl of Lambeth resumed

"It was as bad as old man Rhett said it was. Sundays his do'yard looked like a militia muster. They told it on him that he hadn't cut a stick of wood since Polly was risin' twelve. I reckon, without exaggeration, I fit every unmarried man in that end of the county, and two lookin' widowers from Nashville. I served notice on to them that I'd attend to that woodpile of old man Rhett's fo' the future; that I was qualifying fo' to be his son-in-law, and seekin' his indorsement as a provider. I took 'em on one at a time as they happened along, and lambasted 'em all over the place. As fo' the Nashville widowers," said Cavendish with a chuckle, and a nod to Polly, "I pretty nigh drownded one of 'em in the Elk. We met in mid-stream and fit it out there; and the other quit the county. That was fo'teen years ago; but, mind you, I'd do it all over again to-morrow."

"But, Dick, you ain't telling Mr. Yancy nothin' about yo' title," expostulated Polly.

"I'd admire to hear mo' about that," said Yancy.

"I'm gettin' round to that. It was my great grandfather come over here from England. His name was Richard Keppel Cavendish, same as mine is. He lived back yonder on the Carolina coast and went to raisin' tobacco. I've heard my grandfather tell how he'd heard folks say his father was always hintin' in his licker that he was a heap better than he seemed, and if people only knowed the truth about him they'd respect him mo', and mebby treat him better. Well, sir, he married and riz a family; there was my grandfather and a passel of girls

- and that crop of children was the only decent crop he ever riz. I've heard my grandfather tell how, when he got old enough to notice such things, he seen that his father had the look of a man with something mysterious hangin' over him, but he couldn't make it out what it was, though he gave it a heap of study. He seen, too, that let him get a taste of licker and he'd begin to throw out them hints, how if folks only knowed the truth they'd be just naturally fallin' over themselves fo' to do him a favor, instead of pickin' on him and tryin' to down him.

"My grandfather said he never knowed a man, either, with the same aversion agin labor as his father had. Folks put it down to laziness, but they misjudged him, as come out later, yet he never let on. He just went around sorrowful-like, and when there was a piece of work fo' him to do he'd spend a heap of time studyin' it, or mebby he'd just set and look at it until he was ready fo' to give it up. Appeared like he couldn't bring himself down to toil.

"Then one day he got his hands on a paper that had come acrost in a ship from England. He was readin' it, settin' in the shade; my grandfather said he always noticed he was partial to the shade, and his wife was pesterin' of him fo' to go and plow out his truck-patch, when, all at once, he lit on something in the paper, and he started up and let out a yell like he'd been shot. 'By gum, I'm the Earl of Lambeth!' he says, and took out to the nearest tavern and got b'ilin' full. Afterward he showed 'em the paper and they seen with their own eyes where Richard Keppel Cavendish, Earl of Lambeth, had died in London. My great grandfather told 'em that was his uncle; that when he left home there was several cousins - which was printed in the paper, too - but they'd up and died, so the title naturally come to him.

"Well, sir, that was the first the family ever knowed of it, and then they seen what it was he'd meant when he throwed out them hints about bein' a heap better than he seemed. He said perhaps he wouldn't never have told, only he couldn't bear to be misjudged like he'd always been.

"He never done a lick of work after that. He said he couldn't bring himself down to it; that it was demeanin' fo' a person of title fo' to labor with his hands like a nigger or a common white man. He said he'd leave it to his family to see he didn't come to want, it didn't so much matter about them; and he lived true to his principles to the day of his death, and never riz his hand except to feed himself."

Cavendish paused. Yancy was feeling that in his own person he had experienced some of the best symptoms of a title.

"Then what?" he asked.

"Well, sir, he lived along like that, never complainin', my grandfather said, but mighty sweet and gentlelike as long as there was plenty to eat in the house. He lived to be nigh eighty, and when he seen he was goin' to die he called my grandfather to him and says, 'She's yours, Dick,' - meanin' the title - and then he says, 'There's one thing I've kep' from you. You've been a viscount ever since I come into the title, and then he went on and explained what he wanted cut on his tombstone, and had my grandfather write it out, so there couldn't be any mistake. When he'd passed away, my grandfather took the title. He said it made him feel mighty solemn and grand-like, and it come over him all at once why it was his father hadn't no heart fo' work."

"Does it always take 'em that way?" inquired Yancy.

"It takes the Earls of Lambeth that way. I reckon you might say it was hereditary with 'em. Where was I at?"

"Your grandpap, the second earl," prompted Polly.

"Oh, yes - well, he 'lowed he'd emigrate back to England, but while he was studying how he could do this, along come the war.

He said he couldn't afford to fight agin his king, so he pulled out and crossed the mountings to avoid being drug into the army. He said he couldn't let it get around that the Earls of Lambeth was shootin' English soldiers."

"Of course he couldn't," agreed Yancy.

"It's been my dream to take Polly and the children and go back to England and see the king about my title. I 'low he'd be some surprised to see us. I'd like to tell him, too, what the Earls of Lambeth done fo' him - that they was always loyal, and thought a heap better of him than their neighbors done, and mebby some better than he deserved. Don't you reckon that not hearin' from us, he's got the notion the Cavendishes has petered out?"

Mr. Yancy considered this likely, and said so.

"You might send him writin' in a letter," he suggested.

The furious shrieking of a steam-packet's whistle broke in upon them.

"It's another of them hawgs, wantin' all the river!" said Mr. Cavendish, and fled in haste to the steering oar.

During all the long days that followed, Mr. Yancy was forced to own that these titled friends of his were, despite their social position, uncommon white in their treatment of him. The Earl of Lambeth consorted with him in that fine spirit that recognizes the essential brotherhood of man, while his Lady Countess was, as Yancy observed, on the whole, a person of simple and uncorrupted tastes. She habitually went barefoot, both as a matter of comfort and economy, and she smoked her cob-pipe as did those other ladies of Lincoln County who had married into far less exalted stations than her own. He put these simple survivals down to her native goodness of heart, which would not allow of her succumbing to mere pride and vainglory, for he no more doubted their narrative than they, doubted it themselves, which was not at all.

CHAPTER XIX

THE JUDGE SEES A GHOST

Charley Norton's good offices did not end when he had furnished judge Price with a house, for Betty required of him that he should supply that gentleman with legal business as well. When she pointed out the necessity of this, Norton demurred. He had no very urgent need of a lawyer, and had the need existed, Slocum Price would not have been his choice. Betty knit her brows.

"He must have a chance; perhaps if people knew you employed him it would give them confidence - you must realize this, Charley; it isn't enough that he has a house - he can't wear it nor eat it!"

"And fortunately he can't drink it, either. I don't want to discourage you, but his looks are all against him, Betty. If you take too great an interest in his concerns I am afraid you are going to have him permanently on your hands."

"Haven't you some little scrap of business that really doesn't matter much, Charley? You might try him - just to please me -" she persisted coaxingly.

"Well, there's land I'm buying - I suppose I could get him to look up the title, I know it's all right anyhow," said Norton, after a pause.

Thus it happened that judge Price, before he had been three days in Raleigh, received a civil note from Mr. Norton asking him to search the title to a certain timber tract held by one Joseph Quaid; a communication the effect of which was out of all proportion to the size of the fee involved. The judge, powerfully excited, told Mahaffy he was being understood and appreciated; that the tide of prosperity was clearly setting his way; that intelligent foresight, not chance, had determined him when he selected Raleigh instead of Memphis. Thereafter he spoke of Charley Norton only as "My client," and exalted him for his breeding, wealth and position, refusing to admit that any man in the county was held in quite the same esteem. All of which moved Mahaffy to flashes of grim sarcasm.

The immediate result of Norton's communication had been to send the judge up the street to the courthouse. He would show his client that he could be punctual and painstaking. He should have his abstract of title without delay; moreover, he had in mind a scholarly effort entirely worthy of himself. The dull facts should be illuminated with an occasional striking phrase. He considered that it would doubtless be of interest to Mr. Norton, in this connection, to know something, too, of mediaeval land tenure, ancient Roman and modern English. He proposed artfully to pander to his client's literary tastes - assuming that he had such tastes. But above all, this abstract must be entirely explanatory of himself, since its final purpose was to remove whatever doubts his mere appearance might have bred in Mr. Norton's mind.

"If my pocket could just be brought to stand the strain of new clothes before the next sitting of court, I might reasonably hope for a share of the pickings," thought the judge.

Entering the court-house, he found himself in a narrow hall. On his right was the jury-room, and on his left the county clerk's office, stuffy little holes, each lighted by a single window. Beyond, and occupying the full width of the building, was the court-room, with its hard, wooden benches and its staring white walls. Advancing to the door, which stood open, the judge surveyed the room with the greatest possible satisfaction. He could fancy it echoing to that eloquence of which he felt himself to be the master. He would show the world, yet, what was in him, and especially Solomon Mahaffy, who clearly had not taken his measure.

Turning away from the agreeable picture his mind had conjured up, he entered the county clerk's office. He was already known to this official, whose name was Saul, and he now greeted him with a pleasant air of patronage. Mr. Saul removed his feet from the top of his desk and motioned his visitor to a chair; at the same time he hospitably thrust forward a square box filled with sawdust. It was plain he labored under the impression that the judge's call was of an unprofessional character.

"A little matter of business brings me here, sir," began the judge, with a swelling chest and mellow accents. "No, sir, I'll not be seated - another time I'll share your leisure if I may - now I am in some haste to look up a title for my client, Mr. Norton."

"What Norton?" asked Mr. Saul, when he had somewhat recovered from the effect of this announcement.

"Mr. Charles Norton, of Thicket Point," said the judge.

"I reckon you mean that timber tract of old Joe Quaid's." Mr. Saul viewed the judge's ruinous exterior with a glance of respectful awe, for clearly a man who could triumph over such a handicap must possess uncommon merit of some sort. "So you're looking after Charley Norton's business for him, are you?" he added.

"He's a client of mine. We have mutual friends, sir - I refer to Miss Malroy," the judge vouchsafed to explain.

"You're naming our best people, sir, when you name the Malroys and the Nortons; they are pretty much in a class by themselves," said Mr. Saul, whose awe of the judge was momentarily increasing.

"I don't underestimate the value of a social endorsement, sir, but I've never stood on that," observed the judge. "I've come amongst you unheralded, but I expect you to find me out. Now, sir, if you'll be good enough, I'll glance at the record."

Mr. Saul scrambled up out of the depths of his chair and exerted himself in the judge's behalf.

"This is what you want, sir. Better take the ledger to the window, the light in here ain't much." He drew forward a chair as he spoke, and the judge, seating himself, began to polish his spectacles with great deliberation. He felt that he had reached a crisis in his career, and was disposed to linger over the hope that was springing up in his heart.

"How does the docket for the next term of court stand?" he inquired.

"Pretty fair, sir," said Mr. Saul.

"Any litigation of unusual interest in prospect?" The judge was fitting his glasses to the generous arch of his nose, a feature which nicely indexed its owner's habits.

"No, sir, just the ordinary run of cases."

"I hoped to hear you say different."

"You've set on the bench, sir?" suggested Mr. Saul.

"In one of the eastern counties, but my inclination has never been toward the judiciary. My temperament, sir, is distinctly aggressive - and each one according to the gifts with which God has been graciously pleased to endow him! I am frank to say, however, that my decisions have received their meed of praise from men thoroughly competent to speak on such matters." He was turning the leaves of the ledger as he spoke. Suddenly the movement of his hand was arrested.

"Found it?" asked Mr. Saul. But the judge gave him no answer; absorbed and aloof he was staring down at the open pages of the book. "Found the entry?" repeated Mr. Saul.

"Eh? - what's that? No -" he appeared to hesitate. "Who is this man Quintard?" The question cost him an effort, that was plain.

"He's the owner of a hundred-thousand-acre tract in this and abutting counties," said Mr. Saul.

The judge continued to stare down at the page.

"Is he a resident of the county?" he asked, at length.

"No, he lives back yonder in North Carolina."

"A hundred thousand acres!" the judge muttered thoughtfully.

"There or thereabouts - yes, sir."

"Who has charge of the land?"

"Colonel Fentress; he was old General Ware's law partner. I've heard it was the general who got this man Quintard to make the investment, but that was before my time in these parts."

The judge lapsed into a heavy, brooding silence.

A step sounded in the narrow hall. An instant later the door was pushed open, and grateful for any interruption that would serve to take Mr. Saul's attention from himself, the judge abruptly turned his back on the clerk and began to examine the record before him. Engrossed in this, he was at first scarcely aware of the conversation that was being carried on within a few feet of him. Insensibly, however, the cold, level tones of the voice that was addressing itself to Mr. Saul quickened the beat of his pulse, the throb of his heart, and struck back through the years to a day from which he reckoned time. The heavy, calf-bound volume in his hand shook like a leaf in a gale. He turned slowly, as if in dread of what he might see.

What he saw was a man verging on sixty, lean and dark, with thin, shaven cheeks of a bluish cast above the jaw, and a strongly aquiline profile. Long, black locks swept the collar of his coat, while his tall, spare figure was habited in sleek broadcloth and spotless linen. For a moment the judge seemed to struggle with doubt and uncertainty, then his face went a ghastly white and the book slipped from his nerveless fingers to the window ledge.

The stranger, his business concluded, swung about on his heel and quitted the office. The judge, his eyes starting from their sockets, stared after him; the very breath died on his lips; speechless and motionless, he was still seeing that tall, spare figure as it had passed before him, but his memories stripped a weight of thirty years from those thin shoulders. At last, heavy-eyed and somber, he glanced about him. Mr. Saul, bending above his desk, was making an entry in one of his ledgers. The judge shuffled to his side.

"Who was that man?" he asked thickly, resting a shaking hand on the clerk's arm.

"That? - Oh, that was Colonel Fentress I was just telling you about." He looked up from his writing. "Hello! You look like you'd seen a ghost!"

"It's the heat in here - I reckon -" said the judge, and began to mop his face.

"Ever seen the colonel before?" asked Mr. Saul curiously.

"Who is he?"

"Well, sir, he's one of our leading planters, and a mighty fine lawyer."

"Has he always lived here?"

"No, he came into the county about ten years ago, and bought a place called The Oaks, over toward the river."

"Has he - has he a family?" The judge appeared to be having difficulty with his speech.

"Not that anybody knows of. Some say he's a widower, others again say he's an old bachelor; but he don't say nothing, for the colonel is as close as wax about his own affairs. So it's pure conjecture, sir." There was a brief silence. "The county has its conundrums, and the colonel's one of them," resumed Mr. Saul.

"Yes?" said the judge.

"The colonel's got his friends, to be sure, but he don't mix much with the real quality."

"Why not?" asked the judge.

"He's apparently as high-toned a gentleman as you'd meet with anywhere; polished, sir, so smooth your fingers would slip if you tried to take hold of him, but it's been commented on that when a horsethief or counterfeiter gets into trouble the colonel's always first choice for counsel."

"Get's 'em off, does he?" The judge spoke somewhat grimly.

"Mighty nigh always. But then he has most astonishing luck in the matter of witnesses. That's been commented on too." The judge nodded comprehendingly. "I reckon you'd call Tom Ware, out at Belle Plain, one of Fentress' closest friends. He's another of your conundrums. I wouldn't advise you to be too curious about the colonel."

"Why not?" The judge was frowning now.

"It will make you unpopular with a certain class. Those of us who've been here long enough have learned that there are some of these conundrums we'd best not ask an answer for."

The judge pondered this.

"Do you mean to tell me, sir, that freedom of speech is not allowed?" he demanded, with some show of heat.

"Perfect freedom, if you pick and choose your topic," responded Mr. Saul.

"Humph!" ejaculated the judge.

"Now you might talk to me with all the freedom you like, but I'd recommend you were cautious with strangers. There have been those who've talked freely that have been advised to keep still or harm would come of it."

"And did harm come of it?" asked the judge.

"They always kept still."

"What do you mean by talking freely?"

"Like asking how so and so got the money to buy his last batch of niggers," explained Mr. Saul rather vaguely.

"And Colonel Fentress is one of those about whose affairs it is best not to show too much curiosity?"

"He is, decidedly. His friends appear to set a heap by him. Another of his particular intimates is a gentleman by the name of Murrell."

The judge nodded.

"I've met him," he said briefly. "Does he belong hereabouts?"

"No, hardly; he seems to hold a sort of roving commission. His home is, I believe, near Denmark, in Madison County."

"What's his antecedents?"

"He's as common a white man as ever came out of the hills, but he appears to stand well with Colonel Fentress."

"Colonel Fentress!" The judge spat in sheer disgust.

"You don't appear to fancy the colonel -" said Mr. Saul.

"I don't fancy wearing a gag - and damned if I do!" cried the judge.

"Oh, it ain't that exactly; it's just minding your own business. I reckon you'll find there's lot's to be said in favor of goin' ca'mly on attending strictly to your own affairs, sir," concluded Mr. Saul.

Acting on a sudden impulse, the judge turned to the door. The business and the hope that had brought him there were forgotten. He muttered something about returning later, and hastily quitted the office.

"Well, I reckon he's a conundrum too!" reflected Mr. Saul, as the door swung shut.

In the hall the judge's steps dragged and his head was bowed. He was busy with his memories, memories that spanned the desolate waste of years in which he had walked from shame to shame, each blacker than the last. Then passion shook him.

"Damn him - may God-for ever damn him 1" he cried under his breath, in a fierce whisper. A burning mist before his eyes, he shuffled down the hall, down the steps, and into the shaded, trampled space that was known as the court-house yard. Here he paused irresolutely. Across the way was the gun-maker's shop, the weather-beaten sign came within range of his vision, and the dingy white letters on their black ground spelled themselves out. The words seemed to carry some message, for the judge, with his eyes fixed on the sign as on some beacon of hope, plunged across the dusty road and entered the shop.

At supper that night it was plain to both Mr. Mahaffy and Hannibal that the judge was in a state of mind best described as beatific. The tenderest consideration, the gentlest courtesy flowed from him as from an unfailing spring; not that he was ever, even in his darkest hours, socially remiss, but there was now a special magnificence to his manner that bred suspicion in Mahaffy's soul. When he noted that the judge's shoes were extremely dusty, this suspicion shaped itself definitely. He was convinced that on the strength of his prospective fee the judge had gone to Belle Plain, for what purpose Mr. Mahaffy knew only too well.

"It took you some time to get up that abstract, didn't it, Price?" he presently said, with artful indirection.

"I shall go on with that in the morning, Solomon; my interest was dissipated this evening," rejoined the judge.

"Looks as though you had devoted a good part of your time to pedestrianism," suggested Mahaffy.

"Quite right, so I did, Solomon."

"Were you at Belle Plain?" demanded Mahaffy harshly and with a black scowl. The judge had agreed to keep away from Belle Plain.

"No, Solomon, you forget our pact."

"Well, I am glad you remembered it."

They finished supper, the dishes were cleared away and the candles lighted, when the judge produced a mysterious leather-covered case. This he placed upon the table and opened, and Mahaffy and Hannibal, who had drawn near, saw with much astonishment that it held a handsome pair of dueling pistols, together with all their necessary paraphernalia.

"Where did you get 'em, Judge? - Oh, ain't they beautiful!" cried Hannibal, circling about the table in his excitement.

"My dear lad, they were purchased only a few hours ago," said the judge quietly, as he began to load them.

"For Heaven's sake, Price, do be careful!" warned Mahaffy, who had a horror of pistols that extended to no other species of firearm.

"I shall observe all proper caution, Solomon," the judge assured him sweetly.

"Judge, may I try 'em some day?" asked Hannibal.

"Yes, my boy, that's part of a gentleman's education."

"Well, look out you don't shoot him before his education begins," snapped Mahaffy.

"Where did you buy 'em?" Hannibal was dodging about the judge, the better to follow the operation of loading.

"At the gunsmith's, dear lad. It occurred to me that we required small arms. If you'll stand quietly at my elbow and not hop around, you'll relieve Mr. Mahaffy's apprehension."

"I declare, Price, you need a guardian, if ever a man did!" cried Mahaffy, in a tone of utter exasperation.

"Why, Solomon?"

"Why? - they are absolutely useless. It was a waste of good money that you'll be sorry about."

"Bless you, Solomon - they ain't paid for!" said the judge, with a thick little chuckle.

"I didn't do you the injustice to suppose they were; but you haven't any head for business; aren't you just that much nearer the time when not a soul here will trust you? That's just like you, to plunge ahead and use up your credit on gimcracks!" Mahaffy prided himself on his acquaintance with the basic principles of economics.

"I can sell 'em again," observed the judge placidly.

"For less than half what they are worth! - I never knew so poor a manager!"

The pistols were soon loaded, and the judge turned to Hannibal. "I regretted that you were not with me out at Boggs' this evening, Hannibal; you would have enjoyed seeing me try these weapons there. Now carry a candle into the kitchen and place it on the table."

Mahaffy laughed contemptuously, but was relieved to know the purpose to which the judge had devoted the afternoon.

"What aspersion is rankling for utterance within you now, Solomon?" said the judge tolerantly. Assuming a position that gave him an unobstructed view across the two rooms, he raised the pistol in his hand and discharged it in that brief instant when he caught the candle's flame between the notches of the sight, but he failed to snuff the candle, and a look of bitter disappointment passed over his face. He picked up the other pistol. "This time -" he muttered under his breath.

"Try blowing it out try the snuffers!" jeered Mahaffy.

"This time!" repeated the judge, unheeding him, and as the

pistol-shot rang out the light vanished. "By Heaven, I did it!" roared the judge, giving way to an uncontrollable burst of feeling. "I did it - and I can 'do it again - light the candle, Hannibal!"

He began to load the pistols afresh with feverish haste, and Mahaffy, staring at him in amazement, saw that of a sudden the sweat was dripping from him. But the judge's excitement prevented his attempting another shot at once, twice his hand was raised, twice it was lowered, the third time the pistol cracked and the candle's flame was blown level, fluttered for a brief instant, and went out.

"Did I nick the tallow, Hannibal?" The judge spoke anxiously.

"Yes, sir, both shots."

"We must remedy that," said the judge. Then, as rapidly as he could load and fire, bullet after bullet was sent fairly through the flame, extinguishing it each time. Mahaffy was too astonished at this display of skill even to comment, while Hannibal's delight knew no bounds. "That will do!" said the judge at last. He glanced down at the pistol in his hand. "This is certainly a gentleman's weapon!" he murmured.

CHAPTER XX

THE WARNING

Norton had ridden down to Belle Plain ostensibly to view certain of those improvements that went so far toward embittering Tom Ware's existence. Gossip had it that he kept the road hot between the two places, and this was an added strain on the planter. But Norton did not go to Belle Plain to see Mr. Ware. If that gentleman had been the sole attraction, he would have made just one visit suffice; had it preceded his own, he would have attended Tom's funeral, and considered that he had done a very decent thing. On the present occasion he and Betty were strolling about the rehabilitated grounds, and Norton was exhibiting that interest and enthusiasm which Betty always expected of him.

"You are certainly making the old place look up!" he said, as they passed out upon the terrace. He had noted casually when he rode up the lane half an hour before that a horse was tied near Ware's office; a man now issued from the building and swung himself into the saddle. Norton turned abruptly to Betty. "What's that fellow doing here?" he asked.

"I suppose he comes to see Tom," said Betty.

"Is he here often?"

"Every day or so." Betty's tone was indifferent. For reasons which had seemed good and sufficient she had never discussed

Captain Murrell with Norton.

"Every day or so?" repeated Norton. "But you don't see him, Betty?"

"No, of course I don't."

"Tom has no business allowing that fellow around; if he don't know this some one ought to tell him!" Norton was working himself up into a fine rage.

"He doesn't bother me, Charley, if that's what you're thinking of. Let's talk of something else."

"He'd better not, or I'll make it a quarrel with him."

"Oh, you mustn't think of that, Charley, indeed you mustn't!" cried Betty in some alarm, for young Mr. Norton was both impulsive and hot-headed.

"Well, just how often is Murrell here?" he demanded.

"I told you - every few days. He and Tom seem wonderfully congenial."

They were silent for a moment.

"Tom always sees him in his office," explained Betty. She might have made her explanation fuller on this point had she cared to do so.

"That's the first decent thing I ever heard of Tom!" said Norton with warmth. "But he ought to kick him off the place the first chance he gets."

"Do you think Belle Plain is ever going to look as it did, Charley? - as we remember it when we were children?" asked Betty, giving a new direction to the conversation.

"Why, of course it is, dear, you are doing wonders!"

"I've really been ashamed of the place, the way it looked - and I can't understand Tom!"

"Don't try to," advised Norton. "Look here, Betty, do you remember it was right on this terrace I met you for the first time? My mother brought me down, and I arrived with a strong prejudice against you, young lady, because of the clothes I'd been put into - they were fine but oppressive."

"How long did the prejudice last, Charley?"

"It didn't last at all, I thought you altogether the nicest little girl I'd ever seen - just what I think now, I wish you could care for me, Betty, just a little; just enough to marry me."

"But, Charley, I do care for you! I'm very, very fond of you."

"Well, don't make such a merit of it," he said, and they both laughed. "I'm at an awful disadvantage, Betty, from having proposed so often. That gives it a humorous touch which doesn't properly reflect the state of my feeling at all - and you hear me without the least emotion; so long as I keep my distance we might just as well be discussing the weather!"

"You are very good about that -"

"Keeping my distance, you mean? - Betty, if you knew how much resolution that calls for! I wonder if that isn't my mistake -" And Norton came a step nearer and took her in his arms.

With her hands on his shoulders Betty pushed him back, while the rich color came into her cheeks. She was remembering Bruce Carrington, who had not kept his distance.

"Please, Charley," she said half angrily, "I do like you tremendously, but I simply can't bear you when you act like this - let me got"

"Betty, I despair of you ever caring for me!" and as Norton turned abruptly away he saw Tom Ware appear from about a corner of the house. "Oh, hang it, there's Tom!"

"You are very nice, anyway, Charley -" said Betty hurriedly, fortified by the planter's approach.

Ware stalked toward them. Having dined with Betty as recently as the day before, he contented himself with a nod in her direction. His greeting to Norton was a more ambitious undertaking; he said he was pleased to see him; but in so far as facial expression might have indorsed the statement this pleasure was well disguised, it did not get into his features. Pausing on the terrace beside them, he indulged in certain observations on the state of the crops and the weather.

"You've lost a couple of niggers, I hear?" he added with an oblique glance.

"Yes," said Norton.

"Got on the track of them yet?" Norton shook his head. "I understand you've a new overseer?" continued Ware, with another oblique glance.

"Then you understand wrong - Carrington's my guest," said Norton. "He's talking of putting in a crop for himself next season, so he's willing to help me make mine."

Betty turned quickly at the mention of Carrington's name. She had known that he was still at Thicket Point, and having heard him spoken of as Norton's new overseer, had meant to ask Charley if he were really filling that position. An undefined sense of relief came to her with Norton's reply to Tom's question.

"Going to turn farmer, is he?" asked Ware.

"So he says." Feeling that the only subjects in which he had ever known Ware to take the slightest interest, namely, crops and slaves, were exhausted, Norton was extremely disappointed when the planter manifested a disposition to play the host and returned to the house with them, where his mere presence, forbidding and sullen, was such a hardship that Norton shortly took his leave.

"Well, hang Tom!" he said, as he rode away from Belle Plain. "If he thinks he can freeze me out there's a long siege ahead of him!"

Issuing from the lane he turned his face in the direction of home, but he did not urge his horse off a walk. To leave Belle Plain and Betty demanded always his utmost resolution. His way took him into the solemn twilight of untouched solitudes. A cool breath rippled through the depths of the woods and shaped its own soft harmonies where it lifted the great branches that arched the road. He crossed strips of bottom land where the water stood in still pools about the gnarled and moss-covered trunks of trees. At intervals down some sluggish inlet he caught sight of the yellow flood that was pouring past, or saw the Arkansas coast beyond, with its mighty sweep of unbroken forest that rose out of the river mists and blended with the gray distance that lay along the horizon.

He was within two miles of Thicket Point when, passing about a sudden turn in the road, he found himself confronted by three men, and before he could gather up his reins which he held loosely, one of them had seized his horse by the bit. Norton was unarmed, he had not even a riding-whip. This being the case he prepared to make the best of an unpleasant situation which he felt he could not alter. He ran his eye over the three men.

"I am sorry, gentlemen, but I reckon you have hold of the wrong person -"

"Get down!" said one of the men briefly.

"I haven't any money, that's why I say you have hold of the wrong person."

"We don't want your money." The unexpectedness of this reply somewhat disturbed Norton.

"What do you want, then?" he asked.

"We got a word to say to you."

"I can hear it in the saddle."

"Get down!" repeated the man, a surly, bull-necked fellow. "Come - hurry up!" he added.

Norton hesitated for an instant, then swung himself out of the saddle and stood in the road confronting the spokesman of the party.

"Now, what do you wish to say to me?" he asked.

"Just this - you keep away from Belle Plain."

"You go to hell!" said Norton promptly. The man glowered heavily at hire through the gathering gloom of twilight.

"We want your word that you'll keep away from Belle Plain," he said with sullen insistence.

"Well, you won't get it!" responded Norton with quiet decision.

"We won't?"

"Certainly you won't!" Norton's eyes began to flash. He wondered if these were Tom Ware's emissaries. He was both quick-tempered and high-spirited. Falling back a step, he sprang forward and dealt the bullnecked man a savage blow. The latter grunted heavily but kept his feet. In the same instant one of the men who had never taken his eyes off Norton from the moment he quitted the saddle, raised his fist and struck the young planter in the back of the neck.

"You cur!" cried Norton, blind and dizzy, as he wheeled on him.

"Damn him - let him have it!" roared the bullnecked man.

Afterward Norton was able to remember that the three rushed on him, that he was knocked down and kicked with merciless brutality, then consciousness left him. He lay very still in the trampled dust of the road. The bull-necked man regarded the limp figure in grim silence for a moment.

"That'll do, he's had enough; we ain't to kill him this time," he said. An instant later he, with his two companions, had vanished silently into the woods.

Norton's horse trotted down the road. When it entered the yard at Thicket Point half an hour later, Carrington was on the porch.

"Is that you, Norton?" he called, but there was no response, and he saw the horse was riderless. "Jeff!" he cried, summoning Norton's servant from the house.

"What's the matter, Mas'r?" asked the negro, as he appeared in the open door.

"Why, here's Mr. Norton's horse come home without him. Do you know where he went this afternoon?"

"I heard him say he reckoned he'd ride over to Belle Plain, Mas'r," answered Jeff, grinning. "I 'low the hoss done broke away and come home by himself - he couldn't a-throwed Mas'r Charley!"

"We'll make sure of that. Get lanterns, and a couple of the

boys!" said Carrington.

It was mid-afternoon of the day following before Betty heard of the attack on Charley Norton. Tom brought the news, and she at once ordered her horse saddled and was soon out on the river road with a black groom trailing along through the dust in her wake. Tom's version of the attack was that Charley, had been robbed and all but murdered, and Betty never drew rein until she reached Thicket Point. As she galloped into the yard Bruce Carrington came from the house. At sight of the girl, with her wind-blown halo of bright hair, he paused uncertainly. By a gesture Betty called him to her side.

"How is Mr. Norton?" she asked, extending her hand.

"The doctor says he'll be up and about inside of a week, anyhow, Miss Malroy," said Carrington.

Betty gave a great sigh of relief.

"Then his hurts are not serious?"

"No," said Carrington, "they are not in any sense serious."

"May I see him?"

"He's pretty well bandaged up, so he looks worse off than he is. If you'll wait on the porch, I'll tell him you are here," for Betty had dismounted.

"If you please."

Carrington passed on into the house. His face wore a look of somber repression. Of course it was all right for her to come and see Norton - they were old, old friends. He entered the room where Norton lay.

"Miss Malroy is here," he said shortly.

"Betty? - bless her dear heart!" cried Charley rather weakly. "Just toss my clothes into the closet and draw up a chair . . . There-thank you, Bruce, that will do - let her come along in now." And as Carrington quitted the room, Norton drew himself up on the pillows and faced the door. "This is worth several beatings, Betty!" he exclaimed as she appeared on the threshold. But much cotton and many bandages lent him a rather fearful aspect, and Betty paused with a little gasp of dismay. "I'm lots better than I look, I expect," said Norton. "Couldn't you arrange to come a little closer?" he added, laughing.

He bent to kiss the hand she gave him, but groaned with the exertion. Then he looked up into her face and saw her eyes swimming with tears.

"What - tears? Tears for me, Betty?" and he was much moved.

"It's a perfect outrage! Who did it, Charley?" she asked.

"You sit down and I'll tell you all about it," said Norton happily.

"Now tell me, Charley!" when she had seated her. self.

"Who fetched you, Betty - old Tom?"

"No, I came alone."

"Well, it's mighty kind of you. I'll be all right in a day or so. What did you hear? - that I'd been attacked and half-killed?"

"Yes - and robbed."

"There were three of the scoundrels. They made me climb out of the saddle, and as I was unarmed they did as they pleased with me, which was to stamp me flat in the road -"

"Charley!"

"I might almost be inclined to think they were friends of yours, Betty - or at least friends of friends of yours."

"What do you mean, Charley - friends of mine?"

"Well, you see they started in by stipulating that I should keep away from Belle Plain, and the terms they proposed being on the face of them preposterous, trouble quickly ensued - trouble for me, you understand. But never mind, dear, the next man who undertakes to grab my horse by the bit won't get off quite so easy."

"Why should any one care whether you come to Belle Plain or not?"

"I wonder if my amiable friend, Tom, could have arranged this little affair; it's sort of like old Tom to move in the dark, isn't it?"

"He couldn't - he wouldn't have done it, Charley!" but she looked troubled, not too sure of this.

"Couldn't he? Well, maybe he couldn't - but he's afraid you'll marry me - and I'm only afraid you won't. Betty, hasn't it ever seemed worth your while to marry me just to give old Tom the scare of his life?"

"Please, Charley -" she began.

"I'm in a dreadful state of mind when I think of you alone at Belle Plain - I wish you could love me, Betty!"

"I do love you. There is no one I care half so much for, Charley."

Norton shook his bandaged head and heaved a prodigious sigh.

"That's merely saying you don't love any one." He dropped

back rather wearily on his pillow. "Does Tom know about this?" he added.

"Yes."

"Was he able to show a proper amount of surprise?"

"He appeared really shocked, Charley."

"Well, then, it wasn't Tom. He never shows much emotion, but what he does show he usually feels, I've noticed. I had rather hoped it was Tom, I'd be glad to think that he was responsible; for if it wasn't Tom, who was it? - who is it to whom it makes any difference how often I see you?"

"I don't know, Charley;" but her voice was uncertain.

"Look here, Betty; for the hundredth time, won't you marry me? I've loved you ever since I was old enough to know what love meant. You've been awfully sweet and patient with me, and I've tried to respect your wishes and not speak of this except when it seemed necessary -" he paused, and they both laughed a little, but he looked weak and helpless with his bloodless face showing between the gaps in the bandages that swathed him. Perhaps it was this sense of his helplessness that roused a feeling in Betty that was new to her.

"You see, Charley, I fear - I am sure I don't love you the way I should - to marry you -"

Charley, greatly excited, groaned and sat up, and groaned again.

"Oh, please, Charley-lie still!" she entreated.

"That's all right - and you needn't pull your hand away - you like me better than any one else, you've told me so; well, don't you see that's the beginning of really loving me?"

"But you wouldn't want to marry me at once?"

"Yes I would - right away - as soon as I am able to stir around!" said Charley promptly. "Don't you see the immediate necessity there is of my being in a position to care for you, Betty? I wasn't served this trick for nothing."

"You must try not to worry, Charley."

"But I shall - I expect it's going to retard my recovery," said the young man gloomily. "I couldn't be worse off! Here I am flat on my back; I can't come to you or keep watch over you. Let me have some hope, dear - let me believe that you will marry me!"

She looked at him pityingly, and with a certain latent tenderness in her mood.

"Do you really care so much for me, Charley?"

"I love you, Betty! - I want you to say you will marry me as soon as I can stand by your side - you're not going? - I won't speak of this again if it annoys you, dear!" for she had risen.

"I must, Charley -"

"Oh, don't - well, then, if you will go, I want Carrington to ride back with you."

"But I brought George with me -"

"Yes, I know, but I want you to take Carrington - the Lord knows what we are coming to here in West Tennessee; I must have word that you reach home safe."

"Very well, then, I'll ask Mr. Carrington. Good-by, Charley dear!"

Norton seemed to summon all his fortitude.

"You couldn't have done a kinder thing than come here, Betty; I can't begin to tell you how grateful I am - and as for my loving you - why, I'll just keep on doing that to the end. I can see myself a bent, old man still pestering you with my attentions, and you a sweet, old lady with snow-white hair and pink cheeks, still obdurate - still saying no! Oh, Lord, isn't it awful!" He had lifted himself on his elbow, and now sank back on his pillow.

Betty paused irresolutely.

"Charley -"

"Yes, dear?"

"Can't you be happy without me?"

"No,"

"But you don't try to be!"

"No use in my making any such foolish effort, I'd be doomed to failure."

"Good-by, Charley - I really must go -"

He looked up yearningly into her face, and yielding to a sudden impulse, she stooped and kissed him on the forehead, then she fled from the room.

"Oh, come back - Betty -" cried Norton, and his voice rose to a wail of entreaty, but she was gone. She had been quite as much surprised by her act as Charley himself.

In the yard, Carrington was waiting for her. Jeff had just brought up Norton's horse, and though he made no display of weapons, the Kentuckian had fully armed himself.

"I am going to ride to Belle Plain with you, Miss Malroy," he said, as he lifted her into her saddle.

"Do you think it necessary?" she asked, but she did not look at him.

"I hope not. I'll keep a bit in advance," he added, as he mounted his horse, and all Betty saw of him during their ride of five miles was his broad back. At the entrance to Belle Plain he reined in his horse.

"I reckon it's all right, now," he said briefly.

"You will return at once to Mr. Norton?" she asked. He nodded. "And you will not leave him while he is helpless?"

"No, I'll not leave him," said Carrington, giving her a steady glance.

"I am so glad, I - his friends will feel so much safer with you there. I will send over in the morning to learn how he passed the night. Good-by, Mr. Carrington." And still refusing to meet his eyes, she gave him her hand.

But Carrington did not quit the mouth of the lane until she had crossed between the great fields of waving corn, and he had seen her pass up the hillside beyond to the oak grove, where the four massive chimneys of Belle Plain house showed their gray stone copings among the foliage. With this last glimpse of her he turned away.

CHAPTER XXI

THICKET POINT

It WAS a point with Mr. Ware to see just as little as possible of Betty. He had no taste for what he called female chatter. A sane interest in the price of cotton or pork he considered the only rational test of human intelligence, and Betty evinced entire indifference where those great staples were concerned, hence it was agreeable to him to have most of his meals served in his office.

At first Betty had sought to adapt herself to his somewhat peculiar scheme of life, but Tom had begged her not to regard him, his movements from hour to hour were cloaked in uncertainty. The man who had to overlook the labor of eighty or ninety field hands was the worst sort of a slave himself; the niggers knew when they could sit down to a meal; he never did.

But for all his avoidance of Betty, he in reality kept the closest kind of a watch on her movements, and when he learned that she had visited Charley Norton - George, the groom, was the channel through which this information reached him - he was both scandalized and disturbed. He felt the situation demanded some sort of a protest.

"Isn't it just hell the way a woman can worry you?" he lamented, as he hurried up the path from the barns to the house. He found Betty at supper.

"I thought I'd have a cup of tea with you, Bet - what else have you that's good?" he inquired genially, as he dropped into a chair.

"That was nice of you; we don't see very much of each other, do we, Tom?" said Betty pleasantly.

Mr. Ware twisted his features, on which middle age had rested an untender hand, into a smile.

"When a man undertakes to manage a place like Belle Plain his work's laid out for him, Betty, and an old fellow like me is pretty apt to go one of two ways; either he takes to hard living to keep himself in trim, or he pampers himself soft."

"But you aren't old, Tom!"

"I wish I were sure of seeing forty-five or even forty-eight again - but I'm not," said Tom.

"But that isn't really old," objected Betty.

"Well, that's old enough, Bet, as you'll discover for yourself one of these days."

"Mercy, Tom!" cried Betty.

Mr. Ware consumed a cup of tea in silence.

"You were over to see Norton, weren't you, Bet? How did you find him?" he asked abruptly.

"The doctor says he will soon be about again," answered Betty.

Tom stroked his chin and gazed at her reflectively.

"Betty, I wish you wouldn't go there again - that's a good girl!" he said tactfully, and as he conceived it, affectionately, even, paving the way for an exercise of whatever influence might be his, a point on which he had no very clear idea. Betty glanced up quickly.

"Why, Tom, why shouldn't I go there?" she demanded.

"It might set people gossiping. I reckon there's been pretty near enough talk about you and Charley Norton. A young girl can't be too careful." The planter's tone was conciliatory in the extreme, he dared not risk a break by any open show of authority.

"You needn't distress yourself, Tom. I don't know that I shall go there again," said Betty indifferently.

"I wouldn't if I were you." He was charmed to find her so reasonable. "You know it isn't the thing for a young girl to call on a man, you'll get yourself talked about in a way you won't like - take my word for it! If you want to be kind and neighborly send one of the boys over to ask how he is - or bake a cake with your own hands, but you keep away. That's the idea! - send him something to eat, something you've made yourself, he'll appreciate that."

"I'm afraid he couldn't eat it if I did, Tom. It's plain you have no acquaintance with my cooking," said Betty, laughing.

"Did Norton say if he had any idea as to the identity of the men who robbed him?" inquired Tom casually.

"Their object wasn't robbery," said Betty.

"No?" Ware's glance was uneasy.

"It seems that some one objects to his coming here, Tom - here to Belle Plain to see me, I suppose," added Betty. The planter moved uncomfortably in his seat, refusing to meet her eyes.

"He shouldn't put out a yarn like that, Bet. It isn't just the thing for a gentleman to do -"

"He isn't putting it out, as you call it! He has told no one, so far as I know," said Betty quickly. Mr. Ware fell into a brooding silence. "Of course, Charley wouldn't mention my name in any such connection!" continued Betty.

"Who cares how often he comes here? You don't, and I don't. There's more back of this than Charley would want you to know. I reckon he's got his enemies; some one's had a grudge against him and taken this way to settle it." The planter's tone and manner were charged with an unpleasant significance.

"I don't like your hints, Tom," said Betty. Her heightened color and the light in her eyes warned Tom that he had said enough. In some haste he finished his second cup of tea, a beverage which he despised, and after a desultory remark or two, withdrew to his office.

Betty went up-stairs to her own room, where she tried to finish a letter she had begun the day before to Judith Ferris, but she was in no mood for this. She was owning to a sense of utter depression and she had been at home less than a month. Struggle as she might against the feeling, it was borne in upon her that she was wretchedly lonely. She had seated herself by an open window. Now, resting her elbows on the ledge and with her chin between her palms, she gazed off into the still night. A mile distant, on what was called "Shanty Hill," were the quarters of the slaves. The only lights she saw were there, the only sounds she heard reached her across the intervening fields. This was her world. A half-savage world with its uncouth army of black dependents.

Tom's words still rankled. Betty's temper flared up belligerently as she recalled them. He had evidently meant to insinuate that Charley had lied outright when he told her the motive for the attack, and he had followed it up by that covert slur on his character. Charley's devotion was the thing that redeemed the dull monotony of existence. She became suddenly humble and tenderly penitent in her mood toward him; he loved her much better than she deserved, and she suspected that her own attitude had been habitually ungenerous and selfish. She had accepted all and yielded nothing. She wondered gravely why it was she did not love him; she was fond of him - she was very, very fond of him; she wondered if after all, as he said, this were not the beginning of love, the beginning of that deeper feeling which she was not sure she understood, not sure she should ever experience.

The thought of Charley's unwavering affection gave her a great sense of peace; it was something to have inspired such devotion, she could never be quite desperate while she had him. She must try to make him understand how possible an ideal friendship was between them, how utterly impossible anything else. She would like to have seen Charley happily married to some nice girl - "I wonder whom!" thought Betty, gazing deep into the night through her drooping lashes. She considered possible candidates for the happiness she herself seemed so willing to forego, but for one reason or another dismissed them all. "I am not sure I should care to see him marry," she confessed under her breath. "It would spoil everything. Men are much nicer than girls!" And Charley possessed distinguished merits as a man; he was not to be too hastily disposed of, even for his own good. She viewed him in his various aspects, his character and disposition came under her critical survey. Nature had given the young planter a handsome presence; wealth and position had come to him as fortuitously. The first of these was no great matter, perhaps; Betty herself was sometimes burdened with a sense of possession, but family was indispensable.

In theory, at least, she was a thoroughgoing little aristocrat. A gentleman was always a gentleman. There were exceptions, like Tom, to be sure, but even Tom could have reached up and seized the title had he coveted it. She rarely forgot that she was the mistress of Belle Plain and a Malroy. Just wherein a Malroy differed from the rest of the sons of men she had never paused to consider, it sufficed that there was a hazy Malroy genealogy that went back to tidewater Virginia, and then if one were not meanly curious, and would skip a generation or two that could not be accounted for in ways any Malroy would accept, one might triumphantly follow the family to a red-roofed Sussex manor house. Altogether, it was a highly satisfactory genealogy and it had Betty's entire faith. The Nortons were every bit as good as the Malroys, which was saying a great deal. Their history was quite as pretentious, quite as vague, and as hopelessly involved in the mists of tradition.

Inexplicably enough, Betty found that her thoughts had wandered to Carrington; which was very singular, as she had long since formed a resolution not to think of him at all. Yet she remembered with satisfaction his manner that afternoon, it left nothing to be desired. He was probably understanding the impassable gulf that separated them - education, experience, feeling, everything that made up the substance of life but deepened and widened this gulf. He belonged to that shifting, adventurous population which was far beneath the slave-holding aristocracy, at least he more nearly belonged to this lower order than to any other. She fixed his status relentlessly as something to be remembered when they should meet again. At last, with a little puckering of the brows and a firm contraction of the lips, she dismissed the Kentuckian from her thoughts.

Betty complied with Tom's expressed wish, for she did not again visit Thicket Point, but then she had not intended doing so. However, the planter was greatly shocked by the discovery he presently made that she was engaged in a vigorous correspondence with Charley.

"I wish to blazes Murrell had told those fellows to kick the life clean out of him while they were about it!" he commented savagely, and fell to cursing impotently. Brute force was a factor to be introduced with caution into the affairs of life, but if you were going to use it, his belief was that you should use it to the limit. You couldn't scare Norton, he was in love with that pink-faced little fool. Keep away? - he'd never think of it, he'd stuff his pockets full of pistols and the next man who stopped him on the road would better look out! It made him sick - the utter lack of sense manifested by Murrell, and his talk, whenever they met, was still of the girl. He couldn't see anything so damn uncommon about that red-and-white chit. She wasn't worth running your neck into a halter for - no woman that ever lived was worth that.

The correspondence, so far as Betty was responsible for it, bore just on one point. She wanted Charley to promise that for a time, at least, he would not attempt to see her. It seemed such a needless risk to take, couldn't he be satisfied if he heard from her every day?

Charley was regretful, but firm. Just as soon as he could mount his horse he would ride down to Belle Plain. She was not to distress herself on his account; he had been surprised, but this should not happen again.

The calm manner in which he put aside her fears for his safety exasperated Betty beyond measure. She scolded him vigorously. Charley accepted the scolding with humility, but his resolution was unshaken; he did not propose to vacate the public roads at any man's behest; that would be an unwise precedent to establish.

Betty replied that this was not a matter in which silly vanity should enter, even if his life was of no value to himself it did not follow that she held it lightly. It required some eight closely written pages for Charley to explain why existence would be an unsupportable burden if he were denied the sight of her.

A week had intervened since the attack, and from Jeff, who always brought Charley's letters, Betty learned more of Charley's condition than Charley himself had seen fit to tell. According to Jeff his master was now able to get around pretty tolerable well, though he had a powerful keen misery in his side.

"That was whar' they done kicked him most, Miss," he added Betty shuddered.

"How much longer will he be confined to the house?" she asked.

"I heard him 'low to Mas'r Carrington, Miss, as how he reckoned he'd take a hossback ride to-morrow evenin' if the black and blue was all come out of his features -"

"Oh -" gasped Betty.

"Seems like they was mighty careless whar' they put their feet, don't it, Miss?" said Jeff.

It was this information she gleaned from Jeff that led Betty to desperate lengths, to the making of what her cooler judgment told her was a desperate bargain.

At Thicket Point Charley Norton, greatly excited, hobbled into the library in search of Carrington. He found him reading by the open window.

"Look here, Bruce!" he cried. "It's settled; she's going to marry me!"

The book slipped unheeded from Carrington's hand to the floor. For a moment he sat motionless, then he slowly pulled himself up out of his chair.

"What's that?" he asked a trifle thickly.

"Betty Malroy is going to marry me," said Norton. Carrington gazed at him in silence.

"It's settled, is it?" he asked at length. He saw his own hopes go down in miserable wreck; they had been utterly futile from the first. He had known all along that Norton loved her, the young planter had made no secret of it. He had been less frank.

"I swear you take it quietly enough," said Norton.

"Do I?"

"Can't you wish me joy?"

Carrington held out his hand.

"You are not going to take any risks now, you have too much to live for," he said haltingly.

"No, I'm to keep away from Belle Plain," said Norton happily. "She insists on that; she says she won't even see me if I come there. Everything is to be kept a secret; nothing's to be known until we are actually married; it's her wish -"

"It's to be soon then?" Carrington asked, still haltingly.

"Very soon."

There was a brief silence. Carrington, with face averted, looked from the window.

"I am going to stay here as long as you need me," he presently said. "She - Miss Malroy asked me to, and then I am going back to the river where I belong."

Norton turned on him quickly.

"You don't mean you've abandoned the notion of turning planter?" he demanded in surprise.

"Well, yes. What's the use of my trying my hand at a business I don't know the first thing about?"

"I wouldn't be in too big a hurry to decide finally on that point," urged Norton.

"It has decided itself," said Carrington quietly.

But Norton was conscious of a subtle change in their relation. Carrington seemed a shade less frank than had been habitual with him; all at once he had removed his private affairs from the field of discussion. Afterward, when Norton considered the matter, he wondered if it were not that the Kentuckian felt himself superfluous in this new situation that had grown up.

Charley Norton's features recovered their accustomed hue, but he did not go near Belle Plain; with resolute fortitude he confined himself to his own acres. He was tolerably familiar with certain engaging little peculiarities of Mr. Ware's; he knew, for instance, that the latter was a gentleman of excessively regular habits; once each fortnight, making an excuse of business, he spent a day in Memphis, neither more nor less. Norton told himself with satisfaction that Tom was destined to return to the surprise of his life from the next of these trips. This conviction was the one thing which sustained Charley for some ten days. They were altogether the longest ten days he had ever known, and he had about reached the limit of his endurance when Betty's groom arrived with a letter which threw him into a state of ecstatic happiness. The sober-minded Tom would devote the morrow to Memphis and business. This meant that he would leave Belle Plain at sun-up and return after nightfall.

"You may not like Tom, but you can always count on him," said Norton. Then he ordered his horse and rode off in the direction of Raleigh, but before leaving the house, he scribbled a line or two to be handed Carrington, who had gone down to the nearest river landing.

It was nightfall when the Kentuckian returned, Hearing his step in the hall, Jeff came from the dining-room, where he was laying the cloth for supper.

"Mas'r Charley has rid to Raleigh, Sah," said he; "but he done lef' this fo' me to han' to yo" - extending the letter.

Carrington took it. He guessed its contents. Breaking the seal he read the half dozen lines.

"To-morrow -" he muttered under his breath, and slowly tore the sheet of note-paper into thin ribbons. He turned to Jeff. "Mr. Charley won't be home until late," he said.

"Then I 'low yo' want yo' supper now, Sar?" But Carrington shook his head.

"No, you needn't bother, Jeff," he said, as he turned toward the stairs.

Ten minutes later and he had got together his belongings and was ready to quit Thicket Point. He retraced his steps to the floor below. In the hall he paused and glanced about him. He seemed to feel her presence - and very near - to-morrow she would enter there as Norton's wife. With his pack under his arm he entered the dining-room in search of Jeff.

"Tell your master I have gone to Memphis," he said briefly.

"Ain't yo' goin' to have a hoss, Mas'r Carrington?" demanded Jeff in some surprise. He had come to regard the Kentuckian as a fixture.

"No," said Carrington. "Good-by, Jeff," he added, turning away.

But when he left Thicket Point he did not take the Memphis road, but the road to Belle Plain. Walking rapidly, he reached the entrance to the lane within the hour. Here he paused irresolutely, it was as if the force of his purpose had already spent itself. Then he tossed his pack into a fence corner and kept on toward the house.

CHAPTER XXII

AT THE CHURCH DOOR

There was the patter of small feet beyond Betty's door, and little Steve, who looked more like a nice fat black Cupid than anything else, rapped softly; at the same time he effected to squint through the keyhole.

"Supper served, Missy," he announced, then he turned no less than seven handsprings in the upper hall and slid down the balustrade to the floor below. He was far from being a model house servant.

His descent was witnessed by the butler. Now in his own youth big Steve with as fair a field had cut similar capers, yet he was impelled by his sense of duty to do for his grandson what his own father had so often done for him, and in no perfunctory manner. It was only the sound of Betty's door opening and closing that stayed his hand as he was making choice of a soft and vulnerable spot to which he should apply it. Little Steve slid under the outstretched arm that menaced him and fled to the dining-room.

Betty came slowly down the stairs. Four hours since Jeff had ridden away with the letter. Already there had come to her moments when, she would have given much could she have recalled it, when she knew with dread certainty that whatever her feeling for Charley, it was not love; moments when she realized that she had been cruelly driven by circumstances into a situation that offered no escape.

"Mas'r Tom he say he won't come in to supper, Missy; he 'low he's powerful busy, gittin' ready to go to Memphis in the mo'ning," explained Steve, as he followed Betty into the dining-room.

His mistress nodded indifferently as she seated herself at the table; she was glad to be alone just then; she was in no mood to carry on the usual sluggish conversation with Tom; her own thoughts absorbed hermore and more they became terrifying things to her.

She ate her supper with big Steve standing behind her chair and little Steve balancing himself first on one foot and then on the other near the door. Little Steve's head was on a level with the chair rail and but for the rolling whites of his eyes he was no more than a black shadow against the walnut wainscoting; he formed the connecting link between the dining-room and the remote kitchen. Betty suspected that most of the platters journeyed down the long corridor deftly perched on top of his woolly head. She frequently detected him with greasy or sticky fingers, which while it argued a serious breach of trust also served to indicate his favorite dishes. These two servitors were aware that their mistress was laboring under some unusual stress of emotion. In its presence big Steven, who, with the slightest encouragement, became a medium through which the odds and ends of plantation gossip reached Betty's ears, held himself to silence; while little Steve ceased to shift his weight from foot to foot, the very dearth of speech fixed his attention.

The long French windows, their curtains drawn, stood open. All day a hot September sun had beaten upon the earth, but with the fall of twilight a soft wind had sprung up and the candles in their sconces flared at its touch. It came out of wide solitudes laden with the familiar night sounds. It gave Betty a sense of vast unused spaces, of Belle Plain clinging on the edge of an engulfing wilderness, of her own loneliness. She needed Charley as much as he seemed to think he needed her. The life she had been living had become suddenly impossible of continuance; that it had ever been possible was because of Charley; she knew this now as she had never known it before.

Her thoughts dealt with the past. In her one great grief, her mother's death, it had been Charley who had sustained and comforted her. She was conscious of a choking sense of gratitude as she recalled his patient tenderness at that time, the sympathy and understanding he had shown; it was something never to be forgotten.

Unrest presently sent her from the house. She wandered down to the terrace. Before her was the wide sweep of the swampy fore-shore, and beyond just beginning to silver in the moon-light, the bend of the river growing out of the black void. With her eyes on the river and her hands clasped loosely she watched the distant line of the Arkansas coast grow up against the sky; she realized that the moon was rising on Betty Malroy for the last time.

She liked Charley; she needed some one to take care of her and her belongings, and he needed her. It was best for them both that she should marry him. True she might have gone back to Judith Ferris; that would have been one solution of her difficulties. Why hadn't she thought of doing this before? Of course, Charley would have followed her East. Charley met the ordinary duties and responsibilities of his position somewhat recklessly; it was only where she was concerned that he became patiently determined.

"I suppose the end would have been the same there as here," thought Betty.

A moment later she found herself wondering if Charley had told Carrington yet; certainly the Kentuckian would not remain at Thicket Point when he knew. She was sure she wished him to leave not Thicket Point merely, but the neighborhood. She did not wish to see him again - not see him again - not see him again - She found herself repeating the words over and over; they shaped themselves into a dreadful refrain. A nameless terror of the future swept in upon her. She was cold and sick. It was as though an icy hand was laid upon her heart. The words ran on in endless repetition - not see him again - they held the very soul of tragedy for her, yet she was roused to passionate protest. She must not think of him, he was nothing to her. She was to be married to another man, even now she was almost a wife - but battle as she might the struggle went on.

There was the sound of a step on the path. Betty turned, supposing it to be Tom; but it was not Tom, it was Carrington himself who stood before her, his face haggard and drawn. She uttered an involuntary exclamation and shrank away from him. Without a word he stepped to her side and took her hands rather roughly.

For a moment there was silence between them, Betty stared up into his face with wide scared eyes, while he gazed down at her as if he would fasten something on his mind that must never be forgotten. Suddenly he lifted her soft cold hands to his lips and kissed them passionately again and again; then he held them in his own against his cheek, his glance still fixed intently upon her; it held something of bitterness and reproach, but now she kept her eyes under their quivering lids from him.

"What am I to do without you?" - his voice was almost a whisper. "What is this thing you have done?" Betty's heart was beating with dull sickening throbs, but she dared not trust herself to answer him. He took both her hands in one of his, and, slipping the other under her chin, raised her face so that he could look into her eyes; then he put his arm loosely about her, holding her hands against his breast. "If I could have had one moment out of all the years for my own - only one. I am glad you don't care, dear; it hurts when you reach the end of something that has been all your hope and filled all your days. I have come to say good-by, Betty; this is the last time I shall see you. I am going away."

All in an instant Betty pressed close to him, hiding her face in his arm; she clung to him in a panic of pain and horror. She felt something stir within her that had never been there before, as a storm of passionate longing swept through her. Her words, her promise to another man, became as nothing. All her pride was forgotten. Without this man the days stretched away before her a blank. His arm drew her closer still, until she felt her heart throb against his.

"Do you care?" he said, and seemed to wonder that she should.

"Bruce, Bruce, I didn't know - and now - Oh, my dear, my dear -" He pressed his lips against the bright little head that rested in such miserable abandon against his shoulder.

"Do you love me?" he whispered. The blood ran riot in his veins.

"Why have you stayed away - why didn't you come to me? I have promised him -" she gasped.

"I know," he said, and shut his lips. There was another silence while she waited for him to speak. She felt that she was at his mercy, that whether right or wrong, as he decided so it would be. At length he said. "I thought it wasn't fair to him, and it seemed so hopeless after I came here. I had nothing - and a man feels that - so I kept away." He spoke awkwardly with something of the reserve that was habitual to him.

"If you had only come!" she moaned.

"I did - once," he muttered.

"You didn't understand; why did you believe anything I said to you? It was only that I cared - that in my heart I knew I cared - I've cared about you ever since that trip down the river, and now I am going to be married to-morrow - to-morrow, Bruce - do you realize I have given my promise? I am to meet him at the Spring Bank church at ten o'clock - and it's tomorrow!"

she cried, in a laboring choked voice. For answer he drew her closer. "Bruce, what can I do? - tell me what I can do."

Carrington made an involuntary gesture of protest.

"I can't tell you that, dear - for I don't know." His voice was steady, but it came from lips that quivered. He knew that he might have urged the supreme claim of his love and in her present desperate mood she would have listened, but the memory of Norton would have been between them always a shame and reproach; as surely as he stood there with his arms about her, as surely as she clung to him so warm and near, he would have lived to see the shadow of that shame in her eyes.

"I can not do it - I can not, Bruce!" she panted.

"Dear - dear - don't tempt me!" He held himself in check.

"I am going to tell you - just this once, BruceI love you - you are my own for this one moment out of my life!" and she abandoned herself to the passionate caressing with which he answered her. "How can I give you up?" he said, his voice hoarse with emotion. He put her from him almost roughly, and leaning against the trunk of a tree buried his face in his hands. Betty watched him for a moment in wretched silence.

"Don't feel so bad, Bruce," she said brokenly. "I am not worth it. I tried not to love you - I didn't want to." She raised a white face to his.

"I am going now, Betty. You - you shouldn't stay here any longer with me." He spoke with sudden resolution.

"And I shall not see you again?" she asked, in a low, stifled voice.

"It's good-by -" he muttered.

"Not yet - oh, not yet, Bruce -" she implored. "I can not -"

"Yes - now, dear. I don't dare stay - I may forget -" but he turned again to her in entreaty. "Give me something to remember in all the years that are coming when I shall be alone - let me kiss you on the lips - let me - just this once - it's good-by we're saying - it's good-by, Betty!"

She went to him, and, as he bent above her, slipped her arms about his neck.

"Kiss me -" she breathed.

He kissed her hair, her soft cheek, then their lips met.

He helped her as she stumbled blindly along the path to the house, and half lifted her up the steps to the door. They paused there for a moment. At last he turned from her abruptly in silence. A step away he halted.

"If you should ever need me -"

"Never as now," she said.

She saw his tall figure pass down the path, and her straining eyes followed until it was lost in the mild wide spaces of the night.

Another hot September sun was beating upon the earth as Betty galloped down the lane and swung her horse's head in the direction of Raleigh. Her grief had worn itself out and she carried a pale but resolute face. Carrington was gone; she would keep her promise to Charley and he should never know what his happiness had cost her. She nerved herself for their meeting; somewhere between Belle Plain and Thicket Point Norton would be waiting for her.

He joined her before she had covered a third of the distance that separated the two plantations.

"Thank God, my darling!" he cried fervently, as he ranged up alongside of her.

"Then you weren't sure of me, Charley?"

"No, I wasn't sure, Betty - but I hoped. I have been haunting the road for more than an hour. You are making one poor unworthy devil happy, unless -"

"Unless what, Charley?" she prompted.

"Unless you came here merely to tell me that after all you couldn't marry me." He put out his hand and covered hers that held the reins. "I'll never give you cause to regret it - you know how I love you, dear?"

"Yes, Charley - I know." She met his glance bravely.

"We are to go to the church. Mr. Bowen will be there; I arranged with him last night; he will drive over with his wife and daughter, who will be our witnesses, dear. We could have gone to his house, but I thought it would seem more like a real wedding in a church, you know."

Betty did not answer him, her eyes were fixed straight ahead, the last vestige of color had faded from her face and a deathly pallor was there. This was the crowning horror. She felt the terrible injustice she was doing the man at her side, the depth and sincerity of his devotion was something for which she could make no return. Her lips trembled on the verge of an avowal of her love for Carrington. Presently she saw the church in its grove of oaks, in the shade of one of these stood Mr. Bowen's horse and buggy.

"We won't have to wait on him!" said Norton.

"No -" Betty gasped out the monosyllable.

"Why - my darling - what's the matter?" he asked tenderly, his glance bent in concern on the frightened face of the girl.

"Nothing - nothing, Charley

They had reined in their horses. Norton sprang to the ground and lifted her from the saddle.

"It will only take a moment, dear!" he whispered encouragingly in the brief instant he held her in his arms.

"Oh, Charley, it isn't that - it's dreadfully serious -" she said, with a wild little laugh that was almost hysterical.

"I wouldn't have it less than that," he said gravely.

Afterward Betty could remember standing before the church in the fierce morning light; she heard Mr. Bowen's voice, she heard Charley's voice, she heard another voice - her own, though she scarcely recognized it. Then, like one aroused from a dream, she looked about her - she met Charley's glance; his face was radiant and she smiled back at him through a sudden mist that swam before her eyes.

Mr. Bowen led her toward the church door. As they neared it they caught the clatter of hoofs, and Tom Ware on a hard-ridden horse dashed up; he was covered with dust and inarticulate with rage. Then a cry came from him that was like the roar of some mortally wounded animal.

"I forbid this marriage!" he shrieked, when he could command speech.

"You're too late to stop it, Tom, but you can attend it," said Norton composedly.

"You - you -" Words failed the planter; he sat his horse the picture of a grim and sordid despair.

Mr. Bowen divided a look of reproach between his wife and daughter; his own conscience was clear; he had told no one of the purpose of Norton's call the night before.

"I'll tie the horses, Betty," said Norton.

Ware turned fiercely to Bowen.

"You knew better than to be a party to this, and by God! - if you go on with it you shall live to regret it!"

The minister made him no answer, he thoroughly disapproved of the planter. It was well that Betty should have a proper protector, this half-brother was hardly that measured by any standard.

Norton, leading the horses, had reached the edge of the oaks when from the silent depths of the denser woods came the sharp report of a rifle. The shock of the bullet sent the young fellow staggering back among the mossy and myrtle-covered graves.

For a moment no one grasped what had happened, only there was Norton who seemed to grope strangely among the graves. Black spots danced before his eyes, the little group by the church merged into the distance - always receding, always more remote, as he, stumbled helplessly over the moss and the thick dank myrtle and among the round graves that gave him a treacherous footing; and then he heard Betty's agonized cry. He had fallen now, and his strength went from him, but he kept his face turned on the group before the church in mute appeal, and even as the shadows deepened he was aware that Betty was coming swiftly toward him.

"I'm shot -" he said, speaking with difficulty.

"Charley - Charley -" she moaned, slipping her strong young arms about him and gathering him to her breast.

He looked up into her face.

"It's all over -" he said, but as much in wonder as in fear. "But I knew you would come to me - dear -" he added in a whisper.

She felt a shudder pass through him. He did not speak again. His lips opened once, and closed on silence.

CHAPTER XXIII

THE JUDGE OFFERS A REWARD

The news of Charley Norton's murder spread quickly over the county. For two or three days bands of armed men scoured the woods and roads, and then this activity quite unproductive of any tangible results ceased, matters were allowed to rest with the constituted authorities, namely Mr. Betts the sheriff, and his deputies.

No private citizen had shown greater zeal than Judge Slocum Price, no voice had clamored more eloquently for speedy justice than his. He had sustained a loss that was in a peculiar sense personal, he explained. Mr. Norton was his friend and client; they had much in common; their political ideals were in the strictest accord and he had entertained a most favorable opinion of the young man's abilities; he had urged him to enter the national arena and carve out a career for himself; he had promised him his support. The judge so worked upon his own feelings that presently any mention of Norton's name utterly unmanned him. Well, this was life. One could only claim time as it was doled out by clock ticks; we planned for the years and could not be certain of the moments.

He spent two entire days at the church and in the surrounding woods, nor did any one describe the murder with the vividness he achieved in his description of it. The minister's narrative was pale and colorless by comparison, and those who came from a distance went away convinced that they had talked with an eyewitness to the tragedy and esteemed themselves fortunate. In short, he imposed himself on the situation with such brilliancy that in the end his account of the murder became the accepted version from which all other versions differed to their discredit.

In the same magnificent spirit of public service he would have assumed the direction of the search for the murderer, but Mr. Betts' jealousy proved an obstacle to his ambitious design. In view of this he was regretful, but not surprised when the hard-ridden miles covered by dusty men and reeking horses yielded only failure.

"If I had shot that poor boy, I wouldn't ask any surer guarantee of safety than to have that fool Betts with his microscopic brain working in unhampered asininity on the case," he told Mahaffy.

"Is it your idea that you are enlarging your circle of intimate friends by the way you go about slamming into folks?" inquired Mahaffy, with harsh sarcasm.

Later, the judge was shocked at what he characterized as official apathy. It became a point on which he expressed himself with surpassing candor.

"Do they think the murderer's going to come in and give himself up? - is that the notion?" he demanded heatedly of Mr. Saul.

"The sheriff owns himself beat, Sir; the murderer's got safely away and left no clue to his identity."

The judge waived this aside.

"Clues, sir? If you mean physical evidence the eye can apprehend, I grant it; the murderer has got away; certainly he's been given all the time he needed, but what about the motive that prompted the crime? An intelligently conducted examination such as I am willing to undertake might still bring it to light. Isn't it known that Norton was attacked a fortnight ago as he was leaving Belle Plain? He recovers and is about to be married to Miss Malroy when he is shot at the church door; I'll hazard the opinion the attack was in the nature of a warning for him to keep away from Belle Plain. Now, had he a rival? Clear up these points and you get a clue!" The judge paused impressively.

"Tom Ware has acted in a straightforward manner. He's stated frankly he was opposed to the match, that when he heard about it on his way to Memphis he turned back and made every effort to get to the church in time to stop it if he could," said Mr. Saul.

"Mr. Ware need not be considered," observed the judge.

"Well, there's been a heap of talk."

"If he'd inspired the firing of the fatal shot he'd have kept away from the church. No, no, Mr. Saul, is there anybody hereabout who aspired to Miss Malroy's hand - any rejected suitor?"

"Not that we know of."

"Under ordinary circumstances, sir, I am opposed to measures that ignore the constituted authorities, but we find ourselves living under extraordinary conditions, and the law - God save the name - has proved itself abortive. It is time for the better element to join bands; we must get together, sir. I am willing to take the initial steps and issue the call for a mass meeting of our best citizens. I am prepared to address such a meeting." The very splendor of his conception dazzled the judge; this promised a gorgeous publicity with his name flying broadcast over the county. He continued:

"I am ready to give my time gratuitously to directing the activities of a body of picked men who shall rid the county of the lawless element. God knows, sir, I desire the repose of a private career, yet I am willing to sacrifice myself. Is it your opinion, Mr. Saul, that I should move in this matter?"

"I advise you didn't," said Mr. Saul, with disappointing alacrity.

The judge looked at him fixedly.

"Am I wrong in supposing, Mr. Saul, that if I determine to act as I have outlined I shall have your indorsement?" he demanded. Mr. Saul looked extremely uncomfortable; he was finding the judge's effulgent personality rather compelling. "There is no gentleman whose support I should value in quite the same sense that I should value yours, Mr. Saul; I should like to feel my course met with your full approval," pursued the judge, with charming deference.

"You'll get yourself shot full of holes," said Mr. Saul.

"What causes me to hesitate is this: my name is unfamiliar to your citizens. You know their prejudices, Mr. Saul; how would they regard me if I put myself forward?"

"Can't say how they would take it," rejoined Mr. Saul.

Again the judge gave him a fixed scrutiny. Then ha shook him warmly by the hand.

"Think of what I have said; ponder it, sir, and let me have your answer at another time." And he backed from Mr. Saul's presence with spectacular politeness.

"A cheap mind!" thought the judge, as he hurried up the street.

He broached the subject to Mr. Wesley the postmaster, to Mr. Ellison the gunsmith, to Mr. Pegloe, employing much the same formula he had used with Mr. Saul, and with results almost identical. He imagined there must be some conspiracy afoot to keep him out of the public eye, and in the end he managed to lose his temper.

"Hasn't Norton any friends?" he demanded of Pegloe. "Who's going to be safe at this rate? We want to let some law into west Tennessee, a hanging or two would clear the air!" His emotions became a rage that blew through him like a gale, shaking him to his center.

Two mornings later he found where it had been placed under his door during the night a folded paper. It contained a single line of writing:

"You talk too much. Shut up, or you'll go where Norton went."

Now the judge was accessible to certain forms of fear. He was, for instance, afraid of snakes - both kinds - and mobs he had dreaded desperately since his Pleasantville experience; but beyond this, fear remained an unexplored region to Slocum Price, and as he examined the scrawl a smile betokening supreme satisfaction overspread his battered features. He was agreeably affected by the situation; indeed he was delighted. His activities were being recognized; he had made his impression; the cutthroats had selected him to threaten. Well, the damned rascals showed their good sense; he'd grant them that! Swelling with pride, he carried the scrawl to Mahaffy.

"They are forming their estimate of me, Solomon; I shall have them on the run yet!" he declared.

"You are going out of your way to hunt trouble - as if you hadn't enough at the best of times, Price! Let these people manage their own affairs, don't you mix up in them," advised the conservative Mahaffy.

The judge drew himself up with an air of lofty pride.

"Do you think I am going to be silenced, intimidated, by this sort of thing? No, sir! No, Solomon, the stopper isn't made that will fit my mouth."

A few moments later he burst in on Mr. Saul.

"Glance at that, my friend!" he cried, as he tossed the paper on
the clerk's desk. "Eh, what? - no joke about that, Mr. Saul. I
found it under my door this morning." Mr. Saul glanced at the
penciled lines and drew in his breath sharply. "What do you
make of it, sir?" demanded the judge anxiously.

"Well, of course, you'll do as you please, but I'd keep still."

"You mean you regard this as an authentic expression, sir, and
not as the joke of some irresponsible humorist?"

"It's authentic enough," said Mr. Saul impatiently.

The judge gave a sigh of relief; he could have hugged the little
clerk who had put to rest certain miserable doubts that had
assailed him.

"Sir, I wish it known that I hold the writer and his threats in
contempt; if I have given offense it is to an element I shall
never seek to conciliate." Mr. Saul was clearly divided between
his admiration for the judge's courage and fear for his safety.
"One thing is proven, sir," the judge went on; "the man who
murdered that poor boy is in our midst; that point can no
longer be disputed. Now, where are their fine-spun theories as
to how he crossed to the Arkansas coast? What does their mass
of speculation and conjecture amount to in the face of this?"
He breathed deep. "My God, sir, the murderer may be the
very next man you pass the time of day with!" Mr. Saul
shivered uncomfortably. "And the case in the hands of that
pin-headed fool, Betts!" The judge laughed derisively as he
bowed himself out. He left it with Mr. Saul to disseminate the
news. The judge strutted home with his hat cocked over one
eye, and his chest expanded to such limits that it menaced all
his waistcoat buttons. Perhaps he was under observation. Ah,
let the cutthroats look their full at him!

He established himself in his office. He had scarcely done so when Mr. Betts knocked at the door. The sheriff came direct from Mr. Saul and arrived out of breath, but the letter was not mentioned by the judge. He spoke of the crops, the chance of rain, and the intricacies of county politics. The sheriff withdrew mystified, wondering why it was he had not felt at liberty to broach the subject which was uppermost in his mind. His place was taken by Mr. Pegloe, and on the heels of the tavern-keeper came Mr. Bowen. Judge Price received them with condescension, but back of the condescension was an air of reserve that did not invite questions. The judge discussed the extension of the national roads with Mr. Pegloe, and the religion of the Persian fire-worshipers with Mr. Bowen; he permitted never a pause and they retired as the sheriff had done without sight of the letter.

The judge's office became a perfect Mecca. for the idle and the curious, and while he overflowed with high-bred courtesy he had never seemed so unapproachable - never so remote from matters of local and contemporary interest.

"Why don't you show 'em the letter?" demanded Mr. Mahaffy, when they were alone. "Can't you see they are suffering for a sight of it?"

"All in good time, Solomon." He became thoughtful. "Solomon, I am thinking of offering a reward for any information that will lead to the discovery of my anonymous correspondent," he at length observed with a finely casual air, as if the idea had just occurred to him, and had not been seething in his brain all day.

"There you go, Price -" began Mahaffy.

"Solomon, this is no time for me to hang back. I shall offer a reward of five thousand dollars for this information." The judge's tone was resolute. "Yes, sir, I shall make the figure commensurate with the poignant grief I feel. He was my friend and client -" The moisture gathered in his eyes.

"I should think that fifty dollars was nearer to being your figure," suggested the cautious Mahaffy.

"Inadequate and most insulting," said the judge.

"Well, where do you expect to get five thousand dollars?" cried Mahaffy in a tone of absolute exasperation.

"Where would I get fifty?" inquired the judge mildly.

For once Mahaffy frankly owned himself beaten. A gleam of admiration lit up his glance.

"Price, you have a streak of real greatness!" he declared.

Before the day was over it was generally believed that the judge was wearing his gag with humility; interest in him declined, still the public would have been grateful for a sight of that letter.

"Shucks, he's nothing but an old windbag!" said Mr. Pegloe to a group of loungers gathered before his tavern in the early evening.

As he spoke, the judge's door opened and that gentleman appeared on his threshold with a lighted candle in each hand. Glancing neither to the right nor the left he passed out and up the street. Not a breath of wind was blowing and the flames of the two candles burnt clear and strong, lighting up his stately advance.

At the corner of the court-house green stood a row of locust hitching posts. Two of these the judge decorated with his candles, next he measured off fifteen paces, strides as liberal as he could make them without sacrifice to his dignity; he scored a deep line in the dust with the heel of his boot, toed it squarely, and drew himself up to his fullest height. His right hand was seen to disappear under the frayed tails of his coat, it reappeared and was raised with a movement quicker than the eye could follow and a pistol shot rang out. One of the candles was neatly snuffed.

The judge allowed himself a covert glance in the direction of the loungers before the tavern. He was aware that a larger audience was assembling. A slight smile relaxed the firm set of his lips. The remaining candle sputtered feebly. The judge walked to the post and cleared the wick from tallow with his thumb-nail. There was no haste in any of his movements; his was the deliberation of conscious efficiency. Resuming his former station back of the line he had drawn in the dusty road he permitted his eye to gauge the distance afresh, then his hand was seen to pass deftly to his left hip pocket, the long barrel of the rifle pistol was leveled, the piece cracked, and the candle's yellow flame vanished.

The judge pocketed his pistol, walked down the street, and with never a glance toward the tavern reentered his house.

The next morning it was discovered that sometime during the night the judge had tacked his anonymous communication on the court-house door; just below it was another sheet of paper covered with bold script:

"TO WHOM IT MAY CONCERN: Judge Slocum Price assumes that the above was intended for him since he found it under his office door on the morning of the twenty-fifth inst.

"Judge Price begs leave to state it as his unqualified conviction that the writer is a coward and a cur, and offers a reward of five thousand dollars for any information that will lead to his identification.

"Judge Price has stated that he would conduct an intelligently directed investigation of the Norton murder mystery without remuneration. He has the honor to assure his friends that he is still willing to do so; however, he takes this opportunity to warn the public that each day's delay is a matter of the utmost gravity.

"Furthermore, judge Price avails himself on this occasion to say that he has no wish to avoid personal conclusions with the murderers and cutthroats who are terrorizing this community; on the contrary, he will continue earnestly to seek such personal conclusions."

CHAPTER XXIV

THE CABIN ACROSS THE BAYOU

Tom Ware was seated alone over his breakfast. He had left his bed as the pale morning light crept across the great fields that were alike his pride and his despair - what was the use of trying to sleep when sleep was an impossibility! The memory of that tragedy at the church door was a black horror to him; it gave substance to his dreams, it brought him awake with writhing lips that voiced his fear in the dead stillness of the night. The days were scarcely less terrible. Steeled and resolute as his will could make him, he was not able to speak of what he had seen with composure. Being as he was in this terribly perturbed state he had shirked his morning toilet and presented a proportionately haggard and unkempt appearance. He was about to quit the table when big Steve entered the room to say there was a white fellow at the door wished to see him.

"Fetch him along in here," said Ware briefly, without lifting his bloodshot eyes.

Brought into his presence the white fellow delivered a penciled note which proved to be from Murrell, and then on Ware's invitation partook of whisky. When he was gone, the planter ordered his horse, and while he waited for it to be brought up from the stables, reread Murrell's note. The expression of his unprepossessing features indicated what was passing in his mind, his mood was one of sullen rebellion. He felt Murrell was bent on committing him to an aggregate of crime he would never have considered possible, and all for love of a girl - a pink-cheeked, white-faced chit of a girl - disgust boiled up within him, rage choked him; this was the rotten spot in Murrell's make-up, the man was mad-stark mad!

As Ware rode away from Belle Plain he cursed him under his breath with vindictive thoroughness. His own inclination toward evil was never very robust; he could have connived and schemed over a long period of years to despoil Betty of her property, he would have counted this a legitimate field for enterprise; but murder and abduction was quite another thing. He would wash his hands of all further connection with Murrell, he had other things to lose besides Belle Plain, and the present would be as good a time as any to let the outlaw know he could be coerced and bullied no longer. But he had a saving recollection of the way in which Murrell dealt with what he counted treachery; an unguarded word, and he would not dare to travel those roads even at broad noon-day, while to pass before a lighted window at night would be to invite death; nowhere would he be safe.

Three miles from Belle Plain he entered a bridle path that led toward the river; he was now traversing a part of the Quintard tract. Two miles from the point where he had quitted the main road he came out upon the shores of a wide bayou. Looking across this he saw at a distance of half a mile what seemed to be a clearing of considerable extent, it was the first sign of human occupation he had seen since leaving Belle Plain.

An impenetrable swamp defended the head of the bayou which he skirted. Doubling back as though he were going to retrace his steps to Belle Plain, finally he gained a position opposite the clearing which still showed remotely across the wide reach of sluggish water. Here he dismounted and tied his horse, then as one tolerably familiar with the locality and its resources, he went down to the shore and launched a dugout which he found concealed in some bushes; entering it he pointed its blunt bow in the direction of the clearing opposite. A growth of small timber was still standing along the water's edge, but as he drew nearer, those betterments which the resident of that lonely spot had seen fit to make for his own convenience, came under his scrutiny; these consisted of a log cabin and several lesser sheds. Landing and securing his dug-out by the simple expedient of dragging half its length out of the water, he advanced toward the cabin. As he did so he saw two women at work heckling flax under an open shed. They were the wife and daughter of George Hicks, his overseer's brother.

"Morning, Mrs. Hicks," he said, addressing himself to the mother, a hulking ruffian of a woman.

"Howdy, sir?" she answered. Her daughter glanced indifferently in Ware's direction. She was a fine strapping girl, giving that sense of physical abundance which the planter admired.

"They'd better keep her out of Murrell's way!" he thought; aloud he said, "Anybody with the captain?"

"Colonel Fentress is."

"Humph!" muttered Ware. He moved to the door of the cabin and pushing it open, entered the room where Murrell and Fentress were seated facing each other across the breakfast table. The planter nodded curtly. He had not seen Murrell since the murder, and the sight of him quickened the spirit of antagonism which he had been nursing. "You roust a fellow out early enough!" he grumbled, rubbing his unshaven chin with the back of his hand.

"I was afraid you'd be gone somewhere. Sit down - here, between the colonel and me," said Murrell.

"Well, what the devil do you want of me anyhow?" demanded the planter.

"How's your sister, Tom?" inquired Murrell.

"I reckon she's the way you'd expect her to be." Ware dropped his voice to a whisper. Those women were just the other side of the logs, he could hear them at their work.

"Who's at Belle Plain now?" continued Murrell.

"Bowen's wife and daughter have stayed," answered Ware, still in a whisper.

"For how long, Tom? Do you know?"

"They were to go home after breakfast this morning; the daughter's to come out again to-morrow and stay with Betty until she leaves."

"What's that you're saying?" cried Murrell.

"She's going back to North Carolina to those friends of hers; it's no concern of mine, she does what she likes without consulting me." There was a brief pause during which Murrell scowled at the planter.

"I reckon your heart's tender, too!" he presently said. Ware's dull glance shifted to Fentress, but the colonel's cold and impassive exterior forbade the thought that his sympathy had been roused.

"It isn't that," Ware muttered, moistening his lips. He felt the utter futility of opposition. "I am for letting things rest just where they are," again his voice slid into a husky whisper. "You'll be running all our heads into a halter, the first thing you know - and this isn't any place to talk over such matters, there are too many people about."

"There's only Bess and the old woman busy outside," said Murrell.

"What's to hinder them from sticking an ear to a chink in the logs?"

"Go on, and finish what you've got to say, and get it off your mind," said Murrell.

"Well, then, I want to tell you that I consider you didn't regard me at all in the way you managed that business at the church! If I had known what was due to happen there, do you think I'd have gone near the place? But you let me go! I met you on the road and you told me you'd learned Norton had been to see Bowen, you told me that much, but you didn't tell me near all you might!" Ware was bitter and resentful; again he felt the sweat of a mortal terror drip from him.

"It was the best thing for you that it happened the way it did," rejoined Murrell coolly. "No one will ever think you had a hand in it."

"It wasn't right! You placed me in the meanest kind of a situation," objected Ware sullenly, mopping his face.

"Did you think I was going to let the marriage take place? You knew he had been warned to keep away from her," said Murrell. There was a movement overhead in the loft, the loose clapboards with which it was floored creaked under a heavy tread.

"Who's that? Hicks?" asked Ware.

"It isn't Hicks - never mind who it is, Tom," answered Murrell quietly.

"I thought you'd sent him out of the county?" muttered Ware, his face livid.

"Look here, Tom, I don't ask your help, but I won't stand your interference. I'm going to have the girl."

"John, you'll ruin yourself with your damned crazy infatuation!" It was Fentress, no longer able to control himself, who spoke.

"No, I won't, Colonel, but I'm not going to discuss that. All I want is for Tom to go to Memphis and stay there for a couple of days. When he comes back Belle Plain and its niggers will be as good as his. I am going to take the girl away from there to-night. I don't ask your help and you needn't ask what comes of her afterward. That will be my affair." Murrell's burning eyes shifted from one to the other.

"A beautiful and accomplished young lady - a great heiress - is to disappear and no solution of the mystery demanded by the public at large!" said Fentress with an acid smile. Murrell laughed contemptuously.

"What's all this fuss over Norton's death amounted to?" he said.

"Are you sure you have come to the end of that, John?" inquired Fentress, still smiling.

"I don't propose to debate this further," rejoined Murrell haughtily. Instantly the colonel's jaw became rigid. The masterful airs of this cutthroat out of the hills irked him beyond measure. Murrell turned to Ware.

"How soon can you get away from here, Tom?" he asked abruptly.

"By God, I can't go too soon!" cried the planter, staggering to his feet. He gave Fentress a hopeless beaten look. "You're my witness that first and last I've no part in this!" he added.

The colonel merely shrugged his shoulders. Murrell reached out a detaining hand and rested it on Ware's arm.

"Keep your wits about you, Tom, and within a week people will have forgotten all about Norton and your sister. I am going to give them something else to worry over."

Ware went from the cabin, and as the door swung shut

Fentress faced Murrell across the table.

"I've gone as far with you in this affair as I can go; after all, as you say, it is a private matter. You reap the benefits – you and Tom between you - I shall give you a wide berth until you come to your senses. Frankly, if you think that in this late day in the world you can carry off an unwilling girl, your judgment is faulty."

"Hold on, Colonel - how do you know she is going to prove unwilling?" objected Murrell, grinning.

Fentress gave him a glance of undisguised contempt and rose from his seat.

"I admit your past successes, John - that is, I take your word for them - but Miss Malroy is a lady."

"I have heard enough!" said Murrell angrily.

"So have I, John," retorted the colonel in a tone that was unvexed but final, "and I shall count it a favor if you will never refer to her in my hearing." He moved in the direction of the door.

"Oh, you and I are not going to lose our tempers over this!" began Murrell. "Come, sit down again, Colonel!" he concluded with great good nature.

"We shall never agree, John - you have one idea and I another."

"We'll let the whole matter drop out of our talk. Look here, how about the boy - are you ready for him if I can get my hands on him?"

Fentress considered. From the facts he had gathered he knew that the man who called himself Judge Price must soon run his course in Raleigh, and then as inevitably push out for fresh fields. Any morning might find him gone and the boy with him.

"I can't take him to my place as I had intended doing; under the circumstances that is out of the question," he said at length.

"Of course; but I'll send him either up or down the river and place him in safe keeping where you can get him any time you want."

"This must be done without violence, John!" stipulated Fentress.

"Certainly, I understand that perfectly well. It wouldn't suit your schemes to have that brace of old sots handled by the Clan. Which shall it be - up or down river?"

"Could you take care of him for me below, at Natchez?" inquired Fentress.

"As well there as anywhere, Colonel, and he'll pass into safe hands; he won't give me the slip the second time!"

"Good!" said Fentress, and took his leave.

From the window Murrell watched him cross the clearing, followed by the girl, Bess, who was to row him over to the opposite shore. He reflected that these men - the Wares and Fentresses and their like - were keen enough where they had schemes of their own they wished put through; it was only when he reached out empty hands that they reckoned the consequences.

Three-quarters of an hour slipped by, then, piercing the silence, Murrell heard a shrill whistle; it was twice repeated; he saw Bess go down to the landing again. A half-hour elapsed and a man issued from the scattering growth of bushes that screened the shore. The new-comer crossed the clearing and entered the cabin. He was a young fellow of twenty-four or five, whose bronzed and sunburnt face wore a somewhat reckless expression.

"Well, Captain, what's doing?" he asked, as he shook hands with Murrell.

"I've been waiting for you, Hues," said Murrell. He continued, "I reckon the time's here when nothing will be gained by delay."

Hues dropped down on a three-legged stool and looked at the outlaw fixedly and in silence for a moment. At length he nodded understandingly.

"You mean?"

"If anything's to be done, now is the time. What have you to report?"

"Well, I've seen the council of each Clan division. They are ripe to start this thing off."

Murrell gave him a moment of moody regard.

"Twice already I've named the day and hour, but now I'm going to put it through!" He set his teeth and thrust out his jaw.

"Captain, you're the greatest fellow in America! Inside of a week men who have never been within five hundred miles of you will be asking each other who John Murrell is!"

Murrell had expected to part with Hues then and there and for all time, but Hues possessed qualities which might still be of use to him.

"What do you expect to do for yourself?" he demanded. The other laughed shortly.

"Captain, I'm going to get rich while I have the chance. Ain't that what we are all after?"

"How?" inquired Murrell quietly. Hues shifted his seat.

"I'm sensitive about calling things by their short names;" he gave way to easy laughter; "but if you've got anything special you're saving for yourself, I'm free to say I'd rather take chances with you than with another," he finished carelessly.

"Hues, you must start back across Tennessee. Make it Sunday at midnight - that's three days off." Unconsciously his voice sank to a whisper.

"Sunday at midnight," repeated Hues slowly.

"When you have passed the word into middle Tennessee, turn south and make the best of your way to New Orleans. Don't stop for anything - push through as fast as you can. You'll find me there. I've a notion you and I will quit the country together."

"Quit the country! Why, Captain, who's talking of quitting the country?"

"You speak as though you were fool enough to think the niggers would accomplish something!" said Murrell coolly. "There will be confusion at first, but there are enough white men in the southwest to handle a heap better organized insurrection than we'll be able to set going. Our fellows will have to use their heads as well as their hands or they are likely to help the nigger swallow his medicine. I look for nothing else than considerable of a shake-up along the Mississippi . . . what with lynchers and regulators a man will have to show a clean bill of health to be allowed to live, no matter what his color - just being white won't help him any!"

"No, you're right, it won't!" and again Hues gave way to easy laughter.

"When you've done your work you strike south as I tell you and join me. I'm going to keep New Orleans for myself - it's my ambition to destroy the city Old Hickory saved!"

"And then it's change your name and strike out for Texas with what you've picked up!"

"No, it isn't! I'll have my choice of men - a river full of ships. Look here, there's South America, or some of those islands in the gulf with a black-and-tan population and a few white mongrels holding on to civilization by their eye-teeth; what's to hinder our setting up shop for ourselves? Two or three hundred Americans could walk off with an island like Hayti, for instance - and it's black with niggers. What we'd done here would be just so much capital down there. We'd make it a stamping-ground for the Clan! In the next two years we could bring in a couple of thousand Americans and then we'd be ready to take over their government, whether they liked it or not, and run it at a profit. We'd put the niggers back in slavery where they belong, and set them at work raising sugar and tobacco for their new bosses. Man, it's the richest land in the world, I tell you - and the mountains are full of gold!"

Hues had kindled with a ready enthusiasm while Murrell was speaking.

"That sounds right, Captain - we'd have a country and a flag of our own - and I look at those free niggers as just so much boot!"

"I shall take only picked men with me - I can't give ship room to any other - but I want you. You'll join me in New Orleans?" said Murrell.

"When do you start south?" asked Hues quickly.

"Inside of two days. I've got some private business to settle before I leave. I'll hang round here until that's attended to."

CHAPTER XXV

THE JUDGE EXTENDS HIS CREDIT

That afternoon Judge Price walked out to Belle Plain. Solomon Mahaffy had known that this was a civility Betty Malroy could by no means escape. He had been conscious of the judge's purpose from the moment it existed in the germ state, and he had striven to divert him, but his striving had been in vain, for though the judge valued Mr. Mahaffy because of certain sterling qualities which he professed to discern beneath the hard crust that made up the external man, he was not disposed to accept him as his mentor in nice matters of taste and gentlemanly feeling. He owed it to himself personally to tender his sympathy. Miss Malroy must have heard something of the honorable part he had played; surely she could not be in ignorance of the fact that the lawless element, dreading his further activities, had threatened him. She must know, too, about that reward of five thousand dollars. Certainly her grief could not blind her to the fact that he had met the situation with a largeness of public spirit that was an impressive lesson to the entire community.'

These were all points over which he and Mahaffy had wrangled, and he felt that his friend, in seeking to keep him away from Belle Plain, was standing squarely in his light. He really could not understand Solomon or his objections. He pointed out that Norton had probably left a will - no one knew yet - probably his estate would go to his intended wife - what more likely? He understood Norton had cousins

Vaughan Kester

somewhere in middle Tennessee - there was the attractive possibility of extended litigation. Miss Malroy needed a strong, clear brain to guide her past those difficulties his agile fancy assembled in her path. He beamed on his friend with a wide sunny smile.

"You mean she needs a lawyer, Price?" insinuated Mahaffy.

"That slap at me, Solomon, is unworthy of you. Just name some one, will you, who has shown an interest comparable to mine? I may say I have devoted my entire energy to her affairs, and with disinterestedness. I have made myself felt. Will you mention who else these cutthroats have tried to browbeat and frighten? They know that my theories and conclusions are a menace to them! I got 'em in a panic, sir - presently some fellow will lose his nerve and light out for the tall timber - and it will be just Judge Slocum Price who's done the trick - no one else!"

"Are you looking for some one to take a pot shot at you?" inquired Mahaffy sourly.

"Your remark uncovers my fondest hope, Solomon - I'd give five years of my life just to be shot at - that would round out the episode of the letter nicely;" again the judge beamed on Mahaffy with that wide and sunny smile of his.

"Why don't you let the boy go alone, Price?" suggested Mahaffy. He lacked that sense of sublime confidence in the judge's tact and discretion of which the judge, himself, entertained never a doubt.

"I shall not obtrude myself, Solomon; I shall merely walk out to Belle Plain and leave a civil message. I know what's due Miss Malroy in her bereaved state - she has sustained no ordinary loss, and in no ordinary fashion. She has been the center of a striking and profoundly moving tragedy! I would give a good deal to know if my late client left a will -"

"You might ask her," said Mahaffy cynically. "Nothing like going to headquarters for the news!"

"Solomon, Solomon, give me credit for common sense - go further, and give me credit for common decency! Don't let us forget that ever since we came here she has manifested a charmingly hospitable spirit where we are concerned!"

"Wouldn't charity hit nearer the mark, Price?"

"I have never so regarded it, Solomon," said the judge mildly. "I have read a different meaning in the beef and flour and potatoes she's sent here. I expect if the truth could be known to us she is wondering in the midst of her grief why I haven't called, but she'll appreciate the considerate delicacy of a gentleman. I wish it were possible to get cut flowers in this cussed wilderness!"

The judge had been occupied with a simple but ingenious toilet. He had trimmed the frayed skirts of, his coat; then by turning his cuffs inside out and upside down a fresh surface made its first public appearance. Next his shoes had engaged his attention. They might have well discouraged a less resolute and resourceful character, but with the contents of his ink-well he artfully colored his white yarn socks where they showed though the rifts in the leather. This the judge did gaily, now humming a snatch of song, now listening civilly to Mahaffy, now replying with undisturbed cheerfulness. Last of all he clapped his dingy beaver on his head, giving it an indescribably jaunty slant, and stepped to the door.

"Well, wish me luck, Solomon, I'm off - come, Hannibal!" he said. At heart he cherished small hope of seeing Betty, advantageous as he felt an interview might prove. However, on reaching Belle Plain he and Hannibal were shown into the cool parlor by little Steve. It was more years than the judge cared to remember since he had put his foot inside such a house, but with true grandeur of soul he rose to the occasion; a sublimated dignity shone from every battered feature, while he fixed little Steve with so fierce a glance that the grin froze on his lips.

"You are to say that judge Slocum Price presents his compliments and condolences to Miss Malroy - have you got that straight, you pinch of soot?" he concluded affably. Little Steve, impressed alike by the judge's air of condescension and his easy flow of words, signified that he had. "You may also say that judge Price's ward, young Master Hazard, presents his compliments and condolences -" What more the judge might have said was interrupted by the entrance of Betty, herself.

"My dear young lady -" the judge bowed, then he advanced toward her with the solemnity of carriage and countenance he deemed suitable to the occasion, and her extended hand was engulfed between his two plump palms. He rolled his eyes heavenward. "It's the Lord's to deal with us as His own inscrutable wisdom dictates," he murmured with pious resignation. "We are all poorer, ma'am, that he has died - just as we were richer while he lived!" The rich cadence of the judge's speech fell sonorously on the silence, and that look of horror which had never quite left Betty's eyes since they saw Charley Norton fall, rose out of their clear depths again. The judge, instantly stricken with a sense of the inadequacy of his words, doubled on his spiritual tracks. "In a round-about way, ma'am, we're bound to believe in the omnipresence of Providence - we must think it - though a body might be disposed to hold that west Tennessee had got out of the line of divine supervision recently. Let me lead you to a chair, ma'am!"

Hannibal had slipped to Betty's side and placed his hand in hers. The judge regarded the pair with great benevolence of expression. "He would come, and I hadn't the heart to forbid it. If I can be of any service to you, ma'am, either in the capacity of a friend - or professionally - I trust you will not hesitate to command me -" The judge backed toward the door.

"Did you walk out, Judge Price?" asked Betty kindly.

"Nothing more than a healthful exercise - but we will not detain you, ma'am; the pleasure of seeing you is something we had not reckoned on!" The judge's speech was thick and unctuous with good feeling. He wished that Mahaffy might have been there to note the reserve and dignity of his deportment.

"But you must let me order luncheon for you," said Betty. At least this questionable old man was good to Hannibal.

"I couldn't think of it, ma'am -"

"You'll have a glass of wine, then," urged Betty hospitably. For the moment she had lost sight of what was clearly the judge's besetting sin.

The judge paused abruptly. He endured a moment of agonizing irresolution.

"On the advice of my physician I dare not touch wine - gout, ma'am, and liver - but this restriction does not apply to corn whisky - in moderation, and as a tonic - either before meals, immediately after meals or at any time between meals — always keeping in mind the idea of its tonic properties -" The judge seemed to mellow and ripen. This was much better than having the dogs sicked on you! His manner toward Betty became almost fatherly. Poor young thing, so lonely and desolate in the midst of all this splendor - he surreptitiously wiped away a tear, and when little Steve presented himself and was told to bring whisky, audibly smacked his lips - a whole lot better, surely!

"I am sorry you think you must hurry away, Judge Price," said Betty. She still retained the small brown hand Hannibal had thrust into hers.

"The eastern mail gets in to-day, ma'am, and I have reason to think my share of it will be especially heavy, for it brings the bulk of my professional correspondence." In ten years the judge had received just one communication by mail - a bill which had followed him through four states and seven counties. "I expect my secretary -" boldly fixing Solomon Mahaffy's status, "is already dipping into it; an excellent assistant, ma'am, but literary rather than legal."

Little Steve reappeared bearing a silver tray on which was a decanter and glass.

"Since you insist, ma'am," the judge poured himself a drink, "my best respects -" he bowed profoundly.

"If you are quite willing, judge, I think I will keep Hannibal. Miss Bowen, who has been here - since -" her voice broke suddenly.

"I understand, ma'am," said the judge soothingly. He gave her a glance of great concern and turned to Hannibal. "Dear lad, you'll be very quiet and obedient, and do exactly as Miss alroy says? When shall I come for him, ma'am?"

"I'll send him to you when he is ready to go home. I am thinking of visiting my friends in North Carolina, and I should like to have him spend as much time as possible with me before I start for the East."

It had occurred to Betty that she had done little or nothing for the child; probably this would be her last opportunity.

The state of the judge's feelings was such that with elaborate absence of mind he poured himself a second drink of whisky; and that there should be no doubt the act was one of inadvertence, said again, "My best respects, ma'am," and bowed as before. Putting down the glass he backed toward the door.

"I trust you will not hesitate to call upon me if I can be of any use to you, ma'am - a message will bring me here without a moment's delay." He was rather disappointed that no allusion had been made to his recent activities. He reasoned correctly that Betty was as yet in ignorance of the somewhat dangerous eminence he had achieved as the champion of law and order. However, he reflected with satisfaction that Hannibal, in remaining, would admirably serve his ends.

Betty insisted that he should be driven home, and after faintly protesting, the judge gracefully yielded the point, and a few moments later rolled away from Belle Plain behind a pair of sleek-coated bays, with a negro in livery on the box. He was conscious of a great sense of exaltation. He felt that he should paralyze Mahaffy. He even temporarily forgot the blow his hopes had sustained when Betty spoke of returning to North Carolina. This was life - broad acres and niggers - principally to trot after you toting liquor - and such liquor! - he lolled back luxuriantly with half-closed eyes.

"Twenty years in the wood if an hour!" he muttered. "I'd like to have just such a taste in my mouth when I come to die - and probably she has barrels of it!" he sighed deeply, and searched his soul for words with which adequately to describe that whisky to Mahaffy.

But why not do more than paralyze Solomon - that would be pleasant but not especially profitable. The judge came back quickly to the vexed problem of his future. He desired to make some striking display of Miss Malroy's courtesy. He knew that his credit was experiencing the pangs of an early mortality; he was not sensitive, yet for some days he had been sensible of the fact that what he called the commercial class was viewing him with open disfavor, but he must hang on in Raleigh a little longer - for him it had become the abode of hope. The judge considered the matter. At least he could let people see something of that decent respect with which Miss Malroy treated him.

They were entering Raleigh now, and he ordered the coachman to pull his horses down to a walk. He had decided to make use of the Belle Plain turnout in creating an atmosphere of confidence and trust - especially trust. To this end he spent the best part of an hour interviewing his creditors. It amounted almost to a mass-meeting of the adult male population, for he had no favorites. When he invaded virgin territory he believed in starting the largest possible number of accounts without delay. The advantage of his system, as he explained its workings to Mahaffy, was that it bred a noble spirit of emulation. He let it be known in a general way that things were looking up with him; just in what quarter he did not specify, but there he was, seated in the Belle Plain carriage and the inference was unavoidable that Miss Malroy was to recognize his activities in a substantial manner.

Mahaffy, loafing away the afternoon in the county clerk's office, heard of the judge's return. He heard that Charley Norton had left a will; that Thicket Point went to Miss Malroy; that the Norton cousins in middle Tennessee were going to put up a fight; that Judge Price had been retained as counsel by Miss Malroy; that he was authorized to begin an independent search for Charley Norton's murderer, and was to spare no expense; that Judge Price was going to pay his debts. Mahaffy grinned at this and hurried home. He could believe all but the last, that was the crowning touch of unreality.

The judge explained the situation.

"I wouldn't withhold hope from any man, Solomon; it's the cheapest thing in the world and the one thing we are most miserly about extending to our fellows. These people all feel better - and what did it cost me? - just a little decent consideration; just the knowledge of what the unavoidable associations of ideas in their own minds would do for them!"

What had seemed the corpse of credit breathed again, and the judge and Mahaffy immediately embarked upon a character-istic celebration. Early candlelight found them making a beginning; midnight came - the gray and purple of dawn - and they were still at it, back of closed doors and shuttered windows.

CHAPTER XXVI

BETTY LEAVES BELLE PLAIN

Hannibal had devoted himself loyally to the judge's glorification, and Betty heard all about the letter, the snuffing of the candles and the reward of five thousand dollars. It vastly increased the child's sense of importance and satisfaction when he discovered she had known nothing of these matters until he told her of them.

"Why, where would Judge Price get so much money, Hannibal?" she asked, greatly astonished.

"He won't have to get it, Miss Betty; Mr. Mahaffy says he don't reckon no one will ever tell who wrote the letter - he 'lows the man who done that will keep pretty mum - he just dassent tell!" the boy explained.

"No, I suppose not -" and Betty saw that perhaps, after all, the judge had not assumed any very great financial responsibility. "He can't be a coward, though, Hannibal!" she added, for she understood that the risk of personal violence which he ran was quite genuine. She had formed her own unsympathetic estimate of him that day at Boggs' race-track; Mahaffy in his blackest hour could have added nothing to it. Twice since then she had met him in Raleigh, which had only served to fix that first impression.

"Miss Betty, he's just like my Uncle Bob was- he ain't afraid of nothing! He totes them pistols of his - loaded - if you notice good you can see where they bulge out his coat!" Hannibal's eyes, very round and big, looked up into hers.

"Is he as poor as he seems, Hannibal?" inquired Betty.

"He never has no money, Miss Betty, but I don't reckon he's what a body would call pore."

It might have baffled a far more mature intelligence than Hannibal's to comprehend those peculiar processes by which the judge sustained himself and his intimate fellowship with adversity - that it was his magnificence of mind which made the squalor of his daily life seem merely a passing phase - but the boy had managed to point a delicate distinction, and Betty grasped something of the hope and faith which never quite died out in Slocum Price's indomitable breast.

"But you always have enough to eat, dear?" she questioned anxiously. Hannibal promptly reassured her on this point. "You wouldn't let me think anything that was not true, Hannibal - you are quite sure you have never been hungry?"

"Never, Miss Betty; honest!"

Betty gave a sigh of relief. She had been reproaching herself for her neglect of the child; she had meant to do so much for him and had done nothing! Now it was too late for her personally to interest herself in his behalf, yet before she left for the East she would provide for him. If she had felt it was possible to trust the judge she would have made him her agent, but even in his best aspect he seemed a dubious dependence. Tom, for quite different reasons, was equally out of the question. She thought of Mr. Mahaffy.

"What kind of a man is Mr. Mahaffy, Hannibal?"

"He's an awful nice man, Miss Eetty, only he never lets on; a body's got to find it out for his own self - he ain't like the judge."

"Does he - drink, too, Hannibal?" questioned Betty.

"Oh, yes; when he can get the licker, he does." It was evident that Hannibal was cheerfully tolerant of this weakness on the part of the austere Mahaffy. By this time Betty was ready to weep over the child, with his knowledge of shabby vice, and his fresh young faith in those old tatterdemalions.

"But, no matter what they do, they are very, very kind to you?" she continued quite tremulously.

"Yes, ma'am - why, Miss Betty, they're lovely men!"

"And do you ever hear the things spoken of you learned about at Mrs. Ferris' Sunday-school?"

"When the judge is drunk he talks a heap about 'em. It's beautiful to hear him then; you'd love it, Miss Betty," and Hannibal smiled up sweetly into her face.

"Does he have you go to Sunday-school in Raleigh?"

The boy shook his head.

"I ain't got no clothes that's fitten to wear, nor no pennies to give, but the judge, he 'lows that as soon as he can make a raise I got to go, and he's learning me my letters - but we ain't a book. Miss Betty, I reckon it'd stump you some to guess how he's fixed it for me to learn?"

"He's drawn the letters for you, is that the way?" In spite of herself, Betty was experiencing a certain revulsion of feeling where the judge and Mahaffy were concerned. They were doubtless bad enough, but they could have been worse.

"No, ma'am; he done soaked the label off one of Mr. Pegloe's whisky bottles and pasted it on the wall just as high as my chin, so's I can see it good, and he's learning me that-a-ways! Maybe you've seen the kind of bottle I mean - Pegloe's Mississippi Pilot: Pure Corn Whisky?" But Hannibal's bright little face fell. He was quick to see that the educational system devised by the judge did not impress Betty at all favorably. She drew him into her arms.

"You shall have my books - the books I learned to read out of when I was a little girl, Hannibal!"

"I like learning from the label pretty well," said Hannibal loyally.

"But you'll like the books better, dear, when you see them. I know just where they are, for I happened on them on a shelf in the library only the other day."

After they had found and examined the books and Hannibal had grudgingly admitted that they might possess certain points of advantage over the label, he and Betty went out for a walk. It was now late afternoon and the sun was sinking behind the wall of the forest that rose along the Arkansas coast. Their steps had led them to the terrace where they stood looking off into the west. It was here that Betty had said good-by to Bruce Carrington - it might have been months ago, and it was only days. She thought of Charley - Charley, with his youth and hope and high courage - unwittingly enough she had led him on to his death! A sob rose in her throat.

Hannibal looked up into her face. The memory of his own loss was never very long absent from his mind, and Miss Betty had been the victim of a similarly sinister tragedy. He recalled those first awful days of loneliness through which he had lived, when there was no Uncle Bob - soft-voiced, smiling and infinitely companionable.

"Why, Hannibal, you are crying - what about, dear?" asked Betty suddenly.

"No, ma'am; I ain't crying," said Hannibal stoutly, but his wet lashes gave the lie to his words.

"Are you homesick - do you wish to go back to the judge and Mr. Mahaffy?"

"No, ma'am - it ain't that - I was just thinking -"

"Thinking about what, dear?"

"About my Uncle Bob." The small face was very wistful.

"Oh - and you still miss him so much, Hannibal?"

"I bet I do - I reckon anybody who knew Uncle Bob would never get over missing him; they just couldn't, Miss Betty! The judge is mighty kind, and so is Mr. Mahaffy - they're awful kind, Miss Betty, and it seems like they get kinder all the time - but with Uncle Bob, when he liked you, he just laid himself out to let you know it!"

"That does make a great difference, doesn't it?" agreed Betty sadly, and two piteous tearful eyes were bent upon him.

"Don't you reckon if Uncle Bob is alive, like the judge says, and he's ever going to find me, he had ought to be here by now?" continued Hannibal anxiously.

"But it hasn't been such a great while, Hannibal; it's only that so much has happened to you. If he was very badly hurt it may have been weeks before he could travel; and then when he could, perhaps he went back to that tavern to try to learn what had become of you. But we may be quite certain he will never abandon his search until he has made every possible effort to find you, dear! That means he will sooner or later come to west Tennessee, for there will always be the hope that you have found your way here."

"Sometimes I get mighty tired waiting, Miss Betty," confessed the boy. "Seems like I just couldn't wait no longer" He sighed gently, and then his face cleared. "You reckon he'll come most any time, don't you, Miss Betty ?"

"Yes, Hannibal; any day or hour!"

"Whoop!" muttered Hannibal softly under his breath. Presently he asked: "Where does that branch take you to?" He nodded toward the bayou at the foot of the terraced bluff.

"It empties into the river," answered Betty.

Hannibal saw a small skiff beached among the cottonwoods that grew along the water's edge and his eyes lighted up instantly. He had a juvenile passion for boats.

"Why, you got a boat, ain't you, Miss Betty?" This was a charming and an important discovery.

"Would you like to go down to it?" inquired Betty.

"'Deed I would! Does she leak any, Miss Betty?"

"I don't know about that. Do boats usually leak, Hannibal?"

"Why, you ain't ever been out rowing in her, Miss Betty, have you? - and there ain't no better fun than rowing a boat!" They had started down the path.

"I used to think that, too, Hannibal; how do you suppose it is that when people grow up they forget all about the really nice things they might do?"

"What use is she if you don't go rowing in her?" persisted Hannibal.

"Oh, but it is used. Mr. Tom uses it in crossing to the other side where they are clearing land for cotton. It saves him a long walk or ride about the head of the bayou."

"Like I should take you out in her, Miss Betty?' demanded Hannibal with palpitating anxiety.

They had entered the scattering timber when Betty paused suddenly with a startled exclamation, and Hannibal felt her fingers close convulsively about his. The sound she had heard might have been only the rustling of the wind among the branches overhead in that shadowy silence, but Betty's nerves, the placid nerves of youth and perfect health, were shattered.

"Didn't you hear something, Hannibal?" she whispered fearfully.

For answer Hannibal pointed mysteriously, and glancing in the direction he indicated, Betty saw a woman advancing along the path toward them. The look of alarm slowly died out of his eyes.

"I think it's the overseer's niece," she told Hannibal, and they kept on toward the boat.

The girl came rapidly up the path, which closely followed the irregular line of the shore in its windings. Once she was seen to stop and glance back over her shoulder, her attitude intent and listening, then she hurried forward again. Just by the boat the three met.

"Good evening!" said Betty pleasantly.

The girl made no reply to this; she merely regarded Betty with a fixed stare. At length she broke silence abruptly.

"I got something I want to say to you - you know who I am, I reckon?" She was a girl of about Betty's own age, with a certain dark, sullen beauty and that physical attraction which Tom, in spite of his vexed mood, had taken note of earlier in the day.

"You are Bess Hicks," said Betty.

"Make the boy go back toward the house a spell - I got something I want to say to you." Betty hesitated. She was offended by the girl's manner, which was as rude as her speech. "I ain't going to hurt you - you needn't be afraid of me, I got something important to say - send him off, I tell you; there ain't no time to lose!" The girl stamped her foot impatiently.

Betty made a sign to Hannibal and he passed slowly back along the path. He went unwillingly, and he kept his head turned that he might see what was done, even if he were not to hear what was said.

"That will do, Hannibal - wait there - don't go any farther!" Betty called after him when he had reached a point sufficiently distant to be out of hearing of a conversation carried on in an ordinary tone. "Now, what is it? Speak quickly if you have anything to tell me!"

"I got a heap to say," answered the girl with a scowl. Her manner was still fierce and repellent, and she gave Betty a certain jealous regard out of her black eyes which the latter was at a loss to explain. "Where's Mr. Tom?" she demanded.

"Tom? Why, about the place, I suppose - in his office, perhaps." So it had to do with Tom. . . . Betty felt sudden disgust with the situation.

"No, he ain't about the place, either! He done struck out for Memphis two hours after sun-up, and what's more, he ain't coming back here to-night -" There was a moment of silence. The girl looked about apprehensively. She continued, fixing her black eyes on Betty: "You're here alone at Belle Plain - you know what happened when Mr. Tom started for Memphis last timeI reckon you-all ain't forgot that!"

Betty felt a pallor steal over her face. She rested a hand that shook on the trunk of a tree to steady herself. The girl laughed shortly.

"Don't be so scared; I reckon Belle Plain's as good as his if anything happened to you?"

By a great effort Betty gained a measure of control over herself. She took a step nearer and looked the girl steadily in the face.

"Perhaps you will stop this sort of talk, and tell me what is going to happen to me - if you know?" she said quietly.

"Why do you reckon Mr. Norton was shot? I can tell you why - it was all along of you - that was why!" The girl's furtive glance, which searched and watched the gathering shadows, came back as it always did to Betty's pale face. "You ain't no safer than he was, I tell you!" and she sucked in her breath sharply between her full red lips.

"What do you mean?" faltered Betty.

"Do you reckon you're safe here in the big house alone? Why do you reckon Mr. Tom cleared out for Memphis? It was because he couldn't be around and have anything happen to you - that was why!" and the girl sank her voice to a whisper. "You quit Belle Plain now - to-night - just as soon as you can!"

"This is absurd - you are trying to frighten me!"

"Did they stop with trying to frighten Charley Norton?" demanded Bess with harsh insistence.

Whatever the promptings that inspired this warning, they plainly had nothing to do with either liking or sympathy. Her dominating emotion seemed to be a sullen sort of resentment which lit up her glance with a dull fire; yet her feelings were so clearly and so keenly personal that Betty understood the motive that had brought her there. The explanation, she found, left her wondering just where and how her own fate was linked with that of this poor white.

"You have been waiting some time to see me?" she asked.

"Ever since along about noon."

"You were afraid to come to the house?"

"I didn't want to be seen there."

"And yet you knew I was alone."

"Alone - but how do you know who's watching the place?"

"Do you think there was reason to be afraid of that?" asked Betty.

Again the girl stamped her foot with angry impatience.

"You're just wastin' time - just foolin' it away - and you ain't got none to spare!"

"You must tell me what I have to fear - I must know more or I shall stay just where I am!"

"Well, then, stay!" The girl turned away, and then as quickly turned back and faced Betty once more. "I reckon he'd kill me if he knew - I reckon I've earned that already -"

"Of whom are you speaking?"

"He'll have you away from here to-night!"

"He? . . . who? . . . and what if I refuse to go?"

"Did they ask Charley Norton whether he wanted to live or die?" came the sinister question.

A shiver passed through Betty. She was seeing it all again - Charley as he groped among the graves with the hand of death heavy upon him.

A moment later she was alone. The girl had disappeared. There was only the shifting shadows as the wind tossed the branches of the trees, and the bands of golden light that slanted along the empty path. The fear of the unknown leaped up afresh in Betty's soul, in an instant her flying feet had borne her to the boy's side.

"Come - come quick, Hannibal!" she gasped out, and seized his hand.

"What is it, Miss Betty? What's the matter?" asked Hannibal as they fled panting up the terraces.

"I don't know - only we must get away from here just as soon as we can!" Then, seeing the look of alarm on the child's face, she added more quietly, "Don't be frightened, dear, only we must go away from Belle Plain at once." But where they were to go, she had not considered.

Reaching the house, they stole up to Betty's room. Her well-filled purse was the important thing; that, together with some necessary clothing, went into a small hand-bag.

"You must carry this, Hannibal; if any one sees us leave the house they'll think it something you are taking away," she explained. Hannibal nodded understandingly.

"Don't you trust your niggers, Miss Betty?" he whispered as they went from the room.

"I only trust you, dear!"

"What makes you go? Was it something that woman told you? Are they coming after us, Miss Betty? Is it Captain Murrell?"

"Captain Murrell?" There was less of mystery now, but more of terror, and her hand stole up to her heart, and, white and slim, rested against the black fabric of her dress.

"Don't you be scared, Miss Betty!" said Hannibal.

They went silently from the house and again crossed the lawn to the terrace. Under the leafy arch which canopied them there was already the deep purple of twilight.

"Do you reckon it were Captain Murrell shot Mr. Norton, Miss Betty?" asked Hannibal in a shuddering whisper.

"Hush - Oh, hush, Hannibal! It is too awful to even speak of -" and, sobbing and half hysterical, she covered her face with her hands.

"But where are we going, Miss Betty?" asked the boy.

"I don't know, dear!" she had an agonizing sense of the night's approach and of her own utter helplessness.

"I'll tell you what, Miss Betty, let's go to the judge and Mr. Mahaffy!" said Hannibal.

"Judge Price?" She had not thought of him as a possible protector.

"Why, Miss Betty, ain't I told you he ain't afraid of nothing? We could walk to Raleigh easy if you don't want your niggers to hook up a team for you."

Betty suddenly remembered the carriage which had taken the judge into town; she was sure it had not yet returned.

"We will go to the judge, Hannibal! George, who drove him into Raleigh, has not come back; if we hurry we may meet him on the road."

Screened by the thick shadows, they passed up the path that edged the bayou; at the head of the inlet they entered a clearing, and crossing this they came to the corn-field which lay between the house and the highroad. Following one of the shock rows they hurried to the mouth of the lane.

"Hannibal, I don't want to tell the judge why I am leaving Belle Plain - about the woman, I mean," said Betty.

"You reckon they'd kill her, don't you, Miss Betty, if they knew what she'd done?" speculated the boy. It occurred to him that an adequate explanation of their flight would require preparation, since the judge was at all times singularly alive to the slightest discrepancy of statement. They had issued from the cornfield now and were going along the road toward Raleigh. Suddenly Betty paused.

"Hark!" she whispered.

"It were nothing, Miss Betty," said Hannibal reassuringly, and they hurried forward again. In the utter stillness through which they moved Betty heard the beating of her own heart, and the soft, and all but inaudible patter of the boy's bare feet on the warm dust of the road. Vague forms that resolved themselves into trees and bushes seemed to creep toward them out of the night's black uncertainty. Once more Betty paused.

"It were nothing, Miss Betty," said Hannibal as before, and he returned to his consideration of the judge. He sensed something of that intellectual nimbleness which his patron's physical make-up in nowise suggested, since his face was a mask that usually left one in doubt as to just how much of what he heard succeeded in making its impression on him; but the boy knew that Slocum Price's blind side was a shelterless exposure.

"You don't think the carriage could have passed us while we were crossing the corn-field?" said Betty.

"No, I reckon we couldn't a-missed hearing it," answered Hannibal. He had scarcely spoken when they caught the rattle of wheels and the beat of hoofs. These sounds swept nearer and nearer, and then the darkness disgorged the Belle Plain team and carriage.

"George!" cried Betty, a world of relief in her tones.

"Whoa, you!" and George reined in his horses with a jerk. "Who's dar?" he asked, bending forward on the box as he sought to pierce the darkness with his glance.

"George -"

"Oh, it you, Missy?"

"Yes, I wish you to drive me into Raleigh," said Betty, and she and Hannibal entered the carriage.

"All right, Missy. Yo'-all ready fo' me to go along out o' here?"

"Yes - drive fast, George!" urged Betty.

"It's right dark fo' fas' drivin' Missy, with the road jes' aimin' fo' to bus' yo' springs with chuckholes!" He had turned his horses' heads in the direction of Raleigh while he was speaking. "It's scandalous black in these heah woods, Missy I 'clar' I never seen it no blacker!"

The carriage swung forward for perhaps a hundred yards, then suddenly the horses came to a dead stop.

"Go along on, dar!" cried George, and struck them with his whip, but the horses only reared and plunged.

"Hold on, nigger!" said a rough voice out of the darkness.

"What yo' doin' ?" the coachman gasped. "Don' yo' know dis de Belle Plain carriage? Take yo' han's offen to dem hosses' bits!"

Two men stepped to the side of the carriage.

"Show your light, Bunker," said the same rough voice that had spoken before. Instantly a hooded lantern was uncovered, and

Hannibal uttered a cry of terror. He was looking into the face of Slosson, the tavern-keeper.

CHAPTER XXVII

PRISONERS

In the face of Betty's indignant protest Slosson and the man named Bunker climbed into the carriage.

"Don't you be scared, ma'am," said the tavernkeeper, who smelt strongly of whisky. "I wouldn't lift my hand ag'in no good looking female except in kindness."

"How dare you stop my carriage?" cried Betty, with a very genuine anger which for the moment dominated all her other emotions. She struggled to her feet, but Slosson put out a heavy hand and thrust her back.

"There now," he urged soothingly. "Why make a fuss? We ain't going to harm you; we wouldn't for no sum of money. Drive on, Jim - drive like hell!" This last was addressed to the man who had taken George's place on the box, where a fourth member of Slosson's band had forced the coachman down into the narrow space between the seat and dashboard, and was holding a pistol to his head while he sternly enjoined silence.

With a word to the horses Jim swung about and the carriage rolled off through the night at a breakneck' pace. Betty's shaking hands drew Hannibal closer to her side as she felt the surge of her terrors rise within her. Who were these men - where could they be taking her - and for what purpose? The events of the past weeks linked themselves in tragic sequence in her mind.

What was it she had to fear? Was it Tom who had inspired Norton's murder? Was it Tom for whom these men were acting? Tom who would profit greatly by her disappearance or death.

They swept past the entrance at Belle Plain, past a break in the wall of the forest where the pale light of stars showed Betty the corn-field she and Hannibal had but lately crossed, and then on into pitchy darkness again. She clung to the desperate hope that they might meet some one on the road, when she could cry out and give the alarm. She held herself in readiness for this, but there was only the steady pounding of the big bays as Jim with voice and whip urged them forward. At last he abruptly checked them, and Bunker and Slosson sprang from their seats.

"Get down, ma'am!" said the latter.

"Where are you taking me?" asked Betty, in a voice that shook in spite of her efforts to control it.

"You must hurry, ma'am," urged Slosson impatiently.

"I won't move until I know where you intend taking me!" said Betty, "If I am to die -"

Mr. Slosson laughed loudly and indulgently.

"You ain't. If you don't want to walk, I'm man enough fo' to tote you. We ain't far to go, and I've tackled jobs I'd a heap less heart fo' in my time," he concluded gallantly. From the opposite side of the carriage Bunker swore nervously. He desired to know if they were to stand there talking all night. "Shut your filthy mouth, Bunker, and see you keep tight hold of that young rip-staver," said Slosson. "He's a perfect eel - I've had dealings with him afore!"

"You tried to kill my Uncle Bob - at the tavern, you and Captain Murrell. I heard you, and I seen you drag him to the river!" cried Hannibal.

Slosson gave a start of astonishment at this.

"Why, ain't he hateful?" he exclaimed aghast. "See here, young feller, that's no kind of a way fo' you to talk to a man who has riz his ten children!"

Again Bunker swore, while Jim told Slosson to make haste. This popular clamor served to recall the tavernkeeper to a sense of duty.

"Ma'am, like I should tote you, or will you walk?" he inquired, and reaching out his hand took hold of Betty.

"I'll walk," said the girl quickly, shrinking from the contact.

"Keep close at my heels. Bunker, you tuck along after her with the boy."

"What about this nigger?" asked the fourth man.

"Fetch him along with us," said Slosson. They turned from the road while he was speaking and entered a narrow path that led off through the woods, apparently in the direction of the river. A moment later Betty heard the carriage drive away. They went onward in silence for a little time, then Slosson spoke over his shoulder.

"Yes, ma'am, I've riz ten children but none of 'em was like him - I trained 'em up to the minute!" Mr. Slosson seemed to have passed completely under the spell of his domestic recollections, for he continued with just a touch of reminiscent sadness in his tone. "There was all told four Mrs. Slossons: two of 'em was South Carolinians, one was from Georgia, and the last was a widow lady out of east Tennessee. She'd buried three husbands and I figured we could start perfectly even."

The intrinsic fairness of this start made its strong appeal. Mr. Slosson dwelt upon it with satisfaction. "She had three to her credit, I had three to mine; neither could crow none over the other."

As they stumbled forward through the thick obscurity he continued his personal revelations, the present enterprise having roused whatever there was of sentiment slumbering in his soul. At last they came out on a wide bayou; a white mist hung above it, and on the low shore leaf and branch were dripping with the night dews. Keeping close to the water's edge Slosson led the way to a point where a skiff was drawn up on the bank.

"Step in, ma'am," he said, when he had launched it.

"I will go no farther!" said Betty in desperation. She felt an overmastering fear, the full horror of the unknown lay hold of her, and she gave a piercing cry for help. Slosson swung about on his heel and seized her. For a moment she struggled to escape, but the man's big hands pinioned her.

"No more of that!" he warned, then he recovered himself and laughed. "You could yell till you was black in the face, ma'am, and there'd be no one to hear you."

"Where are you taking me?" and Betty's voice faltered between the sudden sobs that choked her.

"Just across to George Hicks's."

"For what purpose?"

"You'll know in plenty of time." And Slosson leered at her through the darkness.

"Hannibal is to go with me?" asked Betty tremulously.

"Sure!" agreed Slosson affably. "Your nigger, too - quite

a party."

Betty stepped into the skiff. She felt her hopes quicken - she was thinking of Bess; whatever the girl's motives, she had wished her to escape. She would wish it now more than ever since the very thing she had striven to prevent had happened. Slosson seated himself and took up the oars, Bunker followed with Hannibal and they pushed off. No word was spoken until they disembarked on the opposite shore, when Slosson addressed Bunker. "I reckon I can manage that young rip-staver, you go back after Sherrod and the nigger," he said.

He conducted his captives up the bank and they entered a clearing. Looking across this Betty saw where a cabin window framed a single square of light. They advanced toward this and presently the dark outline of the cabin itself became distinguishable. A moment later Slosson paused, a door yielded to his hand, and Betty and the boy were thrust into the room where Murrell had held his conference with Fentress and Ware. The two women were now its only occupants and the mother, gross and shapeless, turned an expressionless face on the intruders; but the daughter shrank into the shadow, her burning glance fixed on Betty.

"Here's yo' guests, old lady!" said Mr. Slosson. Mrs. Hicks rose from the three-legged stool on which she was sitting.

"Hand me the candle, Bess," she ordered.

At one side of the room was a steep flight of stairs which gave access to the loft overhead. Mrs. Hicks, by a gesture, signified that Betty and Hannibal were to ascend these stairs; they did so and found themselves on a narrow landing inclosed by a partition of rough planks, this partition was pierced by a low door. Mrs. Hicks, who had followed close at their heels, handed the candle to Betty.

"In yonder!" she said briefly, nodding toward the door.

"Wait!" cried Betty in a whisper.

"No," said the woman with an almost masculine surliness of tone. "I got nothing to say." She pushed them into the attic, and, closing the door, fastened it with a stout wooden bar.

Beyond that door, which seemed to have closed on every hope, Betty held the tallow dip aloft, and by its uncertain and flickering light surveyed her prison. The briefest glance sufficed. The room contained two shakedown beds and a stool, there was a window in the gable, but a piece of heavy plank was spiked before it.

"Miss Betty, don't you be scared," whispered Hannibal. "When the judge hears we're gone, him and Mr. Mahaffy will try to find us. They'll go right off to Belle Plain - the judge is always wanting to do that, only Mr. Mahaffy never lets him but now he won't be able to stop him."

"Oh, Hannibal, Hannibal, what can he do there - what can any one do there?" And a dead pallor overspread the girl's face. To speak of the blind groping of her friends but served to fix the horror of their situation in her mind.

"I don't know, Miss Betty, but the judge is always thinking of things to do; seems like they was mostly things no one else would ever think of."

Betty had placed the candle on the stool and seated herself on one of the beds. There was the murmur of voices in the room below; she wondered if her fate was under consideration and what that fate was to be. Hannibal, who had been examining the window, returned to her side.

"Miss Betty, if we could just get out of this loft we could steal their skiff and row down to the river; I reckon they got just the one boat; the only way they could get to us would be to swim out, and if they done that we could pound 'em over the head with the oars the least little thing sinks you when you're in the water." But this murderous fancy of his failed to interest Betty.

Presently they heard Sherrod and Bunker come up from the shore with George. Slosson joined them and there was a brief discussion, then an interval of silence, and the sound of voices again as the three white men moved back across the field in the direction of the bayou. There succeeded a period of utter stillness, both in the cabin and in the clearing, a somber hush that plunged Betty yet deeper in despair. Wild thoughts assailed her, thoughts against which she struggled with all the strength of her will.

In that hour of stress Hannibal was sustained by his faith in the judge. He saw his patron's powerful and picturesque intelligence applied to solving the mystery of their disappearance from Belle Plain; it was inconceivable that this could prove otherwise than disastrous to Mr. Slosson and he endeavored to share the confidence he was feeling with Betty, but there was something so forced and unnatural in the girl's voice and manner when she discussed his conjectures that he quickly fell into an awed silence. At last, and it must have been some time after midnight, troubled slumbers claimed him. No moment of forgetfulness came to Betty. She was waiting for what - she did not know! The candle burnt lower and lower and finally went out and she was left in darkness, but again she was conscious of sounds from the room below. At first it was only a word or a sentence, then the guarded speech became a steady monotone that ran deep into the night; eventually this ceased and Betty fancied she heard sobs.

At length points of light began to show through chinks in the logs. Hannibal roused and sat up, rubbing his eyes with the backs of his hands.

"Wasn't you able to sleep none?" he inquired. Betty shook her head. He looked at her with an expression of troubled concern. "How soon do you reckon the judge will know?" he asked.

"Very soon now, dear." Hannibal was greatly consoled by

this opinion.

"Miss Betty, he will love to find us -"

"Hark! What was that?" for Betty had caught the distant splash of oars. Hannibal found a chink in the logs through which by dint of much squinting he secured a partial view of the bayou. "They're fetching up a keel boat to the shore, Miss Betty - it's a whooper!" he announced. Betty's heart sank, she never doubted the purpose for which that boat was brought into the bayou, or that it nearly concerned herself.

Half an hour later Mrs. Hicks appeared with their breakfast. It was in vain that Betty attempted to engage her in conversation, either she cherished some personal feeling of dislike for her prisoner, or else the situation in which she herself was placed had little to recommend it, even to her dull mind, and her dissatisfaction was expressed in her attitude toward the girl.

Betty passed the long hours of morning in dreary speculation concerning what was happening at Belle Plain. In the end she realized that the day could go by and her absence occasion no alarm; Steve might reasonably suppose George had driven her into Raleigh or to the Bowens' and that she had kept the carriage. Finally all her hope centered on Judge Price. He would expect Hannibal during the morning, perhaps when the boy did not arrive he would be tempted to go out to Belle Plain to discover the reason of his nonappearance. She wondered what theories would offer themselves to his ingenious mind, for she sensed something of that indomitable energy which in the face of rebuffs and laughter carried him into the thick of every sensation.

At noon, Mrs. Hicks, as sullen as in the morning, brought them their dinner. She had scarcely quitted the loft when a shrill whistle pierced the silence that hung above the clearing. It was twice repeated, and the two women were heard to go from the cabin. Perhaps half an hour elapsed, then a step became audible on the packed earth of the dooryard; some one entered the room below and began to ascend the narrow stairs, and Betty's fingers closed convulsively about Hannibal's. This was neither Mrs. Hicks nor her daughter, nor Slosson with his clumsy shufe. There was a brief pause when the landing was reached, but it was only momentary; a hand lifted the bar, the door was thrown open, and its space framed the figure of a man. It was John Murrell.

Standing there he regarded Betty in silence, but a deep-seated fire glowed in his sunken eyes. The sense of possession was raging through him, his temples throbbed, a fever stirred his blood. Love, such as it was, he undoubtedly felt for her and even his giant project with all its monstrous ramifications was lost sight of for the moment. She was the inspiration for it all, the goal and reward toward which he struggled.

"Betty!" the single word fell softly from his lips. He stepped into the room, closing the door as he did so.

The girl's eyes were dilating with a mute horror, for by some swift intuitive process of the mind, which asked nothing of the logic of events, but dealt only with conclusions, Murrell stood revealed as Norton's murderer. Perhaps he read her thoughts, but he had lived in his degenerate ambitions until the common judgments or the understanding of them no longer existed for him. That Betty had loved Norton seemed inconsequential even; it was a memory to be swept away by the force of his greater passion. So he watched her smilingly, but back of the smile was the menace of unleashed impulse.

"Can't you find some word of welcome for me, Betty?" he asked at length, still softly, still with something of entreaty in his tone.

"Then it was you - not Tom - who had me brought here!" She could have thanked God had it been Tom, whose hate was not to be feared as she feared this man's love.

"Tom - no!" and Murrell laughed. "You didn't think I'd give

you up? I am standing with a halter, about my neck, and all for your sake - who'd risk as much for love of you?" he seemed to expand with savage pride that this was so, and took a step toward her.

"Don't come near me!" cried Betty. Her eyes blazed, and she looked at him with' loathing.

"You'll learn to be kinder," he exulted. "You wouldn't see me at Belle Plain; what was left for me but to have you brought here?" While Murrell was speaking, the signal that had told of his own presence on the opposite shore of the bayou was heard again. This served to arrest his attention. A look of uncertainty passed over his face, then he made an impatient gesture as if he dismissed some thought that had forced itself upon him, and turned to Betty.

"You don't ask what my purpose is where you are concerned; have you no curiosity on that score?" She endeavored to meet his glance with a glance as resolute, then her eyes sought the boy's upturned face. "I am going to send you down river, Betty. Later I shall join you in New Orleans, and when I leave the country you shall go with me -"

"Never!" gasped Betty.

"As my wife, or however you choose to call it. I'll teach you what a man's love is like," he boasted, and extended his hand. Betty shrank from him, and his hand fell at his side. He looked at her steadily out of his deep-sunk eyes in which blazed the fires of his passion, and as he looked, her face paled and flushed by turns. "You may learn to be kind to me, Betty," he said. "You may find it will be worth your while." Betty made no answer, she only gathered Hanniba closer to her side. "Why not accept what I have to offer, Betty?" again he went nearer her, and again she shrank from him, but the madness of his mood was in the ascendant. He seized her and drew her to him. She struggled to free herself, but his fingers tightened about hers.

"Let me go!" she panted. He laughed his cool laugh of triumph.

"Let you go - ask me anything but that, Betty! Have you no reward for patience such as mine? A whole summer has passed since I saw you first -"

There was the noisy shuffling of feet on the stairs, and releasing Betty, Murrell swung about on his heel and faced the door. It was pushed open an inch at a time by a not too confident hand and Mr. Slosson thus guardedly presented himself to the eye of his chief, whom he beckoned from the room.

"Well?" said Murrell, when they stood together on the landing.

"Just come across to the keel boat!" and Slosson led the way down the stairs and from the house.

"Damn you, Joe; you might have waited!" observed the outlaw. Slosson gave him a hardened grin. They crossed the clearing and boarded the keel boat which rested against the bank. As they did so, the cabin in the stern gave up a shattered presence in the shape of Tom Ware. Murrell started violently. "I thought you were hanging out in Memphis, Tom?" he said, and his brow darkened as, sinister and forbidding, he stepped closer to the planter. Ware did not answer at once, but looked at Murrell out of heavy bloodshot eyes, his face pinched and ghastly. At last he said, speaking with visible effort,

"I stayed in Memphis until five o'clock this morning."

"Damn your early hours!" roared Murrell. "What are you doing here? I suppose you've been showing that dead face of yours about the neighborhood - why didn't you stay at Belle Plain since you couldn't keep away?"

"I haven't been near Belle Plain, I came here instead. How am I going to meet people and answer questions?" His teeth were chattering. "Is it known she's missing?" he added.

"Hicks raised the alarm the first thing this morning, according to the instructions I'd given him."

"Yes?" gasped Ware. He was dripping from every pore and the sickly color came and went on his unshaven cheeks. Murrell dropped a heavy hand on his shoulder.

"You haven't been at Belle Plain, you say, but has any one seen you on the road this morning?"

"No one, John," cried Ware, panting between each word. There was a moment's pause and Ware spoke again. "What are they doing at Belle Plain?" he demanded in a whisper. Murrell's lips curled.

"I understand there is talk of suicide," he said.

"Good!" cried Ware.

"They are dragging the bayou down below the house. It looks as though you were going to reap the rewards of the excellent management you have given her estate. They have been trying to find you in Memphis, so the sooner you show yourself the better," he concluded significantly.

"You are sure you have her safe, John, no chance of discovery? For God's sake, get her away from here as soon as you can, it's an awful risk you run!"

"She'll be sent down river to-night," said Murrell.

"Captain," began Slosson who up to this had taken no part in the conversation. "When are you going to cross to t'other side of the bayou?"

"Soon," replied Murrell. Slosson laughed.

"I didn't know but you'd clean forgot the Clan's business. I want to ask another question - but first I want to say that no one thinks higher or more frequent of the ladies than just me, I'm genuinely fond of 'em and I've never lifted my hand ag'in' 'em except in kindness." Mr. Slosson looked at Ware with an exceedingly virtuous expression of countenance. He continued. "Yo' orders are that we're to slip out of this a little afore midnight, but suppose there's a hitch - here's the lady knowing what she knows and here's the boy knowing what he knows."

"There can be no hitch," rasped out Murrell arrogantly.

"I never knew a speculation that couldn't go wrong; and by rights we should have got away last night."

"Well, whose fault is it you didn't?" demanded Murrell.

"In a manner it were mine, but the ark got on a sandbank as we were fetching it in and it took us the whole damn night to get clear."

"Well?" prompted Murrell, with a sullen frown.

"Suppose they get shut of that notion of theirs that the lady's done drowned herself, suppose they take to watching the river? Or suppose the whole damn bottom drops out of this deal? What then? Why, I'll tell you what then - the lady, good looking as she is, knows enough to make west Tennessee mighty onhealthy for some of us. I say suppose it's a flash in the pan and you have to crowd the distance in between you and this part of the world, you can't tell me you'll have any use for her then." Slosson paused impressively. "And here's Mr. Ware feeling bad, feeling like hell," he resumed. "Him and me don't want to be left in no trap with you gone God only knows where."

"I'll send a man to take charge of the keel boat. I can't risk any more of your bungling, Joe."

"That's all right, but you don't answer my question," persisted Slosson, with admirable tenacity of purpose.

"What is your question, Joe?"

"A lot can happen between this and midnight -"

"If things go wrong with us there'll be a blaze at the head of the bayou; does that satisfy you?"

"And what then?"

Murrell hesitated.

"What about the girl?" insisted Slosson, dragging him back to the point at issue between them. "As a man I wouldn't lift my hand ag'in' no good looking woman except like I said - in kindness, but she can't be turned loose, she knows too much. What's the word, Captain - you say it!" he urged. He made a gesture of appeal to Ware.

"Look for the light; better still, look for the man I'll send." And with this Murrell would have turned away, but Slosson detained him.

"Who'll he be?"

"Some fellow who knows the river."

"And if it's the light?" asked the tavern-keeper in a hoarse undertone. Again he looked toward Ware, who, dry-lipped and ashen, was regarding him steadfastly. Glance met glance, for a brief instant they looked deep into each other's eyes and then the hand Slosson had rested on Murrell's shoulder dropped at his side.

CHAPTER XXVIII

THE JUDGE MEETS THE SITUATION

The judge's and Mr. Mahaffy's celebration of the former's rehabilitated credit had occupied the shank of the evening, the small hours of the night, and that part of the succeeding day which the southwest described as soon in the morning; and as the stone jug, in which were garnered the spoils of the highly confidential but entirely misleading conversation which the judge had held with Mr. Pegloe after his return from Belle Plain, lost in weight, it might have been observed that he and Mr. Mahaffy seemed to gain in that nice sense of equity which should form the basis of all human relations. The judge watched Mr. Mahaffy, and Mr. Mahaffy watched the judge, each trustfully placing the regulation of his private conduct in the hands of his friend, as the one most likely to be affected by the rectitude of his acts.

Probably so extensive a consumption of Mr. Pegloe's corn whisky had never been accomplished with greater highmindedness. They honorably split the last glass, the judge scorning to set up any technical claim to it as his exclusive property; then he stared at Mahaffy, while Mahaffy, dark-visaged and forbidding, stared back at him.

The judge sighed deeply. He took up the jug and inverted it. A stray drop or so fell languidly into his glass.

"Try squeezing it, Price," said Mahaffy.

The judge shook the jug, it gave forth an empty sound, and he sighed again; he attempted to peer into it, closing one watery eye as he tilted it toward the light.

"I wonder no Yankee has ever thought to invent a jug with a glass bottom," he observed.

"What for?" asked Mahaffy.

"You astonish me, Solomon," exclaimed the judge. "Coming as you do from that section which invented the wooden nutmeg, and an eight-day clock that has been known to run as much as four or five hours at a stretch. I am aware the Yankees are an ingenious people; I wonder none of 'em ever thought of a jug with a glass bottom, so that when a body holds it up to the light he can see at a glance whether it is empty or not. Do you reckon Pegloe has sufficient confidence to fill the jug again for us?"

But Mahaffy's expression indicated no great confidence in Mr. Pegloe's confidence.

"Credit," began the judge, "is proverbially shy; still it may sometimes be increased, like the muscles of the body and the mental faculties, by judicious use. I've always regarded Pegloe as a cheap mind. I hope I have done him an injustice." He put on his hat, and tucking the jug under his arm, went from the house.

Ten or fifteen minutes elapsed. Mahaffy considered this a good sign, it didn't take long to say no, he reflected. Another ten or fifteen elapsed. Mahaffy lost heart. Then there came a hasty step beyond the door, it was thrown violently open, and the judge precipitated himself into the room. A glance showed Mahaffy that he was laboring under intense excitement.

"Solomon, I bring shocking news. God knows what the next few hours may reveal!" cried the judge, mopping his brow. "Miss Malroy has disappeared from Belle Plain, and Hannibal

Vaughan Kester

has gone with her!"

"Where have they gone?" asked Mahaffy, and his long jaw dropped.

"Would to God I had an answer ready for that question, Solomon!" answered the judge, with a melancholy shake of the head. He gazed down on his friend with an air of large tolerance. "I am going to Belle Plain, but you are too drunk. Sleep it off, Solomon, and join me when your brain is clear and your legs steady."

Mahaffy jerked out an oath, and lifting himself off his chair, stood erect. He snatched up his hat.

"Stuff your pistols into your pockets, and come on, Price!" he said, and stalked toward the door.

He flitted up the street, and the judge puffed and panted in his wake. They gained the edge of the village without speech.

"There is mystery and rascality here!" said the judge.

"What do you know, Price, and where did you hear this?" Mahaffy shot the question back over his shoulder.

"At Pegloe's, the Belle Plain overseer had just fetched the news into town."

Again they were silent, all their energies being absorbed by the physical exertion they were making. The road danced before their burning eyes, it seemed to be uncoiling itself serpentwise with hideous undulations. Mr. Mahaffy was conscious that the judge, of whom he caught a blurred vision now at his right side, now at his left, was laboring painfully in the heat and dust, the breath whistling from between his parched lips.

"You're just ripe for apoplexy, Price!" he snarled, moderating his pace.

"Go on," said the judge, with stolid resolution.

Two miles out of the village they came to a roadside spring, here they paused for an instant. Mahaffy scooped up handfuls of the clear water and sucked it down greedily. The judge dropped on his stomach and buried his face in the tiny pool, gulping up great thirsty swallows. After a long breathless instant he stood erect, with drops of moisture clinging to his nose and eyebrows. Mahaffy was a dozen paces down the road, hurrying forward again with relentless vigor. The judge shuffled after him. The tracks they left in the dust crossed and re-crossed the road, but presently the slanting lines of their advance straightened, the judge gained and held a fixed place at Mahaffy's right, a step or so in the rear. His oppulent fancy began to deal with the situation.

"If anything happens to the child, the man responsible for it would better never been born - I'll pursue him with undiminished energy from this moment forth!" he panted.

"What could happen to him, Price?" asked Mahaffy.

"God knows, poor little lad!"

"Will you shut up!" cried Mahaffy savagely.

"Solomon!"

"Why do you go building on that idea? Why should any one harm him - what earthly purpose -"

"I tell you, Solomon, we are the pivotal point in a vast circle of crime. This is a blow at me - this is revenge, sir, neither more nor less! They have struck at me through the boy, it is as plain as day."

"What did the overseer say?"

"Just that they found Miss Malroy gone from Belle Plain this morning, and the boy with her."

"This is like you, Price! How do you know they haven't spent the night at some neighbor's?"

"The nearest neighbor is five or six miles distant. Miss Malroy and Hannibal were seen along about dusk in the grounds at Belle Plain, do you mean to tell me you consider it likely that they set out on foot at that hour, and without a word to any one, to make a visit?" inquired the judge; but Mahaffy did not contend for this point.

"What are you going to do first, Price?"

"Have a look over the grounds, and talk with the slaves."

"Where's the brother - wasn't he at Belle Plain last night?"

"It seems he went to Memphis yesterday."

They plodded forward in silence; now and again they were passed by some man on horseback whose destination was the same as their own, and then at last they caught sight of Belle Plain in its grove of trees.

All work on the plantation had stopped, and the hundreds of slaves - men, women and children - were gathered about the house. Among these moved the members of the dominant race. The judge would have attached himself to the first group, but he heard a whispered question, and the answer,

"Miss Malroy's lawyer."

Clearly it was not for him to mix with these outsiders, these curiosity seekers. He crossed the lawn to the house, and mounted the steps. In the doorway was big Steve, while groups of men stood about in the hall, the hum of busy purposeless talk pervading the place. The judge frowned. This was all wrong.

"Has Mr. Ware returned from Memphis?" he asked of Steve.

"No, Sah;; not yet."

"Then show me into the library," said the judge with bland authority, surrendering his hat to the butler. "Come along, Mahaffy!" he added. They entered the library, and the judge motioned Steve to close the door. "Now, boy, you'll kindly ask those people to withdraw - you may say it is Judge Price's orders. Allow no one to enter the house unless they have business with me, or as I send for them - you understand? After you have cleared the house, you may bring me a decanter of corn whisky - stop a bit - you may ask the sheriff to step here."

"Yes, Sah." And Steve withdrew.

The judge drew an easy-chair up to the flat-topped desk that stood in the center of the room, and seated himself.

"Are you going to make this the excuse for another drunk, Price? If so, I feel the greatest contempt for you," said Mahaffy sternly.

The judge winced at this.

"You have made a regrettable choice of words, Solomon," he urged gently.

"Where's your feeling for the boy?"

"Here!" said the judge, with an eloquent gesture, resting his hand on his heart.

"If you let whisky alone, I'll believe you, otherwise what I have said must stand."

The door opened, and the sheriff slouched into the room. He was chewing a long wheat straw, and his whole appearance was one of troubled weakness.

"Morning," he said briefly.

"Sit down, Sheriff," and the judge indicated a meek seat for the official in a distant corner. "Have you learned anything?" he asked.

The sheriff shook his head.

"What you turning all these neighbors out of doors for?" he questioned.

"We don't want people tracking in and out the house, Sheriff. Important evidence may be destroyed. I propose examining the slaves first - does that meet with your approval?"

"Oh, I've talked with them, they don't know nothing," said the sheriff. "No one don't know nothing."

"Please God, we may yet put our fingers on some villain who does," said the judge.

Outside it was noised about that judge Price had taken matters in hand - he was the old fellow who had been warned to keep his mouth shut, and who had never stopped talking since. A crowd collected beyond the library windows and feasted its eyes on the back of this hero's bald head.

One by one the house servants were ushered into the judge's presence. First he interrogated little Steve, who had gone to Miss Betty's door that morning to rouse her, as was his custom. Next he examined Betty's maid; then the cook, and various house servants, who had nothing especial to tell, but told it at considerable. length; and lastly big Steve.

"Stop a bit," the judge suddenly interrupted the butler in the midst of his narrative. "Does the overseer always come up to the house the first thing in the morning?"

"Why, not exactly, Sah, but he come up this mo'ning, Sah. He was talking to me at the back of the house, when the women run out with the word that Missy was done gone away."

"He joined in the search?"

"Yes, Sah."

"When was Miss Malroy seen last?" asked the judge.

"She and the young gemman you fotched heah were seen in the gyarden along about sundown. I seen them myself."

"They had had supper?"

"Yes, Sah."

"Who sleeps here?"

"Just little Steve and three of the women, they sleeps at the back of the house, Sah."

"No sounds were heard during the night?"

"No, Sah."

"I'll see the overseer - what's his name? - Hicks? Suppose you go for him!" said the judge, addressing the sheriff.

The sheriff was gone from the room only a few moments, and returned with the information that Hicks was down at the bayou, which was to be dragged.

"Why?" inquired the judge.

"Hicks says Miss Malroy's been acting mighty queer ever since Charley Norton was shot - distracted like! He says he noticed it, and that Tom Ware noticed it."

"How does he explain the boy's disappearance?"

"He reckons she threw herself in, and the boy tried to drag her out, like he naturally would, and got drawed in."

"Humph! I'll trouble Mr. Hicks to step here," said the judge quietly.

"There's Mr. Carrington and a couple of strangers outside who've been asking about Miss Malroy and the boy, seems like the strangers knowed her and him back yonder in No'th Carolina," said the sheriff as he turned away.

"I'll see them." The sheriff went from the room and the judge dismissed the servants.

"Well, what do you think, Price?" asked Mahaffy anxiously when they were alone.

"Rubbish! Take my word for it, Solomon, this blow is leveled at me. I have been too forward in my attempts to suppress the carnival of crime that is raging through west Tennessee. You'll observe that Miss Malroy disappeared at a moment when the public is disposed to think she has retained me as her legal adviser, probably she will be set at liberty when she agrees to drop the matter of Norton's murder. As for the boy, they'll use him to compel my silence and inaction." The judge took a long breath. "Yet there remains one point where the boy is concerned that completely baffles me. If we knew just a little more of his antecedents it might cause me to make a startling and radical move."

Mahaffy was clearly not impressed by the vague generalities in which the judge was dealing.

"There you go, Price, as usual, trying to convince yourself that you are the center of everything!" he said, in a tone of much exasperation. "Let's get down to business! What does this man Hicks mean by hinting at suicide? You saw Miss

Malroy yesterday?"

"You have put your finger on a point of some significance," said the judge. "She bore evidence of the shock and loss she had sustained; aside from that she was quite as she has always been."

"Well, what do you want to see Hicks for? What do you expect to learn from him?"

"I don't like his insistence on the idea that Miss Malroy is mentally unbalanced. It's a question of some delicacy - the law, sir, fully recognizes that. It seems to me he is overanxious to account for her disappearance in a manner that can compromise no one."

Here they were interrupted by the opening of the door, and big Steve admitted Carrington and the two men of whom the sheriff had spoken.

"A shocking condition of affairs, Mr. Carrington!" said the judge by way of greeting.

"Yes," said Carrington shortly.

"You left these parts some time ago, I believe?" continued the judge.

"The day before Norton was shot. I had started home for Kentucky. I heard of his death when I reached Randolph on the second bluff," explained Carrington, from whose cheeks the weather-beaten bloom had faded. He rested his hand on the edge of the desk and turned to the men who had followed him into the room. "This is the gentleman you wish to see," he said. And stepped to one of the windows; it overlooked the terraces where he had said good-by to Betty scarcely a week before.

The two men had paused by the door. They now advanced.

One was gaunt and haggard, his face disfigured by a great red scar, the other was a shockheaded individual who moved with a shambling gait. Both carried rifles and both were dressed in coarse homespun.

"Morning, sir," said the man with the scar. "Yancy's my name, and this gentleman 'lows he'd rather be known now as Mr. Cavendish."

The judge started to his feet.

"Bob Yancy?" he cried.

"Yes, sir, that's me." The judge passed nimbly around the desk and shook the Scratch Hiller warmly by the hand. "Where's my nevvy, sir - what's all this about him and Miss Betty?" Yancy's soft drawl was suddenly eager.

"Please God we'll recover him soon!" said the judge.

By the window Carrington moved impatiently. No harm could come to the boy, but Betty - a shudder went through him.

"They've stolen him." Yancy spoke with conviction. "I reckon they've started back to No'th Carolina with him - only that don't explain what's come of Miss Betty, does it?" and he dropped rather helplessly into a chair.

"Bob are just getting off a sick bed. He's been powerful porely in consequence of having his head laid open and then being throwed into the Elk River, where I fished him out," explained Cavendish, who still continued to regard the judge with unmixed astonishment, first cocking his shaggy head on one side and then on the other, his bleached eyes narrowed to a slit. Now and then he favored the austere Mahaffy with a fleeting glance. He seemed intuitively to understand the comradeship of their degradation.

"Mr. Cavendish fetched me here on his raft. We tied up to the sho' this morning. It was there we met Mr. Carrington - I'd knowed him slightly back yonder in No'th Carolina," continued Yancy. "He said I'd find Hannibal with you. I was counting a heap on seeing my nevvy."

Carrington, no longer able to control himself, swung about on his heel.

"What's been done?" he asked, with fierce repression. "What's going to be done? Don't you know that every second is precious?"

"I am about to conclude my investigations, sir," said the judge with dignity.

Carrington stepped to the door. After all, what was there to expect of these men? Whatever their interest, it was plainly centered in the boy. He passed out into the hall.

As the door closed on him the judge turned again to the Scratch Hiller.

"Mr. Yancy, Mr. Mahaffy and I hold your nephew in the tenderest regard, he has been our constant companion ever since you were lost to him. In this crisis you may rely upon us; we are committed to his recovery, no matter what it involves." The judge's tone was one of unalterable resolution.

"I reckon you-all have been mighty good and kind to him," said Yancy huskily.

"We have endeavored to be, Mr. Yancy - indeed I had formed the resolution legally to adopt him should you not come to claim him. I should have given him my name, and made him my heir. His education has already begun, under my supervision," and the judge, remembering the high use to which he had dedicated one of Pegloe's trade labels, fairly glowed with philanthropic fervor.

"Think of that!" murmured Yancy softly. He was deeply moved. So was Mr. Cavendish, who was gifted with a wealth of ready sympathy. He thrust out a hardened hand to the judge.

"Shake!" he said. "You're a heap better than you look." A thin ripple of laughter escaped Mahaffy, but the judge accepted Chills and Fever's proffered hand. He understood that here was a simple genuine soul.

"Price, isn't it important for us to know why Mr. Yancy thinks the boy has been taken back to North Carolina?" said Mahaffy.

"Just what kin is Hannibal to you, Mr. Yancy?" asked the judge resuming his seat.

"Strictly speaking, he ain't none. That he come to live with me is all owing to Mr. Crenshaw, who's a good man when left to himself, but he's got a wife, so a body may say he never is left to himself," began Yancy; and then briefly he told the story of the woman and the child much as he had told it to Bladen at the Barony the day of General Quintard's funeral.

The judge, his back to the light and his face in shadow, rested his left elbow on the desk and with his cbin sunk in his palm, followed the Scratch Hiller's narrative with the closest attention.

"And General Quintard never saw him - never manifested any interest in him?" the words came slowly from the judge's lips, he seemed to gulp down something that rose in his throat. "Poor little lad!" he muttered, and again, "Poor little lad!"

"Never once, sir. He told the slaves to keep him out of his sight. We-all wondered, fo' you know how niggers will talk. We thought maybe he was some kin to the Quintards, but we couldn't figure out how. The old general never had but one child and she had been dead fo' years. The child couldn't have been hers no how." Yancy paused.

The judge drummed idly on the desk.

"What implacable hate - what iron pride!" he murmured, and swept his hand across his eyes. Absorbed and aloof, he was busy with his thoughts that spanned the waste of yearsyears that seemed to glide before him in review, each bitter with its hideous memories of shame and defeat. Then from the smoke of these lost battles emerged the lonely figure of the child as he had seen him that June night. His ponderous arm stiffened where it rested on the desk, he straightened up in his chair and his face assumed its customary expression of battered dignity, while a smile at once wistful and tender hovered about his lips.

"One other question," he said. "Until this man Murrell appeared you had no trouble with Bladen? He was content that you should keep the child - your right to Hannibal was never challenged?"

"Never, sir. All my troubles began about that time."

"Murrell belongs in these parts," said the judge.

"I'd admire fo' to meet him," said Yancy quietly.

The judge grinned.

"I place my professional services at your disposal," he said. "Yours is a clear case of felonous assault."

"No, it ain't, sir - I look at it this-a-ways; it's a clear case of my giving him the damnedest sort of a body beating!"

"Sir," said the judge, "I'll hold your hat while you are about it!"

Hicks had taken his time in responding to the judge's summons, but now his step sounded in the hall and throwing open the door he entered the room. Whether consciously or not he had acquired something of that surly, forbidding manner which was characteristic of his employer. A curt nod of the head was his only greeting.

"Will you sit down?" asked the judge. Hicks signified by another movement of the head that he would not. "This is a very dreadful business!" began the judge softly.

"Ain't it?" agreed Hicks. "What you got to say to me?" he added petulantly.

"Have you started to drag the bayou?" asked the judge. Hicks nodded. "That was your idea?" suggested the judge.

"No, it wa'n't," objected Hicks quickly. "But I said she had been actin' like she was plumb distracted ever since Charley Norton got shot -"

"How?" inquired the judge, arching his eyebrows. Hicks was plainly disturbed by the question.

"Sort of out of her head. Mr. Ware seen it, too -"

"He spoke of it?"

"Yes, sir; him and me discussed it together."

The judge regarded Hicks long and intently and in, silence. His magnificent mind was at work. If Betty had been distraught he had not observed any sign of it the previous day. If Ware were better informed as to her true mental state why had he chosen this time to go to Memphis?

"I suppose Mr. Ware asked you to keep an eye on Miss Malroy while he was away from home?" said the judge. Hicks, suspicious of the drift of his questioning, made no answer. "I suppose you told the house servants to keep her under observation?" continued the judge.

"I don't talk to no niggers," replied Hicks, "except to give 'em my orders."

"Well, did you give them that order?"

"No, I didn't."

The sudden and hurried entrance of big Steve brought the judge's examination of Mr. Hicks to a standstill.

"Mas'r, you know dat 'ar coachman George - the big black fellow dat took you into town las' evenin'? I jes' been down at Shanty Hill whar Milly, his wife, is carryin' on something scandalous 'cause George ain't never come home!" Steve was laboring under intense excitement, but he ignored the presence of the overseer and addressed himself to Slocum Price.

"Well, what of that?" cried Hicks quickly.

"Thar warn't no George, mind you, Mas'r, but dar was his team in de stable this mo'ning and lookin' mighty nigh done up with hard driving."

"Yes." interrupted Hicks uneasily; "put a pair of lines in a nigger's hands and he'll run any team off its legs!"

"An' the kerriage all scratched up from bein' thrashed through the bushes," added Steve.

"There's a nigger for you!" said Hicks. "She took the rascal out of the field, dressed him like he was a gentleman and pampered him up, and now first chance he gets he runs off!"

"Ah!" said the judge softly. "Then you knew this?"

"Of course I knew - wa'n't it my business to know? I reckon he was off skylarking, and when he'd seen the mess he'd made, the trifling fool took to the woods. Well, he catches it when I lay hands on him!"

"Do you know when and under what circumstances the team was stabled, Mr. Hicks?" inquired the judge.

"No, I don't, but I reckon it must have been along after dark," said Hicks unwillingly. "I seen to the feeding just after sundown like I always do, then I went to supper," Hicks vouchsafed to explain.

"And no one saw or heard the team drive in?"

"Not as I know of," said Hicks.

"Mas'r Ca'ington's done gone off to get a pack of dawgs - he 'lows hit's might' important to find what's come of George," said Steve.

Hicks started violently at this piece of news.

"I reckon he'll have to travel a right smart distance to find a pack of dogs," he muttered. "I don't know of none this side of Colonel Bates' down below Girard."

The judge was lost in thought. He permitted an interval of silence to elapse in which Hicks' glance slid round in a furtive circle.

"When did Mr. Ware set out for Memphis?" asked the judge at length.

"Early yesterday. He goes there pretty often on business."

"You talked with Mr. Ware before he left?" Hicks nodded. "Did he speak of Miss Malroy?" Hicks shook his head. "Did you see her during the afternoon?"

"No - maybe you think these niggers ain't enough to keep a man stirring?" said Hicks uneasily and with a scowl. The judge noticed both the uneasiness and the scowl.

"I should imagine they would absorb every moment of your time, Mr. Hicks," he agreed affably.

"A man's got to be a hog for work to hold a job like mine," said Hicks sourly.

"But it came to your notice that Miss Malroy has been in a disturbed mental state ever since Mr. Norton's murder? I am interested in this point, Mr. Hicks, because your experience is so entirely at variance with my own. It was my privilege to see and speak with her yesterday afternoon; I was profoundly impressed by her naturalness and composure." The judge smiled, then he leaned forward across the desk. "What were you doing up here early this morning - hasn't a hog for work like you got any business of his own at that hour?" The judge's tone was suddenly offensive.

"Look here, what right have you got to try and pump me?" cried Hicks.

For no discernible reason Mr. Cavendish spat on his palms.

"Mr. Hicks," said the judge, urbane and gracious, "I believe in frankness."

"Sure," agreed Hicks, mollified by the judge's altered tone.

"Therefore I do not hesitate to say that I consider you a damned scoundrel!" concluded the judge.

Mr. Cavendish, accepting the judge's ultimatum as something which must debar Hicks from all further consideration, and being, as he was, exceedingly active and energetic by nature, if one passed over the various forms of gainful Industry, uttered a loud whoop and threw himself on the overseer. There was a brief struggle and Hicks went down with the Earl of Lambeth astride of him; then from his boot leg that knightly soul flashed a horn-handled tickler of formidable dimensions.

The judge, Yancy, and Mahaffy, sprang from their chairs. Mr. Mahaffy was plainly shocked at the spectacle of Mr. Cavendish's lawless violence. Yancy was disturbed too, but not by the moral aspects of the case; he was doubtful as to just how his friend's act would appeal to the judge. He need not have been distressed on that score, since the judge's one idea was to profit by it. With his hands on his knees he was now bending above the two men.

"What do you want to know, judge?" cried Cavendish, panting from his exertions. "I'll learn this parrot to talk up!"

"Hicks," said the judge, "it is in your power to tell us a few things we are here to find out." Hicks looked up into the judge's face and closed his lips grimly. "Mr. Cavendish, kindly let him have the point of that large knife where he'll feel it most!" ordered the judge.

"Talk quick!" said Cavendish with a ferocious scowl. "Talk - or what's to hinder me slicing open your woozen?" and he pressed the blade of his knife against the overseer's throat.

"I don't know anything about Miss Betty," said Hicks in a sullen whisper.

"Maybe you don't, but what do you know about the boy?" Hicks was silent, but he was grateful for the judge's question. From Tom Ware he had learned of Fentress' interest in the boy. Why should he shelter the colonel at risk to himself? "If you please, Mr. Cavendish!" said the judge quietly nodding toward the knife.

"You didn't ask me about him," said Hicks quickly.

"I do now," said the judge.

"He was here yesterday."

"Mr. Cavendish -" and again the judge glanced toward

the knife.

"Wait!" cried Hicks. "You go to Colonel Fentress."

"Let him up, Mr. Cavendish; that's all we want to mow," said the judge.

CHAPTER XXIX

COLONEL FENTRESS

The judge had not forgotten his ghost, the ghost he had seen in Mr. Saul's office that day he went to the court-house on business for Charley Norton. Working or idling - principally the latter - drunk or sober - principally the former - the ghost, otherwise Colonel Fentress, had preserved a place in his thoughts, and now as he moved stolidly up the drive toward Fentress' big white house on the hill with Mahaffy, Cavendish, and Yancy trailing in his wake, memories of what had once been living and vital crowded in upon him. Some sense of the wreck that littered the long years, and the shame of the open shame that had swept away pride and self-respect, came back to him out of the past.

He only paused when he stood on the portico before Fentress' open door. He glanced about him at the wide fields, bounded by the distant timber lands that hid gloomy bottoms, at the great log barns in the hollow to his right; at the huddle of whitewashed cabins beyond; then with his big fist he reached in and pounded on the door. The blows echoed loudly through the silent house, and an instant later Fentress' tall, spare figure was seen advancing from the far end of the hall.

"Who is it?" he asked.

"Judge Price - Colonel Fentress" said the judge.

"Judge Price," uncertainly, and still advancing.

"I had flattered myself that you must have heard of me," said the judge.

"I think I have," said Fentress, pausing now.

"He thinks he has!" muttered the judge under his breath.

"Will you come in?" it was more a question than an invitation.

"If you are at liberty." The colonel bowed. "Allow me," the judge continued. "Colonel Fentress - Mr. Mahaffy, Mr. Yancy and Mr. Cavendish." Again the colonel bowed.

"Will you step into the library?"

"Very good," and the judge followed the colonel briskly down the hall.

When they entered the library Fentress turned and took stock of his guests. Mahaffy he had seen before; Yancy and Cavendish were of course strangers to him, but their appearance explained them; last of all his glance shifted to the judge. He had heard something of those activities by means of which Slocum Price had striven to distinguish himself, and he had a certain curiosity respecting the man. It was immediately satisfied. The judge had reached a degree of shabbiness seldom equaled, and but for his mellow, effulgent personality might well have passed for a common vagabond; and if his dress advertised the state of his finances, his face explained his habits. No misconception was possible about either.

"May I offer you a glass of liquor?" asked Fentress, breaking the silence. He stepped to the walnut centertable where there was a decanter and glasses. By a gesture the judge declined the invitation. Whereat the colonel looked surprised, but not so surprised as Mahaffy. There was another silence.

"I don't think we ever met before?" observed Fentress. There was something in the fixed stare his visitor was bending upon him that he found disquieting, just why, he could not have told.

But that fixed stare of the judge's continued. No, the man had not changed - he had grown older certainly, but age had not come ungracefully; he became the glossy broadcloth and spotless linen he wore. Here was a man who could command the good things of life, using them with a rational temperance. The room itself was in harmony with his character; it was plain but rich in its appointments, at once his library and his office, while the well-filled cases ranged about the walls showed his tastes to be in the main scholarly and intellectual.

"How long have you lived here?" asked the judge abruptly. Fentress seemed to hesitate; but the judge's glance, compelling and insistent, demanded an answer.

"Ten years."

"You have known many men of all classes as a lawyer and a planter?" said the judge. Fentress inclined his head. The judge took a step nearer him. "People have a great trick of coming and going in these western states - all sorts of damned riffraff drift in and out of these new lands." A deadly earnestness lifted the judge's words above mere rudeness. Fentress, cold and distant, made no reply. "For the past twenty years I have been looking for a man by the name of Gatewood - David Gatewood." Disciplined as he was, the colonel started violently. "Ever heard of him, Fentress?" demanded the judge with a savage scowl.

"What's all this to me?" The words came with a gasp from Fentress' twitching lips. The judge looked at him moody and frowning.

"I have reason to think this man Gatewood came to west Tennessee," he said.

"If so, I have never heard of him."

"Perhaps not under that name - at any rate you are going to hear of him now. This man Gatewood, who between ourselves was a damned scoundrel" - the colonel winced - "this man Gatewood had a friend who threw money and business in his way - a planter he was, same as Gatewood. A sort of partnership existed between the pair. It proved an expensive enterprise for Gatewood's friend, since he came to trust the damned scoundrel more and more as time passed - even large sums of his money were in Gatewood's hands - "the judge paused. Fentress' countenance was like stone, as expressionless and as rigid.

By the door stood Mahaffy with Yancy and Cavendish; they understood that what was obscure and meaningless to them held a tragic significance to these two men. The judge's heavy face, ordinarily battered and debauched, but infinitely good-natured, bore now the markings of deep passion, and the voice that rumbled forth from his capacious chest came to their ears like distant thunder.

"This friend of Gatewood's had a wife -" The judge's voice broke, emotion shook him like a leaf, he was tearing open his wounds. He reached over and poured himself a drink, sucking it down with greedy lips. "There was a wife -" he whirled about on his heel and faced Fentress again. "There was a wife, Fentress -" he fixed Fentress with his blazing eyes.

"A wife and child. Well, one day Gatewood and the wife were missing. Under the circumstances Gatewood's friend was well rid of the pair - he should have been grateful, but he wasn't, for his wife took his child, a daughter; and Gatewood a trifle of thirty thousand dollars his friend had intrusted to him!"

There was another silence.

"At a later day I met this man who had been betrayed by his wife and robbed by his friend. He had fallen out of the race

- drink had done for him - there was just one thing he seemed to care about and that was the fate of his child, but maybe he was only curious there. He wondered if she had lived, and married -" Once more the judge paused.

"What's all this to me?" asked Fentress.

"Are you sure it's nothing to you?" demanded the judge hoarsely. "Understand this, Fentress. Gatewood's treachery brought ruin to at least two lives. It caused the woman's father to hide his face from the world, it wasn't enough for him that his friends believed his daughter dead; he knew differently and the shame of that knowledge ate into his soul. It cost the husband his place in the world, too - in the end it made of him a vagabond and a penniless wanderer."

"This is nothing to me," said Fentress.

"Wait!" cried the judge. "About six years ago the woman was seen at her father's home in North Carolina. I reckon Gatewood had cast her off. She didn't go back empty-handed. She had run away from her husband with a child - a girl; after a lapse of twenty years she returned to her father with a boy of two or three. There are two questions that must be answered when I find Gatewood: what became of the woman and what became of the child; are they living or dead; did the daughter grow up and marry and have a son? When I get my answer it will be time enough to think of Gatewood's punishment!" The judge leaned forward across the table, bringing his face close to Fentress' face. "Look at me - do you know me now?"

But Fentress' expression never altered. The judge fell back a step.

"Fentress, I want the boy," he said quietly.

"What boy?"

"My grandson."

"You are mad! What do I know of him - or you?" Fentress was gaining courage from the sound of his own voice.

"You know who he is and where he is. Your business relations with General Ware have put you on the track of the Quintard lands in this state. You intend to use the boy to gather them in."

"You're mad!" repeated Fentress.

"Unless you bring him to me inside of twenty-four hours I'll smash you!" roared the judge. "Your name isn't Fentress, it's Gatewood; you've stolen the name of Fentress, just as you have stolen other things. What's come of Turberville's wife and child? What's come of Turberville's money? Damn your soul! I want my grandson! I'll pull you down and leave you stripped and bare! I'll tell the world the false friend you've been - the thief you are! I'll strip you and turn you out of these doors as naked as when you entered the world!" The judge seemed to tower above Fentress, the man had shot up out of his deep debasement. "Choose! Choose!" he thundered, his shaggy brows bent in a menacing frown.

"I know nothing about the boy," said Fentress slowly.

"By God, you lie!" stormed the judge.

"I know nothing about the boy," and Fentress took a step toward the door.

"Stay where you are!" commanded the judge. "If you attempt to leave this room to call your niggers I'll kill you on its threshold!"

But Yancy and Cavendish had stepped to the door with an intention that was evident, and Fentress' thin face cast itself in haggard lines. He was feeling the judge's terrible capacity, his unexpected ability to deal with a supreme situation. Even Mahaffy gazed at his friend in wonder. He had only seen him spend himself on trifles, with no further object than the next meal or the next drink; he had believed that as he knew him so he had always been, lax and loose of tongue and deed, a noisy tavern hero, but now he saw that he was filling what must have been the measure of his manhood.

"I tell you I had no hand in carrying off the boy," said Fentress with a sardonic smile.

"I look to you to return him. Stir yourself, Gatewood, or by God, I'll hold so fierce a reckoning with you -"

The sentence remained unfinished, for Fentress felt his overwrought nerves snap, and giving way to a sudden blind fury struck at the judge.

"We are too old for rough and tumble," said the judge, who had displayed astonishing agility in avoiding the blow. "Furthermore we were once gentlemen. At present I am what I am, while you are a hound and a blackguard! We'll settle this as becomes our breeding." He poured himself a second glass of liquor from Fentress' decanter. "I wonder if it is possible to insult you," and he tossed glass and contents in Fentress' face. The colonel's thin features were convulsed. The judge watched him with a scornful curling of the lips. "I am treating you better than you deserve," he taunted.

"To-morrow morning at sun-up at Boggs' racetrack!" cried Fentress. The judge bowed with splendid courtesy.

"Nothing could please me half so well," he declared. He turned to the others. "Gentlemen, this is a private matter. When I have met Colonel Fentress I shall make a public announcement of why this appeared necessary to me; until then I trust this matter will not be given publicity. May I ask your silence?" He bowed again, and abruptly passed from the room.

His three friends followed in his steps, leaving Fentress standing by the table, the ghost of a smile on his thin lips.

As if the very place were evil, the judge hurried down the drive toward the road. At the gate he paused and turned on his companions, but his features wore a look of dignity that forbade comment or question. He held out his hand to Yancy.

"Sir," he said, "if I could command the riches of the Indies, it would tax my resources to meet the fractional part of my obligations to you."

"Think of that!" said Yancy, as much overwhelmed by the judge's manner as by his words.

"His Uncle Bob shall keep his place in my grandson's life! We'll watch him grow into manhood together." The judge was visibly affected. A smile of deep content parted Mr. Yancy's lips as his muscular fingers closed about the judge's hand with crushing force.

"Whoop!" cried Cavendish, delighted at this recognition of Yancy's love for the boy, and he gleefully smote the austere Mahaffy on the shoulder. But Mahaffy was dumb in the presence of the decencies, he quite lacked an interpreter. The judge looked back at the house.

"Mine!" he muttered. "The clothes he stands inthe food he eats - miine! Mine!"

CHAPTER XXX

THE BUBBLE BURSTS

At about the same hour that the judge was hurling threats and insults at Colonel Fentress, three men were waiting ten miles away at the head of the bayou which served to isolate Hicks' cabin. Now no one of these three had ever heard of Judge Slocum Price; the breath of his fame had never blown, however gently, in their direction, yet they were preparing to thrust opportunity upon him. To this end they were lounging about the opening in the woods where the horses belonging to Ware and Murrell were tied.

At length the dip of oars became audible in the silence and one of the trio stole down the path, a matter of fifty yards, to a point that overlooked the bayou. He was gone but a moment.

"It's Murrell all right!" he said in an eager whisper. "Him and another fellow - the Hicks girl is rowing them." He glanced from one to the other of his companions, who seemed to take firmer hold of themselves under his eye. "It'll be all right," he protested lightly. "He's as good as ours. Wait till I give you the word." And he led the way into an adjacent thicket.

Meantime Ware and Murrell had landed and were coming along the path, the outlaw a step or two in advance of his friend. They reached the horses and were untying them when the thicket suddenly disgorged the three men; each held a cocked pistol; two of these pistols covered Murrell and the third was leveled at Ware.

"Hues!" cried Murrell in astonishment, for the man confronting him was the Clan's messenger who should have been speeding across the state.

"Toss up your hands, Murrell," said Hues quietly.

One of the other men spoke.

"You are under arrest!"

"Arrest!"

"You are wanted for nigger-stealing," said the man. Still Murrell did not seem to comprehend. He looked at Hues in dull wonder.

"What are you doing here?" he asked.

"Waiting to arrest you - ain't that plain?" said Hues, with a grim smile.

The outlaw's hands dropped at his side, limp and helpless. With some idea that he might attempt to draw a weapon one of the men took hold of him, but Murrell was nerveless to his touch; his face had gone a ghastly white and was streaked with the markings of terror.

"Well, by thunder!" cried the man in utter amazement.

Murrell looked into Hues' face.

"You - you -" and the words thickened on his tongue becoming an inarticulate murmur.

"It's all up, John," said Hues.

"No!" said Murrell, recovering himself. "You may as well turn me loose - you can't arrest me!"

"I've done it," answered Hues, with a laugh. "I've been on your track for six months."

"How about this fellow?" asked the man, whose pistol still covered Ware. Hues glanced toward the planter and shook his head.

"Where are you going to take me?" asked Murrell quickly. Again Hues laughed.

"You'll find that out in plenty of time, and then your friends can pass the word around if they like; now you'll come with me!"

Ware neither moved nor spoke as Hues and his prisoner passed back along the path, Hues with his hand on Murrell's shoulder, and one of his companions close at his heels, while the third man led off the outlaw's horse.

Presently the distant clatter of hoofs was borne to Ware's ears - only that; the miracle of courage and daring he had half expected had not happened. Murrell, for all his wild boasting, was like other men, like himself. His bloodshot eyes slid around in their sockets. There across the sunlit stretch of water was Betty - the thought of her brought him to quick choking terrors. The whole fabric of crime by which he had been benefited in the past or had expected to profit in the future seemed toppling in upon him, but his mind clutched one important fact. Hues, if he knew of Betty's disappearance, did not connect Murrell with it. Ware sucked in comfort between his twitching lips. Stealing niggers! No one would believe that he, a planter, had a hand in that, and for a brief instant he considered signaling Bess to return. Slosson must be told of Murrell's arrest; but he was sick with apprehension, some trap might have been prepared for him, he could not know; and the impulse to act forsook him.

He smote his hands together in a hopeless, beaten gesture. And Murrell had gone weak - with his own eyes he had seen it - Murrell - whom he believed without fear! He felt that he had been grievously betrayed in his trust and a hot rage poured through him. At last he climbed into the saddle, and swaying like a drunken man, galloped off.

When he reached the river road he paused and scanned its dusty surface. Hues and his party had turned south when they issued from the wood path. No doubt Murrell was being taken to Memphis. Ware laughed harshly. The outlaw would be free before another dawn broke.

He had halted near where Jim had turned his team the previous night after Betty and Hannibal had left the carriage; the marks of the wheels were as plainly distinguishable as the more recent trail left by the four men, and as he grasped the significance of that wide half circle his sense of injury overwhelmed him again. He hoped to live to see Murrell hanged!

He was so completely lost in his bitter reflections that he had been unaware of a mounted man who was coming toward him at a swift gallop, but now he heard the steady pounding of hoofs and, startled by the sound, looked up. A moment later the horseman drew rein at his side.

"Ware!" he cried.

"How are you, Carrington?" said the planter.

"You are wanted at Belle Plain," began Carrington, and seemed to hesitate.

"Yes - yes, I am going there at once - now -" stammered Ware, and gathered up his reins with a shaking hand.

"You've heard, I take it?" said Carrington slowly.

"Yes," answered Ware, in a hoarse whisper. "My God, Carrington, I'm heart sick; she has been like a daughter to me!" he fell silent mopping his face.

"I think I understand your feeling," said Carrington, giving him a level glance.

"Then you'll excuse me," and the planter clapped spurs to his horse. Once he looked back over his shoulder; he saw that Carrington had not moved from the spot where they had met.

At Belle Plain, Ware found his neighbors in possession of the place. They greeted him quietly and spoke in subdued tones of their sympathy. The planter listened with an air of such abject misery that those who had neither liked nor respected him, were roused to a sudden generous feeling where he was concerned, they could not question but that he was deeply affected. After all the man might have a side to his nature with which they had never come in contact.

When he could he shut himself in his room. He had experienced a day of maddening anxiety, he had not slept at all the previous night, in mind and body he was worn out; and now he was plunged into the thick of this sensation. He must keep control of himself, for every word he said would be remembered. In the present there was sympathy for him, but sooner or later people would return to their sordid unemotional judgments.

He sought to forecast the happenings of the next few hours. Murrell's friends would break jail for him, that was a foregone conclusion, but the insurrection he had planned was at an end. Hues had dealt its death blow. Moreover, though the law might be impotent to deal with Murrell, he could not hope to escape the vengeance of the powerful class he had plotted to destroy; he would have to quit the country. Ware gloated in this idea of craven flight. Thank God, he had seen the last of him!

But as always his thoughts came back to Betty. Slosson would wait at the Hicks' place for the man Murrell had promised him, and failing this messenger, for the signal fire, but there would be neither; and Slosson would be left to determine his own course of action. Ware felt certain that he would wait through the night, but as sure as the morning broke, if no word had reached him, he would send one of his men across the bayou, who must learn of Murrell's arrest, escape, flight - for in Ware's mind these three events were indissolubly associated. The planter's teeth knocked together. He was having a terrible acquaintance with fear, its very depths had swallowed him up; it was a black pit in which he sank from horror to horror. He had lost all faith in the Clan which had terrorized half a dozen states, which had robbed and murdered with apparent impunity, which had marketed its hundreds of stolen slaves. He had utterly collapsed at the first blow dealt the organization, but he was still seeing Murrell, pallid and shaken.

A step sounded in the hall and an instant later Hicks entered the room without the formality of knocking. Ware recognized his presence with a glance of indifference, but did not speak. Hicks slouched to his employer's side and handed him a note which proved to be from Fentress. Ware read and tossed it aside.

"If he wants to see me why don't he come here?" he growled.

"I reckon that old fellow they call Judge Price has sprung something sudden on the colonel," said Hicks.

"He was out here the first thing this morning; you'd have thought he owned Belle Plain. There was a couple of strangers with him, and he had me in and fired questions at me for half an hour, then he hiked off up to The Oaks."

"Murrell's been arrested," said Ware in a dull level voice. Hicks gave him a glance of unmixed astonishment.

"No!" he cried.

"Yes, by God!"

"Who'd risk it?"

"Risk it? Man, he almost fainted dead away - a damned coward. Hell!"

"How do you know this?" asked Hicks, appalled.

"I was with him when he was taken - it was Hues the man he trusted more than any other!" Ware gave the overseer a ghastly grin and was silent, but in that silence he heard the drumming of his own heart. He went on. "I tell you to save himself John Murrell will implicate the rest of us; we've got to get him free, and then, by hell - we ought to knock him in the head; he isn't fit to live!"

"The jail ain't built that'll hold him!!" muttered Hicks.

"Of course, he can't be held," agreed Ware. "And 'he'll never be brought to trial; no lawyer will dare appear against him, no jury will dare find him guilty; but there's Hues, what about him?" He paused. The two men looked at each other for a long moment.

"Where did they carry the captain?" inquired Hicks.

"I don't know."

"It looks like the Clan was in a hell-fired hole - but shucks! What will be easier than to fix Hues? - and while they're fixing folks they'd better not overlook that old fellow Price. He's got some notion about Fentress and the boy." Mr. Hicks did not consider it necessary to explain that he was himself largely responsible for this.

"How do you know that?" demanded Ware.

"He as good as said so." Hicks looked uneasily at the planter. He knew himself to be compromised. The stranger named Cavendish had forced an admission from him that Murrell would not condone if it came to his knowledge. He had also acquired a very proper and wholesome fear of Judge Slocum Price. He stepped close to Ware's side. "What'll come of the girl, Tom? Can you figure that out?" he questioned, sinking his voice almost to a whisper. But Ware was incapable of speech, again his terrors completely overwhelmed him. "I reckon you'll have to find another overseer. I'm going to strike out for Texas," said Hicks.

Ware's eyes met his for an instant. He had thought of flight, too, was still thinking of it, but greed was as much a part of his nature as fear; Belle Plain was a prize not to be lightly cast aside, and it was almost his. He lurched across the room to the window. If he were going to act, the sooner he did so the better, and gain a respite from his fears. The road down the coast slid away before his heavy eyes, he marked each turn; then a palsy of fear shook him, his heart beat against his ribs, and he stood gnawing his lips while he gazed up at the sun.

"Do you get what I say, Tom? I am going to quit these parts," said Hicks. Ware turned slowly from the window.

"All right, Hicks. You mean you want me to settle with you, is that it?" he asked.

"Yes, I'm going to leave while I can, maybe I can't later on," said Hicks stolidly. He added: "I am going to start down the coast as soon as it turns dark, and before it's day again I'll have put the good miles between me and these parts."

"You're going down the coast?" and Ware was again conscious of the quickened beating of his heart. Hicks nodded. "See you don't meet up with John Murrell," said Ware.

"I'll take that chance. It seems a heap better to me than staying here."

Ware looked from the window. The shadows were lengthening across the lawn.

"Better start now, Hicks," he advised.

"I'll wait until it turns dark."

"You'll need a horse."

"I was going to help myself to one. This ain't no time to stand on ceremony," said Hicks shortly.

"Slosson shouldn't be left in the lurch like this - or your brother's folks -"

"They'll have to figure it out for themselves same as me," rejoined Hicks.

"You can stop there as you go by."

"No," said Hicks; "I never did believe in this damn foolishness about the girl, and I won't go near George's -"

"I don't ask you to go there, you can give them the signal from the head of the bayou. All I want is for you to stop and light a fire on the shore. They'll know what that means. I'll give you a horse and fifty dollars for the job."

Hicks' eyes sparkled, but he only said

"Make it twice that and maybe we can deal."

Racked and tortured, Ware hesitated; but the sun was slipping into the west, his windows blazed with the hot light.

"You swear you'll do your part?" he said thickly. He took his purse from his pocket and counted out the amount due Hicks. He named the total, and paused irresolutely.

"Don't you want the fire lighted?" asked Hicks. He was familiar with his employer's vacillating moods.

"Yes," answered Ware, his lips quivering; and slowly, with shaking fingers, he added to the pile of bills in Hicks' hand.

"Well, take care of yourself," said Hicks, when the count was complete. He thrust the roll of bills into his pocket and moved to the door.

Alone again, the planter collapsed into his chair, breathing heavily, but his terrors swept over him and left him with a savage sense of triumph. This passed, he sprang up, intending to recall Hicks and unmake his bargain. What had he been thinking of - safety lay only in flight! Before he reached the door his greed was in the ascendant. He dropped down on the edge of his bed, his eyes fixed on the window. The sun sank lower. From where he sat he saw it through the upper half of the sash, blood-red and livid in a mist of fleecy clouds.

It was in the tops of the old oaks now, which sent their shadows into his room. Again maddened by his terrors he started up and backed toward the door; but again his greed, the one dominating influence in his life, vanquished him.

He watched the sun sink. He watched the red splendor fade over the river; he saw the first stars appear. He told himself that Hicks would soon be gone - if the fire was not to be lighted he must act at once! He stole to the window. It was dusk now, yet he could distinguish the distant wooded boundaries of the great fields framed by the darkening sky. Then in the silence he heard the thud of hoofs.

CHAPTER XXXI

THE KEEL BOAT

"PRICE " began Mahaffy. They were back in Raleigh in the room the judge called his office, and this was Mahaffy's first opportunity to ease his mind on the subject of the duel, as they had only just parted from Yancy and Cavendish, who had stopped at one of the stores to make certain purchases for the raft.

"Not a word, Solomon - it had to come. I am going to kill him. I shall feel better then."

"What if he kills you?" demanded Mahaffy harshly. The judge shrugged his shoulders.

"That is as it may be."

"Have you forgotten your grandson?" Mahaffy's voice was still harsh and rasping.

"I regard my meeting with Fentress as nothing less than a sacred duty to him."

"We know no more than we did this morning," said Mahaffy. "You are mixing up all sorts of side issues with what should be your real purpose."

"Not at all, Solomon - not at all! I look upon my grandson's speedy recovery as an assured fact. Fentress dare not hold him. He knows he is run to earth at last."

"Price -"

"No, Solomon - no, my friend, we will not speak of it again. You will go back to Belle Plain with Yancy and Cavendish; you must represent me there. We have as good as found Hannibal, but we must be active in Miss Malroy's behalf. For us that has an important bearing on the future, and since I can not, you must be at Belle Plain when Carrington arrives with his pack of dogs. Give him the advantage of your sound and mature judgment, Solomon; don't let any false modesty keep you in the background."

"Who's going to second you?" snapped Mahaffy.

The judge was the picture of indifference.

"It will be quite informal, the code is scarcely applicable; I merely intend to remove him because he is not fit to live."

"At sun-up!" muttered Mahaffy.

"I intend to start one day right even if I never live to begin another," said the judge, a sudden fierce light flashing from his eyes. "I feel that this is the turning point in my career, Solomon!" he went on. "The beginning of great things! But I shall take no chances with the future, I shall prepare for every possible contingency. I am going to make you and Yancy my grandson's guardians. There's a hundred thousand acres of land hereabout that must come to him. I shall outline in writing the legal steps to be taken to substantiate his claims. Also he will inherit largely from me at my death."

Something very like laughter escaped from Mahaffy's lips.

"There you go, Solomon, with your inopportune mirth! What in God's name have I if I haven't hope? Take that from me and what would I be? Why, the very fate I have been fighting off with tooth and nail would overwhelm me. I'd sink into unimportance - my unparalleled misfortunes would degrade me to a level with the commonest! No, sir, I've never been without hope, and though I've fallen I've always got up. What Fentress has is based on money he stole from me. By God, the days of his profit-taking are at an end! I am going to strip him. And even if I don't live to enjoy what's mine, my grandson shall! He shall wear velvet and a lace collar and ride his pony yet, by God, as a gentleman's grandson should!"

"It sounds well, Price, but where's the money coming from to push a lawsuit?"

The judge waved this aside.

"The means will be found, Solomon. Our horizon is lifting - I can see it lift! Don't drag me back from the portal of hope! We'll drink the stuff that comes across the water; I'll warm the cockles of your heart with imported brandy. I carry twenty years' hunger and thirst under my wes-coat and I'll feed and drink like a gentleman yet!" The judge smacked his lips in an ecstasy of enjoyment, and dropping down before the table which served him as a desk, seized a pen.

"It's good enough to think about, Price," admitted Mahaffy grudgingly.

"It's better to do; and if anything happens to me the papers I am going to leave will tell you how it's to be done. Man, there's a million of money in sight, and we've got to get it and spend it and enjoy it! None of your swinish thrift for me, but life on a big scale - company, and feasting, and refined surroundings!"

"And you are going to meet Fentress in the morning?" asked Mahaffy. "I suppose there's no way of avoiding that?"

"Avoiding it?" almost shouted the judge. "For what have I

been living? I shall meet him, let the consequences be what they may. To-night when I have reduced certain facts to writing I shall join you at Belle Plain. The strange and melancholy history of my life I shall place in your hands for safe keeping. In the morning I can be driven back to Boggs'."

"And you will go there without a second?"

"If necessary; yes."

"I declare, Price, you are hardly fitted to be at large! Why, you act as if you were tired of life. There's Yancy - there's Cavendish!"

The judge gave him an indulgent but superior smile.

"Two very worthy men, but I go to Boggs' attended by a gentleman or I go there alone. I am aware of your prejudices, Solomon; otherwise I might ask this favor of you."

Mr. Mahaffy snorted loudly and turned to the door, for Yancy and Cavendish were now approaching the house, the latter with a meal sack slung over his shoulder.

"Here, Solomon, take one of my pistols," urged the judge hastily. "You may need it at Belle Plain. Goodby, and God bless you!"

Just where he had parted from Ware, Carrington sat his horse, his brows knit and his eyes turned in the direction of the path. He was on his way to a plantation below Girard, the owner of which had recently imported a pack of bloodhounds; but this unexpected encounter with Ware had affected him strangely. He still heard Tom's stammering speech, he was still seeing his ghastly face, and he had come upon him with startling suddenness. He had chanced to look back over his shoulder and when he faced about there had been the planter within a hundred yards of him.

Presently Carrington's glance ceased to follow the windings of the path. He stared down at the gray dust and saw the trail left by Hues and his party. For a moment he hesitated; if the dogs were to be used with any hope of success he had no time to spare, and this was the merest suspicion, illogical conjecture, based on nothing beyond his distrust of Ware. In the end he sprang from the saddle and leading his horse into the woods, tied it to a sapling.

A hurried investigation told him that five men had ridden in and out of that path. Of the five, all coming from the south, four had turned south again, but the fifth man - Ware, in other words - had gone north. He weighed the possible significance of these facts.

"I am only wasting time!" he confessed reluctantly, and was on the point of turning away, when, on the very edge of the road and just where the dust yielded to the hard clay of the path, his glance lighted on the print of a small and daintily shod foot. The throbbing of his heart quickened curiously.

"Betty!" The word leaped from his lips.

That small foot had left but the one impress. There were other signs, however, that claimed his attention; namely, the bootprints of Slosson and his men; and he made the inevitable discovery that these tracks were all confined to the one spot. They began suddenly and as suddenly ceased, yet there was no mystery about these; he had the marks of the wheels to help him to a sure conclusion. A carriage had turned just here, several men had alighted, they had with them a child or a woman. Either they had reentered the carriage and driven back as they had come, or they had gone toward the :fiver. He felt the soul within him turn sick.

He stole along the path; the terror of the river was ever in his thoughts, and the specter of his fear seemed to flit before him and lure him on. Presently he caught his first glimpse of the bayou and his legs shook under him; but the path wound deeper still into what appeared to be an untouched solitude, wound on between the crowding tree forms, a little back from the shore, with an intervening tangle of vines and bushes. He scanned this closely as he hurried forward, scarcely conscious that he was searching for some trampled space at the water's edge; but the verdant wall preserved its unbroken continuity, and twenty minutes later he came within sight of the Hicks' clearing and the keel boat, where it rested against the bank.

A little farther on he found the spot where Slosson had launched the skiff the night before. The keel of his boat had cut deep into the slippery clay; more than this, the impress of the small shoe was repeated here, and just beside it was the print of a child's bare foot.

He no longer doubted that Betty and Hannibal had been taken across the bayou to the cabin, and he ran back up the path the distance of a mile and plunged into the woods on his right, his purpose being to pass around the head of the expanse of sluggish water to a point from which he could later approach the cabin. But the cabin proved to be better defended than he had foreseen; and as he advanced, the difficulties of the task he had set himself became almost insurmountable; yet sustained as he was by his imperative need, he tore his way through the labyrinth of trailing vines, or floundered across acre-wide patches of green slime and black mud, which at each step threatened to engulf him in their treacherous depths, until at the end of an hour he gained the southern side of the clearing and a firmer footing within the shelter of the woods.

Here he paused and took stock of his surroundings. The two or three buildings Mr. Hicks had erected stood midway of the clearing and were very modest improvements adapted to their owner's somewhat flippant pursuit of agriculture. While Carrington was still staring about him, the cabin door swung open and a woman stepped forth. It was the girl Bess. She went to a corner of the building and called loudly:

"Joe! Oh, Joe!"

Carrington glanced in the direction of the keel boat and an instant later saw Slosson clamber over its side. The tavern-keeper crossed to the cabin, where he was met by Bess, who placed in his hands what seemed to be a wooden bowl. With this he slouched off to one of the outbuildings, which he entered. Ten or fifteen minutes slipped by, then he came from the shed and after securing the door, returned to the cabin. He was again met by Bess, who relieved him of the bowl; they exchanged a few words and Slosson walked away and afterward disappeared over the side of the keel boat.

This much was clear to the Kentuckian: food had been taken to some one in the shed - to Betty and the boy! - more likely to George.

He waited now for the night to come, and to him the sun seemed fixed in the heavens. At Belle Plain Tom Ware was watching it with a shuddering sense of the swiftness of its flight. But at last the tops of the tall trees obscured it; it sank quickly then and blazed a ball of fire beyond the Arkansas coast, while its dying glory spread aslant the heavens, turning the flanks of the gray clouds to violet and purple and gold.

With the first approach of darkness Carrington made his way to the shed. Hidden in the shadow he paused to listen, and fancied he heard difficult breathing from within. The door creaked hideously on its wooden hinges when he pushed it open, but as it swung back the last remnant of the day's light showed him some dark object lying prone on the dirt floor. He reached down and his hand rested on a man's booted foot.

"George -" Carrington spoke softly, but the man on the floor gave no sign that he heard, and Carrington's questioning touch stealing higher he found that George - if it were George - was lying on his side with his arms and legs securely bound. Thinking he slept, the Kentuckian shook him gently to arouse him.

"George?" he repeated, still bending above him. This time an inarticulate murmur answered him. At the same instant the woolly head of the negro came under his fingers and he discovered the reason of his silence. He was as securely gagged as he was bound.

"Listen, George - it's Carrington - I am going to take off this gag, but don't speak above a whisper - they may hear us!" And he cut the cords that held the gag in place.

"How yo' get here, Mas'r Ca'ington?" asked the negro guardedly, as the gag fell away.

"Around the head of the bayou."

"Lawd!" exclaimed George, in a tone of wonder.

"Where's Miss Betty?"

"She's in the cabin yonder - fo' the love of God, cut these here other ropes with yo' knife, Mas'r Ca'ington - I'm perishin' with 'em!" Carrington did as he asked, and groaning, George sat erect. "I'm like I was gone to sleep all over," he said.

"You'll feel better in a moment. Tell me about Miss Malroy?"

"They done fetched us here last night. I was drivin' Missy into Raleigh - her and young Mas'r Hazard - when fo' men stop us in the* road."

"Who were they, do you know?" asked Carrington.

"Lawd - what's that?"

Carrington, knife in hand swung about on his heel. A lantern's light flashed suddenly in his face and Bess Hicks, with a low startled cry breaking from her lips, paused in the doorway. Springing forward, Carrington seized her by the wrist.

"Hush!" he grimly warned.

"What are you doin' here?" demanded the girl, as she endeavored to shake off his hand, but Carrington drew her into the shed, and closing the door, set his back against it. There was a brief silence during which Bess regarded the Kentuckian with a kind of stolid fearlessness. She was the first to speak. "I reckon you-all have come after Miss Malroy," she observed quietly.

"Then you reckon right," answered Carrington. The girl studied him from beneath her level brows.

"And you-all think you can take her away from here," she speculated. "I ain't afraid of yo' knife - you-all might use it fast enough on a man, but not on me. I'll help you," she added. Carrington gave her an incredulous glance. "You don't believe me? What's to hinder my calling for help? That would fetch our men up from the keel boat. No - yo'-all's knife wouldn't stop me!"

"Don't be too sure of that," said Carrington sternly. The girl met the menace of his words with soft, fullthroated laughter.

"Why, yo' hand's shakin' now, Mr. Carrington!"

"You know me?"

"Yes, I seen you once at Boggs'." She made an impatient movement. "You can't do nothing against them fo' men unless I help you. Miss Malroy's to go down river to-night; they're only waiting fo' a pilot - you-all's got to act quick!"

Carrington hesitated.

"Why do you want Miss Malroy to escape?" he said.

The girl's mood changed abruptly. She scowled at him.

"I reckon that's a private matter. Ain't it enough fo' you-all to know that I do? I'm showing how it can be done. Them four men on the keel boat are strangers in these parts, they're waiting fo' a pilot, but they don't know who he'll be. I've heard you-all was a riverman; what's to hinder yo' taking the pilot's place? Looks like yo' was willing to risk yo' life fo' Miss Malroy or you wouldn't be here."

"I'm ready," said Carrington, his hand on the door.

"No, you ain't - jest yet," interposed the girl hastily. "Listen to me first. They's a dugout tied up 'bout a hundred yards above the keel boat; you must get that to cross in to the other side of the bayou, then when yo're ready to come back yo're to whistle three times - it's the signal we're expecting - and I'll row across fo' you in one of the skiffs."

"Can you see Miss Malroy in the meantime?"

"If I want to, they's nothin' to hinder me," responded Bess sullenly.

"Tell her then -" began Carrington, but Bess interrupted him.

"I know what yo' want. She ain't to cry out or nothin' when she sees you-all. I got sense enough fo' that."

Carrington looked at her curiously.

"This may be a serious business for your people," he said significantly, and watched her narrowly.

"And you-all may get killed. I reckin if yo' want to do a thing bad enough you don't mind much what comes after," she answered with a hard little laugh, as she went from the shed.

"Come!" said Carrington to the negro, when he had seen the cabin door close on Bess and her lantern; and they stole across the clearing. Reaching the bayou side they began a noiseless search for the dugout, which they quickly found, and Carrington turned to George. "Can you swim?" he asked.

"Yes, Mas'r."

"Then go down into the water and drag the canoe farther along the shore - and for God's sake, no sound!" he cautioned.

They placed a second hundred yards between themselves and the keel boat in this manner, then he had George bring the dug-out to the bank, and they embarked. Keeping within the shadow of the trees that fringed the shore, Carrington paddled silently about the head of the bayou.

"George," he at length said, bending toward the negro; "my horse is tied in the woods on the right-hand side of the road just above where you were taken from the carriage last night - you can be at Belle Plain inside of an hour."

"Look here, Mas'r Ca'ington, those folks yonder is kin to Boss Hicks. If he get his hand on me first don't you reckon he'll stop my mouth? I been here heaps of times fotchin' letters fo' Mas'r Tom," added George.

"Who were the letters for?" asked the Kentuckian, greatly surprised.

"They was fo' that Captain Murrell; seems like him and Mas'r Tom was mixed up in a sight of business."

"When was this - recently?" inquired Carrington. He was turning this astonishing statement of the slave over in his mind.

"Well, no, Mas'r; seems like they ain't so thick here recently."

"I reckon you'd better keep away from the big house yet a while," said Carrington. "Instead of going there, stop at the Belle Plain landing. You'll find a raft tied up to the shore, it belongs to a man named Cavendish. Tell him what you know. That I've found Miss Malroy and the boy, tell him to cast off and drift down here. I'll run the keel boat aground the first chance I get, so tell him to keep a sharp lookout."

A few minutes later they had separated, George to hurry away in search of the horse, and Carrington to pass back along the shore until he gained a point opposite the clearing. He whistled shrilly three times, and after an interval of waiting heard the splash of oars and presently saw a skiff steal out of the gloom.

"Who's there?" It was Bess who asked the question.

"Carrington," he answered.

"Lucky you ain't met the other man!" she said as she swept her skiff alongside the bank.

"Lucky for him, you mean. I'll take the oars," added Carrington as he entered the skiff.

Slowly the clearing lifted out of the darkness, then the keel boat became distinguishable; and Carrington checked the skiff by a backward stroke of the oars.

"Hello!" he called.

There was no immediate answer to his hail, and he called again as he sent the skiff forward. He felt that he was risking all now.

"What do you want?" asked a surly voice.

"You want Slosson!" quickly prompted the girl in a whisper.

"I want to see Slosson!" said Carrington glibly and with confidence, and once more he checked the skiff.

"Who be you?"

"Murrell sent you," prompted the girl again, in a hurried whisper.

"Murrell -" And in his astonishment Carrington spoke aloud.

"Murrell?" cried the voice sharply.

" - sent me!" said Carrington quickly, as though completing an unfinished sentence. The girl laughed nervously under her breath.

"Row closter!" came the sullen command, and the Kentuckian did as he was bidden. Four men stood in the bow of the keel boat, a lantern was raised aloft and by its light they looked him over. There was a moment's silence broken by Carrington, who asked:

"Which one of you is Slosson?" And he sprang lightly aboard the keel boat.

"I'm Slosson," answered the man with the lantern. The previous night Mr. Slosson had been somewhat under the enlivening and elevating influence of corn whisky, but now he was his own cheerless self, and rather jaded by the passing of the hours which he had sacrificed to an irksome responsibility. "What word do you fetch from the Captain, brother?" he demanded.

"Miss Malroy is to be taken down river," responded Carrington. Slosson swore with surpassing fluency.

"Say, we're five able-bodied men risking our necks to oblige him! You can get married a damn sight easier than this if you go about it right - I've done it lots of times." Not understanding the significance of Slosson's allusion to his own matrimonial career, Carrington held his peace. The tavern-beeper swore again with unimpaired vigor. "You'll find mighty few men with more experience than me," he asserted, shaking his head. "But if you say the word -"

"I'm all for getting shut of this!" answered Carrington promptly, with a sweep of his arm. "I call these pretty close quarters!" Still shaking his head and muttering, the tavern-keeper sprang ashore and mounted the bank, where his slouching figure quickly lost itself in the night.

Carrington took up his station on the flat roof of the cabin which filled the stern of the boat. He was remembering that day in the sandy Barony road - and during all the weeks and months that had intervened, Murrell, working in secret, had moved steadily toward the fulfilment of his desires! Unquestionably he had been back of the attack on Norton, had inspired his subsequent murder, and the man's sinister and mysterious power had never been suspected. Carrington knew that the horse-thieves and slave stealers were supposed to maintain a loosely knit association; he wondered if Murrell were not the moving spirit in some such organization.

"If I'd only pushed my quarrel with him!" he thought bitterly.

He heard Slosson's shuffling step in the distance, a word or two when he spoke grufy to some one, and a moment later he saw Betty and the boy, their forms darkly silhouetted against the lighter sky as they moved along the top of the bank. Slosson, without any superfluous gallantry, helped his captives down the slope and aboard the keel boat, where he locked them in the cabin, the door of which fastened with a hasp and wooden peg.

"You're boss now, pardner!" he said, joining Carrington at the steering oar.

"We'll cast off then," answered Carrington.

Thus far nothing had occurred to mar his plans. If they could but quit the bayou before the arrival of the man whose place he had taken, the rest would be if not easy of accomplishment, at least within the realm of the possible.

"I reckon you're a river-man?" observed Slosson.

"All my life."

The line had been cast off, and the crew with their setting poles were forcing the boat away from the bank. All was quietly done; except for an occasional order from Carrington no word was spoken, and soon the unwieldy craft glided into the sluggish current and gathered way. Mr. Slosson, who clearly regarded his relation to the adventure as being of an official character, continued to stand at Carrington's elbow.

"What have we, between here and the river?" inquired the latter. It was best, he felt, not to give Slosson an opportunity to ask questions.

"It narrows considerably, pardner, but it's a straight course," said Slosson. "Black in yonder, ain't it?" he added, nodding ahead.

The shores drew rapidly together; they were leaving the lakelike expanse behind. In the silence, above the rustling of the trees, Carrington heard the first fret of 'the river against its bank. Slosson yawned prodigiously.

"I reckon you ain't needing me?" he said.

"Better go up in the bow and get some sleep," advised Carrington, and Slosson, nothing loath, clambered down from the roof of the cabin and stumbled forward.

The ceaseless murmur of the rushing waters grew in the stillness as the keel boat drew nearer the hurrying yellow flood, and the beat of the Kentuckian's pulse quickened. Would he find the raft there? He glanced back over the way they had come. The dark ranks of the forest walled off the clearing, but across the water a dim point of light was visible. He fixed its position as somewhere near the head of the bayou. Apparently it was a lantern, but as he looked a ruddy glow crept up against the sky-line.

From the bow Bunker had been observing this singular phenomenon. Suddenly he bent and roused Slosson, who had fallen asleep. The tavern-keeper sprang to his feet and Bunker pointed without speaking.

"Mebby you can tell me what that light back yonder means?" cried Slosson, addressing himself to Carrington; as he spoke he snatched up his rifle.

"That's what I'm trying to make out," answered Carrington.

"Hell!" cried Slosson, and tossed his gun to his shoulder.

What seemed to be a breath of wind lifted a stray lock of Carrington's hair, but his pistol answered Slosson in the same second. He fired at the huddle of men in the bow of the boat and one of them pitched forward with his arms outspread.

"Keep back, you!" he said, and dropped off the cabin roof.

His promptness had bred a momentary panic, then Slosson's bull-like voice began to roar commands; but in that brief instant of surprise and shock Carrington had found and withdrawn the wooden peg that fastened the cabin door. He had scarcely done this when Slosson came tramping aft supported by the three men.

Calling to Betty and Hannibal to escape in the skiff which was towing astern the Kentuckian rushed toward the bow. At his back he heard the door creak on its hinges as it was pushed open by Betty and the boy, and again he called to them to escape by the skiff. The fret of the current had grown steadily and from beneath the wide-flung branches of the trees which here met above his head, Carrington caught sight of the starspecked arch of the heavens beyond. They were issuing from the bayou. He felt the river snatch at the keel boat, the buffeting of some swift eddy, and saw the blunt bow swing off to the south as they were plunged into the black shore shadows.

But what he did not see was a big muscular hand which had thrust itself out of the impenetrable gloom and clutched the side of the keel boat. Coincident with this there arose a perfect babel of voices, high-pitched and shrill.

"Sho - I bet it's him! Sho' - it's Uncle Bob's nevvy! Sho', you can hear 'em! Sho', they're shootin' guns! Sho'!"

Carrington cast a hurried glance in the direction of these sounds. There between the boat and the shore the dim outline of a raft was taking shape. It was now canopied by a wealth of pale gray smoke that faded from before his eyes as the darkness lifted. Turning, he saw Slosson and his men clearly. Surprise and consternation was depicted on each face.

The light increased. From the flat stone hearth of the raft ascended a tall column of flame which rendered visible six pygmy figures, tow-headed and wonderfully vocal, who were toiling like mad at the huge sweeps. The light showed more than this. It showed a lady of plump and pleasing presence smoking a cobpipe while she fed the fire from a tick stuffed with straw. It showed two bark shanties, a line between them decorated with the never-ending Cavendish wash. It showed a rooster perched on the ridge-pole of one of these shanties in the very act of crowing lustily.

Hannibal, who had climbed to the roof of the cabin, shrieked for help, and Betty added her voice to his.

"All right, Nevvy!" came the cheerful reply, as Yancy threw himself over the side of the boat and grappled with Slosson.

"Uncle Bob! Uncle Bob!" cried Hannibal.

Slosson uttered a cry of terror. He had a simple but sincere faith in the supernatural, and even with the Scratch Hiller's big hands gripping his throat, he could not rid himself of the belief that this was the ghost of a murdered man.

"You'll take a dog's licking from me, neighbor?" said Yancy grimly. "I been saving it fo' you!"

Meanwhile Mr. Cavendish, whose proud spirit never greatly inclined him to the practice of peace, had prepared for battle; Springing aloft he knocked his heels together.

"Whoop! I'm a man as can slide down a thorny locust and never get scratched!" he shouted. This was equivalent to setting his triggers; then he launched himself nimbly and with enthusiasm into the thick of the fight. It was Mr. Bunker's unfortunate privilege to sustain the onslaught of the Earl of Lambeth.

The light from the Cavendish hearth continued to brighten the scene, for Polly was recklessly sacrificing her best straw tick. Indeed her behavior was in every way worthy of the noble alliance she had formed. Her cob-pipe was not suffered to go out and with Connie's help she kept the six small Cavendishes from risking life and limb in the keel boat, toward which they were powerfully drawn. Despite these activities she found time to call to Betty and Hannibal on the cabin roof.

"Jump down here; that ain't no fittin' place for you-all to stop in with them gentlemen fightin'!"

An instant later Betty and Hannibal stood on the raft with the little Cavendishes flocking about them. Mr. Yancy's quest of his nevvy had taken an enduring hold on their imagination. For weeks it had constituted their one vital topic, and the fight became merely a satisfying background for this interesting restoration.

"Sho', they'd got him! Sho' - he wa'n't no bigger than Richard! Sho'!"

"Oh!" cried Betty, with a fearful glance toward the keel boat. "Can't you stop them?"

"What fo'?" asked Polly, opening her black eyes very wide.

"Bless yo' tender heart!-you don't need to worry none, we got them strange gentlemen licked like they was a passel of children! Connie, you-all mind that fire!"

She accurately judged the outcome of the fight. The boat was little better than a shambles with the havoc that had been wrought there when Yancy and Carrington dropped over its side to the raft. Cavendish followed them, whooping his triumph as he came.

CHAPTER XXXII

THE RAFT AGAIN

Yancy and Cavendish threw themselves on the sweeps and worked the raft clear of the keel boat, then the turbulent current seized the smaller craft and whirled it away into the night; as its black bulk receded from before his eyes the Earl of Lambeth spoke with the voice of authority and experience.

"It was a good fight and them fellows done well, but not near well enough." A conclusion that could not be gainsaid. He added, "No one ain't hurt but them that had ought to have got hurt. Mr. Yancy's all right, and so's Mr. Carrington - who's mighty welcome here." The earl's shock of red hair was bristling like the mane of some angry animal and his eyes still flashed with the light of battle, but he managed to summon up an expression of winning friendliness.

"Mr. Carrington's kin to me, Polly," explained Yancy to Mrs. Cavendish. His voice was far from steady, for Hannibal had been gathered into his arms and had all but wrecked the stoic calm with which the Scratch Hiller was seeking to guard his emotions.

Polly smiled and dimpled at the Kentuckian. Trained to a romantic point of view she had a frank liking for handsome stalwart men. Cavendish was neither, but none knew better than Polly that where he was most lacking in appearance he was richest in substance. He carried scars honorably earned in those differences he had been prone to cultivate with less generous natures; for his scheme of life did not embrace the millennium.

"Thank God, you got here when you did!" said Carrington.

"We was some pushed fo' time, but we done it," responded the earl modestly. He added, "What now? - do we make a landing?"

"No - unless it interferes with your plans not to. I 'want to get around the next bend before we tie up. Later we'll all go back. Can I count on you?"

"You shorely can. I consider this here as sociable a neighborhood as I ever struck. It pleases me well. Folks are up and doing hereabout."

Carrington looked eagerly around in search of Betty. She was sitting on an upturned tub, a pathetic enough figure as she drooped against the wall of one of the shanties with all her courage quite gone from her. He made his way quickly to her side.

"La!" whispered Polly in Chills and Fever's ear. "If that pore young thing yonder keeps a widow it won't be because of any encouragement she gets from Mr. Carrington. If I ever seen marriage in a man's eye I seen it in his this minute!"

"Bruce!" cried Betty, starting up as Carrington approached. "Oh, Bruce, I am so glad you have come - you are not hurt?" She accepted his presence without question. She had needed him and he had not failed her.

"We are none of us hurt, Betty," he said gently, as he took her hand.

He saw that the suffering she had undergone during the preceding twenty-four hours had left its record on her tired face and in her heavy eyes. She retained a shuddering consciousness of the unchecked savagery of those last moments on the keel boat; she was still hearing the oaths of the men as they struggled together, the sound of blows, and the dreadful silences that had followed them. She turned from him, and there came the relief of tears.

"There, Betty, the danger is over now and you were so brave while it lasted. I can't bear to have you cry!"

"I was wild with fear - all that time on the boat, Bruce -" she faltered between her sobs. "I didn't know but they would find you out. I could only wait and hope - and pray!"

"I was in no danger, dear. Didn't the girl tell you I was to take the place of a man Slosson was expecting? He never doubted that I was that man until a light - a signal it must have been - on the shore at the head of the bayou betrayed me."

"Where are we going now, Bruce? Not the way they went -" and Betty glanced out into the black void where the keel boat had merged into the gloom.

"No, no - but we can't get the raft back up-stream against the current, so the best thing is to land at the Bates' plantation below here; then as soon as you are able we can return to Belle Plain," said Carrington.

There was an interval broken only by the occasional sweep of the great steering oar as Cavendish coaxed the raft out toward the channel. The thought of Charley Norton's murder rested on Carrington like a pall. Scarcely a week had elapsed since he quitted Thicket Point and in that week the hand of death had dealt with them impartially, and to what end? Then the miles he had traversed in his hopeless journey up-river translated themselves into a division of time as well as space. They were just so much further removed from the past with its blight of tragic terror. He turned and glanced at Betty. He saw that her eyes held their steady look of wistful pity that was for the dead man; yet in spite of this, and in spite of the bounds beyond which he would not let his imagination carry him, the future enriched with sudden promise unfolded itself. The deep sense of recovered hope stirred within him. He knew there must come a day when he would dare to speak of his love, and she would listen.

"It's best we should land at Bates' place - we can get teams there," he went on to explain. "And, Betty, wherever we go we'll go together, dear. Cavendish doesn't look as if he had any very urgent business of his own, and I reckon the same is true of Yancy, so I am going to keep them with us. There are some points to be cleared up when we reach Belle Plain - some folks who'll have a lot to explain or else quit this part of the state! And I intend to see that you are not left alone until - until I have the right to take care of you for good and all - that's what you want me to do one of these days, isn't it, darling?" and his eyes, glowing and infinitely tender, dwelt on her upturned face.

But Betty shrank from him in involuntary agitation.

"Oh, not now, Bruce - not now - we mustn't speak of that - it's wrong - it's wicked - you mustn't make me forget him!" she cried brokenly, in protest.

"Forgive me, Betty, I'll not speak of it again," he said.

"Wait, Bruce, and some time - Oh, don't make me say it," she gasped, "or I shall hate myself!" for in his presence she was feeling the horror of her past experience grow strangely remote, only the dull ache of her memories remained, and to these she clung. They were silent for a moment, then Carrington said:

"After I'm sure you'll be safe here perhaps I'll go south into the Choctaw Purchase. I've been thinking of that recently; but I'll find my way back here - don't misunderstand me - I'll not come too soon for even you, Betty. I loved Norton. He was one of my best friends, too," he continued gently. "But you know - and I know - dear, the day will come when no matter where you are I shall find you again - find you and not lose you!"

Betty made no answer in words, but a soft and eloquent little hand was slipped into his and allowed to rest there.

Presently a light wind stirred the dead dense atmosphere, the mist lifted and enveloped the shore, showing them the river between piled-up masses of vapor. Apparently it ran for their raft alone. It was just twenty-four hours since Carrington had looked upon such another night but this was a different world the gray fog was unmasking - a world of hopes, and dreams, and rich content. Then the thought of Norton - poor Norton who had had his world, too, of hopes and dreams and rich content -

The calm of a highly domestic existence had resumed its interrupted sway on the raft. Mr. Cavendish, associated in Betty's memory with certain earsplitting manifestations of ferocious rage, became in the bosom of his family low-voiced and genial and hopelessly impotent to deal with his five small sons; while Yancy was again the Bob Yancy of Scratch Hill, violence of any sort apparently had no place in his nature. He was deeply absorbed in Hannibal's account of those vicissitudes which had befallen him during their separation. They were now seated before a cheerful fire that blazed on the hearth, the boy very close to Yancy with one hand clasped in the Scratch Hiller's, while about them were ranged the six small Cavendishes sedately sharing in the reunion of uncle and nevvy, toward which they felt they had honorably labored.

"And you wa'n't dead, Uncle Bob?" said Hannibal with a deep breath, viewing Yancy unmistakably in the flesh.

"Never once. I been floating peacefully along with these here titled friends of mine; but I was some anxious about you, son."

"And Mr. Slosson, Uncle Bob - did you smack him like you

smacked Dave Blount that day when he tried to steal me?" asked Hannibal, whose childish sense of justice demanded reparation for the wrongs they had suffered.

Mr. Yancy extended a big right hand, the knuckle of which was skinned and bruised.

"He were the meanest man I ever felt obliged fo' to hit with my fist, Nevvy; it appeared like he had teeth all over his face."

"Sho - where's his hide, Uncle Bob?" cried the little Cavendishes in an excited chorus. "Sho - did you forget that?" They themselves had forgotten the unique enterprise to which Mr. Yancy was committed, but the allusion to Slosson had revived their memory of it.

"Well, he begged so piteous to be allowed fo' to keep his hide, I hadn't the heart to strip it off," explained Mr. Yancy pleasantly. "And the winter's comin' onat this moment I can feel a chill in the air - don't you-all reckon he's goin' to need it fo' to keep the cold out,' Sho', you mustn't be bloody-minded!"

"What was it about Mr. Slosson's hide, Uncle Bob?" demanded Hannibal. "What was you a-goin' to do to that?"

"Why, Nevvy, after he beat me up and throwed me in the river, I was some peevish fo' a spell in my feelings fo' him," said Yancy, in a tone of gentle regret. He glanced at his bruised hand. "But I'm right pleased to be able to say that I've got over all them oncharitable thoughts of mine."

"And you seen the judge, Uncle Bob?" questioned Hannibal.

"Yes, I've seen the judge. We was together fo' part of a day. Me and him gets on fine."

"Where is he now, Uncle Bob?"

"I reckon he's back at Belle Plain by this time. You see we left him in Raleigh along after noon to 'tend tosome business he had on hand. I never seen a gentleman of his weight so truly spry on his legs - and all about you, Nevvy; while as to mind! Sho - why, words flowed out of him as naturally as water out of a branch."

Of Hannibal's relationship to the judge he said nothing. He felt that was a secret to be revealed by the judge himself when he should see fit.

"Uncle Bob, who'm I going to live with now?" questioned Hannibal anxiously.

"That p'int's already come up, Nevvy - him and me's decided that there won't be no friction. You-all will just go on living with him."

"But what about you, Uncle Bob?" cried Hannibal, lifting a wistful little face to Yancy's.

"Oh, me? - well, you-all will go right on living with me."

"And what will come of Mr. Mahaffy?"

"I reckon you-all will go right on living witli him, too."

"Uncle Bob, you mean you reckon we are all going to live in one house?"

"I 'low it will have to be fixed that-a-ways," agreed Yancy.

CHAPTER XXXIII

THE JUDGE RECEIVES A LETTER

After he had parted with Solomon Mahaffy the judge applied himself diligently to shaping that miracle-working document which he was preparing as an offset to whatever risk he ran in meeting Fentress. As sanguine as he was sanguinary he confidently expected to survive the encounter, yet it was well to provide for a possible emergency - had he not his grandson's future to consider? While thus occupied he saw the afternoon stage arrive and depart from before the City Tavern.

Half an hour later Mr. Wesley, the postmaster, came sauntering up the street. In his hand he carried a letter.

"Howdy," he drawled, from just beyond the judge's open door.

The judge glanced up, his quill pen poised aloft.

"Good evening, sir; won't you step inside and be seated?" he asked graciously. His dealings with the United States mail service were of the most insignificant description, and in personally delivering a letter, if this was what had brought him there, he felt Mr. Wesley had reached the limit of official courtesy and despatch.

"Well, sir; it looks like you'd never told us more than two-thirds of the truth!" said the postmaster. He surveyed the judge curiously.

"I am complimented by your opinion of my veracity," responded that gentleman promptly. "I consider two-thirds an enormously high per cent to have achieved."

"There is something in that, too," agreed Mr. Wesley. "Who is Colonel Slocum Price Turberville?"

The judge started up from his chair.

"I have that honor," said he, bowing.

"Well, here's a letter come in addressed like that, and as you've been using part of the name I am willing to assume you're legally entitled to the rest of it. It clears up a point that off and on has troubled me considerable. I can only wonder I wa'n't smarter;"

"What point, may I ask?"

"Why, about the time you hung out your shingle here, some one wrote a letter to General Jackson. It was mailed after night, and when I seen it in the morning I was clean beat. I couldn't locate the handwriting and yet I kept that letter back a couple of days and give it all my spare time. It ain't that I'm one of your spying sort - there's nothing of the Yankee about me!"

"Certainly not," agreed the judge.

"Candid, Judge, I reckon you wrote that letter, seeing this one comes under a frank from Washington. No, sir - I couldn't make out who was corresponding with the president and it worried me, not knowing, more than anything I've had to contend against since I came into office. I calculate there ain't a postmaster in the United States takes a more personal interest in the service than me. I've frequently set patrons right when they was in doubt as to the date they had mailed such and such *f* letter." As Mr. Wesley sometimes canceled as many as three or four stamps in a single day he might have been pardoned his pride in a brain which thus lightly dealt with the burden of official business. He surrendered the letter with marked reluctance.

"Your surmise is correct," said the judge with dignity. "I had occasion to write my friend, General Jackson, and unless I am greatly mistaken I have my answer here." And with a fine air of indifference he tossed the letter on the table.

"And do you know Old Hickory?" cried Mr. Wesley.

"Why not? Does it surprise you?" inquired the judge. It was only his innate courtesy which restrained him from kicking the postmaster into the street, so intense was his desire to be rid of him.

"No, I don't know as it does, judge. Naturally a public man like him is in the way of meeting with all sorts. A politician can't afford to be too blame particular. Well, next time you write you might just send him my regards - G. W. M. de L. Wesley's regards - there was considerable contention over my getting this office; I reckon he ain't forgot. There was speeches made, I understand the lie was passed between two United States senators, and that a quid of tobacco was throwed in anger." Having thus clearly established the fact that he was a more or less national character, Mr. Wesley took himself off.

When he had disappeared from sight down the street, the judge closed the door. Then he picked up the letter. For along minute he held it in his hand, uncertain, fearful, while his mind slipped back into the past until his inward searching vision ferreted out a handsome soldierly figure - his own.

"That's what Jackson remembers if he remembers anything!" he muttered, as with trembling fingers he broke the seal. Almost instantly a smile overspread his battered features. He hitched his chin higher and squared his ponderous shoulders.

"I am not forgotten - no, damn it - no!" he exulted under his breath, "recalls me with sincere esteem and considers my services to the country as well worthy of recognition -" the judge breathed deep. What would Mahaffy find to say now! Certainly this was well calculated to disturb the sour cynicism of his friend. His bleared eyes brimmed. After all his groping he had touched hands with the realities at last! Even a federal judgeship, though not an office of the first repute in the south. had its dignity - it signified something! He would make Solomon his clerk! The judge reached for his hat. Mahaffy must know at once that fortune had mended for them. Why, at that moment he was actually in receipt of an income!

He sat down, the better to enjoy the unique sensation. Taxes were being levied and collected with no other end in view than his stipend - his ardent fancy saw the whole machinery of government in operation for his benefit. It was a singular feeling he experienced. Then promptly his spendthrift brain became active. He needed clothes - so did Mahaffy - so did his grandson; they must take a larger house; he would buy himself a man servant; these were pressing necessities as he now viewed them.

Once again he reached for his hat, the desire to rush off to Belle Plain was overmastering.

"I reckon I'd be justified in hiring a conveyance from Pegloe," he thought, but just here he had a saving memory of his unfinished task; that claimed precedence and he resumed his pen.

An hour later Pegloe's black boy presented himself to the judge. He came bearing a gift, and the gift appropriately enough was a square case bottle of respectable size. The judge was greatly touched by this attention, but he began by making a most temperate use of the tavern-keeper's offering; then as the formidable document he was preparing took shape under his hand he more and more lost that feeling of Spartan fortitude which had at first sustained him in the presence of temptation. He wrote and sipped in complete and quiet luxury, and when at last he had exhausted the contents of the bottle it occurred to him that it would be only proper personally to convey his thanks to Pegloe. Perhaps he was not uninspired in this by ulterior hopes; if so, they were richly rewarded. The resources of the City Tavern were suddenly placed at his disposal. He attributed this to a variety of causes all good and sufficient, but the real reason never suggested itself, indeed it was of such a perfidious nature that the judge, open and generous-minded, could not have grasped it.

By six o'clock he was undeniably drunk; at eight he was sounding still deeper depths of inebriety with only the most confused memory of impending events; at ten he collapsed and was borne up-stairs by Pegloe and his black boy to a remote chamber in the kitchen wing. Here he was undressed and put to bed, and the tavernkeeper, making a bundle of his clothes, retired from the room, locking the door after him, and the judge was doubly a prisoner.

Rousing at last from a heavy dreamless sleep the judge was aware of a faint impalpable light in his room, the ashen light of a dull October dawn. He was aware, too, of a feeling of profound depression. He knew this was the aftermath of indulgence and that he might look forward to forty-eight hours of utter misery of soul, and, groaning aloud, he closed his eyes, Sleep was the thing if he could compass it. Instead, his memory quickened. Something was to happen at sunup - he could not recall what it was to be, though he distinctly remembered that Mahaffy had spoken of this very matter - Mahaffy, the austere and implacable, the disembodied conscience whose fealty to duty had somehow survived his own spiritual ruin, so that he had become a sort of moral sign-post, ever pointing the way yet never going it himself. The judge lay still and thought deeply as the light intensified itself. What was it that Mahaffy had said he was to do at sun-up? The very hour accented his suspicions. Probably it was no more than some cheerless obligation to be met, or Mahaffy would not have been so concerned about it. Eventually he decided to refer everything to Mahaffy. He spoke his friend's name weakly and in a shaking voice, but received no answer.

"Solomon!" he repeated, and shifting his position, looked in what should have been the direction of the shake-down bed his friend occupied. Neither the bed nor Mahaffy were there. The judge gasped he wondered if this were not a premonition of certain hallucinations to which he was not a stranger. Then all in a flash he remembered Fentress and the meeting at Boggs', something of how the evening had been spent, and a spasm of regret shook him.

"I had other things to think of. This must never happen again!" he told himself remorsefully.

He was wide-awake now. Doubtless Pegloe had put him to bed. Well, that had been thoughtful of Pegloe - he would not forget him - the City Tavern should continue to enjoy his patronage. It would be something for Pegloe to boast of that judge Slocum Price Turberville always made his place headquarters when in Raleigh. Feeling that he had already conferred wealth and distinction on the fortunate Pegloe the judge thrust his fat legs over the side of his bed and stood erect. Stooping he reached for his clothes. He confidently expected to find them on the floor, but his hand merely swept an uncarpeted waste. The judge was profoundly astonished.

"Maybe I've got 'em on, I don't recall taking them off!" he thought hopefully. He moved uncertainly in the direction of the window where the light showed him his own bare extremities. He reverted to his original idea that his clothes were scattered about the floor.

He was beginning to experience a great sense of haste, it was two miles to Boggs' and Fentress would be there at sun-up. Finally he abandoned his quest of the missing garments and turned to the door. To say that he was amazed when he found it locked would have most inadequately described his emotions. Breathing deep, he fell back a step or two, and then with all the vigor he could muster launched himself at the door. But it resisted him. "It's bolted on the other side!" he muttered, the full measure of Pegloe's perfidy revealing itself to his mind.

He was aghast. It was a plot to discredit him. Pegloe's hospitality had been inspired by his enemy, for Pegloe was Fentress' tenant.

Again he attacked the door; he believed it might be possible to force it from its hinges, but Pegloe had done his work too well for that, and at last, spent and breathless, the judge dropped down on the edge of his bed to consider the situation. He was without clothes and he was a prisoner, yet his mind rose splendidly to meet the difficulties that beset him. His greatest activities were reserved for what appeared to be only a season of despair. He armed himself with a threelegged stool he had found and turned once more to the door, but the stout planks stood firm under his blows.

"Unless I get out of here in time I'm a ruined man!" thought the judge. "After this Fentress will refuse to meet me!"

The window next engaged his attention. That, too, Pegloe had taken the precaution to fasten, but a single savage blow of the stool shattered glass and sash and left an empty space that framed the dawn's red glow. The judge looked out and shook his head dubiously. It was twelve feet or more to the ground, a risky drop for a gentleman of his years and build. The judge considered making a rope of his bedding and lowering himself to the ground by means of it, he remembered to have read of captives in that interesting French prison, the Bastille, who did this. However, an equally ingenious but much more simple use for his bedding occurred to him; it would form a soft and yielding substance on which to alight. He gathered it up into his arms, feather-tick and all, and pushed it through the window, then he wriggled out across the ledge, feet first, and lowering himself to the full length of his arms, dropped.

He landed squarely on the rolled-up bed with a jar that shook him to his center. Almost gaily he snatched up a quilt, draping it about him after the manner of a Roman, toga, and thus lightly habited, started across Mr. Pegloe's truck-patch, his one thought Boggs' and the sun. It would have served no purpose to have gone home, since his entire wardrobe, except for the shirt on his back, was in the tavern-keeper's possession, besides he had not a moment to lose, for the sun was peeping at him over the horizon.

Unobserved he gained the edge of the town and the highroad that led past Boggs' and stole a fearful glance over his shoulder. The sun was clear of the treetops, he could even feel the lifeless dust grow warm beneath his feet; and wrapping the quilt closer about him he broke into a labored run.

Some twenty minutes later Boggs' came in sight. He experienced a moment of doubt - suppose Fentress had been there and gone! It was a hideous thought and the judge groaned. Then at the other end of the meadow near the woods he distinguished several men, Fentress and his friends beyond question. The judge laughed aloud. In spite of everything he was keeping his engagement, he was plucking his triumph out of the very dregs of failure. The judge threw himself over the fence, a corner of the quilt caught on one of the rails; he turned to release it, and in that instant two pistol shots rang out sharply in the morning air.

Vaughan Kester

CHAPTER XXXIV

THE DUEL

It had been with no little reluctance that Solomon Mahaffy accompanied Yancy and Cavendish to Belle Plain; he would have preferred to remain in Raleigh in attendance upon judge Price. Intimately acquainted with the judge's mental processes, he could follow all the devious workings of that magnificent mind; he could fathom the simply hellish ingenuity he was capable of putting forth to accomplish temporary benefits. Permitting his thoughts to dwell upon the mingled strength and weakness which was so curiously blended in Slocum Price's character, he had horrid visions of that great soul, freed from the trammels of restraint, confiding his melancholy history to Mr. Pegloe in the hope of bolstering his fallen credit at the City Tavern.

Always where the judge was concerned he fluctuated between extremes of doubt and confidence. He felt that under the urgent spur of occasion his friend could rise to any emergency, while a sustained activity made demands which he could not satisfy; then his efforts were discounted by his insane desire to realize at once on his opportunities; in his haste he was for ever plucking unripe fruit; and though he might keep one eye on the main chance the other was fixed just as resolutely on the nearest tavern.

With the great stake which fate had suddenly introduced into their losing game, he wished earnestly to believe that the judge would stay quietly in his office and complete the task he had set himself; that with this off his hands the promise of excitement at Belle Plain would compel his presence there, when he would pass somewhat under the restraining influence which he was determined to exert; in short, to Solomon, life embraced just the one vital consideration, which was to maintain the judge in a state of sobriety until after his meeting with Fentress.

The purple of twilight was stealing over the land when he and his two companions reached Belle Plain. They learned that Tom Ware had returned from Memphis, that the bayou had been dragged but without results, and that as yet nothing had been heard from Carrington or the dogs he had gone for.

Presently Cavendish and Yancy set off across the fields. They were going on to the raft, to Polly and the six little Cavendishes, whom they had not seen since early morning; but they promised to be back at Belle Plain within an hour.

By very nature an alien, Mahaffy sought out a dark corner on the wide porch that overlooked the river to await their return. The house had been thrown open, and supper was being served to whoever cared to stay and partake of it. The murmur of idle purposeless talk drifted out to him; he was irritated and offended by it. There was something garish in this indiscriminate hospitality in the very home of tragedy. As the moments slipped by his sense of displeasure increased, with mankind in general, with himself, and with the judge - principally with the judge - who was to make a foolish target of himself in the morning. He was going to give the man who had wrecked his life a chance to take it as well. Mahaffy's cold logic dealt cynically with the preposterous situation his friend had created.

In the midst of his angry meditations he heard a clock strike in the hall and counted the strokes. It was nine o'clock. Surely Yancy and Cavendish had been gone their hour! He quitted his seat and strolled restlessly about the house. He felt deeply indignant with everybody and everything. Human intelligence seemed but a pitiable advance on brute instinct. A whole day had passed and what had been accomplished? Carrington, the judge, Yancy, Cavendish - the four men who might have worked together to some purpose had widely separated themselves; and here was the duel, the very climax of absurdity. He resumed his dark corner and waited another hour. Still no Carrington, and Yancy and Cavendish had not come up from the raft.

"Fools!" thought Mahaffy bitterly. "All of them fools!"

At last he decided to go back to the judge; and a moment later was hurrying down the lane in the direction of the highroad, but, jaded as he was by the effort he had already put forth that day, the walk to Raleigh made tremendous demands on him, and it was midnight when he entered the little town.

It can not be said that he was altogether surprised when he found their cottage dark and apparently deserted. He had half expected this. Entering, and not stopping to secure a candle, he groped his way up-stairs to the room on the second floor which he and the judge shared.

"Price!" he called, but this gained him no response, and he cursed softly under his breath.

He hastily descended to the kitchen, lighted a candle, and stepped into the adjoining room. On the table was a neat pile of papers, and topping the pile was the president's letter. Being burdened by no false scruples, and thinking it might afford some clue to the judge's whereabouts, Mahaffy took it up and read it. Having mastered its contents he instantly glanced in the direction of the City Tavern, but it was wrapped in darkness.

"Price is drunk somewhere," was his definite conclusion. "But he'll be at Boggs' the first thing in the morning - most likely so far gone he can hardly stand!" The letter, with its striking news, made little or no impression on him just then; it merely furnished the clue he had sought. The judge was off somewhere marketing his prospects.

After a time Mahaffy went up-stairs, and, without removing his clothes, threw himself on the bed. He was worn down to the point of exhaustion, yet he could not sleep, though the deep silence warned him that day was not far off. What if - but he would not let the thought shape itself in his mind. He had witnessed the judge's skill with the pistol, and he had even a certain irrational faith in that gentleman's destiny. He prayed God that Fentress might die quickly and decently with the judge's bullet through his brain. Over and over in savage supplication he muttered his prayer that Fentress might die.

He began to watch for the coming of the dawn, but before the darkness lifted he had risen from the bed and gone downstairs, where he made himself a cup of wretched coffee. Then he blew out his candle and watched the gray light spread. He was impatient now to be off, and fully an hour before the sun, set out for Boggs', a tall, gaunt figure in the shadowy uncertainty of that October morning. He was the first to reach the place of meeting, but he had scarcely entered the meadow when Fentress rode up, attended by Tom Ware. They dismounted, and the colonel lifted his hat. Mahaffy barely acknowledged the salute; he was in no mood for courtesies that meant nothing. Ware was clearly of the same mind.

There was an awkward pause, then Fentress and Ware spoke together in a low tone. The planter's speech was broken and hoarse, and his heavy, bloodshot eyes were the eyes of a haunted man; this was all a part of Fentress' scheme to face the world, and Ware still believed that the fires Hicks had kindled had served his desperate need.

When the first long shadows stole out from the edge of the woods Fentress turned to Mahaffy, whose glance was directed toward the distant corner of the field, where he knew his friend must first appear.

"Why are we waiting, sir?" he demanded, his tone cold and formal.

"Something has occurred to detain Price," answered Mahaffy.

The colonel and Ware exchanged looks. Again they spoke together, while Mahaffy watched the road. Ten minutes slipped by in this manner, and once more Fentress addressed Mahaffy.

"Do you know what could have detained him?" he inquired, the ghost of a smile curling his thin lips.

"I don't," said Mahaffy, and relapsed into a moody and anxious silence. He held dueling in very proper abhorrence, and only his feeling of intense but never-declared loyalty to his friend had brought him there.

Another interval of waiting succeeded.

"I have about reached the end of my patience; I shall wait just ten minutes longer," said Fentress, and drew out his watch.

"Something has happened -" began Mahaffy.

"I have kept my engagement; he should have kept his," Fentress continued, addressing Ware. "I am sorry to have brought you here for nothing, Tom."

"Wait!" said Mahaffy, planting himself squarely before Fentress.

"I consider this comic episode at an end," and Fentress pocketed his watch.

"Scarcely!" rejoined Mahaffy. His long arm shot out and the open palm of his hand descended on the colonel's face. "I am here for my friend," he said grimly.

The colonel's face paled and colored by turns.

"Have you a weapon?" he asked, when he could command his voice. Mahaffy exhibited the pistol he had carried to Belle Plain the day before.

"Step off the ground, Tom." Fentress spoke quietly. When Ware had done as he requested, the colonel spoke again. "You are my witness that I was the victim of an unprovoked attack."

Mr. Ware accepted this statement with equanimity, not to say indifference.

"Are you ready?" he asked; he glanced at Mahaffy, who by a slight inclination of the head signified that he was. "I reckon you're a green hand at this sort of thing?" commented Tom evilly.

"Yes," said Mahaffy tersely.

"Well, listen: I shall count, one, two, three; at the word three you will fire. Now take your positions."

Mahaffy and the colonel stood facing each other, a distance of twelve paces separating them. Mahaffy was pale but dogged, he eyed Fentress unflinchingly. Quick on the word Fentress fired, an instant later Mahaffy's pistol exploded; apparently neither bullet had taken effect, the two men maintained the rigid attitude they had assumed; then Mahaffy was seen to turn on his heels, next his arm dropped to his side and the pistol slipped from his fingers, a look of astonishment passed over his face and left it vacant and staring while his right hand stole up toward his heart; he raised it slowly, with difficulty, as though it were held down by some invisible weight.

A hush spread across the field. It was like one of nature's invisible transitions. Along the edge of the woods the song of birds was stricken into silence. Ware, heavy-eyed Fentress, his lips twisted by a tortured smile, watched Mahaffy as he panted for breath, with his hand clenched against his chest. That dead oppressive silence lasted but a moment, from out of it came a cry that smote on the wounded man's ears and reached his consciousness.

"It's Price -" he gasped, his words bathed in blood. and he pitched forward on his face.

Ware and Fentress had heard the cry, too, and running to their horses threw themselves into the saddle and galloped off. The judge midway of the meadow roared out a furious protest but the mounted men turned into the highroad and vanished from sight, and the judge's shaking legs bore him swiftly in the direction of the gaunt figure on the ground.

Mahaffy struggled to rise, for he was hearing his friend's voice now, the voice of utter anguish, calling his name. At last painful effort brought him to his knees. He saw the judge, clothed principally in a gaily colored bed-quilt, hatless and shoeless, his face sodden and bleary from his night's debauch. Mahaffy stood erect and staggered toward him, his hand over his wound, his features drawn and livid, then with a cry he dropped at his friend's feet.

"Solomon! Solomon!" And the judge knelt beside him.

"It's all right, Price; I kept your appointment," whispered Mahaffy; a bloody spume was gathering on his lips, and he stared up at his friend with glassy eyes.

In very shame the judge hid his face in his hands, while sobs shook him.

"Solomon - Solomon, why did you do this?" he cried miserably.

The harsh lines on the dying man's face erased themselves.

"You're the only friend I've known in twenty years of

loneliness, Price. I've loved you like a brother," he panted, with a pause between each word.

Again the judge buried his face in his hands.

"I know it, Solomon - I know it!" he moaned wretchedly.

"Price, you are still a man to be reckoned with. There's the boy; take your place for his sake and keep it - you can."

"I will - by God, I will!" gasped the judge. "You hear me? You hear me, Solomon? By God's good help, I will!"

"You have the president's letter - I saw it " said Mahaffy in a whisper.

"Yes!" cried the judge. "Solomon, the world is changing for us!"

"For me most of all," murmured Mahaffy, and there was a bleak instant when the judge's ashen countenance held the full pathos of age and failure. "Remember your oath, Price," gasped the dying man. A moment of silence succeeded. Mahaffy's eyes closed, then the heavy lids slid back. He looked up at the judge while the harsh lines of his sour old face softened wonderfully. "Kiss me, Price," he whispered, and as the judge bent to touch him on the brow, the softened lines fixed themselves in death, while on his lips lingered a smilc that was neither bitter nor sneering.

CHAPTER XXXV

A CRISIS AT THE COURT-HOUSE

In that bare upper room they had shared, the judge, crushed and broken, watched beside the bed on which the dead man lay; unconscious of the flight of time he sat with his head bowed in his hands, having scarcely altered his position since he begged those who carried Mahaffy up the narrow stairs to leave him alone with his friend.

He was living over the past. He recalled his first meeting with Mahaffy in the stuffy cabin of the small river packet from which they had later gone ashore at Pleasantville; he thanked God that it had been given him to see beneath Solomon's forbidding exterior and into that starved heart! He reviewed each phase of the almost insensible growth of their intimacy; he remembered Mahaffy's fine true loyalty at the time of his arrest - he thought of Damon and Pythias - Mahaffy had reached the heights of a sublime devotion; he could only feel enobled that he had inspired it.

At last the dusk of twilight invaded the room. He lighted the candles on the chimneypiece, then he resumed his seat and his former attitude. Suddenly he became aware of a small hand that was resting on his arm and glanced up; Hannibal had stolen quietly into the room. The boy pointed to the still figure on the bed.

"Judge, what makes Mr. Mahaffy lie so quiet - is he dead?" he asked in a whisper.

"Yes, dear lad," began the judge in a shaking voice as he drew Hannibal toward him, "your friend and mine is dead - we have lost him." He lifted the boy into his lap, and Hannibal pressed a tear-stained face against the judge's shoulder. "How did you get here?" the judge questioned gently.

"Uncle Bob fetched me," said Hannibal. "He's down-stairs, but he didn't tell me Mr. Mahaffy was dead-"

"We have sustained a great loss, Hannibal, and we must never forget the moral grandeur of the man. Some day, when you are older, and I can bring myself to speak of it, I will tell you of his last moments." The judge's voice broke, a thick sob rose chokingly in his throat. "Poor Solomon! A man of such tender feeling that he hid it from the world, for his was a rare nature which only revealed itself to the chosen few he honored with his love." The judge lapsed into a momentary brooding silence, in which his great arms drew the boy closer against his heart. "Dear lad, since I left you at Belle Plain a very astonishing knowledge has come to me. It was the Hand of Providence - I see it now - that first brought us together. You must not call me judge any more; I am your grandfather your mother was my daughter."

Hannibal instantly sat erect and looked up at the judge, his blue eyes wide with amazement at this extraordinary statement.

"It is a very strange story, Hannibal, and its links are not all in my hands, but I am sure because of what I already know. I, who thought that not a drop of my blood flowed in any veins but my own, live again in you. Do you understand what I am telling you? Your are my own dear little grandson -" and the judge looked down with no uncertain love and pride into the small face upturned to his.

"I am glad if you are my grandfather, judge," said Hannibal

very gravely. "I always liked you."

"Thank you, dear lad," responded the judge with equal gravity, and then as Hannibal nestled back in his grandfather's arms a single big tear dropped from the end of that gentleman's prominent nose.

"There will be many and great changes in store for us," continued the judge. "But as we met adversity with dignity, I am sure we shall be able to endure prosperity with equanimityonly unworthy natures are affected by what is at best superficial and accidental. I mean that the blight of poverty is about to be lifted from our lives."

"Do you mean we ain't going to be pore any longer, grandfather?" asked Hannibal.

The judge regarded him with infinite tenderness of expression; he was profoundly moved.

"Would you mind saying that again, dear lad?"

"Do you mean we ain't going to be pore any longer, grandfather?" repeated Hannibal.

"I shall enjoy an adequate competency which I am about to recover. It will be sufficient for the indulgence of those simple and intellectual tastes I propose to cultivate for the future." In spite of himself the judge sighed. This was hardly in line with his ideals, but the right to choose was no longer his. "You will be very rich, Hannibal. The Quintard lands - your grandmother was a Quintard - will be yours; they run up into the hundred of thousand of acres here about; this land will all be yours as soon as I can establish your identity."

"Will Uncle Bob be rich too?" inquired Hannibal.

"Certainly. How can he be poor when we possess wealth?" answered the judge.

"You reckon he will always live with us, don't you, grandfather?"

"I would not have it otherwise. I admire Mr. Yancy - he is simple and direct, and fit for any company under heaven except that of fools. His treatment of you has placed me under everlasting obligations; he shall share what we have. My one bitter, unavailing regret is that Solomon Mahaffy will not be here to partake of our altered fortunes." And the judge sighed deeply.

"Uncle Bob told me Mr. Mahaffy got hurt in a duel, grandfather?" said Hannibal.

"He was as inexperienced as a child in the use of firearms, and he had to deal with scoundrels who had neither mercy nor generous feeling - but his courage was magnificent."

Presently Hannibal was deep in his account of those adventures he had shared with Miss Betty.

"And Miss Malroy - where is she now?" asked the judge, in the first pause of the boy's narrative.

"She's at Mr. Bowen's house. Mr. Carrington and Mr. Cavendish are here too. Mrs. Cavendish stayed down yonder at the Bates' plantation. Grandfather, it were Captain Murrell who had me stole - do you reckon he was going to take me back to Mr. Bladen?"

"I will see Miss Malroy in the morning. We must combine - our interests are identical. There should be hemp in this for more than one scoundrel! I can see now how criminal my disinclination to push myself to the front has been!" said the judge, with conviction. "Never again will I shrink from what I know to be a public duty."

A little later they went down-stairs, where the judge had Yancy make up a bed for himself and Hannibal on the floor. He would watch alone beside Mahaffy, he was certain this would have been the dead man's wish; then he said good night and mounted heavily to the floor above to resume his vigil and his musings.

Just at daybreak Yancy was roused by the pressure of a hand on his shoulder, and opening his eyes saw that the judge was bending over him.

"Dress!" he said briefly. "There's every prospect of trouble - get your rifle and come with me!"

Yancy noted that this prospect of trouble seemed to afford the judge a pleasurable sensation; indeed, he had quite lost his former air of somber and suppressed melancholy.

"I let you sleep, thinking you needed the rest," the judge went on. "But ever since midnight we've been on the verge of riot and possible bloodshed. They've arrested John Murrell - it's claimed he's planned a servile rebellion! A man named Hues, who had wormed his way into his confidence, made the arrest. He carried Murrell into Memphis, but the local magistrate, intimidated, most likely, declined to have anything to do with holding him. In spite of this, Hues managed to get his prisoner lodged in jail, but along about nightfall the situation began to look serious. Folks were swarming into town armed to the teeth, and Hues fetched Murrell across country to Raleigh -"

"Yes?" said Yancy.

"Well, the sheriff has refused to take Murrell into custody. Hues has him down at the court-house, but whether or not he is going to be able to hold him is another matter!"

Yancy and Hannibal had dressed by this time, and the judge led the way from the house. The Scratch Hiller looked about him. Across the street a group of men, the greater number of whom were armed, stood in front of Pegloe's tavern. Glancing in the direction of the court-house, he observed that the square before it held other groups. But what impressed him more was the ominous silence that was everywhere. At his elbow the judge was breathing deep.

"We are face to face with a very deplorable condition, Mr. Yancy. Court was to sit here to-day, but judge Morrow and the public prosecutor have left town, and as you see, Murrell's friends have gathered for a rescue. There's a sprinkling of the better element - but only a sprinkling. I saw judge Morrow this morning at four o'clock - I told him I would obligate myself to present for his consideration evidence of a striking and sensational character, evidence which would show conclusively that Murrell should be held to await the action of the next grand jury - this was after a conference with Hues - I guaranteed his safety. Sir, the man refused to listen to me! He showed himself utterly devoid of any feeling of public duty." The bitter sense of failure and futility was leaving the judge. The situation made its demands on that basic faith in his own powers which remained imbedded in his character.

They had entered the court-house square. 'On the steps of the building Betts was arguing loudly with Hues, who stood in the doorway, rifle in hand.

"Maybe you don't know this is county property?" the sheriff was saying. "And that you have taken unlawful possession of it for an unlawful purpose? I am going to open them doors-a passel of strangers can't keep folks out of a building their own money has bought and paid for!" While he was speaking, the judge had pushed his way through the crowd to the foot of the steps.

"That was very nicely said, Mr. Betts," observed the judge. He smiled widely and sweetly. The sheriff gave him a hostile glare. "Do you know that Morrow has left town?" the judge went on.

"I ain't got nothing to do with judge Morrow. It's my duty to see that this building is ready for him when he's a mind to open court in it"

"You are willing to assume the responsibility of throwing open these doors?" inquired the judge affably.

"I shorely am," said Betts. "Why, some of these folks are our leading people!"

The judge turned to the crowd, and spoke in a tone of excessive civility. "Just a word, gentlemen! - the sheriff is right; it is your court-house and you should not be kept out of it. No doubt there are some of you whose presence in this building will sooner or later be urgently desired. We are going to let all who wish to enter, but I beg you to remember that there will be five men inside whose prejudices are all in favor of law and order." He pushed past Hues and entered the court-house, followed by Yancy and Hannibal. "We'll let 'em in where I can talk to 'em," he said almost gaily. "Besides, they'll come in anyhow when they get ready, so there's no sense in exciting them."

In the court-house, Murrell, bound hand and foot, was seated between Carrington and the Earl of Lambeth in the little railed-off space below the judge's bench. Fear and suffering had blanched his unshaven cheeks and given a wild light to his deeply sunken eyes. At sight of Yancy a smothered exclamation broke from his lips, he had supposed this man dead these many months!

Hues had abandoned his post and the crowd, suddenly grown clamorous, stormed the narrow entrance. One of the doors, borne from its hinges, went down with a crash. The judge, a fierce light flashing from his eyes, turned to Yancy.

"No matter what happens, this fellow Murrell is not to escape - if he calls on his friends to rescue him he is to be shot!"

The hall was filling with swearing, struggling men, the floor shook beneath their heavy tread; then they burst into the court-room and saluted Murrell with a great shout. But Murrell, bound, in rags, and silent, his lips frozen in a wolfish grin, was a depressing sight, and the boldest felt something of his unrestrained lawlessness go from him.

Less noisy now, the crowd spread itself out among the benches or swarmed up into the tiny gallery at the back of the building. Man after man had hurried forward, intent on passing beyond the railing, but each lead encountered the judge, formidable and forbidding, and had turned aside. Gradually the many pairs of eyes roving over the little group surrounding the outlaw focused themselves on Slocum Price. It was in unconscious recognition of that moral force which was his, a tribute to the grim dignity of his unshaken courage; what he would do seemed worth considering.

He was charmed to hear his name pass in a whisper from lip to lip. Well, it was time they knew him! He squared his ponderous shoulders and made a gesture commanding silence. Battered, shabby and debauched, he was like some old war horse who sniffs the odor of battle that the wind incontinently brings to his nostrils.

"Don't let him speak!" cried a voice, and a tumult succeeded.

Cool and indomitable the judge waited for it to subside. He saw that the color was stealing back into Murrell's face. The outlaw was feeling that he was a leader not overthrown, these were his friends and followers, his safety was their safety too. In a lull in the storm of sound the judge attempted to make himself heard, but his words were lost in the angry roar that descended on him.

"Don't let him speak! Kill him! Kill him!"

A score of men sprang to their feet and from all sides came the click of rifle and pistol hammers as they were drawn to the full cock. The judge's fate seemed to rest on a breath. He swung about on his heel and gave a curt nod to Yancy and Cavendish, who, falling back a step, tossed their guns to their shoulders and covered Murrell. A sudden hush grew up out of the tumult; the cries, angry and jeering, dwindled to a murmur, and a dead pall of silence rested on the crowded room.

The very taste of triumph was in the judge's mouth. Then came a commotion at the back of the building, a whispered ripple of comment, and Colonel Fentress elbowed his way through the crowd. At sight of his enemy the judge's face went from white to red, while his eyes blazed; but for the moment the force of his emotions left him speechless. Here and there, as he advanced, Fentress recognized a friend and bowed coolly to the right and left.

"What does this ridiculous mockery mean?" he demanded harshly. "Mr. Sheriff, as a member of the bar, I protest! Why don't you clear the building?" He did not wait for Betts to answer him, but continued. "Where is this man Hues?"

"Yonder, Colonel, by the captain," said Betts.

"I have a warrant for his arrest. You will take him into custody."

"Wait!" cried the judge. "I represent Mr. Hues. I desire to see that warrant!"

But Fentress ignored him. He addressed the crowded benches.

"Gentlemen, it is a serious matter forcibly to seize a man without authority from the courts and expose him to the danger of mob violence - Mr. Hues will learn this before we have done with him."

Instantly there was a noisy demonstration that swelled into a burst of applause, which quickly spent itself. The struggle seemed to have narrowed to an individual, contest for supremacy between Fentress and the judge. On the edge of the railed off space they confronted each other: the colonel, a tall, well-cared-for presence; the judge shabby and unkempt. For a moment their eyes met, while the judge's face purpled and paled, and purpled again. The silence deepened. Fentress' thin lips opened, twitched, but no sound came from them; then his glance wavered and fell. He turned away.

"Mr. Sheriff!" he called sharply.

"All right, Colonel!"

"Take your man into custody," ordered Fentress. As he spoke he handed the warrant to Betts, who looked at it, grinned, and stepped toward Hues. He would have pushed the judge aside had not that gentleman; bowing civilly, made way for him.

"In my profound respect for the law and properly constituted authority I yield to no man, not even to Colonel Fentress," he said, with a gracious gesture. "I would not place the slightest obstacle in the way of its sanctioned manifestation. Colonel Fentress comes here with that high sanction." He bowed again ceremoniously to the colonel. "I repeat, I respect his dependence upon the law!" He whirled suddenly.

Cavendish - Yancy - Carrington - I call upon you to arrest John Murrell! I do this by virtue of the authority vested in me as a judge of the United States Federal Court. His crime - a mere trifle, my friends - passing counterfeit money! Colonel Fentress will inform you that this is a violation of the law which falls within my jurisdiction," and he beamed blandly on Fentress.

"It's a lie!" cried the colonel.

"You'll answer for that later!" said the judge, with abrupt austerity of tone.

"For all we know you may be some fugitive from justice! Why, your name isn't Price!"

"Are you sure of that?" asked the judge quickly.

"You're an impostor! Your name is Turberville!"

"Permit me to relieve your apprehensions. It is Turberville who has received the appointment. Would you like to examine my credentials? - I have them by me - no? I am obliged for your introduction. It could not have come at a more timely moment!" The judge seemed to dismiss Fentress contempt-uously. Once more he faced the packed benches. "Put down your weapons!" he commanded. "This man Murrell will not be released. At the first effort at rescue he will be shot where he sits - we have sworn it - his plotting is at an end." He stalked nearer the benches. "Not one chance in a thousand remains to him. Either he dies here or he lives to betaken before every judge in the state, if necessary, until we find one with courage to try him! Make no mistake - it will best conserve the ends of justice to allow the state court's jurisdiction in this case; and I pledge myself to furnish evidence which will start him well on his road to the gallows!" The judge, a tremendous presence, stalked still nearer the benches. Outfacing the crowd, a sense of the splendor of the part he was being called upon to play flowed through him like some elixir; he felt that he was transcending himself, that his inspiration was drawn from the hidden springs of the spirit, and that he could neither falter nor go astray. "You don't know what you are meddling with! This man has plotted to lay the South in ruins - he has been arming the negroes - it - it is incredible that you should all know this - to such I say, go home and thank God for your escape! For the others" - his shaggy brows met in a menacing frown - "if they force our hand we will toss them John Murrell's dead carcass - that's our answer to their challenge!"

He strode out among the gun muzzles which wavered where they still covered him. He was thinking of Mahaffy - Mahaffy, who had said he was still a man to be reckoned with. For the comfort of his own soul he was proving it.

"Do you know what a servile insurrection means? - you men

who have wives and daughters, have you thought of their fate? Of the monstrous savagery to which they would be exposed? Do you believe he could limit and control it? Look at him! Why, he has never had a consideration outside of his own safety, and yet he expects you to risk your necks to save his! He would have left the state before the first blow was struck - his business was all down river - but we are going to keep him here to answer for his crimes! The law, as implacable as it is impartial, has put its mark on him - the shadow in which he sits is the shadow of the gallows!"

The judge paused, but the only sound in that expectant silence was the heavy breathing of men. He drew his unwieldy form erect, while his voice rumbled on, aggressive and threatening in its every intonation.

"You are here to defend something that no longer exists. Your organization is wrecked, your signals and passwords are known, your secrets have become public property - I can even produce a list of your members; there are none of you who do not stand in imminent peril - yet understand, I have no wish to strike at those who have been misled or coerced into joining Murrell's band!" The judge's sodden old face glowed now with the magnanimity of his sentiments. "But I have no feeling of mercy for your leaders, none for Murrell himself. Put down your guns! - you can only kill us after we have killed Murrell - but you can't kill the law! If the arch conspirator dies in this room and hour, on whose head will the punishment fall?" He swung round his ponderous arm in a sweeping gesture and shook a fat but expressive forefinger in the faces of those nearest him. "On yours - and yours - and yours!"

Across the space that separated them the judge grinned his triumph at his enemy. He had known when Fentress entered the room that a word or a sign from him would precipitate a riot, but he knew now that neither this word nor this sign would be given. Then quite suddenly he strode down the aisle, and foot by foot Fentress yielded ground before his advance. A murderous light flashed from the judge's bloodshot eyes and his right hand was stealing toward the frayed tails of his coat.

"Look out - he's getting ready to shoot!" cried a frightened voice.

Instantly by doors and windows the crowd, seized with inexplicable panic, emptied itself into the courthouse yard. Fentress was caught up in the rush and borne from the room and from the building. When he reached the graveled space below the steps he turned. The judge was in the doorway, the center of a struggling group; Mr. Bowen, the minister, Mr. Saul and Mr. Wesley were vainly seeking to pinion his arm.

"Draw - damn you!" he roared at Fentress, as he wrenched himself free, and the crowd swayed to right and left as Fentress was seen to reach for his pistol.

Mr. Saul made a last frantic effort to restrain his friend; he seized the judge's arm just as the latter's finger pressed the trigger, and an instant later Fentress staggered back with the judge's bullet in his shoulder.

CHAPTER XXXVI

THE END AND THE BEGINNING

It was not strange that a number of gentlemen in and about Raleigh yielded to an overmastering impulse to visit newer lands, nor was it strange that the initial steps looking toward the indulgence of their desires should have been taken in secrecy. Mr. Pegloe was one of the first to leave; Mr. Saul had informed him of the judge's declared purpose of shooting him on sight. Even without this useful hint the tavern-keeper had known that he should experience intense embarrassment in meeting the judge; this was now a dreary certainty.

"You reckon he means near all he says?" he had asked, his fat sides shaking.

"I'd take his word a heap quicker than I would most folks," answered Mr. Saul with conviction.

Pegloe promptly had a sinking spell. He recalled the snuffing of the candles by the judge, an extremely depressing memory under the circumstances, also the reckless and headlong disregard of consequences which had characterized so many of that gentleman's acts, and his plans shaped themselves accordingly, with this result: that when the judge took occasion to call at the tavern, and the hostile nature of his visit was emphasized by the cautious manner of his approach, he was greatly shocked to discover that his intended victim had sold his business overnight for a small lump sum to Mr. Saul's brother-in-law, who had appeared most opportunely with an offer.

Pegloe's flight created something of a sensation, but it was dwarfed by the sensation that developed a day or so later when it became known that Tom Ware and Colonel Fentress had likewise fled the country. Still later, Fentress' body, showing marks of violence, was washed ashore at a wood-yard below Girard. It was conjectured that he and Ware had set out from The Oaks to cross the river; there was reason to believe that Fentress had in his possession at the time a considerable sum of money, and it was supposed that his companion had murdered and robbed him. Of Ware's subsequent career nothing was ever known.

These were, after all, only episodes in the collapse of the Clan, sporific manifestations of the great work of disintegration that was going forward and which the judge, more than any other, perhaps, had brought about. This was something no one questioned, and he quickly passed to the first phase of that unique and peculiar esteem in which he was ever after held. His fame widened with the succeeding suns; he had offers of help which impressed him as so entirely creditable to human nature that he quite lacked the heart to refuse them, especially as he felt that in the improvement of his own condition the world had bettered itself and was moving nearer those sound and righteous ideals of morality and patriotism which had never lacked his indorsement, no matter how inexpedient it had seemed for him to put them into practice. But he was not diverted from his ultimate purpose by the glamour of a present popularity; he was able to keep his bleared eyes resolutely fixed on the main chance, namely the Fentress estate and the Quintard lands. It was highly important that he should go east to South Carolina to secure documentary evidence that would establish his own and Fentress' identity, to Kentucky, where Fentress had lived prior to his coming to Tennessee.

Early in November the judge set out by stage on his journey east; he was accompanied by Yancy and Hannibal, from neither of whom could he bring himself to be separated; and as the woods, flaming now with the touch of frost, engulfed the little town, he turned in his seat and looked back. He had entered it by that very road, a beggar on foot and in rags; he was leaving it in broadcloth and fine linen, visible tokens of his altered fortunes. More than this, he could thrust his hands deep down into his once empty pockets and hear the clink of gold and silver. The judge slowly withdrew his eyes from the last gray roof that showed among the trees, and faced the east and the future with a serenely confident expression.

Betty Malroy and Carrington had ridden into Raleigh to take leave of their friends. They had watched the stage from sight, had answered the last majestic salute the judge had given them across the swaying top of the coach before the first turn of the road hid it from sight, and then they had turned their horses' heads in the direction of Belle Plain.

"Bruce, do you think judge Price will ever be able to accomplish all he hopes to?" Betty asked when they had left the town behind. She drew in her horse as she spoke, and they went forward at a walk under the splendid arch of the forest and over a carpet of vivid leaves.

"I reckon he will, Betty," responded Carrington. Unfavorable as had been his original estimate of the judge's character, events had greatly modified it.

"He really seems quite sure, doesn't he?" said Betty.

"There's not a doubt in his mind," agreed Carrington.

He was still at Belle Plain, living in what had been Ware's office, while the Cavendishes were domiciled at the big house. He had arranged with the judge to crop a part of that hopeful gentleman's land the very next season; the fact that a lawsuit intervened between the judge and possession seemed a trifling matter, for Carrington had become infected with the judge's point of view, which did not admit of the possibility of failure;

but he had not yet told Betty of his plans. Time enough for that when he left Belle Plain.

His silence concerning the future had caused Betty much thought. She wondered if he still intended going south into the Purchase; she was not sure but it was the dignified thing for him to do. She was thinking of this now as they went forward over the rustling leaves, and at length she turned in the saddle and faced him.

"I am going to miss Hannibal dreadfully - yes, and the judge, and Mr. Yancy!" she began.

"And when I leave - how about me, Betty?" Carrington asked unexpectedly, but he only had in mind leaving Belle Plain.

A little sigh escaped Betty's red lips, for she was thinking of the Purchase, which lay far down the river, many, many miles distant. The sigh was ever so little, but Carrington had heard it.

"I am to be missed, too, am I, Betty?" he inquired, leaning toward her.

"You, Bruce? - Oh, I shall miss you, too - dreadfully - but then, perhaps in five years, when you come back -"

"Five years!" cried Carrington, but he understood, something of what was passing in her mind, and laughed shortly. "Five years, Betty?" he repeated, dwelling on the numeral.

Betty hesitated and looked thoughtful. Presently she stole a surreptitious glance at Carrington from under her long lashes, and went on slowly, as though she were making careful choice of her words.

"When you come back in three years, Bruce -"

Carrington still regarded her fixedly. There was a light in his black eyes that seemed to penetrate to the most secret recesses of her heart and soul.

"Three years, Betty?" he repeated again.

Betty, her eyes cast down, twisted her rein nervously between her slim, white fingers, but Carrington's steady glance never left her sweet face, framed by its halo of bright hair. She stole another look at him from beneath her dark lashes.

"Three years, Betty?" he prompted.

"Bruce, don't stare at me that way, it makes me forget what I was going to say! When you come, back - next year -" and then she lifted her eyes to his and he saw that they were full of sudden tears. "Bruce, don't go away - don't go away at all -"

Carrington slipped from the saddle and stood at her side.

"Do you mean that, Betty?" he asked. He took her hands loosely in his and relentlessly considered her crimsoned face. "I reckon it will always be right hard to refuse you anything - here is one settler the Purchase will never get!" and he laughed softly.

"It was the Purchase - you were going there!" she cried.

"No, I wasn't, Betty; that notion died its natural death long ago. When we are sure you will be safe at Belle Plain with just the Cavendishes, I am going into Raleigh to wait as best I can until spring." He spoke so gravely, that she asked in quick alarm.

"And then, Bruce - what?"

"And then - Oh, Betty, I'm starving -" All in a moment he lifted her slender figure in his arms, gathering her close to him. "And then, this - and this - and this, sweetheart - and more - and - oh, Betty! Betty!"

When Murrell was brought to trial his lawyers were able to produce a host of witnesses whose sworn testimony showed that so simple a thing as perjury had no terrors for them. His fight for liberty was waged in and out of court with incredible bitterness, and, as judge and jury were only human, the outlaw escaped with the relatively light sentence of twelve years' imprisonment; he died, however, before the expiration of his term.

The judge, where he returned to Raleigh, resumed his own name of Turberville, and he allowed it to be known that he would not be offended by the prefix of General. During his absence he had accumulated a wealth of evidence of undoubted authenticity, with the result that his claim against the Fentress estate was sustained by the courts, and when The Oaks with its stock and slaves was offered for sale, he, as the principal creditor, was able to buy it in.

One of his first acts after taking possession of the property was to have Mahaffy reinterred in the grove of oaks below his bedroom windows, and he marked the spot with a great square of granite. The judge, visibly shaken by his emotions, saw the massive boulder go into place.

"Harsh and rugged like the nature of him who lies beneath it — but enduring, too, as he was," he murmured. He turned to Yancy and Hannibal, and added

"You will lay me beside him when I die."

Then when the bitter struggle came and he was wrenched and tortured by longings, his strength was in remembering his promise to the dead man, and it was his custom to go out under the oaks and pace to and fro beside Mahaffy's grave until he had gained the mastery of himself. Only Yancy and Hannibal knew how fierce the conflict was he waged, yet in the end he won that best earned of all victories, the victory over himself.

"My salvation has been a costly thing; it was bought with the blood of my friend," he told Yancy.

It was Hannibal's privilege to give Cavendish out of the vast Quintard tract such a farm as the earl had never dreamed of owning even in his most fervid moments of imagining; and he abandoned all idea of going to England to claim his title. At the judge's suggestion he named the place Earl's Court. He and Polly were entirely satisfied with their surroundings, and never ceased to congratulate themselves that they had left Lincoln County. They felt that their friends the Carringtons at Belle Plain, though untitled people, were still of an equal rank with themselves; while as for the judge, they doubted if royalty itself laid it any over him.

Mr. Yancy accepted his changed fortunes with philosophic composure. Technically he filled the position of overseer at The Oaks, but the judge's activity was so great that this position was largely a sinecure. The most arduous work he performed was spending his wages.

Certain trifling peculiarities survived with the judge even after he had entered what he had once been prone to call the Portal of Hope; for while his charity was very great and he lived with the splendid air of plenty that belonged to an older order, it required tact, patience, and persistence to transact business with him; and his creditors, of whom there were always a respectable number, discovered that he esteemed them as they were aggressive and determined. He explained to Yancy that too great certainty detracted from the charm of living, for, after all, life was a game - a gamble - he desired to be reminded of this. Yet he was held in great respect for his wisdom and learning, which was no more questioned that his courage.

Thus surrounded by his friends, who were devoted to him, he began Hannibal's education and the preparation of his memoirs, intended primarily for the instruction of his grandson, and which he modestly decided to call The History of My Own Times, which clearly showed the magnificence of his mind and its outlook.

Choose from Thousands of 1stWorldLibrary Classics By

Ada Leverson	Charles Ives	Evelyn Everett-green
Adolphus William Ward	Charles Kingsley	Everard Cotes
Aesop	Charles Klein	F. H. Cheley
Agatha Christie	Charles Lathrop Pack	F. J. Cross
Alexander Aaronsohn	Charles Whibley	Federick Austin Ogg
Alexander Kielland	Charles Willing Beale	Ferdinand Ossendowski
Alexandre Dumas	Charlotte M. Braeme	Francis Bacon
Alfred Gatty	Charlotte M. Yonge	Francis Darwin
Alfred Ollivant	Charlotte Perkins Stetson	Frances Hodgson Burnett
Alice Duer Miller	Clair W. Hayes	Frances Parkinson Keyes
Alice Turner Curtis	Clarence Day Jr.	Frank Gee Patchin
Alice Dunbar	Clarence E. Mulford	Frank Harris
Ambrose Bierce	Clemence Housman	Frank Jewett Mather
Amelia E. Barr	Confucius	Frank L. Packard
Andrew Lang	Cornelis DeWitt Wilcox	Frank V. Webster
Andrew McFarland Davis	Cyril Burleigh	Frederic Stewart Isham
Andy Adams	D. H. Lawrence	Frederick Trevor Hill
Anna Sewell	Daniel Defoe	Frederick Winslow Taylor
Annie Besant	David Garnett	Friedrich Kerst
Annie Hamilton Donnell	Don Carlos Janes	Friedrich Nietzsche
Annie Payson Call	Donald Keyhoe	Fyodor Dostoyevsky
Annonaymous	Dorothy Kilner	G.A. Henty
Anton Chekhov	Dougan Clark	G.K. Chesterton
Arnold Bennett	Douglas Fairbanks	Gabrielle E. Jackson
Arthur Conan Doyle	E. Nesbit	Garrett P. Serviss
Arthur M. Winfield	E.P.Roe	Gaston Leroux
Arthur Ransome	E. Phillips Oppenheim	George Ade
Atticus	Edgar Rice Burroughs	Geroge Bernard Shaw
B.H. Baden-Powell	Edith Van Dyne	George Durston
B. M. Bower	Edith Wharton	George Ebers
Baroness Emmuska Orczy	Edward J. O'Biren	George Eliot
Baroness Orczy	Edward S. Ellis	George MacDonald
Basil King	Edwin L. Arnold	George Meredith
Bayard Taylor	Eleanor Atkins	George Orwell
Ben Macomber	Eliot Gregory	George Tucker
Bertha Muzzy Bower	Elizabeth Gaskell	George W. Cable
Bjornstjerne Bjornson	Elizabeth McCracken	George Wharton James
Booth Tarkington	Elizabeth Von Arnim	Gertrude Atherton
Boyd Cable	Ellem Key	Grace E. King
Bram Stoker	Emerson Hough	Grace Gallatin
C. Collodi	Emily Dickinson	Grant Allen
C. E. Orr	Enid Bagnold	Guillermo A. Sherwell
C. M. Ingleby	Enilor Macartney Lane	Gulielma Zollinger
Carolyn Wells	Erasmus W. Jones	Gustav Flaubert
Catherine Parr Traill	Ernie Howard Pie	H. A. Cody
Charles A. Eastman	Ethel Turner	H. B. Irving
Charles Dickens	Ethel Watts Mumford	H.C. Bailey
Charles Dudley Warner	Eugenie Foa	H. G. Wells
Charles Farrar Browne	Eugene Wood	H. H. Munro

H. Irving Hancock
H. Rider Haggard
H. W. C. Davis
Hamilton Wright Mabie
Hans Christian Andersen
Harold Avery
Harold McGrath
Harriet Beecher Stowe
Harry Houidini
Helent Hunt Jackson
Helen Nicolay
Hendrik Conscience
Hendy David Thoreau
Henri Barbusse
Henrik Ibsen
Henry Adams
Henry Ford
Henry Frost
Henry James
Henry Jones Ford
Henry Seton Merriman
Henry W Longfellow
Herbert A. Giles
Herbert N. Casson
Herman Hesse
Homer
Honore De Balzac
Horace Walpole
Horatio Alger Jr.
Howard Pyle
Howard R. Garis
Hugh Lofting
Hugh Walpole
Humphry Ward
Ian Maclaren
Inez Haynes Gillmore
Irving Bacheller
Israel Abrahams
Ivan Turgenev
J.G.Austin
J. Henri Fabre
J. M. Barrie
J. Macdonald Oxley
J. S. Fletcher
J. S. Knowles
J. Storer Clouston
Jack London
Jacob Abbott
James Allen
James Andrews
James Baldwin

James DeMille
James Joyce
James Lane Allen
James Lane Allen
James Oliver Curwood
James Oppenheim
James Otis
James R. Driscoll
Jane Austen
Jens Peter Jacobsen
Jerome K. Jerome
John Burroughs
John Cournos
John F. Kennedy
John Gay
John Glasworthy
John Habberton
John Joy Bell
John Kendrick Bangs
John Milton
John Philip Sousa
Jonas Lauritz Idemil Lie
Jonathan Swift
Joseph A. Altsheler
Joseph Carey
Joseph Conrad
Joseph E. Badger Jr
Joseph Hergesheimer
Joseph Jacobs
Julian Hawthrone
Julies Vernes
Justin Huntly McCarthy
Kakuzo Okakura
Kenneth Grahame
Kenneth McGaffey
Kate Langley Bosher
Kate Langley Bosher
Katherine Cecil Thurston
Katherine Stokes
L. A. Abbot
L. T. Meade
L. Frank Baum
Latta Griswold
Laura Lee Hope
Laurence Housman
Leo Tolstoy
Leonid Andreyev
Lewis Carroll
Lilian Bell
Lloyd Osbourne
Louis Tracy

Louisa May Alcott
Lucy Fitch Perkins
Lucy Maud Montgomery
Lydia Miller Middleton
Lyndon Orr
M. Corvus
M. H. Adams
Margaret E. Sangster
Margaret Vandercook
Margret Penrose
Maria Edgeworth
Maria Thompson Daviess
Mariano Azuela
Marion Polk Angellotti
Mark Overton
Mark Twain
Mary Austin
Mary Catherine Crowley
Mary Cole
Mary Hastings Bradley
Mary Roberts Rinehart
Mary Rowlandson
M. Wollstonecraft Shelley
Maud Lindsay
Max Beerbohm
Myra Kelly
Nathaniel Hawthrone
Nicolo Machiavelli
O. F. Walton
Oscar Wilde
Owen Johnson
P.G. Wodehouse
Paul and Mabel Thorne
Paul G. Tomlinson
Paul Severing
Percy Brebner
Peter B. Kyne
Plato
R. Derby Holmes
R. L. Stevenson
R. S. Ball
Rabindranath Tagore
Rahul Alvares
Ralph Henry Barbour
Ralph Waldo Emmerson
Rene Descartes
Rex Beach
Rex E. Beach
Richard Harding Davis
Richard Jefferies
Richard Le Gallienne

Robert Barr
Robert Frost
Robert Gordon Anderson
Robert L. Drake
Robert Lansing
Robert Lynd
Robert Michael Ballantyne
Robert W. Chambers
Rosa Nouchette Carey
Rudyard Kipling
Samuel B. Allison
Samuel Hopkins Adams
Sarah Bernhardt
Selma Lagerlof
Sherwood Anderson
Sigmund Freud
Standish O'Grady
Stanley Weyman
Stella Benson
Stephen Crane
Stewart Edward White
Stijn Streuvels
Swami Abhedananda

Swami Parmananda
T. S. Ackland
T. S. Arthur
The Princess Der Ling
Thomas A. Janvier
Thomas A Kempis
Thomas Anderton
Thomas Bailey Aldrich
Thomas Bulfinch
Thomas De Quincey
Thomas H. Huxley
Thomas Hardy
Thomas More
Thornton W. Burgess
U. S. Grant
Valentine Williams
Various Authors
Victor Appleton
Virginia Woolf
Walter Camp
Walter Scott
Washington Irving
Wilbur Lawton

Wilkie Collins
Willa Cather
Willard F. Baker
William Dean Howells
William le Queux
W. Makepeace Thackeray
William W. Walter
Winston Churchill
Yei Theodora Ozaki
Yogi Ramacharaka
Young E. Allison
Zane Grey

www.ingramcontent.com/pod-product-compliance
Lightning Source LLC
Chambersburg PA
CBHW030759260626
47169CB00001B/123